GW00712312

A Harmony for Steve

Part 4 of the Song of Suspense series

A Novel by

HALLEE BRIDGEMAN

Published by
Olivia Kimbrell Press™

Olivia Kimbrell Press™

COPYRIGHT NOTICE

PUBLISHED BY: Olivia Kimbrell Press™*, P.O. Box 470, Fort Knox, KY 40121-0470. The *Olivia Kimbrell Press*™ colophon and open book logo are trademarks of Olivia Kimbrell Press™.
Olivia Kimbrell Press™ is a publisher offering true to life, meaningful fiction from a Christian worldview intended to uplift the heart and engage the mind.

Some scripture quotations courtesy of the King James Version of the Holy Bible. Some scripture quotations courtesy of the New King James Version of the Holy Bible, Copyright © 1979, 1980, 1982 by Thomas-Nelson, Inc. Used by permission. All rights reserved.

Cover Art by Romance Cover Creations (www.romance-covers.com)

Library Cataloging Data

Names: Bridgeman, Hallee (Bridgeman Hallee) 1972-

Title: A Harmony for Steve; Song of Suspense Series book 4 / Hallee Bridgeman
414 p. 5 in. × 8 in. (12.70 cm × 20.32 cm)

Description: Olivia Kimbrell Press™ digital eBook edition | Olivia Kimbrell Press™ Trade paperback edition | Kentucky: Olivia Kimbrell Press™, 2015.

Summary: Harmony and Steve draw closer and spiritual war wages when heaven meets hell.

Identifiers: ePCN: 2016915550 | ISBN-13: 978-1-68190-083-4 (hardcover) | 978-1-68190-089-6 (trade) | 978-1-68190-087-2 (POD) | 978-1-939603-44-9 (ebk.)

1. suspenseful thriller 2. clean romance love story 3. Christian fiction mystery 4. women's inspirational 5. music songs recording 6. spiritual warfare family 7. occult satanic worship

PS3558.B7534 H513 2016 [Fic.] 813.6 (DDC 23)

Part 4 of the Song of Suspense series

A Novel by

HALLEE BRIDGEMAN

LOVINGLY DEDICATED TO...

Chaplain Mark and Mrs. Sheri Williams and family. Sometimes people come into your life and you know with absolute certainty that their friendship and support comes directly from God. Thank you for all of your encouragement as this project came together.

♫ ♫ ♫ ♫

Table of Contents

♫ ♫ ♫ ♫

I'D LIKE ACKNOWLEDGE...

... Jessica Pasley, Todd Ballard, and the entire staff at Northeast Christian Church in Lexington, Kentucky, who were so gracious and generous with their time and knowledge and helped me learn everything a laymen could learn about touring Christian bands and the behind-the-scenes work that goes into a Christian music concert.

♫ ♫ ♫ ♫

HARMONY Harper stopped inside the doorway of Sheri Mercer's hospital room and held her hand under the automatic sanitizer dispenser. Her palm filled with the foamy alcohol-based sterilizer, and she rubbed her hands together, making sure she didn't miss a spot on her hands and wrists. She wore purple scrubs with a "volunteer" badge pinned to the shirt pocket.

A large window overlooked the courtyard of the hospital complex, filling the room with natural light. A wallpaper border covered in childlike drawings of grassy hills dotted with flowers ran along the top of the wall. The bright green floor and walls painted the color of apricot jam gave the sterile room a cheerful feeling. Wood paneling over the cupboards and cabinets matched the trim on the blue vinyl couch and chair.

Sheri lay still in the bed, a nasal cannula strapped to her nose, wearing a fuchsia colored knitted cap on her little bald head. A hand-crocheted blanket in green, gold, and white covered the hospital linens, adding warmth and a feeling of home.

"Harmony," Sheri greeted in a weak and wheezy voice, "you made it."

Setting her bag on the floor by the rocking chair, Harmony walked over to the bed and took Sheri's frail hand in hers. Black circles rimmed the child's pale face, and her bones stood out on her shallow cheeks. The decline in her appearance from just a week ago shocked Harmony, though she tried not to show it. "I promised I would," she quietly replied. In the terminally ill children ward of the hospital, even the nurses spoke in hushed, reverent tones. "I'm so sorry to have missed your birthday yesterday."

"Mom was happy it was just family. She wanted the memory of the birthday to be just for them for when I'm gone."

Sheri had always spoken very matter of factually when it came to her mortality. Harmony admired that about her. She herself joined the throng of adults unwilling to accept that this beautiful and talented child would likely not live another week. She looked at the brightly colored Happy Birthday balloon that danced at the foot of the bed. Stuffed animals perched like sentries next to vases of silk flowers on a narrow table by the window. A Mercer family photo sat in the center of the display. A laughing and healthy Sheri stood next to her two sisters and parents as she grinned (or parents, grinning) for the camera. Her cancer diagnosis came six months after the picture was taken. Harmony knew that Sheri had beaten all odds to make it to eleven years old.

"I'm glad that I had a conflict then," Harmony said. "Your mom never said anything about it."

"She loves you too much."

The simple statement gave Harmony's heart a painful squeeze. She knew volunteering at a children's hospital allowed her to give as much support to the parents as she did to the children. God had directed her to the terminal ward. The parents to whom she ministered walked down a long and painful path of mourning that no mother nor father should ever have to walk. Harmony prayed with them, sang to them, spent time with them, and ministered to them as much as she did their children.

"I got you a present," Harmony whispered.

Sheri's eyes widened. "You didn't have to get me anything!"

"I think you'll like this. But I'm going to open it for you and then let the nurses put it in the dishwasher, okay?" This was their little joke. Anything Sheri touched had to be sterilized because her treatments had so fully compromised her immune system. Harmony retrieved a gaily wrapped square package from her bag and opened it as if presenting the grand prize on some game show. "Do you like it?"

She held Melody Mason Montgomery's latest album on CD-ROM in her hand. The case had been autographed by the famous singer. Sheri's smile lit up the room.

"Harmony, I *love* it! Thank you so much!"

"Well, good. I already talked to the nurses. They'll get it loaded onto your MP3 player quick as you like."

"I can hardly wait."

Sheri began to look tired. She had started to sleep much more than she could remain awake recently. Harmony put the CD away and fished around in her bag until she found her dog-eared copy of Wilder's *These Happy Golden Years*. "We're nearly done. Let's see if we can finish this today," she said with a smile, pulling the rocking chair closer to the bed. "I think we left off right before they get married."

As she settled into the chair and found the spot in the book, Sheri, speaking so quietly Harmony nearly didn't hear her, said, "I wish I could find my Almanzo and get married one day."

Sheri did not like it when adults treated her like a dying child. Instead of crying about how unfair it was that Sheri would never even go on a date, Harmony marked her place in the book with her index finger and said, "So do I. I wonder what mine looks like."

Sheri took a deep wheezing breath. "Mine wouldn't be tall. I'm too little."

She pursed her lips and nodded. "But I like tall. How about six feet?"

"Dark?"

"Hmm," Harmony said, thinking of what she found attractive. "I've always been a fan of men with light hair. Red or blond or straw colored."

Sheri touched her cap with a mischievous grin. "I'd go for just hair."

"Oh, honey, you had beautiful hair. I think a dark-haired man would go perfectly with your auburn color."

"He would have to be smart. No dummies."

"Absolutely. Smart is important."

"And handsome," she whispered, her eyes drooping.

"Handsome is definitely on my list." She reached between the bed rails and took her hand. "But, I want a man with a beautiful heart more than a beautiful face. I want him to love God as much as I do. I want him to serve God right along with me."

Sheri leaned toward her and her eyes bored into Harmony's. "You need that. Don't settle for just a pretty face."

For a moment, she stared at the wise little eleven-year-old, then laughed. "I promise. No pretty faces for me."

"And no tattoos. Tattoos are gross."

Harmony nearly chuckled, thinking of a secret she knew about someone very close to her. "If you insist."

Sheri appeared to accept that answer and lay back against the pillows again. "I'm ready to read now. I'd like to hear the end."

She flipped the book back open and gently cleared her throat. "Haste to the Wedding," Harmony said, reading the chapter title.

Harmony had met the Mercers through a charitable wish granting organization for terminal children. As a popular Christian music artist, Harmony helped fulfill Sheri's wish and allowed her to sing at one of her concerts. The talent she'd heard in the little body amazed her. She prayed daily that God would heal Sheri so that her voice could be a gift to the world. As she got sicker, she lost her stamina and the ability to sing for very long, so Harmony sang for her. Once or twice a week, depending on her own schedule, she came to the hospital and softly sang or read to Sheri.

At four in the afternoon, this floor of hospital produced little noise. It was that peaceful time between meals and shift changes at nurses' stations, with most children taking an afternoon nap. Occasionally, Harmony would hear the wheels of a cart or a hospital bed go past the open door of the room as meals were served or patients were relocated for tests and the like, but for the most part, nothing invaded the quiet except the wheezing panting sounds as Sheri battled for her next breath.

As Harmony finished the chapter, she looked up and saw that Sheri had fallen into a deep sleep. Wondering how much of the chapter she'd heard before she gave in to the demands of the disease ravaging her body, Harmony slipped the book back into her bag. "I'll be back Monday to finish the book," she promised, standing and leaning over the bed to press a kiss to the child's forehead. "Try to hang on until then," she whispered. She straightened already perfectly straight covers and made sure Sheri could reach her water cup when she woke up.

Sadness tried to break through the wall of self-control she had carefully constructed. She mustn't let it out. Volunteering with terminally ill children in one of Nashville's largest hospitals did not allow for emotional breakdowns on the ward. She reserved breakdowns for long showers, when she could cry and wail and let it all out and no one would ever witness it except God.

She walked out of the room and the tile floor changed from bright green to bright blue. She passed a painting of a giant whale swimming along the wall then a school of fish. Eventually the tile and walls changed from blue to a light tan. Now crabs and seagulls watched her make her way to the nurses' station. The nurses treated her cordially, used to seeing her by now and no longer overly starstruck. She signed out on the visitor's log, left her badge in the plastic basket next to the clipboard, and waved good-bye to two nurses coming out of one of the rooms.

She didn't have time to stay and chat, so she walked to the bathrooms in the corridor by the elevator. Inside, she quickly stripped out of her purple scrubs and pulled on a long white, sleeveless dress that fell to mid-calf. After wrapping a silk scarf embroidered with lavender flowers around her small waist, she slipped on purple bracelets and purple hoop earrings. Purple heels helped elevate her height three whole inches, helping her barely scrape the five-four mark. Finally, she pulled the clip out of her hair and let the long blonde curls fall well past her shoulders and down her back. Doing a partial spin, she checked to make sure all clothing looked in order before pushing the scrubs and tennis shoes into her bag and rushing from the bathroom.

On the ground floor, she walked along the corridors, smiling and nodding at people who knew her or recognized her, but she did not stop to speak. Once she entered the parking garage, the oppressive heat of the Nashville July day wrapped around her, pushing back the chill of the artificially cool environment of the hospital. In no time, she drove out of the garage and into the Nashville traffic, trying not to look at the clock on the dashboard. Her family would understand her late arrival, of course, but she hated arriving late for anything. Thankfully, the upcoming Independence Day weekend must have lightened the downtown Nashville traffic load because she pulled into her spot in the parking garage of her family's building in record time.

Harmony began singing professionally as a young teenager, and her older brother Franklin managed not only her career, but the career of many other family members. Harper Enterprises was a long-standing name in Christian entertainment. Her father and grandfather cohosted an internationally syndicated daily radio program together and had written dozens of books on marriage and family. In her own right, her mother, a well sought-after song writer, had authored several books on parenting and marriage, and her aunt had written several screenplays and currently managed a Christian film production company.

Today would begin the Harper Enterprises Board of Trustees meeting, which they euphemistically called the Harper Family Meeting. Held on the first Friday of every new quarter, it would probably last until Saturday night, filling the hours with meals, fellowship, prayer, discussions, and business. Harmony hoped they concluded their business by then, because she had to fly to San Francisco on Saturday night for her Sunday July Fourth concert.

The heat of the day immediately enveloped Harmony as she got out of her car, and she wished she'd kept her hair up. She couldn't believe the high temperature so early in July, and had a feeling that the summer would be a hard one this year. She popped her trunk and grabbed her suitcase. In the elevator, she punched a special code that granted her access to the top floor of the building where her brother Franklin, who usually hosted the meeting, lived.

The elevator opened directly onto Franklin's living room. Glass walls offered a breathtaking view of downtown Nashville from twenty stories up. A giant sitting area with a circle of black leather couches took over one end of the room while a long table that seated ten sat under a crystal chandelier on the other end. Near the base of the spiral staircase, which led up to the four bedrooms on the floor above, sat a grand piano.

A uniformed maid greeted her at the elevator and relieved her of her suitcase. Chandra had graying red hair, deep wrinkles on her face, and a thick waist. "Good evening Miss Harmony, the family is out on the roof terrace."

"Oh. Thanks, Chandra," Harmony returned.

"I'll put your bags in Mr. Franklin's room," she said. "He said to tell you he'd be sleeping on the couch instead of you."

"Don't you dare," Harmony replied with a smile as she stepped back into the elevator. "I'll stay on the couch like I always do. I prefer it to his bedroom."

"Yes ma'am," Chandra agreed with a smile dimpling the wrinkles on her cheeks. "I'll just put your bag in there and let y'all fight that fight then make the beds whenever you figure it out."

The ride to the roof took mere seconds. She stepped out and automatically took a deep breath of the fragrant garden. Franklin had spent the better part of ten years transforming the roof of the building into a paradise retreat. A vegetable garden he faithfully tended flourished on one half of the roof. Potted trees and plants lined a large koi pond that ran down the center of the roof with beautiful fountains on either end. The remainder of the roof he left for business and pleasure. Harmony found her family near the large gazebo next to a smoking barbecue grill. Her aunt Dee, her father's sister and award winning screenwriter, stood at a table in the shade of the gazebo, pouring lemonade into frosty glasses.

"There she is," her mother, Alice, said, coming toward her. Harmony had overheard people remarking on just how much she and her mother looked alike her entire life. Her mother had gifted Harmony with golden blonde hair, though she kept hers cut in an attractive bob to her chin. The blue top she wore with white capris made her blue eyes shine.

"Here I am," Harmony said with a smile, hugging her mom tightly. "I was at the hospital this afternoon."

"Franklin told us." Her mom gestured toward her brother, who stood next to the grill in perfectly pressed khaki pants, a white long-sleeved shirt, and a blue and red striped tie. Over his clothes, he wore a black and white pin-striped apron. "Your grandfather had the grill delivered last week. He thought we might enjoy meeting outside if the weather was nice."

Harmony pulled a hair band out of her pocket and wrapped her long hair into a sloppy bun. "It's July, mom, in Tennessee. Why would he think the weather would be nice?"

Her grandfather approached, also wearing a shirt and tie like her brother. "I can hear you, little girl," he said with a smile. "I'm old, not deaf." Stuart Harper had pioneered Christian talk radio and carried his mantle as Harper Enterprises' patriarch very seriously.

"We're just cooking the meal up here," her grandmother, Liz, interjected, slipping her arm into her husband's. "I don't think you can beat grilled chicken on Fourth of July weekend, can you?"

"Even if we do have to work," her father, Grayson, added from his station next to the grill. "I've tried for forty years to get dad to change the meeting in July, but he never has."

His sister, Dee, set the pitcher down and brought Harmony a glass. "I remember one year when you went off to some picnic with friends instead of attending the meeting."

"You only did that once, as I recall," Stuart murmured.

Her father cringed. "Some lessons you only need to learn once."

Harmony laughed and took a sip of her lemonade,

feeling the stress from Sheri Mercer's decline in health gradually fade away amidst the love of her family. She walked over to where her brother manned the grill. "Smells good," she said with a smile.

From behind her, Grayson agreed. "It does. It almost makes me want to give up being a vegetarian." Grayson had become a vegetarian when he started dating Alice. While Franklin and Harmony had grown up that way, no one else in the family ever embraced their food lifestyle.

Using tongs, Franklin picked up a chicken leg and set it on a platter next to the grill. "I balked at the idea of grilling at first, but now I'm glad I caved. Chandra's organizing the caterer inside with all the sides that go with the meat."

"It's hotter over here by the grill," Harmony observed, fanning herself. "How can you stand having your shirt sleeves down?"

Franklin smiled. "When I thought to roll them up, I had sauce on my hands and figured I'd just soldier on. Don't want to get stains all around my cuff links." He set the tongs down and wiped his hands on the apron. "Besides, I think it would ruin my stuffy reputation if I were seen with rolled up sleeves."

Harmony giggled and thought about the anchor tattoo Franklin had gotten in a much, much more wild and rebellious youth. "You just don't want grandpa to see your tattoo," she whispered as she snatched a Brussels sprout out of the pan sitting on the corner of the grill.

"I'm not ashamed of my tattoo," Franklin objected, though he kept his voice very low.

Harmony grinned and said, "I have it on very good authority that little girls think they're gross."

Grayson piped up. "What's gross? Brussels sprouts?"

Harmony hoped he hadn't heard the tattoo remarks. "No, daddy. No one thinks Brussels sprouts are gross."

"Speak for yourself," Stuart chuffed.

Harmony turned back to Franklin. "I don't think a stuffy reputation has anything to do with it."

"It takes many good deeds to build a good reputation, and only one bad one to lose it."

Before Franklin could source the quote, Harmony said, "Benjamin Franklin. I know, Franklin." She patted his shoulder. "Trust me, brother, your reputation as a stuffed shirt is under no threat."

At his mock shock, she laughed and turned toward her aunt, launching into a conversation about the travel arrangements for Sunday's concert. Dee planned to go with her to give her some company and help provide the courage it would take for her to do that concert. Thirty minutes later, the family sat around the dining room table, heads bowed, as Stuart blessed the meal. As soon as he said, "Amen," platters of chicken, grilled vegetables, salad, and bread started getting passed around the table.

She listened to the chatter of family talk as everyone ate. Dee's youngest daughter had just started college and she told a funny anecdote about the new roommate. Harmony felt herself slipping more and more into her head until her grandmother pulled her out of her thoughts with a hand on her wrist.

"How is your little girl at the hospital?" Liz asked.

Harmony looked at her grandmother and thought about the frail body she'd left languishing in a hospital bed just an hour before. She didn't really want to discuss it at the dinner table, so she tried to keep her answer short.

"She's a fighter, but without divine healing, she won't make it through the month."

"It's good, what you do," Grayson said. "Your mother and I are proud of your heart."

Without warning, tears burned her eyes as she thought of the years she had spent volunteering on that wing of the hospital. "I appreciate that. Every time I lose one of them, I tell myself I won't go back. But then I go back so I tell myself I won't get attached. But then I get attached. And then they depart from this world and my heart gets ripped apart and I start all over again."

Dee, who sat to her left, reached over and took her hand. "Not everyone can walk into a children's hospital and give such joy as you do. It's a gift from God. Don't feel like it's something you shouldn't do. Just pray for strength to endure it."

She took a deep shaking breath and prayed she could make it through the next few seconds without bursting into tears. She tried to think of the joy Sheri had shown when she met her for the very first time. Focusing on the beautiful smiling face of the then ten-year-old rather than the gray and sunken face of the now eleven-year-old, she felt her control slip back into place. With Franklin's next words, she stopped thinking of the sick little girl altogether. "Have you told the family about the details of the concert you're doing this weekend?"

Her teeth clenched in frustration. She had argued with him about this concert for two months and felt weary of the subject. She intentionally kept her face blank and looked at him. "I wasn't aware that at twenty-six I still needed their permission to sing in a concert. Or that after hundreds of concerts in my life, they'd be interested in any specific one."

Franklin set his fork down. "A secular concert. You'll be sharing the stage with rappers and heavy metal and—"

"And!" she interrupted, "I'll be singing about God to a captive audience, Franklin. What don't you get about that?" This aspect of Franklin's personality truly baffled her. Performing on stage was just as much her mission on earth as visiting dying children in the hospital.

"This is why I didn't agree with your decision to cross your albums over to pop. I knew it would come to this."

She unceremoniously dropped her fork and crossed her arms as she sat back against the chair. "That it would come to this? I've been crossing over for five years. You're acting like you just walked into the room and caught me summoning a demon."

"Harmony!" Her mother cautioned, then superfluously dabbed at her lips with her napkin and set it on top of her plate. She did not need to elaborate for Harmony to understand the silent message to quit having a temper tantrum at the dinner table. Alice stood and gestured toward the sitting area. "Let's take five minutes and let Chandra clear the table. We'll go ahead and start the business meeting at the couches."

Neither Franklin nor Harmony would dare to continue the argument their mother had very intentionally ended. Instead, they both walked to the circle of couches and chairs and chose seats well away from each other. As the rest of the family made their way over, Dee slipped on a pair of reading glasses and retrieved a stack of papers from the coffee table. "Here is the agenda for the weekend," she announced, handing each person a stapled packet. "We have quite a bit of business to discuss, and you all know that Harmony and I have a flight out tomorrow night, so let's go ahead and get started."

Franklin spoke to Chandra, who cleared dishes from the dining room table. "Whenever you're free, can you bring in the coffee?"

"Sure thing," Chandra confirmed as one of the catering staff joined her in her chore.

Harmony settled into the chair, glad she'd made it to a comfortable arm chair before anyone else. She knew business would occupy the next several hours. Glancing through the agenda, she inwardly cringed when she saw a planned discussion about her new album topping the pop charts.

♫ ♫ ♫ ♫

CHARLES Richard Galton tried to lie very still in his twin-size bed with his ear buds firmly in place. He had to lie perfectly still because his parents had expressly forbidden him to ever play this music. Should they discover his choice of music, it could lead to further revelations and possibly even uncover his very serious and very dark secret.

He lay atop his perfectly made bed fully clothed in dress shoes and socks, khaki dress slacks, and a white button down short-sleeved shirt with a light blue tie and a cross tie pin. His mouse brown hair gripped his skull like a winter watch cap, parted with a geometrically straight part on the left-hand side and combed tightly down then secured in place with a few oily splashes of hair tonic. His skin looked nearly as pale as his white shirt and did nothing to highlight his unremarkable brown eyes.

Anyone looking at Charles Galton would immediately label him as a likely intelligent young man with a sweet temperament and a sunny disposition. He dressed well. He rarely spoke out of turn or offered an unkind word. He had never had a girlfriend. He resided in a Christian home, had been baptized at the age of eleven, and was active in his youth group. He made straight As in a private Christian high school and actively participated in Computer Club. In a few years he would obtain a degree sufficient to begin a lifetime of work as an accountant or an engineer.

In the upper middle class suburban home surrounding him, his bedroom looked exceptionally well ordered, uncluttered, and organized. Most young men in the middle of their sophomore year in high school had some trophies or keepsakes on display and the posters of fast cars or popular sports figures of a few short years before began to make way for posters of beautiful women usually adorned in bikinis. Charles had neither trophies nor posters in his room and never had. Besides the bed, the single bedside table sporting a simple lamp, and the five-drawer chest of drawers, only a bookcase and a small desk broke up the space. No one looking at the picturesque upper middle class suburban home, or catching a glimpse of Charles Galton himself engaged in any public activity, would ever guess the nature of his dark secret.

Lying perfectly still in the very center of his bed, Charles closed his eyes and allowed himself to silently pray a quick prayer to his master. "Oh, Lucifer, bringer of light, make my hand steady and quick that I may serve you well tonight."

The fact that he had inadvertently prayed a little rhyme pleased him and he hoped it also pleased his master. The harsh strains of the acid rock band blaring in his ears made his prayer to Satan feel even more delicious. He opened his eyes and spotted his mother standing in the doorway of his room. He hit pause on his MP3 player and sat up with a warm and welcoming smile.

"Hey, Charlie Brown," his mother greeted. The

nickname made him want to set her on fire and burn her alive but his warm smile never faltered. "I called for you a few times."

Charles' lips twitched and he kept himself from sneering. "Sorry, mommy. I guess the music was too loud."

She clucked at him like a sick chicken. "You know better, Charlie. You'll hurt your ears. Anyway, Frankie D is downstairs. You ready?"

He carefully moved to the edge of the bed and then stood up very smoothly but without revealing any of his newly discovered power. One day she would realize how powerful he was, but he had to deceive her until that day. "All set, mommy."

He picked up his carefully packed backpack and they went downstairs to find Francis Dawkins, aka Frankie D, standing in their entryway speaking with his father about tomorrow's trip to see Harmony Harper playing at the children's benefit. Oh, absolutely standing because sitting down would be imposing. Sitting down would be taking advantage of your hospitality, Mr. and Mrs. Galton. I'll just be a moment and thank you so very much I just couldn't possibly impose.

"There are going to be all kinds of secular groups there, too, of course. But Harmony Harper is worth a tank of gas, I think. We don't have to hang around for any of the more objectionable groups, you know."

Francis Dawkins was the kind of youth minister that passed every kind of parental inspection. He always wore a tie, and he always carried a little black New Testament. He smelled clean, like vanilla and drugstore aftershave. His clothes smelled like dryer sheets and the creases in his slacks could slice carrots. He was perfectly polite at all times and at all costs. He was youthful, single, always had a clean joke, and kept his thick beard shaved so close that his chin almost looked blue. He had warm hazel eyes and a ready smile that conveyed habitual kindness. Charles wanted to be Francis Dawkins when he grew up.

"Well, there he is. Hey there, Charles. How are ya?" The right hand, the hand not crating around the little black New Testament, shot out as if spring loaded, as if activated by the smile of greeting like some kind of zany switchblade knife.

"Hey, Pastor Frank. I'm good." He shook hands and their mutual smiles grew perhaps a bit secretive or even furtive when each of them pressed their fingers into each other's palms in a certain way. Charles knew his parents would never catch on to the secret handshake and the fact that they could do it right there in plain sight made his heart race.

His dad spoke. "What's the agenda?"

Francis replied, "Cookout and bonfire at the church tonight then we'll have the lock-in. At ten in the morning, we'll load into the church van and drive to the concert. It should be terrific."

His father patted him on the shoulder. Charles managed not to shudder in absolute disgust and revulsion. "He's a good boy and works so hard in school. He deserves a treat like this. Have a good time, son." Charles imagined chopping his father's fingers off one by one unless the oaf took them off his shoulder. How had this creature lent him half of his DNA? Perhaps he was really adopted.

His mother appeared from the den. "Speaking of Harmony Harper, have you had a chance to listen to her latest CD?" She shoved a brand new CD case under Pastor

Frank's nose. It was purple, like all of Harmony Harper's CDs, and still had the cellophane wrapper on the outside. "I was picking up my prescription this afternoon when they were delivered to the drugstore. Lucky I got it, really. The news is saying that she sold out in record time today. This is the one with the song with that little sick girl."

Francis Dawkins made his face look beatific, forming his mouth into the shape of an angelic smile. "That is fantastic, Mrs. Galton. Is this copy for Charles?"

She beamed and nodded. "I know how much my Charlie Brown loves her voice. He's always listening to her songs."

Charles tasted bile in the back of his throat but kept his smile intact. Instead of saying how much he wanted to hurt this woman, he managed, "I love you so much, mommy. Thank you. Can I take it with me?"

Francis nodded as if the answer should be obvious. "You better take it with you, man! That will be great! Maybe you can get her to sign it at the concert tomorrow!"

♫ ♫ ♫ ♫

BURNING pain between his fingertips jolted Steven Slayer to awareness. Cursing, he dropped the cigarette butt on the floor and shook his hand. He must have zoned out holding it. Gratefully, the burn was far from where he held his pick. It would not do for the lead singer and guitarist of Abaddon to find himself unable to strum his Stratocaster because of a party foul. With blurry eyes, he found the burnt up butt and ground it beneath the heel of his boot without any consideration for the terra cotta tile floor beneath his heel.

Everywhere he looked, Steve saw intoxicated people—sitting on couches, leaning against walls, lounging on cushions on the floor. Where had they all come from? The loud music and smoky air made his stomach turn. He had to get out. Standing, he stumbled over the body of a woman on the floor at his feet, crashing into the glass coffee table and falling to the ground as glass and bottles and pills went flying. Somehow, he managed to turn his body and land hip-first instead of hand-first, saving his golden tickets from getting slashed to ribbons by the glass, making sure he would live to play his guitar another day.

Someone must have found it amusing, because he heard drunken laughter coming from the low couch covered in bodies. Clumsily, Steve got to his feet and stumbled through the house, pausing in the game room when he saw the circle of girls sitting on his pool table passing around a large bong. Some part of his brain tried to work through the haze of whatever drug he'd last consumed and tell them to get off his forty-thousand-dollar hand carved rosewood table, but his heavy tongue wouldn't form the words. Instead, he pushed through the double doors and stumbled out onto the patio.

A man sitting near a fire pit strummed a guitar. How that person thought he could be overheard from the loud banging Abaddon music coming through the house speakers puzzled Steve's intoxicated brain.

The fresh air brought a moment of clarity. Away. Steve had to get away from this house full of people. He fell off the patio and onto the sand. Now on his hands and knees, he thought if he could just get to the water, a dunk into the cold waters of the Pacific Ocean ought to clear his head.

He fell twice more trying to get to the surf. The farther away from the house he got, the more he could hear the sound of the waves hitting the beach and the fainter the music became. Planning to strip as he walked, he kicked off his leather boots. When he reached to rip off his shirt, Steve realized he wasn't wearing one. When had he taken off his shirt?

He half stumbled, half fell into the water and let the next wave carry him away.

♫ ♫ ♫ ♫

Chapter 2

THE bonfire felt hot against their young faces. The fire cast eerie light and shadows against their crimson robes. It amused Frankie D that the church had funded their purchase as "choir robes" prior to last year's Christmas cantata. They considered themselves warlocks whom Lucifer had granted special supernatural powers. The youth group consisted of six acolytes, all young men like Charles, with Francis acting as the priest. Francis had once studied under a Satanic high priest known only as Railroad in their home state of California, and he had also been to one meeting in Rome. He knew all the rituals.

Charles also knew about the coven of witches in the area, but the priesthood of warlocks would only worship with them once a year and Charles had only joined eight months earlier. Still, they greeted each other when they passed in the hallways at school or saw each other out in town. To all appearances, the witches—girls about his own age—looked exactly as normal as Charles looked give or take a piercing or henna tattoo.

They began to chant as the moon rose. When the moon finally achieved first quarter, they all stood and disrobed. Performing the remainder of the ritual in the nude demonstrated fearlessness. It also made it much easier to clean up any otherwise hard to explain arterial spray that might inadvertently stain their garments, red or not.

Francis had brought the goat, as usual, but tonight Charles had the honor of both slaying the beast and making the sacrifice. The other five acolytes spread-eagled the goat, laughing at the animal's terror. They stood at the five points of the pentagram with the terrified goat in the center. Francis prayed over the dagger, cleansed it in the flames of the bonfire, then handed the hot blade over to Charles.

"Do you bring a sacrifice?" Francis recited.

"I bring suitable sacrifices for my master," Charles answered.

"What sacrifices do you bring?"

Charles turned the dagger in his palm and recited, "I bring the sacrifice of blood."

Francis raised his arms high so that his naked body looked spread-eagled in the firelight. "*Deprecamur, ut sanguis!*" We bring you blood.

With that, Charles struck, stabbing the dagger into the goat's outstretched neck before quickly sawing it out through the throat. The animal shuddered and brayed in gurgling agony and its hot blood blanketed the naked congregation.

As the animal died, Charles carefully cleaned the dagger using the ritual cloth, then poured olive oil over the steel before allowing the flames of the bonfire to once more lick the blade. Francis intoned, "What else do you bring?"

Now the moment of truth had arrived. Charles swallowed, then answered, "I bring the sacrifice of flesh."

Francis rolled his eyes up into his head and muttered, "*Deprecamur, ut in carne.*" We bring you flesh.

After only the smallest of hesitations, Charles used the dagger to slice the very tip of his own left pinkie finger off. In time the wound would heal and barely even leave a mark, and the cut didn't hurt as badly as he had imagined. He had done it. He had made himself into a human sacrifice at the altar of the dark one.

He lifted the flap of severed skin to his lips and touched it to his tongue, symbolically eating the sacrificed flesh, before passing it to Francis. Francis accepted the offering with great ceremony, then touched it to his tongue and passed it around the circle. Charles had now been elevated to the status of Journeyman Acolyte.

When everyone had tasted his flesh, he used the ritual cloth to bandage his skin and stop the bleeding. Francis then intoned, "What else do you bring?"

Charles smiled and answered, "I bring an enemy for the flames." With that, he lifted the Harmony Harper CD from the ground and offered it to Francis.

Francis grinned and stripped the cellophane from it, then removed the CD disk itself from the case. He allowed the case to fall to the ground. It would be an excellent place for Charles to hide a bootleg copy of Steven Slayer or some other true believer's work.

Francis held the CD high and announced, "*Nos vobis inimicus!*" We bring you your enemy. He then tossed the CD into the flames. Harmony Harper's smiling face on the front of the CD melted as the flames engulfed it.

♫ ♫ ♫ ♫

STEVE jerked awake when he felt the toe of a boot nudge him. It took a moment to get his bearings. The pink sun peeked over the rooftops of the row of houses crowding the shore, bracing itself to race into the sky of a newborn day. The early morning light turned the white beach sand shades of pink and crimson and gave the sea foam a golden halo as it blew in with the surf.

He lay face down in the sand. As he pushed himself up to his knees, he realized that he didn't have on a shirt and ocean water had soaked his jeans. His head pounded and his stomach rolled. The cool morning air and the remnants of the chemicals he had put in his bloodstream made him shiver.

"Good morning, sunshine." Though his manager, Cain Proctor, spoke in a normal tone of voice, it sounded like a gong going off inside Steve's head.

Steve pushed himself to a sitting position and drew his legs up. The sand scraping against his bare feet made him wonder where he'd left his shoes. As he moved, he winced at a sudden pain near his hip. Squinting his eyes against the harsh light of the morning sun, he inspected the nasty gash, gingerly prodding it with the tip of a finger. He had no recollection of what had happened.

He tried to swallow, but the taste of salt water and the grit of sand on his tongue and lips made him gag. So thirsty. Steve needed a drink. He took a few deep breaths. The morning air felt cool in his lungs. Deciding he could maybe stand without falling, he rose to his feet. Wobbling slightly, he pushed both hands through his tangled mane of hair. He needed a shower to wash the salt water, blood, and sand from his skin.

Steve patted his damp pockets but came up empty. Without a word exchanged between them, Cain handed him a cigarette and a lighter. As soon as Steve lit the cigarette, Cain held out a little blue pill and a bottle of spring water.

"What's that?"

"It's called you have a concert tonight and you need to function."

He didn't want the pill. He never wanted the pills. Just like he didn't want the party the night before. He knew he would swallow the pill despite the fact that he didn't want it. He had a concert tonight. He did indeed need something to help him function. With a sigh, he popped the pill in his mouth and washed it down with the entire bottle of water. He felt a little better washing the salt water and sand out of his mouth.

He turned and looked at the row of houses behind him, getting his bearings and finding his own blue bungalow. He hadn't wandered too far away this time.

"They're all gone," Cain confirmed.

For the first time, Steve looked at him. Cain took the term Hipster to an all new level. He wore a navy suit with all the edges trimmed in white, making him look like a cartoon drawing. He also wore a red and white checkered shirt buttoned to the neck, horn-rimmed glasses, and black gauges in his ears the size of nickels. Steve wondered when he'd grown the soul patch and thought it looked like Hitler's mustache had moved a few inches south.

"Who are all gone?" The water he'd consumed started to make him feel better, or maybe the little blue pill, and his brain began to lose some of the haze of the hangover.

"The people who were there last night."

"The groupies you invited?" He started walking, knowing that Cain would follow. "I told you I didn't want a party."

"It's the Fourth of July and you're Steven Slayer, lead singer and lead guitarist of Abaddon. You throw parties. Wild parties."

He wanted to rail and scream, but the pounding in his head prevented him from doing anything more than quietly saying, "I don't want any more parties for a while. I need a break."

He felt out of breath walking through the shifting sand. His side ached terribly. He thought he might need to get it looked at. Even as these thoughts flitted through his tired mind, the pill started working its magic. By the time he walked up the steps to his patio, past the fire pit that still smoldered, and entered his house, he forgot about the pain in his side.

A team of cleaners worked on the final touches from cleaning up after the party. There was no telling how early they had arrived to have the house in this perfected condition at dawn. His floor shone. The big white circular couch gleamed. The glass dining room table sparkled. He couldn't even tell he'd had a mass of groupies there the night before, and at this point, he didn't care anymore. Framed gold and platinum records lined the walls in place of any personal photographs. He walked barefoot across the tile floor and headed straight for the large stainless steel refrigerator in the kitchen. Someone had already restocked his supply, and he pulled out a cold green bottle of his favorite beer. He drank most of it before he made it to his bedroom.

Black sheets covered his circular bed that sat on the

platform. On the wall above the bed sat a giant framed painting of him playing his guitar done all in reds and blacks. For some reason, a suitcase sat open on the bed. He frowned at it then remembered he had a show tonight. Obviously, Cain had left him a message that he needed to pack. He belched at the suitcase, then laughed at the hilariousness of the action as he sauntered into his bathroom.

There, he stripped his damp jeans off. While he loaded his toothbrush with toothpaste, he stared at his reflection in the mirror. His normally green eyes stared back at him, red-rimmed and pale gray. His dirty blond hair hung in a tangled mass to his shoulders, and several days' growth of a beard gave him a barbaric look.

He hated himself. He knew it, but occasionally the thought surprised him. As the beer and the pill brought on a mild buzz, he shot his reflection the middle finger before stepping into the steaming shower. He tossed his empty beer bottle in the general direction of the small trash can and jammed the toothbrush into his mouth.

♫ ♫ ♫ ♫

"DUDE, where are we going?" Chaz Acker, Abaddon's drummer, threw himself into the white leather seat next to Steve on the record label's private jet. The rest of the band filled the other seats and the long couch that covered half of the cabin. Faux mahogany paneled walls with brass accents made the cabin feel luxurious and inviting. A uniformed flight attendant closed the double doors to the cockpit, bringing the two halves of the record label's logo together. After securing the door, she went to the bar and began preparing the band members' drinks of preference. The first class sized seating faced both front and rear, lending the small cabin an illusion of space.

"Don't know. Don't care." Steve opened his eyes and looked at Cain, who sat in a chair facing him. "What's this gig on the Fourth of July, man? I'd rather spend my day on the beach and wait for the fireworks."

"It's a benefit concert." Cain looked up from the book in his hands. "They sold out the Giants' stadium. That place holds over eighty thousand seats. This is a big deal."

Steve's heart fell into his stomach. "San Francisco Giants?"

"The very same."

"Benefit for what?" asked Eli Malcom, the Jamaican keyboard player. He lifted a perfectly rolled marijuana joint to his lips and licked the paper to seal it. His dreadlocks stood up at crazy angles all around his head.

"No smoking on this plane. You know that. No excuses. And, does it matter? Eighty thousand seats." Cain picked his book back up and added, "Something for sick kids. Not positive. Whatever."

Steve's pulse rate felt very skittish and his vision started to tunnel. As cold sweat broke out over his whole body, he thought, *a children's benefit concert in San Francisco? What kind of cruel joke is this?* Maybe the god everyone was always babbling about really did exist after all. If so, it looked like that deity had set him up for a serious ironic butt kicking, revenge for all of his wrong doings, maybe.

Eli lifted the joint to his lips and held the flame of his lighter up to the end of it, smirking in Cain's direction. As soon as it started burning, Steve reached out and snatched it from him. He took a long drag on it before passing it back to Eli, then leaned back in his seat and closed his eyes, holding the drug infused smoke in his lungs as long as he could before slowly exhaling.

As his limbs started to tingle, his heartbeat slowed and sweat cooled his body. He must have dozed, because he woke up as the plane's tires hit the ground with a loud chirp. For a moment, he felt complete disorientation, then he remembered.

San Fran. Concert.

"What time do we take the stage?" asked Anton Ramirez, the band's rhythm guitarist. He had short black hair that he kept shaved close to his head and a black pencil thin mustache on the edge of his lip. He wore his standard black leather pants, black turtleneck, and black boots. On a silver chain around his neck hung his Baphomet amulet of a snake eating its tail forming a circle that went around a pentagram containing the image of a ram's head.

Cain stuffed his book into his bag. "Curtain up at eight-thirty."

The band's bassist, Adolf Judge, ran his hands through his long blond hair and scrubbed at his full beard. With his beard and Scandinavian features, he looked like a crazy Viking. He had changed his name from Adam to Adolf on his eighteenth birthday. "Dude, I'm starving."

"We'll have dinner at the stadium." Cain turned his phone on as the plane taxied. "Caterers should have a nice spread laid out by the time we get there."

Steve sat up and unbuckled his seat belt. "I have an errand to run."

Cain stared at him for several seconds before checking the time. "You're scheduled to be on the stage in four hours."

As soon as the flight attendant had the door open, Steve pushed himself to his feet. "See you at the stadium."

"Where...."

Chaz, Steve's best friend since fifth grade, put a hand on Cain's arm. "I'm going with him. We'll see you at the stadium."

Annoyed that Chaz had intervened and simultaneously relieved that he would not have to go alone, Steve gave his best friend a short nod. Chaz knew, and Chaz had his back.

"Don't be late," Cain said. "You have one hour. One. Hour."

Steve stole a glimpse of Chaz's profile as they walked across the tarmac. "You don't need to babysit me, man."

Chaz spun a drumstick in his hand like a baton. He stood shorter than Steve's six feet, with red hair and a red goatee. His green eyes looked at his best friend with a sober expression. "I kind of do, bro."

Steve stopped walking and patted his pockets. "I don't have any...."

"It's all good, bro." Chaz slapped his hip. "I got some cash. We'll catch a cab."

Twenty minutes later, the two men stood in the cemetery and stared at the polished marble headstone. Steve fell to his knees in front of it. As shaky as he felt, his hand was steady as he traced his fingers over the words.

GRACE SLATER
BELOVED DAUGHTER

The wail came out of Steve's soul and he found himself face down in the grass with the tombstone at his head.

"I'm sorry I'm sorry I'm sorry," he whispered, over and over again as the drugs mixed with the grief and made his body feel like the earth spun faster and faster around him, until he gripped the grass with both hands, afraid that the force of the spinning world would throw him off the face of the planet.

BILL Rhodes watched as Francis Dawkins slid from the driver's seat of the church van and walked across the gravel toward him. He slipped his hands into the pockets of his black denim jeans and smiled a cold smile. Few people could pull off the clandestine nature of Francis working as a youth pastor at some mega church while recruiting ripe teens seeking a real master to serve.

Rorschach patterns made of sweat had formed on his light blue linen shirt. After spending the night aboard the overly air conditioned tour bus, he relished the heat of the sun as it thawed him out. Looking up, he could almost detect the line of brown smog over the city of San Francisco as it battled with the El Niño currents.

"Frankie, my man," he said. He let his eyes wander over the crowd of teenagers piling out of the van. "Looks like business is good."

The summer breeze blew a paper bag along the empty

railroad tracks. Overhead, carrion birds squawked as they flew in a circle, watching the lifeless body of a groundhog about a hundred yards away. He always met his network at a designated railroad crossing. Most only knew him as "Railroad." Francis, a childhood friend, served as one of the few exceptions.

"Welcome home, brother," Francis Dawkins replied. "It's been too long."

"This cat never comes to San Fran. In all my years with him, this is the first time," Bill replied. "What's the mission field like?"

"Ripe for the picking, my man." Frankie laughed. He gestured to a black-haired woman in a tight gray halter-top. "This here is, no kidding, Jezebel. She's a student teacher at a local high school and she is brilliant at plucking ripe fruit." Jezebel stepped forward and slipped under Frankie's arm. "We owe a large portion of our congregation to her."

Bill picked up her hand and stared into her gray eyes. He could see the sluggishness of her pupils and some of the attraction he felt for her faded. "This life is so much more intoxicating when you experience it sober," he murmured, turning her hand and running a finger over the tattoo of a contorted railroad symbol that he found on the inside of her wrist. "Why don't you get that way then come see me in a few hours? Frankie here will know where to find me."

She inhaled with a shaky breath and licked her lips. "Yes, Father."

"Good girl." He puckered and placed cold, dry lips atop her tattoo, imitating a kiss, then released her hand and passed Frankie an envelope. "Here are the tickets to the concert. We'll meet for worship at sundown."

"Looking forward to it." The men shook hands and embraced. As Francis guided the students that he'd brought with him back to the church van, Bill met the eyes of one of the boys. Immediately, he felt a connection with a kindred soul.

"Frankie," he called out. When his friend jogged back up to him, he gestured with his chin. "Who's that boy in the white short-sleeved shirt?"

Francis showed all his teeth when he smiled. "He's the one I e-mailed you about. My greatest disciple and a recent journeyman acolyte. The power in him is almost palpable."

"I should spend time with him while I'm in town."

"I was hoping you'd want to."

"I'll make time tonight. Send him with Jezebel. I'll talk to him after."

"You got it."

Excited energy ran up and down Bill's spine as he watched the group drive away. He felt like something amazing approached unseen, crouching just over the horizon. His fingers felt tingly, his eyesight twitched. He hurried back to see to his tasks so he could prepare for his visitors.

♫ ♫ ♫ ♫

JOURNEYMAN Acolyte Charles Galton spread his arms wide and lifted his face to the sky, soaking in the rays of the sun and letting the voice of Steven Slayer and the music of Abaddon wash over him. Frank had secured VIP tickets for himself and the six acolytes. They'd convinced their parents and peers that they attended the concert only to see the insipid Harmony Harper. Once there, they used the VIP restrooms to change into clothes more suitable to their worship.

Like many others, Charles wore black leather pants and a black tank top. They had taken turns using henna to paint satanic symbols on their arms and necks. Charles wished he could get permanent tattoos, but even Frank chose to use the clandestine washable ink. For now, what they did and how they did it must be kept secret. Charles longed for the day when they could come into the light and wear the mark of the beast on their foreheads. Around his neck he wore a silver amulet much like the one worn by Abaddon's Anton Ramirez.

Standing here, in this stadium, surrounded by the metal band's fans, he felt like he could just let loose and let the inner animal inside of him escape. As he danced, he screamed. He chanted. Above all, he offered tribute to his master. The music washed over him like a force of nature, like ocean water, like wind. It lifted him. He felt like he was floating.

His body and soul hummed with pleasure as the music filled the stadium. His head started to move in rhythm to the beat and soon he found himself right in front of the stage, head banging in time with every pulse. He felt something inside of him come to life as he fisted his hands and screamed with bliss.

♫ ♫ ♫ ♫

"TEN minutes, Miss Harper!" The stage manager pounded on Harmony's door. Three hours earlier, the same stage manager had ushered her below the stadium to this green room that had an attached bathroom. The green paint on the cinder block walls had begun to fade and peel in places, but she had access to a full length mirror, a shower, and a lighted makeup mirror. The varnished cement floors felt cool beneath her feet. Someone had laid out a beautiful fruit and cheese buffet on a table against the wall. She and Dee had gorged themselves on crusty sourdough bread and local California cheese until she thought she wouldn't fit into her stage outfit.

"Thank you!" she replied. Seconds later, she enjoyed the break from the sound of the bass thumping through her every pore as the metal band which had taken the stage before her finished their set. She felt incredibly thankful for the several feet of concrete ceiling that had separated her from the loud music and wondered how people in the audience could stand the cacophony.

As Harmony double checked her appearance, she tucked her white tank top into her white jeans and adjusted the wide sparkling purple belt on her hips. Slipping on purple wedge heels, she shot up several inches in height. The thin soles did little to shield her feet from the cool floor. The ends of the purple scarf tied around her head mixed in with the strands of hair painstakingly curled by the stylist. Tilting her head around, she confirmed that her makeup still looked good an hour after having it applied and she just touched up the lipstick. She turned to her aunt Dee, who sat on the brown leather couch. "How do I look?"

Dee smiled and stood, walking toward her. "Like a pop princess, but with more clothes on."

Knowing that those words meant something different coming from her aunt than if they had come from her brother, she shuddered and said, "Don't let Franklin hear you say that."

Dee put her hands on her shoulders. "Hey, as long as you are listening to the voice of the Holy Spirit and you are where He would have you to be, Franklin's opinion is not what you should concern yourself with." Despite the makeup, she framed Harmony's face with her hands, her rings clinking against Harmony's purple hoop earrings. "But heed my warning, child. Stay on the path. Don't let this world you've entered influence you. You are the light that shines in the darkness. Make sure the darkness doesn't overcome you."

Understanding the respect and love her aunt spoke to her, Harmony stepped forward and hugged Dee close. "Thank you," she said. "Thank you for not assuming that it has already influenced me." As she stepped back, she retrieved her bottle of water from the desk where she'd set it and took a careful long pull before she added, "And don't worry. I can sing and play to stadiums of people and witness to them without being influenced by them."

Another knock at her door surprised her. She looked at the clock on the wall, wondering if she'd let too much time go by. When she opened the door and saw country music superstar Bobby Kent standing on the other side, she squealed and threw her arms around him. He stood tall enough that he nearly lifted her from the floor hugging her back.

"I'm so happy to see you!" she exclaimed. "What are you doing here?"

"Singing the National Anthem at tomorrow's game." He slipped his hat off his dark head and stepped back, allowing his daughter, Lisa, to step into the room.

"Surprise!" Lisa exclaimed as Harmony's heart flooded with love and excitement.

"Oh my, look at how you've grown," Harmony exclaimed, pulling the young teen into her arms. "You're as tall as me now."

"It's so good to see you," Lisa said with a smile. "I couldn't believe it when Daddy surprised me with this concert."

"Have you been enjoying it?"

Lisa shrugged. Harmony felt her heart tug at the way the teen had already started to transform into a young woman. "We just got here. There was a rapper first, and I'm not really a fan. And then Abaddon played next. Daddy said any band named for the Hebrew word for hell wasn't one he'd pay good money to sit and listen to."

Harmony grinned. "So you're just here to see me!"

"Yes! And I guess about a hundred thousand other people out there are, too." Lisa hugged her again. "I've missed you."

"I've missed you, too, girl." She stepped back and looked at the clock on the wall again. "I have to run. Can you have dinner with me later, or are you too jet lagged?"

Bobby nodded. "We already have a table reserved at our hotel. We're at the downtown Viscolli."

"Us, too. I'll see you after my set." She looked behind her at Dee. "Thanks for being here, Auntie Dee."

"Wouldn't be anywhere else." She waved at the door. "Evening, Bobby. How about we pray with this girl before she takes the stage?"

Bobby winked and replied with, "Ma'am." He tossed his hat onto the sofa and held out his hands. Harmony took one, Lisa took the other, and they both held hands with Dee. "Father God," Bobby said in a rich voice, "we ask that you speak through Harmony tonight. People out there need to hear her. Open their hearts, open their ears, and let your words flow." As they said, "Amen," he retrieved his hat then extended an elbow to Lisa. "Ready to find our seats, punk?"

Lisa slipped her hand into the crook of his arm and

Harmony let them lead the way out of the room, turning to wave at Dee one last time.

♫ ♫ ♫ ♫

STEVE accepted the cold bottle of beer from Cain as he stepped off the stage. The exhilaration of performing in front of an audience of tens of thousands never got old. His heart raced, sweat poured down his face, and he heard buzzing in his ears from the adrenaline. Hands slapped him on the back as he took a towel from a stagehand and drained the bottle in a few long gulps.

Chaz ran up to him and grabbed him by both shoulders and screamed in his face. He tossed the bottle away and grabbed Chaz's shoulders and returned the scream with the same exuberance. "You rocked!" Chaz yelled. "That was unbelievable!"

He wanted to talk about the concert some more. He felt like maybe this was one of the best in a long time. Cain walked up to them gesturing with his hands. "Let's get rounded up. Next act is on its way."

"I wouldna want to follow us up, man," Elijah interjected. "Listen to 'em. They're crying for us."

As the buzzing faded from Steve's ears, he could make out the chanting of the crowd. "*Abaddon! Abaddon! Abaddon!*"

A wild-eyed Adolf ran up to Anton. "They're calling for hell to come back!"

Anton laughed as he twisted the top off a bottle of beer and flicked it in Adolf's direction. He held the bottle over his head and started head banging to the crowd, chanting with them. Foam poured out of the top of the bottle and splashed all over them.

"Gentlemen, let's clear the path," someone wearing a headset and holding a clipboard yelled. "Miss Harper needs to get through. We have a room ready for you in the back if you'll please make your way there."

Steve stumbled backward as he tried to take a drink of his fresh beer. He tripped over his own boot and turned and spun, falling into a woman with long blonde hair. The shocked look on her face was almost comical as the two stumbled backward into the wall. As soon as he regained his balance, he stepped back, lifting his hands up but laughing so hard he bent over. "Sorry," he laughed, "I...."

She straightened and brushed at her white pants. Who wore white pants to a rock concert? "You spilled beer on me."

He leaned toward her again. "Well, then, we should probably go get you out of these wet clothes," he said on a laugh.

She froze. He didn't think anyone could possibly stand that tall or that straight. Despite having at least eight inches on her, she managed to angle her head so that she looked down at him. Her eyes, a vivid blue, turned almost black as her cheeks flushed.

"Get out of my way," she ordered quietly but with every bit of derision that her body language exhibited. "Now. I need to get on stage."

He raised an eyebrow. "You?" Taking a swig of his beer, he stepped back and bowed, elaborately gesturing to the stage entrance. "By all means, follow me in your purple glitter and white britches, babe."

Anton guffawed. "Good luck with that." The two men fell against each other, laughing as the stage manager and a stagehand elbowed their way through the Abaddon members. "This way, Miss Harper. I'm so sorry about that," he said.

They each took one of her arms and guided her through the throng of Abaddon band members and staff. Steve watched her all the way to the stage entrance before he turned back to his group. "I hate this town. I need to amscray most ricki-tick."

"Me, too," Chaz said, beating on the wall next to him with his drumsticks. "Let's blow."

Cain checked the time. "There's an after party and we have hotel reservations."

Out of nowhere, rage surged through his chest. He lashed out as his vision filled with a red haze. "No parties. No hotels. Take me home."

Cain put a hand on Steve's shoulder. "Dude, what's wrong with you? Chill."

"No. Take me home." He put both hands on Cain's chest and pushed as hard as he could. "Now!" Cain stumbled backward into Adolf, knocking him into Eli. Steve ran his hands through his hair and grabbed a black and silver chair from next to the wall, straddling it. "I'll just wait right here. I'm not going into some backstage party to get high. Get the plane ready."

Cain straightened his jacket and reached into the inside of his coat pocket. He pulled out a metal box and opened it, selected a green pill, and held it out to Steve. "I'll call the plane. You take this. You're obviously still wound up from playing."

Steve glared at the pill. "I don't want that. I don't need that. I just want to go home."

"This? This is nothing. Nada. It'll just relax you. Make the plane ride more bearable. You're jacked up on energy, man. This will bring you back down to a level playing field."

He slapped Cain's hand so that the pill went flying across the room, landing on the concrete floor and sliding under a pallet of boxes. "I don't want any more pills. I just want to get on the plane, get out of this city, and never come back. Clear?"

"Fine. Great. I'll make the call." Cain walked away. Two minutes later, he returned with two beers in his hand. "All taken care of." He passed one to Steve. "Cheers, brother," he said as the bottlenecks clinked together. "No worries."

"Thanks, man." Relieved, Steve took a long pull of his beer and crossed his arms over the top of the chair, waiting.

♫ ♫ ♫ ♫

AS Harmony stepped out onto the unfamiliar stage, she stared at the sea of people filling the stadium. She might have imagined it, but outdoor lighting, with the same ambers in the same stage light rigs, always felt cooler and less draining to her. She enjoyed performing outside so much more because of it. As the last band of the concert, evening quickly approached and a cool ocean-born breeze blew through the stands as the tide in the bay began to shift. The shocks of the sound waves from the crowd's cheers rippled through her body. Thankful for the earplugs she wore, she waved to the crowd, walking all around the stage so she could wave toward every seat.

The smell of the beer on her pants overwhelmed her, but she knew a lot of that was psychosomatic. It threw her off. It made her feel clumsy and out of place here in this crowd. She wondered if all the naysayers and critics tossing out opinions about her cross over into popular music might know something she didn't after all. Should she, minister for Christ, actually take the stage after a band that openly claimed the Hebrew name for hell as their own and had nothing but bad press about drugs, women, and destructive parties?

"Happy Fourth of July, San Francisco!" Within seconds of the band starting to play, the audience began singing her latest hit with her. She wondered if anyone could even hear her. Humble gratitude flooded her chest that an audience who had given the subsequent bands so much attention and affection appeared to know and like her as well.

Aided and encouraged by industry icons like Bobby Kent and Melody Mason Montgomery, Harmony had started allowing her singles to cross over into pop music just five years before. She'd added one or two songs to each album that could go either way—contemporary Christian or popular. To the surprise of many people, she became what they called an overnight sensation despite her decade's worth of work in the Christian music industry. Her mother helped her with the songs and, so far, all of her releases in the pop charts had hit number one. Now she had an entire album rising in the pop ranks—a mostly evangelical, Christ-centered album.

The size of the crowd did not intimidate her. She'd performed for crowds this size many times in the past. What happened backstage made her incredibly uncomfortable. She'd actually felt frightened by the drunken men around her. What would have happened if the stage manager hadn't come when he had?

Determined to put it behind her, praying silently that Franklin would never find out, she focused on the show. She sang through two songs, introduced her band, sang a Christian song, and another crossover song. Then the lights faded on her band and she stepped into the spotlight. The sun had just finished setting, and the sky had turned a brilliant pink and purple. When she finished this song, the fireworks show would begin. She looked out on the crowd and felt the cool breeze blow against her face. Cameras silently flashed as eighty-thousand people held their breath.

She chose to sing this final song without any accompaniment. She would let the power of her voice be the only instrument presenting this timeless hymn.

Taking a deep breath, she began.

Amazing grace! How sweet the sound

That saved a wretch like me!

I once was lost, but now am found;

Was blind, but now I see.

As she sang, the audience quieted until she felt she could hear even a whisper. She had considered shortening the original seven stanzas down to four or maybe five, but while she had such a captive audience, she would continue singing and decided to include all of the verses she knew.

♫ ♫ ♫ ♫

STEVE finished the beer Cain handed him and had started on another when his ears started buzzing and his stomach started to swirl.

No. No! He slipped him a Mickey? Head spinning, he dropped the bottle and watched in fascination as it hit the ground in slow motion, as the amber liquid spurted up, every droplet catching the dim backstage light, forming a perfect cascading fountain framed by the fracturing green glass.

A burst of laughter rose up in his chest, but he tried to

fight it down. He knew he felt angry about something, but at the moment, he couldn't remember what. So he let the laughter out. He got to his unsteady feet.

He had to—

Wait.

What?

Confused, he sat back down and watched as his band members and their entourage headed down a corridor. Must be a party about to start.

"You coming, man?" Anton gestured down the corridor, but it sounded like he spoke from under a foot of water.

Steve nodded, hearing every creak of muscle and pop of bone inside his neck. "Yeah. Yeah. Be right there." He wondered how he'd spoken around a thick and unyielding tongue.

In the back of his mind, some tiny little part of him started screaming, "No! No party! You wanted to go home!" He shook his head to try to shut the voice up.

He stood, intending to follow the group. As he stepped forward, the voice hit him. *"Amazing grace! How sweet the sound—"*

Gracie? He looked around, frantic. Gracie was here? The voice came from the stage. A woman. He remembered, maybe. A woman in white. Gracie? He'd never heard such a strong, commanding voice before.

♫ ♫ ♫ ♫

HARMONY closed her eyes and found the energy to keep her voice strong as she hit the fifth verse.

Yea, when this flesh and heart shall fail,

And mortal life shall cease,

I shall possess, within the veil,

A life of joy and peace.

She almost heard the voice in her ear. She could skip the sixth verse. The fifth was the important one. She signaled to her drummer and he began a very light rhythmic beat. That also signaled the engineers manning the fireworks.

As she began the last verse, she slowed the tempo down and lifted her hands above her head.

When we've been there ten thousand years...

♫ ♫ ♫ ♫

STEVE heard the words through every cell in his body. They tried to rip him apart. "*Yea, when this flesh and heart shall fail.*"

"Gracie!" The scream came from his very soul and he covered his ears with his hands, trying to drive the words away.

"And mortal life shall cease."

"Gracie!" He fell to his knees, screaming and clawing at his ears. Wails from deep in his soul threatened to rip his body apart. Hands grabbed at him and he fought them off with fists and booted feet, crying and screaming for Gracie.

♫ ♫ ♫ ♫

AS Harmony finished the last line from the last verse, the fireworks show began, lighting up the audience with gold, red, white, and blue light even as her voice still echoed through the stadium. The audience's applause after total rapt silence stunned her and forced her to take a step backward before she grinned and bowed at the waist. The stage lights went off so the audience could fully enjoy the fireworks show. In the dark, she ran back up to the microphone as explosions sounded above her and the dark night sky lit in flashes like a dry lightning storm. "God bless you, San Francisco! And God bless America! Happy Independence Day!"

She ran from the stage to the deafening applause of eighty thousand people. In the wings, her Aunt Dee waited. Harmony hugged her tight as she pulled her earplugs out of her ears.

"That was incredible!" Dee said. "I've never seen you perform with that much energy before."

Harmony grinned and nodded as she accepted a bottle of water from a stagehand. She didn't speak as she took a long swallow and hugged Dee again. Her hands shook a bit, and she felt a joy bubbling inside of her that she didn't think she'd ever felt before.

♫ ♫ ♫ ♫

"I get the feeling I'm not telling you anything you don't already know."

His doctor, a large black man with a silver goatee, looked at his chart again. Steve closed his eyes, leaning back against the hospital bed. As soon as they stabilized him in the emergency room, they had moved him to a private room on the sixth floor. He could see the colorful sparks of Roman candles and bottle rockets occasionally light up the night sky from his window, but he could not hear the sounds through the double pane glass.

He hated hospitals. The squeak of shoes on the tile, the smell of disinfectant, the bright fluorescent lights—he hadn't stepped inside a hospital since the day Gracie died. He took a deep breath and tried to think about the words the doctor said.

His head ached. His earlobe throbbed. Nausea rolled through his gut until he thought he would embarrass himself further. Through it all, a deep-seated shame ate at his soul.

"You only have one kidney, Mr. Slayer. The years of drug and alcohol abuse are destroying the one filter you have left in your body. If you don't stop, you are going to die quickly or you are going to live out the remainder of your shortened life on dialysis in misery then die. In summary, you have to stop."

Steve barely remembered how he got here. Some security men had held him down. He fought and scrapped and tried to get free while his heart pounded so hard he thought it might explode. Eventually, an ambulance arrived and they strapped him onto a stretcher. While the paramedic tried to get him to admit to what drugs he had taken, his arms and legs started to jerk uncontrollably. The nurse told him he'd had a seizure and passed out.

He hated his life. Except for Chaz, he hated his band. He definitely hated his music. He hated drugs and parties. He hated Cain and all of the pills he slipped him. Self-loathing welled up inside of him until he curled his upper lip in disgust. Strangely, though, despite a lack of will to want to live, he absolutely knew he did not want to die.

He felt like someone had blow-dried his mouth. Eyes pounding, sinking deeper into his skull with every millisecond, he forced them open and looked at the doctor. "What do I do?"

♫ ♫ ♫ ♫

HARMONY sat back in the comfortably padded chair, cradling her teacup in her hand, and laughed at the humorous story Lisa Kent had just told about some backstage antics during her dad's last tour. Dee had just excused herself to go to their room. Not many patrons remained in the hotel restaurant, and they had the corner table all to themselves. Their waiter returned occasionally to silently fill water glasses, but he did not press for them to leave. The tip Harmony had given him when she paid the bill more than made up for the late hour.

"I will never forget that summer I got to tour with you," she said, taking a sip of her tea. "Your crew is insane."

He laughed. "Nah. They just know how to have a good time."

"I'd go with insane," Lisa interjected, making them all chuckle again.

Harmony took another sip of tea and held back a yawn. She looked at her watch. "Well, no wonder I'm so sleepy," she said as she stood, "it's midnight and I'm on central time, which makes it two in the morning." She stopped at Lisa's chair. "I love you, girl. I'm so happy to see you."

"It was a great show, Harmony."

She put a hand on Bobby's shoulder as she went by his chair. "Please give my love to Carol. I can't wait to see her at Christmas. And enjoy the game tomorrow."

As she walked through the mostly empty hotel dining room, she rolled her head on her neck. The meeting that ended just 24 hours before had exhausted her before she even got to her concert. During the meeting, she discovered that a good portion of her family clearly felt uncomfortable with her stepping out of the Christian music circles. They worried about the influence on her, and worried about her own reputation.

She tried making them understand just how strong she felt the leading of God in this matter, but they wouldn't hear her. Only Dee and her grandfather stood up for her. In the end, they gave the unanimous consensus to give it two more albums and see what everything looked like before making any firm decisions about it. In the meantime, she would simply pray that God would soften their hearts about the good she could do in the secular music world, about the lives her full albums would touch, and about the words she could freely use in interviews that would reach listeners who would never turn on a Christian radio station.

As she walked into her suite, she set her room key on the table near the door and noticed Dee's already sat there. With a smile, she thought of her grandfather always reminding her to leave the key in the same place in every hotel suite. Clearly, his daughter Dee had created the same habits. She slipped off her earrings and kicked off the purple pumps. She swore she could still smell beer. Of course she knew it was all in her mind. As she sat down on the soft gray couch, she propped her feet up on the coffee table and contemplated making a pot of tea. She'd already had so much tonight, though. Dee hadn't come out of her room, so she must have already gone to sleep.

Performing usually wound her up. Between that and catching up with the Kents, she felt a little hum of energy that she knew would make sleep impossible. Wishing she'd brought a book to read, she reached for the television remote control and saw her cell phone sitting on the table right next to it. The little blue light flashed, signaling a missed call or message.

With a sigh, she saw two missed calls from the children's hospital, one from Sheri Mercer's father, and three calls from Franklin. She could only think of one reason why Mr. Mercer would call her.

Ignoring the time difference, thinking only of fragile

Sheri and the disease destroying her body, she called him back. He answered on the first ring. "Harmony."

"Mr. Mercer. I'm so sorry to have missed—"

"Did you get my voice mail?" She could hear the grief in his voice. How many times had she spoken with parents with that very same tone? She knew what he would say.

"No. I just saw the call and immediately called back."

She heard his shaky intake of breath and steeled herself for the news. "I'm afraid that we lost Sheri. She died three hours ago."

Pain, grief, and anger clawed at her throat. "I'm so sorry, Mr. Mercer," she whispered.

"Thank you for loving her as much as you did. It really meant a lot to her." His voice cracked and he disconnected the call.

She set the phone gently on the couch and stumbled to the bedroom, stripping her clothes off as she went. Through the bedroom, into the bathroom—as the water heated up, she took off her earrings, took out her hair clips, and slipped off her bracelets. She crawled into the shower and as the water hit her skin, her grief erupted out of her. Putting her hands to her mouth to try to stifle the wails of pain, she slid down the wall of the shower and pulled her body into the tightest ball she could form.

♫ ♫ ♫ ♫

THE tires crunched on the gravel road. In the rented sedan, Steve leaned back against the seat and stared at the view of Oregon's Mount Jefferson. The snow-covered peaks seemed completely out of place with the digital car thermostat that told him the temperature outside exceeded ninety degrees.

Chaz slowed as he approached a rusted mailbox. He paused, tapped on the steering wheel for a moment, then turned into the driveway that was little more than ruts in the brown grass, pressed in on both sides by evergreen trees and ferns. After about fifty yards, they bounced around a corner and entered a clearing where a little stone house sat.

Next to the house, a wooden shed had collapsed, succumbing to the elements. What looked like a chicken coop leaned precariously close to a wooden rail fence covered in vines. A wooden porch sagged around the cabin, and rose bushes bloomed in wild abandon right in front of the steps.

"Yep," Chaz said, nodding. "This was my gran's. Haven't been here since I was a teenager."

"It's perfect," Steve said hoarsely, thinking of the isolation. His stomach felt like he had filled it with ice water. Despite the heat when he opened the car door, a cold chill wracked his body. The air smelled like pine and damp dirt. He looked at the mountain, at the white snow, and took a deep breath, wanting to breathe in good and exhale bad. It sent him into a coughing fit that had him bent over, trying to catch his breath. He felt his cheeks flush so hot that his ears burned.

"You okay, man?" Chaz asked walking toward him, but not touching him.

Steve rested his hands on his knees and breathed slowly. Finally, he straightened. "Yeah. I will be."

Chaz opened the car door and grabbed the paper grocery bags out of the back seat. Steve threw his backpack over his arm. They carefully worked their way around the thorny rose bushes and over the precarious porch to the front door. Chaz had the key in his hand, but tried the knob first. It opened without resistance.

They walked into a small kitchen with faded linoleum on the floor and a Formica table in the center of the room. A two-burner gas stove with a half-oven sat next to a refrigerator shorter than him. Ceramic containers shaped like mushrooms lined the counter.

"It's small, but Gram lived here for eighty years. I think it'll be good for what you need." Chaz set the bags on the table then led the way through the kitchen and into the living room. A brown plaid couch with a matching chair flanked a cold fireplace. A dusty coffee table sat in front of the couch, and an end table holding a lamp and a set of crocheted coasters sat next to the chair. An olive green rotary phone sat on a telephone table by the front door. A brown and mustard yellow shag carpet covered the floor.

"Electric and gas should be on. Bedroom's this way," Chaz said, gesturing to the small hall. In front of them, a door hid the linen closet that Chaz opened to gesture toward the sheets and towels packed into plastic bags. To the left, Steve could see the bathroom with the white and black tile and an old claw-foot tub, and to the right a bedroom the size of the living room. It had a metal framed bed covered by a crocheted lace spread. A small couch decorated with maroon roses sat by the large window that looked out on Mount Jefferson.

He took in all of the details as if from a distance looking through a fog. Vaguely, he heard Chaz suggest that he wash the towels before using them, but the words didn't make complete sense. Shaking his head to clear it, he tried to focus.

"Gram left me the place when she died." They walked back into the kitchen. He felt like ants crawled all over his skin and it took every single ounce of energy he had not to slap at his arms and legs. He wanted Chaz to shut up and just leave him alone.

"Thanks, man. For the ride and for the place to stay."

Chaz had his hand on the kitchen doorknob. He looked at his friend with narrowed eyes. "You sure about this? I can stay, bro."

Steve pointed to the bags that sat on the table. "I have soup and soap. Just let me do this."

"We can go somewhere official—"

He shook his head. "Rehabs are just a place for the press to find me. Best thing I can do is just hide out." His hands started to shake, so he shoved them in his pockets. "Please—"

"I know. Don't tell anyone where you are. Not even Cain."

"Even under threat." Chaz walked up to him and the men hugged. "I'll call when I'm ready to come back, but I think it will be a while."

"Take your time, brother. I got you covered." He pointed to one of the bags. "When you get that prepaid phone in there going, text me your number. I wrote mine on the package." He set a bank envelope on the table. "There's a couple hundred bucks. I drew a map to town on the back of it."

Steve walked out onto the porch with Chaz. He put his hand against the stone wall. The rock hurt his skin. Nausea rolled in his icy stomach. Chaz opened the door of the rental car. "See you when you're ready," he said before slipping behind the wheel and carefully driving back down the gravel driveway.

Suddenly, Steve wanted to chase after him and hop

into the passenger's seat, drive down to the little town at the end of the road, and find a bar. He wanted to dig through the bags in the back seat and see what kind of narcotic treasures he could find. He wanted—

He wanted to stop. He needed to stop. Even with every cell in his body screaming for relief from the oncoming withdrawal, he determined he would stop.

Steve looked out at the wooded lot. He stared at the snow covering the crown of Mount Jefferson in the distance and breathed in the clean mountain air. As he exhaled, he leaned over the side of the porch railing and threw up.

♫ ♫ ♫ ♫

HARMONY sat near the back row of the funeral home. She wore a black double-breasted suit with a wide gray collar that scooped around her neck, framing her simple pearl necklace. The skirt fell to her knees. She'd twisted her hair into a simple bun on the back of her head and fastened it with a black clip. She clutched a lace-trimmed handkerchief in her hand that she'd already soaked with silent tears. As she stared at the too small coffin in the front of the room, she felt so angry at the unfairness brought into the world in the form of childhood cancer. She wanted to wail and scream at the world, but she didn't. She sat quietly, listening to Sheri's uncle pay tribute to his young niece.

The interior of the Victorian mansion that served as the funeral home fit the outside perfectly. Flowered settees formed sitting areas in rooms all along the hallways. Oriental rugs covered the hardwood floors. Pillars held potted plants and vases of flowers. Brocade curtains in maroons and golds covered every window, shielding the black-clad mourners inside from the morning sunlight outside.

At the podium in the front, Sheri's family took turns telling beautiful stories about her. As she felt the love for Sheri in the room and in the way the young girl's family tried to celebrate her life rather than mourn her disease and death, the grief that gripped her heart so tightly began to loosen. By the time her part came, the tears had dried and the smile on her face didn't feel forced as she made her way to the front of the room. She took the microphone offered to her by the funeral director and turned to face the sea of family and friends.

"I had the privilege of spending many hours with Sheri. I fell so much in love with her, and prayed so hard for her healing so that she could fulfill her dream of becoming a music star. She had an amazing voice. I met her through her wish, which was to perform on stage with me. I was so honored to share the spotlight with her. We had it professionally recorded and produced. Please, enjoy her song."

She stepped to the side of the stage as a screen lowered from the ceiling and the lights dimmed. The professional production began with a photo of the laughing Sheri, arms outstretched as if she embraced the world, and morphed into a section of a recorded interview where she laughingly said her wish was to be a star, but that she'd settle for singing a song with Harmony Harper. That faded to her walking into the spotlight on the stage and singing. A few minutes later, Harmony stepped into the light and finished the song with her. At the conclusion of the song, Sheri, with joy shining from her face waved to the audience as the scene faded and another photo of her appeared with the dates of her birth and death superimposed across the screen.

When the lights came back up, the screen quietly rose

and Harmony stepped forward once again. "Sheri said she'd settle for singing a song with me. I don't think that amazing child should have to settle for anything. The recording of her performance is on the album that released this week. That song along with this video will be the first release from the album. Sheri's parents and I have agreed that all of the proceeds from that video and single will be donated to the children's hospital."

Harmony handed the microphone back to the funeral director and stepped off of the platform to walk down the aisle. Sheri's mother stood up from the front row and embraced her.

"Thank you for loving my girl the way you did," she said into Harmony's ear.

She hugged her back and pulled slightly away so that she could look into the ravaged face of the grieving mother. What would it do to a person to lose a child? As she silently prayed for Mrs. Mercer to have the strength to get through the next day and week and month, she said, "It was my honor to know her. Thank you for sharing her with me."

Mrs. Mercer said, "All you had to do was that one song, but you kept coming back week after week." She paused long enough to swallow the lump in her throat. Her grip on Harmony's wrist tightened involuntarily. "You didn't have to do that. Sheri really loved your visits, and we appreciated every minute you spent with her."

Harmony hugged her one more time and said, "Visiting her and spending time with her meant more to me than I can ever say."

After she reached her seat, she sat for the final words from the minister, then stood with the rest of the audience as Mr. Mercer and his brothers and uncles carried the little coffin down the aisle and out the door. The family followed behind the coffin, row by row, until everyone stepped outside. The bright sunlight surprised Harmony. She had expected the sky to have blackened with grief or raindrops like tears from heaven to have flooded the earth.

With the coffin loaded into the hearse, she walked toward her car. Away from the building and the crowd, she turned a corner and walked into a wall of reporters. As soon as they saw her, they flocked around her, screaming questions at her while photographers snapped stills.

"How long have you been seeing Slayer?"

"Slayer's apparently missing. Has he been in touch with you?"

"Have you had sex with him yet?"

"Harmony? Harmony! Over here!"

"Are you hiding Slayer?"

"Do you do drugs together?"

"Why have you kept your relationship a secret?"

"Harmony! Do you have a comment for the record?"

"Are you pregnant?"

"What will your fans think?"

"Does your family know?"

"Harmony! Harmony!"

"You know where Slayer is, don't you?"

"Are you crossing over to metal?"

Questions came from every side. Absurd questions. Disrespectful questions. Furious, she held up her hands. "Hey! Do you people have any sense of decency? This is neither the time nor the place. This is a funeral! For a little girl. I have no idea what you people are even talking about! Show some respect for the family and take this away from here."

Pushing her way through the throng, she made it to her car where her driver held the door open for her. Even as he shut his own door and started driving, the reporters took pictures through the window and screamed questions at her. In the camel-colored leather backseat of the luxury sedan, she picked up a bottle of water the driver had made ready for her out of the cup holder and took a long swallow. Her hands shook with fury and her heart pounded. How dare they? And what were they talking about?

"They started showing up about ten minutes ago. I thought they were here because of Sheri. Human interest piece and all. I'm so sorry, Miss Harper."

"It's not your fault. We're not going to the graveside service," she declared. "I don't want those vultures intruding on the Mercers. I'll send my apologies to the family."

"Yes, Miss Harper," the driver responded. "Where to?"

"My office, please."

♫ ♫ ♫ ♫

HARMONY pushed her chair back away from her desk and got to her feet. She couldn't sit there any longer. Feeling restless, she paced from her desk to the sitting area. A plush white couch accented with pillows in various shades of purple sat flanked by glossy cherry wood tables that matched her desk. A bookshelf showed her eclectic taste in reading—with everything from memoirs by her favorite musicians to books written by her family to Christian fiction. Framed snapshots of her and the children she worked with filled the shelves, and as she ran a finger over the photographed face of Sheri, fresh tears filled her eyes.

She picked up the photograph and held it to her chest as she silently walked back to her desk, shifting a photo of her grandparents over to add Sheri to the family collection. Unwilling to sit back down and try to complete more work, she turned and looked out over the city of Nashville from her perch on the fourth floor of the Harper Enterprises building. On the next block, a construction company worked on erecting a high-rise building. The crane in the center of the footprint lifted a bundle of steel beams and moved them from one corner to the other. As she watched dozens of workers doing their respective jobs, she found it fascinating that the world just kept going on, buildings kept getting built, traffic kept driving down the street, and she stood here in this bubble of grief fully expecting the world to just stop and mourn that little coffin with her.

She heard her door open and turned to watch Franklin intrude on her solitude without so much as a preemptive knock on her door. He wore a stuffy brown three-piece suit with a light blue shirt and a brown striped tie. He glared at her the entire time he crossed her office. "This is what I've been talking about," he declared, slamming a tabloid paper on top of Harmony's desk.

First the funeral. Then the reporters. Now Franklin barged into her office wanting to start something? Today?

"What?" she asked wearily. She tried to focus on the picture he pointed at, but the image of Sheri's exhausted face the last time Harmony visited her danced across her field of vision.

"This is exactly what I meant when I said I don't think

it's a good idea to be associating yourself with a secular crowd. Will you listen to me now?"

She narrowed her eyes, forced herself to focus, and found she looked at a front-page picture of herself in very close proximity to Steven Slayer backstage at last weekend's concert. The headline screamed "Heaven Meets Hell!" After the funeral, she'd done an internet search of Steven Slayer and Harmony Harper and saw the picture in a thousand different websites. "It's just tabloid trash, Franklin. No one will believe this. It's nothing."

Franklin's thin finger tapped the paper. "Well, you're wrong on a few counts. First of all, it isn't nothing. It's a picture. Secondly, most people will believe just about anything. The only thing the public loves more than a hero is watching a hero fall. So why not educate me, here. Why don't you elaborate for me? What is this?"

Even as she spoke, she knew emotions caused an overreaction. She just couldn't help herself. She felt so broken inside that she needed to lash out and break something, too. "This," she said, spitting out the word and adding meaning to it just like Franklin had, "is me taking a break. I need to get away. From you. From here. From Nashville, even." She walked across her lilac carpet and stopped at the coat hook by the door where she grabbed her purse.

"Get away?" He stormed after her. "What are you talking about?"

She turned and looked at him. He had managed her career to stardom very well. But, he had also tried desperately to manage her life. Quite frankly, she'd had enough.

"I'm going to my cabin. I'm going on a sabbatical. I need to go away. Maybe write."

"What? You're not due to go there until Labor Day."

"So, manager, manage. Adjust things. I'm not on tour and I don't have an album to cut until the Christmas album in September. I'll just go now."

His lips thinned and he shook his head. "Not possible unless I go with you and we work—"

Frustrated, she slammed the palm of her hand against the door frame. "I don't want anyone to go with me. I'm going to my cabin alone. I need to be alone. I need to pray and think and write and I need to do it by myself."

"By yourself?" His brows furrowed with his frown. "I don't think that's a good idea right now with this blast of bad publicity."

"Then it's a good thing that I'm not thirteen anymore and I don't have to listen to what you think or don't think is a good idea. I. Don't. Care." She annunciated every word to make sure he heard her clearly, then opened her door. Halfway down the hall, near her mother's office, she spun back around and stared at her shocked brother who rushed after her. "Don't bother me. Don't come visit. Don't even call. In fact, if I see or hear from you before I contact you again, you're fired." When she turned and saw her mother standing next to her in the doorway, she almost stepped back and retracted everything she'd just said. She might have, except the black hole inside of her threatening to consume her started to take over. So she lifted her chin. "Hello, mama. I'm headed to my cabin. I'm going to take a few weeks off."

Her mother looked her down and up, from the toes of her black shoes to the white pearl necklace she wore with her black and gray suit to the top of her blonde hair pulled back into a simple French twist. "I think that's a good idea, baby. I'll have Leslie buy plane tickets and have a car waiting on you in Portland."

"Mother!" Franklin exclaimed.

Their mother looked at her oldest child. "It's okay, son. I think right now it's important that Harmony takes a break."

"Did you see the papers?"

She smiled at him. "Oh, stuff and fiddlesticks. It will all be all right. Believe me when I tell you this. If you're not getting attacked by Satan then you're not doing something right. Clearly, Harmony's music suddenly reaching so many unbelievers is right. Just as she said." She turned back to her daughter. "Go on home and pack, baby girl. I'll call ahead and get an order of groceries put into a rental for you. Once you're up the mountain, you won't want to go into town for a while."

A sob welled up in Harmony's chest as she grabbed her mother in a hug. "Thank you, mama."

Behind them, Franklin offered a final protest, "You really don't think it would be better to contain the situation?"

"Franklin, you're a good man. Among the best. But you're a man. Harmony is a grown woman. She has to deal with this as a woman. I know you want to protect her, but the best thing you can do is let her work it out."

♫ ♫ ♫ ♫

Chapter 5

BILL "Railroad" Rhodes stood next to the swimming pool in his elaborate backyard. His day job as lighting manager for touring rock bands paid well by American middle class standards. He answered to whatever tour manager ran the show during daylight hours.

However, at night, he worked his real job and his boss went by many names including: the Angel of Light, Beelzebub, Belial, the Son of Perdition, the Father of Lies, the Roaring Lion, the Little Horn, the Liar, the Thief, the Murderer, Lucifer, the Lord of this World and the King of this Age. His position as the leader of a national church, a high priest for Satan, helped him maintain this lavish lifestyle. He lived under a pseudonym that afforded him all of the privacy he needed, while his job gave him reliable physical access to his church membership all over the country.

Abaddon was his main customer, and he had worked almost exclusively for them for years. Abaddon fans were true proselytes. The messages in the music fed their damned souls and encouraged their worship like little else in the mainstream world. A few band members even dabbled in his dark world. Because they promised secrecy, Bill gave them many added benefits. Wherever they went he provided connections to drugs, women, gambling dens, and endless adoration in exchange for doing something no more challenging than strumming on guitar strings or tickling some ivories.

Now, however, it would seem that something had shaken Abaddon's world. He looked at the headline of the newspaper, proclaiming the disappearance of the lead singer, Steven Slayer. Pictures of him in the throes of some intimate grip with the goodie-two-shoes Christian artist Harmony Harper, coupled with photos of EMTs loading him into the back of an ambulance peppered the story. Cain, the manager, had no comment. Bill's curled his upper lip into a snarl. If Cain had nothing to say, it meant he had no information. How had he let things get so out of hand? He would have to contact Cain and get an accounting.

Meanwhile, though, what to do about Harmony Harper? Did she actually pose a serious threat to his kingdom here on earth? Because that's what the demise of Abaddon would mean—a threat.

A splash and feminine laughter interrupted his thoughts. He looked up and watched two young women wearing nothing but bikini bottoms take turns attempting different elaborate dives off the diving board. No, he would not allow anything to threaten his kingdom.

Turning his back on the frolicking brunettes, he went into the house, pulling a phone out of his pocket. Cain answered on the first ring, like a good boy.

"Talk," Bill said.

"If I knew anything, I would have already called you."

He could hear the panic in Cain's voice. It pleased him to know he could invoke fear into someone so arrogant. "You should have called me the instant you knew about it. I certainly shouldn't be reading the story in the paper with no knowledge of what's going on."

After a long pause, Cain agreed. "You're right, Father. I apologize. Most sincerely."

Bill took a deep breath and slowly let it out. The red haze of anger gradually faded. Finally, he said, "Fix this."

"Yes, Father."

♫ ♫ ♫ ♫

HARMONY Harper sat on the deck of her cabin nestled deep in the Cascade Range in Oregon and stared out at the view of Mount Jefferson. Her grandparents both grew up in the little town of Harperville, about eight miles south of her cabin as the crow flies, fifteen miles by car. In fact, her great-great-grandfather had founded the little town just over a hundred years ago. Harmony's grandparents had both grown up there, fallen in love in the little high school, and married the day after graduation. He'd taken her with him when he went to seminary in Tennessee, and the two had worked together in their family focused radio ministry until he semi-retired from his nationally syndicated show two years ago. Her father, Grayson, had very smoothly taken over the reins, having been a regular part of the ministry his entire life.

She loved the legacy of her family. Harmony loved her part in it and prayed that God would bless any of her future children with talents to continue the Harper Enterprises ministry. As much as she loved it, though, the work itself tended to drain her. The constant pressures of performing, interviews, public speaking, and writing exhausted her—as it would anyone.

One her nineteenth birthday, five years into her solo career, her grandfather suggested she find a spot that she could claim as hers alone, a place to retreat and refresh and commune with God. Without a second thought, she knew she would build in Harperville. Harmony found the perfect property, picked the design of the cabin she wanted, and watched as the builders created a beautiful two-story cabin just for her. The cabin had a cathedral front wall made almost entirely of windows that pointed up to the sky, gracing God with all of the credit for the beauty around her. Standing in her living room, her windows framed the view of the snow-covered Mount Jefferson more beautifully than any photograph.

The deck wrapped around the cedar cabin, and a glass door led into the main room—a large open bay room with her living area, dining area, and kitchen combined. Wide sweeping stairways on either side of the room led to the three bedrooms upstairs. She'd utilized the glass-walled landing as an office and set up her large mahogany desk next to her electronic keyboard.

At first, her mother didn't feel overly comfortable with Harmony coming out here alone. With nonexistent cell phone service and a landline that came and went almost at will, she protested the first trip Harmony planned and Harmony had to fight for just a week's vacation. After three small stays over the next couple of years and one big family retreat, her parents no longer worried about her time here. Public figures themselves, they understood the necessity of solitude and how it encouraged mental and spiritual health. The older Harmony got, the more they started encouraging regular stays.

She came to her cabin twice a year, and everyone knew better than to bother her here including Franklin, her mother, and even her grandfather. Harmony rested, read the Bible, sang, wrote songs, and relaxed.

She'd woken up this morning intending to get some song writing done, but after a light breakfast, she went up to her keyboard and found she had absolutely no creative energy. Knowing she still mourned Sheri's illness and death, she poured a cup of tea and found herself sitting on the deck for hours, watching the wildlife in the woods surrounding her cabin.

As Harmony sat, she eventually thought about the reporters at the funeral and the tabloid article. The speed at which that photograph found itself the headlining story kind of shocked her. The national magazine must have stopped the presses and pushed everything aside in order to get it out to the public so soon after the concert. Of course, with the disappearance of Steven Slayer, a buzz already stirred through the entertainment industry. This tabloid simply added fuel to that fire and placed her near the center of his controversy. She imagined Franklin had likely fielded calls from reporters all day yesterday.

She'd never done anything controversial in her career. This swarm of reporters hounding her came as a new experience in her life and her career. Franklin's words rang true. As much as the public loved to elevate a hero, the public loved to watch a hero fall even more. Perfect little Christian Harmony Harper, elevated as a standard of modesty, purity, talent, beauty, and humility, certainly provided the fodder for a scandal. Since it was all untrue gossip, Harmony found herself highly annoyed at the attention. She imagined, though, that Steven Slayer probably often performed controversial acts.

A slow burn of anger over the entire incident

backstage at that July Fourth concert threatened to interrupt the tranquility she'd sought and found out here on the deck. What a waste of life, she thought, to destroy one's body and mind with substances. What a waste of talent. Harmony knew Steven Slayer probably could claim the title of the most celebrated living guitarists in the world at the moment, and yet minutes after playing for eighty-thousand people he could barely stand upright. What would bring a person to such a low state of self-worth?

While she longed to face whatever anger she felt over this incident, which had created a false rumor designed to hurt her reputation, she didn't feel the emotional energy to confront it. Instead, she reined it in and tried to stop thinking about it. She set her teacup down and pulled her legs up to her chest while she watched a doe with two fawns cautiously step out into the clearing of her cabin. Not willing to move, afraid she'd scare them off, she sat very still and watched the beauty of the wild animals as they ate from a patch of wild clover.

Eventually, Harmony found herself praying for Steven Slayer. She prayed for his physical health and for his emotional and spiritual health. A part of her hoped that their paths would cross again so that she would have an opportunity to tell him about the God she loved so much; the same God who loved Steven Slayer so very, very much even while he was still a sinner.

♫ ♫ ♫ ♫

THE first sensation Steve had when he opened his eyes was a dull throbbing ache in the back of his head. His mouth felt so dry it felt chapped. The back of his throat burned with the need for a drink. With shaking limbs, he pushed himself into a sitting position. He didn't know how many days had passed, but a dozen empty water bottles scattered on the floor near the bed informed him of his constant thirst. His stomach rolled, but he didn't think he felt any more nausea. He thought maybe this feeling was a deep unsatiated hunger born of days without sustenance—without any kind of sustenance—be it nourishment or one of those brightly colored pills washed down with his favorite single malt.

No more. His promise to himself resonated around his mind. The single kidney he had couldn't take any more abuse, and even one more binge might be the last. The message from the doctor echoed loud and clear. As much as he had spent the last thirteen years running as far and as fast away from whatever deity reigned above, he had no desire to come face to face with eternity anytime soon. So he'd chill on the drinking and the drugs, and he'd stick to not smoking, even though right now the need for a cigarette screamed through every single pore of his skin almost more intensely than the need for a drink.

When Steve thought he might be able to stand without falling back down or throwing up, he shakily stood and made his way into the bathroom. He barely recognized the man staring back at him from the mirror. Black circles framed red-rimmed eyes. A scraggly beard covered his face and his hair lay in greasy strings all around hollow cheeks that sunk into yellowed skin. Dried blood crusted along the side of his face where he'd apparently ripped out an earring.

Drink. Then shower. Then food.

He turned on the water and bent his head, drinking directly from the faucet, ignoring the coppery taste of the water coming in from the ancient pipes. He remembered, vaguely, Chaz telling him that an old artesian well fed water to the cabin. The ice cold blast took his breath away.

Once he got used to the temperature, he drank until he couldn't imagine swallowing another drop, then turned on the water to fill the big claw-foot bathtub. When he stripped his shirt off, he looked in the mirror again. Bruises lined his torso. He wondered where they'd come from. Had he beaten himself in the throes of detoxing, or was this just a physical result of his body's suffering?

When he turned to look at his back, he felt his eyebrows come together in a frown. A tattoo of a snake wrapped around an apple covered one entire shoulder blade. He tried to remember when he'd gone in to get the red ink added to the design. Pressing his hands to his head, he tried to think back, tried to remember, but came up with nothing. He often lost days at a time in a drug induced haze, and couldn't remember the last time he looked at himself, really looked, in a mirror. An uncomfortable thought about all the things he might not remember, coupled with the things he could remember and was less than proud of, made him uneasy. Could a man hate himself more than he did right now?

He soaked in the bathtub until the lukewarm water turned cold, then filled it again and scrubbed himself clean. With a towel wrapped around his too skinny waist, he used the electric razor he found in his bag and shaved his head and beard. After splashing aftershave on his face, he ran his hands over his smooth head and face.

A fresh start.

A new life.

His stomach rolled again. Hunger or fear?

He left the bathroom and pulled on a pair of jeans and a sweatshirt that he found in his bag. Apparently, he hadn't thought ahead when he packed. He would have to find his way into town at some point and purchase some different clothes. When he went into the kitchen, he discovered some rotten bananas on the counter and a trail of little black ants that went out a crack near the base of the kitchen door. He gingerly picked up the bunch by the stems and opened the back door to toss them out, catching a glimpse of the Oregon wilderness beyond.

While canned soup simmered on the stove, he dug through the freezer. Chaz had left a note on the counter telling him that he could find bread and cold cuts in the fridge. In the back of the fridge, he found a bag of crisp apples and a block of cheese that looked good.

He toasted the bread, topped it with cheese, and set that under the broiler of the oven to melt. When he took the first bite, saliva flooded his mouth and hunger pains hit so rapidly that it left him sweaty, shaky, and weak. Not even bothering to transfer the soup into a bowl, he grabbed a spoon and shoveled it into his mouth from the little pot, alternating bites of cheese toast with soup.

His hunger temporarily sated, he walked on still somewhat shaky legs into the main room of the cabin. A large stone fireplace dominated one wall. He barely remembered the brown furniture and fireplace from the day he'd arrived. He wondered, again, how long he had been there. Long enough for bananas to rot, apparently. How long did that take at this altitude?

He needed to change the sheets on the bed and clean up whatever mess he made after spending the last several days in that room, but first, he needed to rest. His heart beat a weird, thready rhythm, and the need for something —whiskey, drugs, nicotine, sex—something to satisfy him, started to overpower him. He collapsed onto the couch and drew his knees up to his chest while the room spun around him.

♫ ♫ ♫ ♫

Chapter 6

C **HARLES** Richard Galton stood in the checkout line and watched his mother insipidly babble with the woman in line in front of them. He couldn't stand these weekly grocery shopping trips, even though she'd taken him on them every single Thursday for his entire life. While he tried to look anywhere but at her and that cart filled with the best boxes and packages of food America had to offer— because only the best and gluten free and organic and sustainable would do for her little Charlie Brown—he found his gaze resting on the cover of a tabloid newspaper.

The headline "Heaven Meets Hell" filled the top of the tabloid above a picture that deeply shocked him. What was this? Some kind of hoax?

He wanted to snatch the paper up and read it, but he didn't want to draw his mother's attention to it. Instead, he politely interrupted her. "Excuse me for interrupting, mommy. I just need to run and use the little boys' room."

She smiled her infuriating smile and waved a hand in his direction. "Okay, Charlie." As he walked away, he heard her say to the complete stranger, "Oh, he is. He's such a good boy. We are so blessed."

Six aisles away, he snatched one of the papers off the rack and headed to the back of the store. He read the article quickly. "Steven Slayer, lead singer and guitarist for the metal band Abaddon was caught in a rather intimate embrace backstage with popular Contemporary Christian artist Harmony Harper during Sunday's Children's Medical Miracle Benefit concert. It looks like she's about to show him what the term heaven really means."

Infuriated, he balled the paper up in his fists. Why would Slayer get photographed with Harmony Harper? The woman was the epitome of everything wrong in the world, and he was in a corner doing who-knew-what with her backstage? What did that mean? Where could this go?

An ice cold feeling began to fill him starting in his chest and moving toward his extremities. He didn't feel cold. He felt as if he was transforming into something else, as if ice water filled his veins instead of red hot blood. His racing pulse began to slow and emotion made way for razor sharp logic. He believed, in that moment, that this new feeling came with his new office as a Journeyman Acolyte. He relaxed and let the feeling overtake him. He felt more powerful than he had ever felt in his life.

He'd always taken Steven Slayer at face value. Maybe he should do some real digging and see what kind of man he truly was. Was he friend or foe? Was he a true believer or a big fat fake?

Knowing he couldn't take much more time, he tossed the paper onto a shelf that held toilet bowl cleaners and rushed back to the front of the store in time to catch his mother finishing her transaction. He wondered how she couldn't see his power. All she saw was his carefully constructed mask that made him seem meek and tractable. Charles realized more than ever before what fools his parents must be.

♫ ♫ ♫ ♫

STEVE followed the narrow rutted lane for about ten minutes until it came to a somewhat less-rutted two-lane road. To his left, the road went up a hill and took a sharp turn. To his right, he could see the little town down in the valley below. A fat chipmunk skittered across the lane, stopping to look back at him once he safely arrived on the gravel shoulder of the road. The rodent's little black eyes stared at Steve, boring into him, as if leveling an accusation. Never one to back down from a challenge, Steve stood stock still and stared back. Eventually, the human won the staring contest. As he watched the little critter scurry up the trunk of a tree, he caught sight of a big blackberry bush.

He walked over and checked, but most of the berries still looked a bit green. He wondered when they'd ripen, and his mouth watered as he thought about the fat juicy berries. Checking his pockets one more time to make sure he had cash on him, he turned right, ready to step off of the road onto the gravel shoulder if he heard a car.

About halfway to the town, his heart had started beating rapidly and a cold sweat broke out all over his body. He stopped and walked into the woods a bit and leaned against a tree. Bracing his hands on his thighs, he leaned forward and yelled out loud, a frustrated, incoherent sound. His arms quaked and his stomach rolled. Recognizing the symptoms, refusing to give in to the fear and anxiety trying to swamp him, he closed his eyes and breathed through it. Eventually, the worst of the symptoms passed. He felt weaker and a little nauseated, but well enough to keep walking.

By the time he passed a sign welcoming him to Harperville, population who really cares, he couldn't believe how exhausted he felt. His legs felt heavy and the back of his throat felt so dry that he could barely swallow around his swollen tongue. He stopped at a gas station on the edge of town and put three quarters into a drink machine, selecting a bottle of water. As soon as he twisted the cap off the plastic bottle, he chugged half of the contents before even taking a breath. Using the sleeve of his shirt, he wiped the sweat off of his forehead and took another long pull of the cold water. It revived him somewhat and he continued on his way to the wooden row of businesses on Main Street. A coffee shop called Java Java took up the corner next to Cooper's Creamery, which sat next to Martin's Grocery.

When Steve walked into Martin's, the clerk, a tall thin man with white hair holding a paperback novel in a beam of sunlight manned the counter. He lifted his eyes from the pages of his novel and peered at Steve over the rims of his reading glasses. Steve lifted his chin in a greeting and snatched up a little carry basket.

He carefully worked through the small store, trying to think of the last time he had grocery shopped for himself, but found himself unable to remember. He had enough peanut butter, canned soup, and canned spaghetti sauce at the cabin to last him weeks. With that in mind, he added dried pasta, cheese, crackers, bread, some packaged cold cuts, and some hot dogs to his basket. Thinking of eating something that didn't come out of a jar or a can, he bought a single steak, a potato, and a ready-made bag of salad.

As he worked his way to the cash register, he paused at a display of beer. Suddenly, his mouth started watering and he felt the blood roar in his ears. After several moments, he very purposefully turned his body and, with feet feeling like he wore heavy cement shoes, slowly made his way to the front of the store.

At the checkout, the old man stared at him as he rang up the groceries. "Don't think I've seen you around here before," he causally remarked.

He'd lived surrounded by groupies and roadies for the last ten years. People hung on his every word, laughed at his every joke. Women threw themselves at him in exchange for a plastic guitar pick he had touched, and in his circles, everyone knew exactly who Steven Slayer was. Or, who he used to be. What did he say? How did one do small talk with an old man in a little grocery who admitted that he'd never seen him before?

"No," he remarked, "never been here." He held up the backpack. "I'll just put everything in here."

"Just passing through, then?" The old man started handing him the items he'd purchased, starting with the heavy cans.

Was he just passing through? What would happen if he decided to leave his world of rock 'n' roll and all the trappings that came with it and began anew, a faceless person in a little cabin in the Oregon mountains? "I'm here for a little while. Haven't decided how long yet."

He handed the old man the cash. As he finished the transaction and started counting out change, he said, "Well, welcome to Harperville. If you're looking for a church, services start at eleven tomorrow morning at the building on the corner of Main and Church." He handed him the receipt and change. "We'd love to have you."

Thinking of the songs he'd written over the last ten years, Steve thought to himself that the church on the corner of Main and Church would most certainly *not* love to have him. Deciding against outright rudeness, he shoved the change and receipt into his pocket and nodded. "Thanks, man." He zipped the opening of the backpack shut.

"And, son," the man said, "if you're looking for a meeting, they hold them there, too. Every Thursday night. Seven o'clock."

"A meeting?" His confusion must have covered every part of his face.

"AA, son. I saw how you were looking at that beer. There's no shame."

Apparently, he had no secrets. Well, except for his name, and his past, and his possible future. This complete stranger could see Steve's present spelled out in flashing neon letters like a Las Vegas welcome mat. His current addiction was no secret even in Podunk Population Few, USA.

"Thanks, man," he mumbled. "I'll think about it."

The bright sunlight hurt his eyes as he stepped out of the store. Half stumbling, he sat on the wooden bench next to the doorway and fished the bottle of water out of the pocket on the side of his backpack. With shaking hands, he twisted the top off and finished the bottle. Hoping that he kept the water down, he closed his eyes and rested his head against the wall of the store. Eventually, the dizziness receded and he felt like he could safely stand again.

He spotted a community thrift store across the street. Thinking of the two outfits he currently had in his possession, he crossed the street to see about adding to his wardrobe.

♫ ♫ ♫ ♫

HARMONY parked in front of Martin's Grocery. As she got out of her Jeep, she waved at Mrs. Cooper, who swept the sidewalk in front of her ice cream shop. "How's the summer been, Mrs. Cooper?"

"We had a good season. Still a full month before I close." She gestured toward the mountain view. "Lotsa tourists this year. Glad to see people back to looking at God's creation rather than those man-made theme parks."

Harmony nodded. "People will always come back to the mountain views. See you in a few minutes!" She walked into the little store and lifted her hand toward the man behind the counter. "Afternoon, Martin," she said with a smile. "How have you been?"

He set down his paperback novel and looked at her over the top rim of his reading glasses. "Been a good summer 'round here." He gestured toward the back of the store. "Got your order in yesterday. Wondered when you be in."

"Thanks!" She slid the check she'd written to pay for the groceries onto the counter in front of him and slipped her sunglasses onto her head as she walked to the back of the store and into the cooler, where she found a cart loaded with a box of organic vegetables, some fermented tofu, sprouted grains, and organic dairy. She grabbed the handle of the cart and maneuvered it out of the small area, stopping in the storeroom for the box of organic cereals, beans, pastas, and rice. After carefully setting the box of dry goods on the cart, she wheeled it through the store.

"Need help with that?" Martin asked from his perch.

"Nope." Using her hip to open the door, she smiled at him. "I got this. Thanks, Martin."

"One of these days, you're going to come to me and ask me to sell you the biggest steak I got. You know what I'll say?"

With a snort she replied, "You'll say, 'Will that be cash or charge?' Your principles aren't going to stand in the way of a sale, Martin."

"Go on with your rabbit food, then," he said in good nature, "and if you're staying longer, give me three days notice for a new order."

"Yes, sir." She pulled the cart to the edge of the sidewalk and left it there. After opening the door of her Jeep, she tugged the handle and pulled the passenger's seat forward. She loved having a four-wheel drive vehicle in the mountains, but for hauling boxes and groceries, the Jeep was less than ideal. Hefting the box of vegetables, she lifted it into the back seat. While she had her back turned, she heard the unmistakable sound of the cart rolling off of the curb, followed immediately by the sound of boxes tumbling out of it.

"Whoa!" she heard a man say.

As she ducked out of the Jeep, she turned and spotted a man catching a box as it fell out of the cart. "Thank you!" she exclaimed, rushing forward and grabbing a container of yogurt that had started to roll into the street. "That thing clearly needs brakes."

He turned, holding the box. Harmony's eyes widened when she thought she recognized Steven Slayer. He'd shaved his head and face, and looked like he'd lost quite a bit of weight, but she absolutely recognized him. What was the lead singer of Abaddon doing in front of Martin's Grocery in Harperville?

"I think the sidewalk is slanted," he observed, walking around her to set the box in her back seat. He returned to help load the spilled box back up with the groceries. Before she could lift it, he had it in his hands.

"Thanks. I really appreciate your help, Mr. Slayer," she said.

She watched his shoulders stop moving as he paused before continuing to load the box into the back seat. Task complete, he turned from the Jeep, his eyes curious. "Mr. Slayer?"

Immediately wondering if she'd made a mistake, she said, "That is your name, isn't it?"

He shrugged and bent and picked up a backpack. "My name is Steve. Most people just call me Slayer. Or Mr. Slayer. But to your point, no, only fans really call me that. And you are ... ?"

"I'm hardly what one would call a fan." She brushed her hands along the sides of her white jeans. "I'm barely what one would call a colleague, but that's probably the best definition."

Thinking of the indignity she had publicly suffered at his intoxicated hand, she pushed the Jeep seat back and slammed the door. Unfortunately, it caught on the seat belt strap and flew open again. With impatience she hated showing, she pushed the seat belt out of the way and slammed the door again. When it firmly shut, she turned back around and faced her nemesis. "Good day, Mr. Slayer."

"Hey, wait," he said, stepping forward. He started to stumble but put a hand on the hood of her Jeep. Her eyes narrowed as she took in his pale skin, the shine of sweat, the dilated pupils. "Who are you?" His voice had grown weaker.

As she watched his arms start quaking, holding

himself up, she said, "My name is Harmony Harper. We met a little over a week ago at a benefit concert in San Francisco."

He closed his eyes and took several long, deep breaths. When he opened them again, the quaking had stopped, but she noticed the slight tremor in his hands remained. Sweat poured down his face. "I'm sorry. For whatever. The truth is I barely remember that day."

"Never mind that." With a frown, she studied his face. "Are you okay?"

"Me? Yeah. I'm just dandy." He slipped his backpack strap over one arm. "Get those groceries home, Harmony Harper." He stepped away from the Jeep and started walking down Main toward the mountain road. About halfway down the sidewalk, he turned and looked at her. "I remember. You wore white then, too." He lifted a hand in a wave. "'Amazing Grace,' right? I owe you one."

"Yeah," she murmured, thinking about the tabloid and all of the rumors that went with it, "at least one."

She went a few doors down and opened the door to Cooper's Creamery. "There she is," Mrs. Cooper said by way of a greeting. "I thought you'd forget all about me."

"How could I forget about an ice cream sundae dripping with caramel sauce?" Harmony asked with a grin, taking the sundae from the older woman.

"Let's sit outside with a scoop and a coffee and you can tell me how your grandmother's doing," Mrs. Cooper said, hustling Harmony out the door. As she sat at the little wrought iron table, she couldn't help but look down the street as Steven Slayer crossed Church Avenue and kept heading toward the mountain road.

♪ ♪ ♪ ♪

HARMONY sat on the iron chair and chatted with Mrs. Cooper for almost thirty minutes. People came in and out of the grocery store, often stopping to say hi, to pass messages on to her family, or to praise Mrs. Cooper on the spiced peach ice cream that she'd made her weekly special. "I hate to leave, but I need to get these groceries home," she said, tossing her empty cardboard bowl into the garbage can next to the curb. "I'll see you one day next week."

"Always a pleasure, my dear." She looked at her watch. "Afternoon rush should be starting soon, anyhow. I need to get some fresh coffee brewing and some soft serve going."

Harmony slid into the driver's seat of the Jeep and backed out of the parking space. Her mind wandered while she drove, wondering how long she intended to hide up here away from the real world. She had spent the last week grieving like she'd rarely grieved before. Sheri's death had affected her deeply, but somehow she found that as each day passed, she wanted to get back home and get back to work with more kids. She knew that most of them wouldn't survive the year, and she knew she'd grieve and grieve again, but that didn't change the fact that she had the power to brighten a life for even a short time. Without a doubt, God had directed her into that ministry, and to sit up alone on the top of a mountain and nurse her grieving heart didn't play an active role in her mission.

With her mind wandering, she very nearly ran over Steven Slayer. As she went around a curve, she had to jerk hard on the wheel to swerve around him. He knelt on his hands and knees, leaning over the ditch on the side of the road. Putting the Jeep in neutral and setting the parking brake, she rushed out of the Jeep and toward him. "Are you okay?"

"Nothing a shot of whiskey and a cigarette wouldn't fix," he said weakly.

Harmony gasped and bent next to him. "I don't understand."

He rolled over off of his knees until he sat, wiping his mouth with the shoulder of his shirt. "It's just rejection. My body appears to be protesting my recent sobriety," he said. "I'm beginning to wonder if I'm fighting a losing battle."

It suddenly occurred to her what he meant. His body's reaction reminded her of some of her cancer patient friends right after a particularly rough batch of chemo. "What can I do?"

With a raised eyebrow he asked, "Do?"

"Yes, do. Can I help you in any way?"

"Help?"

Closing her eyes and praying for some help or

guidance, she remembered praying for him. Thanking God for the answered prayer and opportunity, she said, "I don't believe you're fighting a losing battle. Can I help you fight?"

As if suddenly understanding, his face softened and he smiled half a smile. "I don't even know how to respond to that. I'm not used to people wanting to help me."

She stood and brushed the dirt off of her pants, then held her hand out. "How about I start by driving you home?"

He stared at her offered hand for several seconds before placing his hand in hers. "Actually, I really would appreciate a ride," he said. She braced herself and helped him up then gestured toward the passenger door.

"Good thing the groceries didn't need the front seat," she said with a smile as they got into the Jeep. She released the parking brake and put it in gear and said, "Where to?"

He pointed with his finger. "That way. At the split, go left."

He leaned back in the seat and briefly closed his eyes. "What are you doing here?" she asked, giving in to the curiosity that had eaten at her from the first moment she recognized him.

"Here in Podunk? Friend loaned me his cabin. Used to be his grandmother's. Thought I could do this alone, but I'm not sure anymore."

She turned left and the road narrowed, becoming little more than a path made from old asphalt now crumbled into chunks of gravel. "Turn here," he said suddenly, pointing at the rusty mailbox in the shape of a birdhouse.

"Oh, you're staying at Mrs. Ackers'?"

"Yeah," he said, rolling his head on the seat back until he looked at her. "Chaz Ackers is my friend."

"She was very proud of him. He's a drummer, she said."

Steve smiled. "Best in the business."

"I know. He has tons of awards." She pulled into the yard of the tiny cabin. "Mrs. Ackers was good people. She loved the Lord."

"I can tell. There's a Bible in every room." He opened the door of the Jeep and hopped out. "Thank you for the ride."

"Wait!" He stopped before he shut the door. "What did you mean when you said you owed me one?"

"You sang 'Amazing Grace' as your closer that night. I haven't heard that since Gracie's funeral. It's been thirteen years and that song did things to my heart...." He cleared his throat and looked at the cabin then back at her. "Beginning of the sobriety. I'm starting a new life. I won't go back to the old one."

He started to shut the door again and she said, "Mr. Slayer?"

"Steve," he corrected.

She paused, then said, "Steve. I meant it when I asked you what I could do." She set the emergency brake and put the Jeep in neutral. "Here, let me give you the number to my cabin." Not finding a piece of paper, she ripped a flap off of one of the cardboard boxes. Using lipstick she had in her purse, she wrote down her landline number. "My cell doesn't work at my cabin, but my land line is usually reliable." She handed it to him and he stared at it a long time before looking at her with a very intense look on his face. "Call day or night. You are not fighting a losing battle."

Steve cleared his throat before he looked back at her and nodded. Then he took a step back and lifted a hand as if to tell her good-bye. Fighting the impulse to go back and offer to pray with him, she simply turned around and went back to her cabin.

♫ ♫ ♫ ♫

STEVE put his groceries away in the little kitchen. Next, he loaded the washing machine he'd found behind the blue gingham curtain in the back of the kitchen with the clothes he'd purchased for himself at the thrift store. He'd managed to get a couple more shirts and another pair of jeans, some shorts, and a brand new pair of running shoes, still in the box. He had no idea how much money he had access to, and didn't want to waste any. Some rational part of his brain that he hadn't accessed in over a decade started prompting him to sit down and make lists, to make plans. He thought doing that would help him get his mind off of the agony his body currently suffered in a desperate plea for substances to abuse.

With the sound of the working washing machine echoing through the small cabin, he found a scratch pad and a ballpoint pen in one of the kitchen drawers. When he opened the cover of the pad, he found a page labeled, "PRAYER REQUESTS." He probably wouldn't have paid much attention, but halfway down the page, he saw his own name. With a frown, he looked closer, reading, "Chaz and his friend Steve Slater. Salvation. Clarity. Wisdom."

Chaz's grandmother had died over a year ago. How often had she prayed for him? Disgust welling up inside of him, he ripped the page out and crumpled it into a ball. What did he care about some old lady talking to her god? Determined to refocus, he uncapped the pen and wrote across the top of the page, "PLAN." Suddenly, his mind blanked out. Plan? What kind of plan?

His eyes wandered from the pad in front of him to the crumpled ball of paper in the corner. What did he care about some old lady praying for him? Praying to her god. His knee-jerk response suddenly felt very weak. Somehow, some way, he cared. Truly cared.

Was this one of those foxhole conversions that he'd heard about? Should he listen for death's knock at his door? If not, then why this sudden and unexplainable interest in someone's prayers for him? His parents had raised him in a churchgoing home. Then they'd used their faith to destroy the little boy who had once called himself their son. Their faith and actions behind it carried as much blame as anything else for the path upon which he set all those years ago. Why in the world would the idea that someone had prayed for him touch him in such a way? It should infuriate him. It should fill him with righteous indignation. He should feel intense and uncompromising mistrust at the idea that someone would appeal to some higher authority on his behalf—as if he couldn't take care of himself.

And yet… and yet he felt awe that as utterly alone as he had often felt during his existence in the world for the last thirteen years, someone had actually cared for him. Someone had prayed for him—someone whom he had never even met.

His mind went back to the man at the grocery store. A man who had no idea of his past, of the—sins—of his heart, invited him to church as if he actually cared whether he chose to go or not. Told him about the AA meeting and said there was "no shame." And a woman, who probably knew more than Steve cared for her to know, despite his heart and his life, put herself out there and offered to help him.

He'd spent so many years with so many people manipulating him to get what they selfishly wanted out of him that he had no idea whatsoever how to handle this generosity he suddenly faced. Looking back at the notebook, under the word "PLAN," he shakily scribbled, "Accept help."

Suddenly, his brain started functioning again. He also made notes about banking, contracts, and in the process, decided to call Chaz.

He'd plugged the cell phone in to charge two days ago, but hadn't turned it on. He found the box where Chaz had written his number and dialed it. His friend answered on the first ring.

"Dude."

"Hey, bro," Steve greeted, feeling nervous for some reason, "good to hear your voice."

"How did it go? You all set?"

He thought back to the other times he'd entered rehab clinics and the intrusive presence of nurses and counselors. "It was both harder and easier to do it alone."

After a pause, Chaz said, "Need me to come get you?"

"Nah, man. I'm not ready. I need to keep going it alone for a little longer."

"Cain calls me every day trying to find out where you are." At the sound of his manager's name, Steve felt a tightening in his neck and a pulse start throbbing in his forehead.

"Don't tell him."

"Dude. You know I wouldn't."

"I mean it. I can't deal with him right now. Tell him

I'm fine and I'll be in touch in a couple of months." He looked at his list. "Can you do me a favor?"

"Absolutely, bro."

"Find out about my bank. Get me a number to call."

After another long pause, Chaz said, "Sure. I'll get on it."

"Thanks, man. Just text it to me."

When he disconnected the phone, he turned it off. He'd had enough contact with the outside world to suit him for some time. His heart pounded and the sides of his vision grayed. Taking a long deep breath, he looked back at his list. When his vision cleared enough to see the lines of the paper again, he added, "STAY SOBER!"

Determined, he changed into shorts and a T-shirt and put on his new running shoes. Perhaps a good workout would help him with his planned detox.

♫ ♫ ♫ ♫

HARMONY sat on the black leather couch with one leg tucked up under her and played with the white shag carpet with the toes of her other foot. She looked at the stone fireplace that took up the opposite wall and couldn't wait until she came here in the fall or winter and could light a fire. Rain splashed against the windows and the light in the room dimmed as the clouds grew darker. She loved watching the rain from the main room of the cabin. Floor to ceiling windows made her feel like she could enjoy the elements outside without actually succumbing to them, while staying warm and dry inside.

The tea kettle whistled, so she pushed herself to her feet and crossed the rug, stepping onto the smooth surface of the wood floor. She stepped up into the kitchen area and went to the stove, flicking off the gas burner. Immediately, the steam screaming out of the kettle ceased, and she poured the boiling water over the tea bag she already put in her mug.

On her way back to the couch, she picked up the handset of the cordless phone and carried it with her to the couch. Claiming her seat again, she sat back to watch more of the storm. Two birds flew in the rain right in front of her window, moving together as if they'd practiced a synchronized dance, until they darted into a tree close to her driveway.

She took a deep breath and slowly released it. As much as she loved the storm, distraction kept her from truly enjoying it. She pursed her lips and stared at the phone sitting next to her on the couch. Finally, she picked it up and dialed her mother's cell phone number. On the third ring, Alice answered. "Harmony, dear, is everything okay?"

She never called from her cabin. Of course her mother would assume something had happened. She suddenly felt guilty for worrying her. Guilt warred with anxiety over her reason for calling. "Everything is fine, mama. I just wanted to let you know that I was thinking about coming home at the end of the week."

After a slight pause, Alice said, "You have nothing pressing here. Stay as long as you'd like. Franklin is busy helping your father with a big project, so he's hardly even complained about you being gone."

"Well...."

"Darling, you have nothing to worry about or to feel guilty about. People who create need to take breaks. People who give of themselves the way you give, need to take breaks. You were at a snapping point two weeks ago.

If another week or two or a month will help solidify you, then take it."

Hearing her mother affirm her wants brought tears of thankfulness to her eyes. "Okay, mama. Thank you."

"Have you written anything at all?"

Harmony looked up the stairwell to the landing where her keyboard and desk sat collecting dust. "Not a bit. I want to, but when I sit down, nothing comes to me. I've just been playing songs over and over again, praying for inspiration."

"When God's ready to give you inspiration, you and I both know it will come in droves." She paused. "Was there something else you needed to talk about?"

Immediately, an image of Steven Slayer's worn face flashed in front of her eyes. Her mother had always shown a deep intuition with her children. "Yes, but I'm not quite sure how to even begin."

Alice chuckled. "Perhaps with the beginning."

"I ran into someone a several days ago. It was quite shocking, actually, especially in context."

"Oh?" She could almost see her mother tipping her chair back and turning to stare out at the Nashville skyline. "Shocking in what way?"

Harmony cleared her throat. "It was Steven Slayer."

It felt like an eternity passed before her mother said, "I beg your pardon?"

"He, ah, helped me load my groceries in front of Martin's."

An incredibly long moment went by. Harmony's neck muscles tensed in anticipation of how Alice would respond. "Why was Steven Slayer in front of Martin's

Grocery in Harperville?"

"His drummer's grandmother was Mrs. Ackers. He said he was staying at her place while he, uh, quits drinking and detoxes from drugs."

She heard her mother's deep breath intake and slow release. "I see."

Relief at admitting the chance meeting flooded through her. Now her family wouldn't be surprised by some tabloid article talking about Steve and her hiding out or vacationing together in the mountains. As her mind let go of the anxiety, a new thought suddenly occurred to her. She spoke before she could change her mind. "Could you do me a favor, mama?"

"Considering the subject matter, I would dare say that depends."

"Can you get me a list of Christian rehabs? He's struggling, and I would really like to see him succeed."

Another pause. "Harmony, honey, how does his struggling with sobriety have anything whatsoever to do with you?"

She spoke before she could convince herself of the bad idea. "Because he's, at this moment, definitely a least of these. Isn't he? If I didn't know who he was, if I hadn't seen him for what he was, I never would have even recognized the man I saw. He is lost and wounded and needs a friend."

"Let me guess. You feel like you need to be that friend? Why is that?"

As her eyebrows came together in a confused frown, she said, "Because, mama, I believe God put me here while he was here. You may disagree, but it makes perfect sense to me."

"Sense? What sense is there in a helpless young woman, miles away from civilization, stepping in to help a strung out drug addict who, by the way, has done more damage to your professional reputation than anything else in your career? Care to enlighten me?"

She felt her teeth set on edge at the helpless implication. "I'm hardly helpless. I'm barely even young. And, I am speaking to you on a very civilized phone. There's nothing dangerous about him. He's weak and alone. If you don't want to help me, that's fine. I can just go to the library in town and research on my own."

"Harmony," her mother said on a breath, "please tread carefully. If anyone in the press even catches wind that you two are in the same little isolated town, then—"

For the first time in her life, she dared to interrupt her mother. "Then! I'm sure some other tabloid editor will get patted on the back for a catchy heaven and hell headline. It doesn't change the truth. I can't allow myself to be swayed by what people think of me."

"I beg to differ." She heard her mother's chair as she likely straightened at her desk. "You have responsibilities. Your fame, your celebrity, and your public podium all come with responsibilities to the people who look up to you. Everything to do with our success is based on public perception. The thing that sets us apart, the wonderful thing, is that how we are perceived is exactly who we really are in our real lives. But it doesn't change the fact that people listen to your father, read my books, watch your aunt's movies, and listen to your music because they believe our family is a good, godly family. Unsubstantiated though they may be, rumors tying you to an actual card-carrying devil worshiping band is going to hurt that reputation and ripple through this entire family. Are you prepared to face those consequences?"

Despite the fact that no one could see her, Harmony lifted her chin. She would not be intimidated by a what-if over something so wrong. "Gossip is evil. The Bible doesn't say to do what you can to avoid being gossiped about. It simply says to refrain from gossip. I will not bear the burden of anyone else's sin. Their sin is their responsibility. Not mine. I'll do what I feel God is leading me to do, and that is to help Steven Slayer." She stood and paced to her big bay window, looking out at the snow-capped mountains. "And if in the end, he comes to know Christ, then won't that amount to a huge victory?" She looked at her watch. "I'm going to head on into town and go to the library to use their internet before they close."

"Harmony—"

"I love you, mama. Good-bye."

She hung up the phone, feeling like she'd just come out of the mouth of the lion. Of course, she knew how her mother would react. Franklin got every bit of his fussiness from her. She'd never actually had her mother disapprove so verbally to some decision she'd made. She wondered whether she should heed her mother's warning and just go on back home to Nashville, or if she truly needed to stand on her principles and help Mr. Slayer. Steve.

Deciding that she ought to pray about it first, she slid down to her knees by the couch. "God, I could really use a touch of wisdom here."

♫ ♫ ♫ ♫

Chapter 8

S TEVE ducked under a fallen tree trunk, putting his hands down on the moist mossy ground as he slipped under the thick wood. The smell of cedar filled his senses and he wanted to just stop and inhale the aroma. As he moved further away, the smell faded and the earthy dampness he'd come to associate with the wooded areas returned. He stopped and marked the tree as he had every hundred paces or so, so that he didn't get lost and end up not finding his way back to the cabin. His booted feet barely made a sound on the soft ground, and the sound of insects and birds accompanied him during his walk.

Peace surrounded him, warming him like a blanket. For the last four days, he'd walked in all directions of the little cabin. Every once in a while, he came across another home, but for the most part, he'd had hours of solitude during his walks. Thankfully, his weak and dizzy spells hadn't recurred since the day he walked into town. Every day, he felt stronger and walked farther. While he walked, he thought and planned and had, somehow, started praying.

Unlike other members of his band, Anton especially, Steve was not an atheist. He wasn't even agnostic. He actually believed in Jehovah God and everything the Bible said about Him. However, his hurt and anger as a teenager had destroyed any love of God he could possibly have in his heart. In an attempt to hurt both God and his parents, he had chosen to record the music he recorded and start living the life he lived. As the years went by any guilt he might have felt about his lifestyle faded. He quit even thinking about God. Instead, he focused on himself and on earthly pleasures.

Eventually, everything in his life turned darker and darker. Symbols that represented his band had gradually morphed into ritualistic demonic symbols, and somehow, in his heart and mind, he hadn't cared. Anton, his rhythm guitarist, even wore an amulet to signify his worship of a satanic influence. Steve himself had discovered that tattoo on his own back, a snake wrapped around an apple—symbolic of Satan's temptation of man and the failure of man to turn his back. He had no idea how many young people in the world had turned to the evil arm of spirituality due to his own direct influence.

He thought of something Anton had said to him—that if you told God you wanted a cookie, God would say, "Be patient. Wait until tomorrow and I will give you a hundred cookies." But, if you told Satan you wanted a cookie, he'd say, "Here! Have a cookie. In fact, indulge in all the cookies you want. Your gratification right now is my pleasure today."

He had certainly sought instant gratification. Lots of it. So now, why would he begin to presume that God would listen to his prayers? He likely had made the "Enemy

Number One" list at least once in his life. While he allowed himself to blame his dependency on drugs and alcohol to account for his lack of handling any business affairs, he knew no amount of drugs or alcohol could explain his purposeful and intentional turning away from God.

Could God possibly forgive someone like him? Should He?

Did Steve really want Him to? To seek forgiveness would almost certainly remove any justification he'd felt in his anger. It would almost cancel out and suggest that the hurt and betrayal that had consumed him for so many years meant nothing.

As he had constantly done since the trip into town a week ago, he pondered and thought and warred with himself about it while he walked, marking trees and stumps so he could find his way back. When he heard a voice singing, he paused, listening, trying to determine the direction from which the voice came. Moving quickly and confidently, he went around a huge patch of blackberries and jumped over a narrow stream, then stepped through a dense patch of ferns, and found himself standing at the edge of a clearing. A cabin made of cedar wood sat in front of him. He saw Harmony Harper standing on the wraparound deck. She wore a purple plaid shirt with the sleeves rolled up to her elbows over a white T-shirt and a pair of worn denim jeans. Her blonde hair hung in a braid down her back. Unobserved, Steve watched her light a gas grill while singing into a set of tongs. After lighting the grill, she disappeared through a glass door and momentarily returned, carrying a plate piled with food. Deciding he had to either make himself known or else leave very quietly, he took a deep breath and stepped into the clearing.

"Hello!" he yelled.

Harmony jumped, as if startled, and spun around, spotting him. For a moment, she looked confused and almost scared, then she smiled and waved. "Steve! Come on up!"

With more confidence than he felt, he walked to the stairs that led to the upper deck and climbed them. She didn't move from her spot by the grill, and continued to load it with vegetables. He recognized Portobello mushrooms, zucchini, and eggplant peppered with spices. "Did you walk all the way here from your cabin?"

When she looked at him, he felt like he really looked at her for the first time, no longer through the haze of alcohol and drugs, no longer inside the fog of withdrawal. He saw violet eyes framed with long lashes, eyes that told him she wanted to hear about his walk. She wore no makeup, yet the beauty of her high cheekbones and rosy lips needed no help or enhancements. He truly didn't think he'd ever looked on such natural beauty before.

Trying to avoid just sitting there and staring like an idiot, he looked out over the woods, back in the direction from which he'd traveled. His mind cleared and he thought he might be able to continue the conversation like an actual grown-up. "I did. I've been walking for about four hours a day."

She smiled and her eyes widened as she nodded. "How are you feeling?"

Embarrassment heated his neck and started to inch up his ears, as he thought about how she had found him at one of his weakest moments. "Much better. Ironically, the cravings for a cigarette seem to be the hardest part of this."

"How interesting." She set the empty plate on the wooden table next to her and gestured at a chair. "Take a seat."

When she moved, he noticed that her T-shirt had purple sequins formed into the shape of a crown, and words that said Daughter of the King.

"Can I get you something to drink? I have lemonade I sweetened with honey or some herbal teas."

"Lemonade would be great. Thank you."

She opened the door to step into the house and he caught a glimpse of hardwood floors and the edge of a black couch. When the door shut behind her, the woods behind him reflected back at him.

Clearly, the glass had some kind of reflective coating that provided her privacy but still allowed one entire wall to be made of glass. He cleared his throat and shifted in the chair, determined to get a handle on this out-of-character reaction to a woman. A beautiful woman, yes, but he'd met throngs of beautiful women in his life. Surely, he could carry on a normal conversation with one.

She returned very quickly, carrying a tray that contained a pitcher and two glasses. "I'm glad that I made this, now. I almost settled for just a slice of lemon in my water."

She poured him a glass and smiled at him as she handed it to him. After checking on the vegetables, she perched on the edge of the table. "Still feeling down?"

Did he still feel down? The question came at him from nowhere. He examined his heart and tried to answer honestly. "Maybe. Sometimes." He ran a palm over his head, feeling the bristles of hair growing back in. "I don't really know how to explain it sufficiently. For thirteen years, I've masked my emotions with alcohol and chemicals. Now, suddenly, it seems like I feel everything in extreme." Relief at verbalizing why he could possibly react this way to her made him relax. Clearly, another part of the detoxing had reared its ugly head,—the part where he learned how to handle normal responses to outside stimuli, pleasure or pain.

She took a sip of her lemonade and nodded. "I imagine that's where some group therapies would come in handy at a qualified rehab center." She grabbed the tongs off of the table and turned the vegetables over on the grill.

"I've done rehab twice. The first time, my manager paid a nurse to slip me drugs on the sly. The second time, I was in for a week and got high the day I got out. Honestly, I don't think I can do it again. That's why I'm here in the woods by myself."

She turned to look at him, her face a mixture of anger and sadness. "Why would he do that?"

"Who?"

"Your manager."

He thought of Cain Proctor, and all of the ways that man had manipulated him over the years. "Because, controlling me is his life's work. And the easiest way to control me is chemically." He took a long pull of the lemonade, enjoying the flavor of the honey. "I am not saying I'm not responsible, I'm just explaining why he did what he did. However, he won't have another opportunity to do it."

"Oh?"

Decisions. He had so many decisions to make. Some would prove easier than others. "I'm going to take a long break from the business, if I don't leave it entirely. I need to figure out how best to handle my future. I think ending my relationship with my number one drug dealer is probably the first good decision I've made in a long time."

A look of sympathy crossed her face. "How hard for you." If she didn't honestly feel sympathy for him, she was a great actress. How could she have such genuine feelings for a virtual stranger?

He shrugged, but didn't want to imply that he had made the decision casually. "What will be hard will be telling the band. It occurs to me that I have a lot of people who rely on me for their livelihood."

She took a sip of her own lemonade and braced a foot on the chair next to her, rather than sitting in it. "They could just go on without you, you know. Bands get new lead singers all the time."

He smiled as he thought about the group of men he had worked and performed with for the last decade. "That's true. I think I could probably sell them the songs I wrote." He cleared his throat. "Quite frankly, I've never truly paid much attention to the business side of things, so I'll have to get an attorney to help me with what I need to do."

Harmony ran her tongue over her teeth before she spoke. "I have a cousin who is an entertainment attorney in Nashville." She opened the lid of the grill and peeked in, then shut it. He caught the scent of the seared squash coated with garlic and basil. "Where are you from?"

"California."

She leaned against it again. "I don't know what good he can do in California, but he might know someone. Would you like me to call him?"

He stared at her. She looked good and clean, something with which he had never really had a lot of experience. Women had always been a faceless sea of bodies to him, constantly throwing themselves at him. Most women he'd interacted with didn't even come with names, not that he ever cared about their names, anyway. Yet, here stood Harmony Harper, an amazing vocalist and character, extending a hand to him to help him. When she shifted and crossed her arms over her chest, he realized he'd been staring and wondered how much time had passed since she'd asked the question. "Sorry. I was thinking."

"Thinking?"

"Yeah, uh," Steve cleared his throat.. "I don't want to lie to you. I don't ever want to lie again."

Harmony uncrossed her arms. "Okay."

"So, yeah. I would appreciate that very much. If you could make the call. And that's the truth."

When she straightened and grabbed the tongs again, he drained his glass and stood. "I should probably go."

"I made some rice to go with these. I have plenty if you'd like to join me for lunch." With nervous movements, she pulled the vegetables off of the grill.

"I'm gonna go."

Halfway down the stairs she stopped him. "Steve, wait."

Nervous, uncomfortable, not sure how to act or react, he simply wanted to escape. How did he say that? With a hand on the rail, he turned and looked at her. "Miss Harper..."

"It's Harmony, Steve." She raised her hand and gestured at the door. "I really do have plenty. And I'd enjoy it very much if you would join me."

After a long pause, he turned around and came back up

the stairs. "Thank you."

♫ ♫ ♫ ♫

HARMONY slid the door open for Steve, who carried the platter of freshly grilled vegetables. She led the way through the main room, past the black leather couches, and over the white shag carpet to the kitchen area and gestured toward the counter. "Just set those there. I'll get the rice." As she made her way to the stove, she pointed toward the cupboard next to the refrigerator. "Plates are in there, if you want to grab a couple."

Had she done the right thing? Should she have let him into her cabin? She didn't know him, she only knew of him, and nothing she knew suggested anything good or moral about him. Maybe next time she prayed to God with a request for exposure to someone to witness to him, she might be a little more specific about how and when he came into her life.

With nervous movements, she turned the burner off and removed the lid from the pot. The smell of the rice flavored steam rising up made her stomach growl. Grabbing the wooden spoon she'd set next to the stove, she turned to the island and loaded the plates Steve had set out. "I have salad in the fridge."

While he went to the stainless steel refrigerator and opened the door, she set the pot back on the stove and grabbed the salad tongs out of the dish drainer. Surely, nothing would happen. Surely, God had orchestrated this. Believing it, she loaded the greens she'd already tossed with vinegar and oil onto the plates.

"I am going to enjoy eating something that didn't come out of a can," Steve said with a smile, loading one of the plates with the vegetables he'd carried in. "I bought a steak that day at the store, but other than that one meal, I've had soup. And then when I get tired of that, I have more soup."

With a smile, she replied, "I could heat up some soup if you'd rather."

"That'd be great," he said with a little laugh. She liked that sound. It brought joy into this room that had seen so much solitude. It filled her heart with joy to hear it.

"They say soup is good food," she teased.

He shook his head. "I say soup is food you eat until you can get some good food."

They carried their full plates back outside and sat at the table on the deck. Steve picked up his fork just as Harmony folded her hands. She couldn't help but be impressed at the way he very gently set his fork back down and bowed his head. "Father God," Harmony said, "thank you for new friends, for this food, and this time of fellowship. Lead and guide us, God. Amen."

She watched as he took the first bite of mushroom and rice. Some feminine part of her felt immense satisfaction at the way he closed his eyes and obviously savored what he tasted. With a smile she couldn't quite control, she took a bite of her salad.

"This is so good," he said, shoveling another forkful into his mouth.

"Thank you." She refreshed their lemonade. "When I want to think, I like to cook." She ate several bites before she looked at him, surprised to find him staring at her.

He chewed and swallowed while he stared at her with intense green eyes. "When I walked up, you were singing into your tongs."

Heat flooded her cheeks. "Well, I was working out the

lyrics to a new song. It's easier for me when I sing them."

When he smiled, it lit his entire face up. "I'm sure the tongs are also essential to the process."

With a gasp and a laugh, she said, "Like you've never sung into your hairbrush."

The smile faded and he ran his hands over his shaved head. Somehow, she felt like she'd said something wrong. He put his fork down and picked up his glass of lemonade, staring into the liquid. "Steve?"

He cleared his throat and looked at her, his eyes welling with tears. After he cleared his throat, he said, "I'm sorry. Overwhelming emotions, remember?"

This wasn't about him singing into a hairbrush. Instinctively, and before she could think about the movement, she leaned forward and took his free hand. "What happened?"

"My, ah, little sister Gracie—" his voice cracked on her name. She remembered him mentioning Gracie's funeral the day she dropped him at the cabin, so she shored herself up and prepared to hear tragedy. He cleared his throat again, "She used to sing into a hairbrush while I played guitar." A single tear rolled down his cheek. He roughly cleared his throat and pulled his hand free then picked up his fork again, using his shoulder to wipe at the tear. "Anyway, that was a long time ago."

This subject clearly hurt him. Without the benefit of the education a trained psychologist received, she had no idea what one did with an emotional subject and a drug addict. Encourage him to talk or allow him to withdraw? Would she damage what progress he'd made by making the wrong decision?

Deciding to play it safe and broach a more recent

topic, she sliced into a piece of eggplant and said, "Did you see the tabloid photo of us?"

His eyebrows knotted together in a frown. "Tabloid photo?"

Her eyes widened. "Oh, you didn't see it? My older brother, who is *my* manager, his name is Franklin by the way, always tries to hide that stuff from me, too. When you ran into me and knocked me backward, someone took a picture. The picture is highly suggestive."

The confused look didn't leave his face. "What are you talking about?"

"You really don't know?" At his nod, she dabbed at her lips with her napkin and stood. "I'll be right back." She went back into the cabin and rushed up the stairs to the landing where her tote bag sat on her desk chair. She'd set it there two weeks ago and hadn't even opened it since she got here. It took no time to find, and she carried it back outside, handing it to Steve.

He set his fork down and put his napkin on top of his empty plate as he took the magazine from her. She watched his face darken as he opened the tabloid and found the article. Not knowing what else to do, she continued to eat as he read. "I ran into you?"

Studying the confusion on his face, she knew he truly didn't remember. "Yes. You were rather unsteady on your feet. I was headed to the stage to perform. You spilled a beer all over my pants and for the first half of my set, all I could smell was beer."

"Is this why you're here?" he finally asked. He gestured all around. "Hiding from the press?"

"Maybe." Was it? Uncomfortable, she set her fork down again and leaned back in her chair. "I don't know. I volunteer at a children's hospital. One of my favorite patients died the night that photo was taken. The tabloid came out on the day of her funeral. It kind of added to the overwhelming turmoil in my life at the moment."

"Harmony," he said on a breath, tossing the magazine on the table away from their plates, "I am sincerely sorry." He looked around, as if searching the edge of the clearing. "I shouldn't be here. Someone might—"

"I want you here, Steve." She knew he would likely repeat what her mother had said, so she reached forward and took his hand again. "I want us to be friends."

"You want to be my friend?" He tossed his head in the direction of the tabloid. "Here's something about me you should know. I don't even remember that happening."

Confused, she frowned. "At the store the other day you said you remembered me."

With a shake of his head, he clarified, "I remembered you singing 'Amazing Grace,' and I barely remember some sort of purple sequined belt or something. But this," with his free hand, he tapped a finger on the photo of him pushing her back against the wall, looking as if the photographer caught them while freshly engaged in a very intimate and consensual pose, "this I have no recollection of whatsoever." He looked down at their joined hands. "The last thing someone as… as good of a person as you needs is a friend like me."

Feeling like he might be about to leave, she grasped his hand with both of hers and looked intently into his eyes. "You might believe that. But, here's what I believe. I believe that you need a friend like me." Releasing his hand, no longer imprisoning him, she sat back in her chair. "And I'm going to be that friend for you."

"Why?" he snarled, pushing his chair back. The metal

legs scraped against the wood deck. "I got nothing for you."

"That's good, because I don't need a thing from you." Guessing that everyone in his life had used him for their own gain, she very calmly said, "I have lots of friends. Some good, some intimate, some casual. I love and am loved. But you," she picked up her glass and took a delicate sip, "you're alone. Christ called us to love our neighbor. You're just about the closest neighbor I have."

He remained seated. She thought that might possibly count as a small victory. "And then what?"

Eyebrow raised she asked, "'Then what' what?"

"What happens after we're friends?"

"Well, I imagine that both of our lives are made better for the friendship." She stood and picked up his plate along with her own. "I personally feel like God brought us together for a reason. I wouldn't even put it past Him to have arranged for that photo at just that time, to get us both here for His purpose."

She entered the house, halfway expecting him to leave. Instead he followed her inside. She set the dishes in the sink and gestured toward the couches that faced the large stone fireplace. "Make yourself at home. Would you like some fresh strawberries and a cup of tea?"

He looked at her as if she had sprouted two extra heads. "You're serious."

"Yes, I am."

"Sure. Strawberries and tea it is." He nodded and stepped down into the living room area, walking over to the mantel. She quickly put together a tea tray while he read the sheet music she had framed and hung above the mantel. In minutes, she carried the tray into the room and set it on the coffee table. She walked up next to him and tapped the glass on the first frame with her fingernail. "This was the first song of mine that topped the Billboard charts. The rest of the songs framed here are the ones that have made it to number one."

"'Daughter of the King'." He gestured at her shirt. "Like your shirt."

"Exactly. These shirts are sold at my concerts."

"Never been in a room with a real live princess before." Harmony chuckled as Steve slipped his hands into his jeans and read the byline at the top of the page. "You wrote it."

With pride that may or may not have been a little puffed up, she grinned. "Yes. When I was fourteen."

He walked down to the end of the line of frames. "Well, look at you. This is quite amazing, Princess."

She chuckled. "I guess that's what I am, by definition. A princess. A daughter of the Most High King. And, I appreciate the compliment. Thank you."

"I'm not saying that lightly." He turned and looked at her. "You're obviously incredibly talented."

She didn't know why that pleased her so much. "I come from a very talented family. We have all turned our gifts over to God for His glory. When people listen to me sing, it is my prayer that they don't hear my voice, but rather that they hear His voice." When he pressed his lips together, she decided to press forward. "Do you believe in God?"

"Is that a requirement for this friendship you talk about?" His voice came out rough and rude.

With a casual shrug, she moved back to the coffee table and poured tea. "Actually, I'm capable of being your friend given all sorts of circumstances." When she picked up the cups and saucers and turned, she found him standing right behind her. She suddenly felt very trapped between him and the couch. She held out the cup and saucer, determined not to act as intimidated as she felt. He took the offered cup and moved away, sitting in a chair across from the couch. Unable to not know, she asked, "What happened to Gracie?"

He had his cup halfway to his lips before she spoke. Instead of taking a sip, he set it down on the table and sat forward in his chair, scrubbing at his face with both hands. "No one really knows this. She was my baby sister. When I was seventeen," he said, his voice gruff, "I killed her."

Harmony froze. Her heart felt like it stopped beating, then kicked back in again, almost painfully thumping. Her hands went cold. With a loud clattering sound, she set the cup and saucer on the table. "What?"

♫ ♫ ♫ ♫

STEVE watched the color drain from Harmony's face and knew he'd shocked her. What thoughts went through her head right now? She probably thought he planned to attack her and bury her in the woods. She would start hyperventilating if he didn't clarify soon. He had intentionally shocked her just to see her reaction. Then he decided to give her a break.

"When I was sixteen, my sister, who was only nine at the time, got really sick. She got a type of strep that attacked her kidneys. She ended up on dialysis and in need of a kidney transplant."

Harmony's face started to regain some color. As he spoke, the panicked look left her eye. She even picked the tea back up and took a sip. "I know a few kids that are waiting on transplants," she said quietly.

"Yeah. That's right. You volunteer at that children's hospital." As he reminisced, memories transported him back to San Francisco, to his parents' living room. Once more, he experienced the moment when he first heard that his sister would likely never receive a donor kidney, and that she would live out the rest of her shortened life on dialysis. "My parents both tested and were found not compatible. It took the doctors to convince them to let me be tested as well."

As memories that he'd buried for thirteen years assaulted him, he took a sip of tea. The horrible taste pulled him out of his self-pity party and dragged him back to the moment. "Ugh. What *is* this?"

"Chamomile." She looked at him with a wide-eyed, innocent look.

"What the h—" He stopped himself and reworded. "What exactly is chamomile?"

"It's a soothing tea. It helps calm and relax."

Avoiding shuddering at the thought of taking another sip of the wretched brew, he set the cup back down and wished he had that lemonade, if for nothing more than to wash the taste from his mouth. "Uh, that certainly wouldn't calm or relax me. In fact, I'm feeling considerably more tense."

"Sorry. Don't mind the tea. Please go on."

"The short story is that I was a close match," he said, continuing his story, "so I gave her one of my kidneys."

"Are you serious?"

"I told you. I don't want to lie to you." Steve raised his shirt slightly. A very long, very ugly scar ran along the bottom of his ribcage on the right side of his body. It looked as if he had been sawed in half. He lowered his shirt.

"The surgery was pretty bad. The pain afterward is hard to describe. I would have to say it was the most pain I have ever experienced. It had to be just as bad or worse for Gracie. She was so little and sick. But then, after a few days, she was able to stop the dialysis." He froze, remembering the next few weeks. "About a week later, she got really sick all of a sudden. No one could figure out why. Eventually, they discovered she'd contracted a staph infection during the surgery. All of the investigations into how that could have happened didn't do any good because she got sicker and sicker and then she just died."

Harmony tilted her head and looked at him as if trying to see him from a different angle. "I'm so sorry for your loss," she said quietly. "How does that mean you killed her?"

"My parents grieved." He felt hot tears burn his eyes, and embarrassment flooded his chest at the thought of crying in front of this woman. "They said my rock music, my evil heart, my guitar—that my sister had died because she was so good and I was so bad. They said that when I gave her a piece of me, her body rejected it."

Harmony gasped and rushed toward him. Before he could even react, she fell to her knees at his feet, gripping his hand in hers. "How could they say that to their own son? After what you went through to try to save her life!"

He looked down into her beautiful face. A strand of hair teased her forehead, and he fought against the impulse to brush it back. "Because it was true. Against their rules, I'd brought music into their home, hidden it in my room, and learned to play guitar to it with headphones on. They didn't have any idea of the stuff I was listening to. I was a bad kid. My friend Chaz and I would sneak whiskey out of his dad's bottles. By the time I was sixteen, I pretty regularly smoked marijuana before school."

Hearing the sincerity and hurt in his voice, Harmony felt her eyes well up with tears.

"Before I was even medically released to go back to school, they kicked me out." He clasped her hands between his.

Tears fell from her eyes and down her cheeks. "How old were you?"

"Just about seventeen. I threw a toothbrush into my guitar case, cleaned out my mom's purse, and Chaz and I hitchhiked from San Francisco down to LA." He bent so close to her that their noses almost touched. "The rest is history. I was picked up almost immediately. Cain put a band together and shot us to the top. Eventually, I didn't even think of my parents anymore."

She sniffled. "I'm so sorry that happened to you, Steve. My heart is broken for the boy you were."

He stared into her wet violet eyes for a long time before kneeling next to her on the floor. "That night you sang 'Amazing Grace,' that was the first time I'd been back to San Fran and the first time I'd heard that song since my baby sister's funeral. I was so stoned on who knows what, more than half drunk, and had a breakdown. They took me to the hospital by ambulance. The doctor told me that my remaining kidney is shot. So I decided it's time to quit trying to kill myself." At her wide-eyed response, he gave a small laugh. "Oh, sure, I know that's what I was trying to do. I don't know why I didn't ever have the courage to just do it right; do it all the way."

She inched closer to him so that their knees touched and released his hands to put her hands on his shoulders.

"You didn't kill your sister, Steve," she insisted. He felt some dark corner of his heart that he had long ago shut and locked start to creak open. "Your parents were wrong. It was not your fault." Her small hands squeezed his shoulders, as if reassuring him. "Steve, I would like to pray for you."

Fear flooded his soul. Panic tried to make him push her away, but he fought and won the battle to stay still. Her hands remained on his shoulders. "God doesn't want to hear from me."

"I don't believe that. In fact, I know that is not the case." When he started to look away, she gave him a little shake. "Look at me." Her eyes, intense on his, bored straight through as if she could see the deepest darkest corners of his being. "God said that He gave us His Son, who is Christ, and that whosoever believes on Him shall not perish, but will have eternal life. So, while you may think that He doesn't want to hear from you, I can assure you that His Word said quite the opposite. Because you're one of those whosoevers."

Emotions flooded his heart and mind and tears fell from his eyes. He couldn't form a coherent thought. The idea that despite everything he'd intentionally done and said, he might still find a way into God's loving arms almost destroyed him. Harmony continued, "Let me pray for you, Steve."

Unable to speak, he simply nodded and bowed his head, resting his forehead on her shoulder. Her arms came around him, and she whispered a prayer of healing for his heart and soul into his ear. His tears soaked into the shoulder of her shirt.

♫ ♫ ♫ ♫

Chapter 9

HARMONY came around the corner and hit the brakes seconds before she plowed into the stack of lumber sitting in front of Steve's borrowed cabin. With a hand to her heart to stop it from racing, she turned the engine off and climbed out of the driver's seat just as Steve came around the corner of the cabin, carrying a crowbar and a bottle of water.

He wore a ball cap, a pair of shorts, and boots. She could see his T-shirt draped over the porch railing. A stylized geometric pattern of lines that resembled the stripes on hard candy wrapped all the way around his right arm to form a highly impressionistic venomous snake tattoo. Over his heart, he had a colorful and detailed tattoo of what she recognized as a Stratocaster guitar. Her eyes immediately located the long diagonal scar along the bottom of his rib cage, and she remembered the story he told last week.

As he walked, he tossed a rotten piece of wood into a large pile. She noticed then that he'd ripped up half of the porch and trimmed the rose bushes down away from the walkway.

"Good morning," she said, glad she'd worn jeans today. "Looks like a project."

He took a sip of water as he walked toward her. "I stepped through the porch two days ago. Thought I better see to fixing that." He gestured toward the lumber with his bottle. "Hardware store delivered that this morning."

In the week since he came upon her cabin while out walking, she'd seen him twice. Once, they'd driven to Mount Jefferson State Park and hiked one of the trails. Another time, she took him deep into her property and showed him the waterfall she'd found a few years ago. She discovered that she really enjoyed spending time with him and watching him discover the new Steve, as he called it, the reborn Steve.

She reached into the Jeep and pulled out a hair clip. "Great! I was going to see if you wanted to go for a walk, but this will be much more productive."

With a raised eyebrow, he said, "What do you know about replacing a porch?"

"About as much as you, I would imagine." She wrapped her hair into a sloppy bun and secured it with the hair clip. "I don't think it's something they teach you in recording studios."

"Very cute," he grinned, "but my father is a contractor. I teethed on a hammer."

"Must be why you're so tough as nails."

With his bark of laugher, she walked over to the demolition pile. "Seriously. Tell me what to do."

He took the leather gloves off of his hands and handed them to her. "I'll rip it up. You discard."

By lunchtime, the entire porch lay in a rubble heap and Harmony's muscles ached from hauling the old wood to the pile. She sat back and watched as Steve laid out the new porch with stakes and string. When he had it fully laid out, he tossed the ball of twine on top of the new tool belt that lay on the ground next to where they worked and wiped his forehead with the back of his arm.

"I'm starving," he announced. "This is a good stopping point."

She pulled the gloves off and tossed them on top of the tool belt, then followed him to the doorway. He grabbed his shirt where he'd hung it from the doorknob and opened the door, hopping through the doorway. He turned and held a hand out for her, half lifting her up into the cabin. For the slightest moment, their bodies brushed in the doorway. He smelled like wood and sunshine and sweat. For the briefest second, they paused, his hand gripping hers and her other hand on the doorframe. She looked up at him, looking into his green eyes. As they darkened, he suddenly released her, stepping back and slipping the shirt over his head.

Determined that she'd made up the "moment", that it had only happened in her head, she refused to act jittery or uncomfortable. Instead, she walked to the sink and turned on the water, putting her hands under the cold stream. She noticed that he had scrubbed the kitchen clean. The empty dish drainer was turned upside down in the sink. Even the curtains in the kitchen window were bright white and freshly ironed.

"I have to say, Steve, I'm so impressed. I wouldn't even know where to begin with building a porch."

"I haven't built one yet." He pulled bread and cheese out of the refrigerator. "I will honestly tell you I had to check a book out of the library." He gestured at the carpentry book that lay open on the counter. "But once I began reading, it started to come back to me." In no time, he had cheese sandwiches grilling on a cast iron griddle over gas flame.

Harmony pulled the old metal ice tray out of the freezer and pulled the handle to crack the ice. She filled glasses with ice, water, and lemon slices, then set them on the table. He flipped the sandwiches while she sliced an apple.

He slid sandwiches off the griddle and set them on the table. When they sat, he held out his hand to her. Pleased and surprised, she lay her fingers against his palm and bowed her head. He prayed a simple prayer over the meal. After he said, "Amen," he held out the platter of sandwiches to her.

"I have a food order coming in today or tomorrow. Would you like to go with me to pick it up?"

For several moments, Steve stared at her, his face solemn and serious. Finally, he shook his head. "I don't think so."

Surprised, she leaned back in her chair. "Why?"

"I don't want anyone to recognize me here."

"It's Martin's Grocery. It's not driving to Portland and going to the newest and hippest grocery. I doubt anyone will recognize you."

He took a bite of sandwich and chewed and swallowed before replying, "I realize they won't immediately recognize me. I look different, and they're not looking for me here. But they'll recognize you. And then they'll wonder who you're with, and someone might use their phone and take a picture of us. Within a day, the vultures would be here, screaming questions, demanding answers."

She felt her eyes widen. "I honestly didn't think about that."

"I imagine you wouldn't. This is your town. It's your safe place." He waved toward the door. "Even if someone sees you here, it's not news. This is where you are when you're not making news." He took a piece of the apple and popped it into his mouth. "I'm needing the seclusion right now."

Understanding, she nodded her head. "I understand. Thank you for your candor. Do you want me to leave?"

His eyebrows furrowed together in a frown. "Leave? No." He leaned forward and took her hand. "I think you're right. I think that God brought us together. I appreciate your company and look forward to seeing you when we're apart." He let her hand go and sat back in the chair. A silly smile crossed her face. "Plus, I don't really know if I can build that porch without a good laborer next to me. You're the only person I know in a thousand miles, so it's kind of you and me."

With a snort, she picked up her water glass. "At least you find me useful."

He stared at her for a second before saying, "Oh, I could find a use for you."

She watched as his eyes widened when he realized what he'd said. Heat fused her cheeks and she actually sat backward. "I don't think…"

"Harmony, I'm sorry. That just slipped out." He took a deep breath and pushed his plate away. "I had everything in my old life in excess." Rubbing his palm over the stubble on his head, he looked down, no longer meeting her stare. "I don't really know what I'm trying to say."

Harmony closed her eyes and took a deep breath, trying to look at it all from a different angle. Finally, she said, "I imagine that you just had to crook your finger and a dozen girls would fall all over themselves to be the one you picked."

He looked up, his face lit by surprise. "Yes! Exactly!"

She nodded. "I appreciate that about your old lifestyle and the things it's trained you to think about the opposite sex. However, I'd like to make it clear that I'm not one of those girls. I'm a woman. As a woman, as a sister in Christ, I am not only worthy of your respect, I require it in order to continue to be your friend."

She couldn't read his expression as he processed her words. Finally, he nodded. "I appreciate *your* candor," he said, mimicking her words. "I really am sorry. I'm working on getting rid of more than one bad habit."

She reached out and squeezed his hand. "You'll get there. You've already come so far."

♫ ♫ ♫ ♫

HARMONY sat on a flat rock. The sun beat down on them. The river rushed by, forming rapids over the rocks in the center. The roar of the water made them have to speak with slightly raised voices. Overhead, two hawks circled and cried out to each other. She looked up, shielding her eyes from the sun, and watched the beauty of their flight. When she looked back at Steve, she saw him bait his hook with a fat worm. Her stomach rolled at the sight. "What are you going to do with a fish if you catch it?" she asked.

He looked over his shoulder at her and winked. "Well, Princess, I'm going to eat it."

She made a face and felt her body actually shudder.

"I'm not cooking it."

He cast the hook into the river and tightened the reel. After a few seconds, he turned the reel a few times, then stopped and waited a few seconds. He looked over his shoulder again. "I'm capable of cooking my own fish." He carefully stepped backward until he reached her rock, then slowly sat down next to her. "You know," he said as he tightened the reel, "Jesus ate fish. He even cooked fish."

With a snort she replied, "Jesus didn't have to deal with toxic mercury levels in His fish." She crisscrossed her legs and rested her elbows on her knees and her chin in her hand. The hot sun beat down on her neck. "Is your real name Slayer? That's not your real name is it?"

He adjusted the bill of his ball cap and glanced at her. "No. It's Slater."

"Steven Slater?"

"Until I was seventeen." He pulled the line in and recast it. "Is your name really Harmony Harper?"

"Of course," she answered. He gave her a skeptical look. "Did you legally change your name to Slayer?"

He shrugged and turned his back to her. "Not that I can remember. I guess I need to add it to my list."

She knew he kept a list of things he needed to handle, business-wise, and a list of things he wanted to investigate further about himself. Pondering his memory gaps for the last thirteen years, she said, "Steve, can I talk to you about something?"

"Just a sec," he said as he stood, straining against the fish fighting on the end of his hook. She smiled as she watched the pole bend almost in half and at his exuberance at the battle. He gradually brought the fish out of the water, then held it up to her, triumphant. As the fish fought and wiggled its tail, water splayed around and she held up her hands, laughing.

Soon, they walked back to his cabin. He carried the now cleaned and gutted Rainbow Trout by the gills. "This should grill up nicely," he said, holding it up. "Sure you don't want some?"

She ate eggs and dairy but she hadn't eaten meat a day in her life. Holding her hand up as if to ward off something unpleasant, she shook her head. "I'll be fine with potato salad and coleslaw," she said, thinking of the salads she had made earlier and left chilling in his refrigerator.

"Fair enough." He grinned. She felt her heart tug in response to the happy look on his face. "I'm going to go put this in the fridge."

"Okay." While he was gone, she retrieved the packet of papers from her Jeep. When she heard the sound of the screen door slam shut, she turned and saw him come out of the house, wiping his hands on a kitchen towel. He wore a red T-shirt and a pair of khaki shorts. He had gained a little bit of weight since the first time she'd seen him outside of Martin's Grocery. The change in the last month since he had started truly seeking a relationship with God had simply put her in awe. She couldn't believe someone could go through such a metamorphosis.

They'd spent hours and hours together since that first day at her cabin. Every second with him, she felt herself grow closer and closer to him. Every day, he got healthier, happier, and more clear-headed.

"You now have my undivided attention," he said with a grin, leaning against the Jeep and crossing his ankles. He turned his head to look at her and she realized how close they stood. "What did you want to talk about?"

She turned so that her shoulder rested against the roll

bar. "I need to go back to Nashville." His eyes lost some of their humor. "I'm recording my annual Christmas album with Melody Montgomery and Bobby Kent. I can't put it off any longer or the production schedule will be delayed."

His eyes searched her face and he surprised her by reaching out and touching her cheek. He had never voluntarily touched her before. Her breath caught in her throat as she suddenly realized that she wished he wanted to. "So why the nervousness? Something's got you on edge."

She licked her lips and held up the papers, immediately missing his touch when he took them from her. "Rehab," she said very quickly. At the dark look that crossed his face, she took one of his hands. "Not like what you know. This one is a Christian rehab. They focus on the love of Christ and the healing power of God. They reinforce that through Christ, you can do anything." She tapped the brochure. "And it's really close to Nashville."

His hand tightened over hers. "You bringing me home like a stray dog, Harmony?"

Hurt sliced through her heart. "Why would you think that? I want to help you."

"Why? What motivation do you have? The second the press gets word of this—"

Speaking before she thought, she blurted out, "Because I really care about you. And, I want you to be near where I live so that I can be there if you need me."

Instead of pulling her closer, he pushed her away and took a step back, panic turning his eyes dark gray. "No. I am absolutely incapable of trusting my emotions right now. I can't—"

"Steve, I know that." She straightened and opened the

Jeep door, pulling out a piece of paper. "Here are twenty other rehabs similar to that one all over the country. And one in Europe." She held the paper out. "If you want to do it away from me, I absolutely understand. You're right. You can't trust your emotions." She smiled. "I'm not in recovery, though, so I can trust mine. And I don't know how this can possibly go anywhere, either. But I'm willing to see you through whatever I need to until you're in a position to trust yourself and we both know how you truly feel."

His eyes narrowed and he spoke, clearly understanding what she didn't say out loud. "As long as I go through rehab, that is."

"Yes. I think so." She shrugged. "I think they'll teach you coping skills to deal with the real world. I think they'll help you grow closer to God. It can only be a good thing." She stepped toward him and he took a step back. "Steve, I am going to go home tomorrow. But on this top paper is all of my contact information. And, I added my number to your phone in the kitchen."

She held the paper out and he took it without stepping toward her. He glanced at the top sheet. "I don't know if I can do this without you here," he confessed.

This time, when she walked toward him, he didn't back away. She put her arms around him and after a moment's hesitation, he wrapped his arms tight around her. For the first time ever, she closed her eyes and rested her cheek on his chest, listening to his heartbeat. She would memorize that sound and hold onto this moment when she left tomorrow. "I know that you can," she said. "I am confident in you and the power of the Holy Spirit."

For several minutes, they stood perfectly still. She breathed him in, memorizing the feel of his arms, the sound of his heart, and the smell of his aftershave. Eventually, they stepped away. Harmony slid her hands into the pockets of her shorts and gestured toward the cabin with her chin. "Ready to grill your fish?"

He looked at the stack of papers in his hand once more before looking at her, his face relaxing and his green eyes shining. "You going to taste it?"

"No. Of course not."

He laughed and led the way into the cabin.

♫ ♫ ♫ ♫

HARMONY sat in the back seat of the car next to her mother and watched the Tennessee landscape rush by. She thought about the difference of the soft leather of this car and the hard seat of the Jeep she'd rented. Her mind drifted far away from the car and soared home to Mount Jefferson.

"You haven't said much since you got back home," Alice observed, closing the cover of her tablet and setting it on the seat beside her. "Would you like to talk about it?"

Harmony thought about the last week. After a tearful good-bye at Steve's cabin, and a hug that neither of them wanted to end, she went back home and packed. Early the next morning she left. A part of her had hoped he'd show up and beg her to stay. A part of her feared that her leaving would cause him to spiral down. Instead, she'd received a text from him wishing her a safe journey. She called when she'd arrived in Nashville, but his signal came and went, and finally they settled for texting long into the night.

She didn't hear from him the next day. Then, two days after she got home, he sent her a text from the Atlanta airport, telling her he had made arrangements to go to one of her suggested rehabilitation clinics in New York City. Four days later, she hadn't heard from him again. She had expected that. His contact with the outside world would be limited for some time.

If she felt offense at the fact that he picked one so far away from her, she didn't allow herself to dwell on it. He needed to do what he needed to do, and as much as she hated to admit it, he probably needed to do it away from her.

For the last week, she'd examined her heart and her mind. Had the feelings she'd felt growing for Steve been a consequence of isolation and heightened emotions? Back in her real world, back in the city, away from the isolation, no longer simply enjoying his presence, she didn't think so. She truly believed that she felt very real feelings, that they existed, and even possibly that God gave them to her.

"What is there to say?" she responded to her mother. "You don't approve of my friendship with him. I'm not going to spend all of my time defending my actions."

Her mom pressed her lips together and looked at her for several moments. "Your friendship with him may damage your career."

Harmony raised an eyebrow. "Do you no longer believe in the redemptive power of the blood of the Lamb, mama?" She closed her eyes and shook her head. "Never mind. I don't want to talk about him with you. I'll say this, and then the subject is closed. Who he was a month ago is not who he is today. I will be his friend and, quite frankly, I don't want nor do I need your permission."

Neither spoke for the rest of the ride. As the car pulled

up outside the studio, Harmony gathered her bag. Alice reached forward and put a hand on her arm. "Harmony, darling, I am very proud of you for standing up for what you believe. I will trust you for now. And, if you need an ear, know that I will listen with the utmost respect and love."

Out of nowhere, tears stung her eyes. How much had she needed that affirmation? She nodded and whispered, "Thank you, mama." The driver opened the door and she slid out of the car. Knowing her mother did not intend to stay, she turned and said, "Please place him in your prayers."

She smiled. "Honey, I have already."

Harmony turned and went into the door of the studio. Bobby Kent and Melody Mason Montgomery had already arrived.

"Hello there, darlin'," Bobby drawled, sweeping her into his arms. She laughed and hugged him, then turned her attention to Melody Montgomery.

"I think you grow more beautiful every time I see you," she said, lifting a long black curl off Melody's shoulder.

"That's just love, hon," her friend grinned, gesturing toward the dark-haired man wearing glasses and typing at the console's computer. "That man I love right there? He makes me feel radiant."

"Hey. What about me? I'm in love," Bobby demanded with his honeyed voice.

Harmony very seriously said, "Yeah. I think you have a radiant glow, too, Kent." Then she couldn't contain it anymore and burst out laughing.

"Hi, James," Harmony said to Melody's husband. "I

didn't know you'd be here today."

He looked up, clearly distracted. Then he smiled. "Montgomery Records needs that special Montgomery touch. It's so good to see you, Harmony."

"How was your sabbatical?" Melody asked, hooking her arm into Harmony's and steering them toward the buffet of food laid out for them.

"Incredible," Harmony truthfully admitted. "I will tell you about it one day."

Melody stepped back and looked at Harmony from head to toe. "Tell me about it, or about him?" When she felt her cheeks fuse with color, Melody smiled and pointed a finger at her. "Thought so. You have a certain radiance, yourself." Looking around, she whispered, "Can't wait to hear about him."

Just as she finished indulging in a plate piled high with fresh fruits, the producer called them into the studio to talk about the organization of the songs. Since she had worked with Bobby and Melody together on four Christmas albums already, the three worked together like a well-oiled machine. In no time, they had completed the first run through of the songs.

Taking a break and sipping some tea with honey, Harmony pulled her phone out of her bag and took the opportunity to read through her e-mails. Her heart almost jumped into her throat to see one from Steve.

HARMONY: I WOULD LIKE TO THANK YOU FOR YOUR PUSH FOR THIS REHAB. IT'S LIKE NOTHING I'VE EVER EXPERIENCED. I CAN'T EXPLAIN WHAT IT'S LIKE TO BE SURROUNDED BY PEOPLE WHO ARE ENCOURAGING ME TO SEEK OUT CHRIST. EVERY MORNING, I WAKE UP WITH

SONGS IN MY HEAD. THEY'VE GIVEN ME A JOURNAL. I'VE
FILLED UP ABOUT A THIRD OF IT WITH JUST SONGS. I KNOW
YOU'RE PRAYING FOR ME. PLEASE KNOW THAT I'VE
STARTED TO PRAY FOR YOU, TOO. STEVE

A tear slid down her cheek as a silly grin covered her face.

Taking the chair next to her, Melody superfluously cleared her throat and announced, "So!" Harmony looked up and met the older woman's eyes and Melody smiled as she started with, "Is," and dragged out that lone one syllable word for so long that Harmony raised an eyebrow at her, waiting for her to continue, before she finally concluded, "this *the* him?"

"It is." Harmony turned the screen off on her phone and looked at her friend. "I can tell you that in my entire life, I've never felt this way."

Melody shot a look at her husband. "I know that feeling." She leaned closer. "Did I ever tell you that James probably could have talked me into marrying him the first day we met?"

Harmony raised an eyebrow and looked over at James, who stood next to the buffet talking to Bobby. "No!"

"It's true. And the thing is, that day I was on a flight back from my honeymoon that didn't happen. Long story. Anyway, James didn't, of course, but I was so enamored with him right away. It wouldn't have been a hard sale."

"And now you're parents of five-year-old daughters." Harmony thought about the little black-haired beauties. "And three foster sons."

"Maybe four." Melody pulled a clip out of her pocket and pulled her hair back. "We have started praying to see if God might bring another boy into our lives.

Harmony felt her heart melt a little bit. "I can't wait to meet him."

"Me, either." She grinned. "You need to come visit. The kids all ask about you."

"I will as soon as I can break away."

Melody tapped Harmony's phone. "And bring him?"

Suddenly uncomfortable, she looked around, making sure no one could overhear them. "Do you believe, truly, that when someone comes to know Christ, they become a new creation?"

Melody raised an eyebrow. "I think that both the Bible and the world are filled with those very testimonies."

"I met a man." She licked her lips and looked around again. "He's quite famous but he was a different person before. Now he's come to know Christ and the change in him has been unbelievable. But, I'm afraid his past is going to be a problem for almost everyone."

"His past?" Melody frowned. "All right, hon. You haven't been pen palling with someone in prison, have you? Like death row?"

Her eyebrows knotted in confusion. "What?" When she realized what Melody asked, she laughed. "No. Nothing like that. I actually spent quite some time with him." She pulled the tabloid out of her bag and handed it to Melody.

Her eyes widened in surprise. "You are kidding me. I thought this was tabloid trash. This was for real?"

Harmony spoke quickly. "No. I didn't know him that day. That was actually just wrong place at the wrong time and a picture taker got lucky to get that photo. But, I met him later. He was sober and clean. We spent a lot of time together. Right now, he's in a Christian rehab."

Melody leaned forward. "Harmony, honey, tread carefully."

"I am." She slipped the magazine back into her bag. "I'm just his friend right now. His emotional state is incredibly tenuous and I would never do anything to damage it." She took a sip of her tea. "I have been reading so much about it. I know not to even pretend to want a relationship with him right now." She lowered her voice. "Though I confess it wouldn't be hard to convince me right now, either."

Melody studied her for a moment. "I imagine Franklin doesn't approve."

Harmony snorted. "Yeah. No doubt." She huffed out a breath. "Franklin would probably actually stroke out and die. I love my brother too much to do that to him. Best wait to see what the future holds."

"Exactly." Melody laughed, then took Harmony's hand. "I will be praying for you. For wisdom and guidance. And, I look forward to meeting this new and improved man. Last time he and I were in the same room, it wasn't really a positive experience. Lucky James didn't find out about it. He would have likely got all manly and protective."

Harmony squeezed her hand. "Thank you for not making a rash judgment."

With a smile, Melody released her hand and stood. "It's not rash, but I'll reserve any new judgment for when I see him again." She gestured toward the studio. "Ready for round two?"

♫ ♫ ♫ ♫

STEVE sat at a picnic table and wrote in his journal. He felt warm sunlight against the back of his neck. The morning breeze felt a little cool here in October in New York City, but he knew the day promised to be warm and beautiful.

He tried to get outside whenever the staff allowed it. Ivy covered the wrought iron fence surrounding the facility, creating a natural shield against the outside world. Oak trees planted throughout the campus offered shade for half of the tables, and the other half sat in the sun. Steve always chose a table in the sun. He felt like the rays of the sun helped his continued healing in a way that probably wouldn't stand up to the scrutiny of medical science, but worked in his mind. He missed the days he could sit on the sandy beach of his own backyard and just let the sun beat down on him.

Without taking his eyes from the page, he took a sip of still hot black coffee, savoring the flavor. Everything tasted much better recently. Intellectually, he knew that had a lot to do with the fact that he no longer smoked tobacco. Emotionally, the rediscovered flavors satisfied his soul in the same ways that rediscovered colors seen in the light of day or pure sensations, like clean sheets and a good shave satisfied.

When someone sat down across from him, he looked up, surprised to see his counselor, Paul Daniels. "Mr. Slater. You've had a request for a visitor."

For a moment, he thought Paul spoke of Harmony. Excited, he shut his journal and capped his pen. "Who?"

"Cain Proctor."

As quickly as the elation had come, it left, leaving him feeling deflated. "You know what? I think I'm ready. Can I see him?"

Paul tilted his head and looked at him. "Honestly, I'd like to be in the room with you when you do. The things you've told me give me a basis for concerns about leaving you alone with him right now."

Steve shook his head. "I can do this. You're welcome to watch, but I would prefer to do it alone." He picked up his journal and stood. "I'm going to have to face the lions eventually."

Paul led the way to the conference room off of the main reception. Steve felt a nervous energy that made him feel a little bit on the aggressive side. Cain hadn't been his primary problem, he knew that, but it didn't make him any less of an accomplice. Inside the conference room, he found Cain sitting impatiently in one of the chairs. As soon as the door opened, he hopped up and charged toward Steve. "Seriously, Slayer, I can't believe you did this."

Determined not to react, Steve gestured at the chairs and pulled one out. He felt his palms sweating, so he clasped his fingers together and silently prayed. "Well, Cain, I had to. The doctor told me I had to quit or die. So, I quit." He paused. "For real this time."

Cain laughed. "Yeah, right." He gestured toward the door. "Let's blow this joint. Tell me what I need to do or who I need to see to spring you."

Calmly, he shook his head. "No."

Cain froze. "No?"

"No. I'm not leaving yet. I need to stay here for several more weeks. Get stronger, learn more coping skills, grow in my faith."

"Your faith?" As if for the first time, Cain looked around, obviously seeing the posters and signs that talked of Christian faith. He actually made air quotes with his fingers when he spoke next. "Your 'faith,' dude, is your music. You're a god to all your fans. You think some mysticism and getting cozy with your imaginary friend is going to keep you clean? I thought you were smarter than this, man."

"The problem is that you've never thought I was smart at all." He glanced at a poster that reminded him that through Christ, all things are possible. "The truth is that you've used me. You've even abused me. You've intentionally strung me out like some sick kind of pimp. Granted, it was with my consent. However, my plan was to fire you as soon as I got out. You coming here just shortened the timeline." He used his thumb to gesture over his shoulder. "I've made arrangements with my financial company to remove you as a signatory from, well, everything. The papers I signed went out via messenger yesterday afternoon. I imagine you've already been informed of that, which is probably how you found me."

Cain moved quickly, gripping the arms of Steve's chair. "Listen to me. I made you. You're nothing without me."

Steve raised an eyebrow with pretended calm. Inside, he seethed. "Actually, in the last couple of months, I've learned exactly how much more I can be." He stood, forcing Cain to back away. "Thank you for the hard work you put into my career. I haven't decided what I want to do next. But, I am officially quitting as lead singer of Abaddon. I'm sure you will continue to represent the other members. Perhaps you can find a new lead. I wish you the best in that."

"You *are* Abaddon and you know it." He punched the table with the side of his closed fist. "It's you, not any of the other members. You're who the fans want."

Steve closed his eyes and shook his head. Why had he thought this conversation would be hard? "Cain, I am done. There is actually and absolutely nothing you can say or do to convince me otherwise. Leaving is the first step toward my staying well."

He went to the door and put his hand on the handle as Cain very quietly said, "I will destroy you."

Steve looked back at him and nodded. "I believe you'll try." He opened the door and walked out. Paul met him in the hallway inside the area restricted to guests.

"I think you handled that well. How do you feel?"

How did he feel? "Relieved is the first word that came to mind. I'm not even remotely worried or scared."

"It's not easy making such a big break."

Steve put a hand on Paul's shoulder. "Doc, nothing about this is easy. In fact, it's incredibly, horribly hard, but making the break is how I will get through. If I went with Cain, the first thing I'd do is wash a pill down with some Scotch whiskey, then light a cigarette. You know that. He and I both know that. And I would do exactly that. That's the truth."

Paul put a hand on his arm. "There will come a day when that won't be the truth."

With a self-recriminating smile, Steve replied, "Just being honest here. I don't really believe that right now."

"One day you will." He gestured toward his office. "Let's go pray."

♫ ♫ ♫ ♫

Chapter 11

S TEVE sat at a computer in one of the little half cubicles in the library. Patients occupied all twenty of the computers, and all around the library, more patients milled about, looking at books, waiting for their turn at the keyboard. Each patient who had graduated to that level had the privilege of twenty minutes a week of computer time on Sunday afternoons. He could hear the clacking of keyboard keys from the woman next to him and the murmuring of a conversation from some patients waiting for their turn. He looked at the timer on the computer. He had about ten minutes left. He read back through the email one more time before hitting "send."

HARMONY: IT WAS GOOD TO HEAR FROM YOU. I'M GLAD THE CHRISTMAS ALBUM IS IN THE CAN. I CAN'T WAIT TO HEAR IT. I MISS HEARING YOUR VOICE.

THANKS FOR THE INFO ABOUT THE PRESS. THERE'S NOTHING I CAN WORRY ABOUT RIGHT NOW, BECAUSE I CAN'T

CHANGE IT. ANYONE WHO WOULD BE IN AN UPROAR OVER THE THINGS THAT CAIN IS SAYING ARE NOT THE PEOPLE WHO WILL BE MY FRIENDS OR FANS IN THE END. I HAD A BAD DREAM LAST NIGHT THAT I ACTUALLY LEFT WITH CAIN LAST WEEK AND HIRED HIM BACK. THEN I REALIZED I WAS DREAMING AND IMAGINED THAT JESUS HIMSELF SAT BETWEEN US IN THE CAR. IT GAVE ME A REALLY GREAT VISUAL TOOL TO USE FOR WHEN I DO GET OUT OF HERE. DOC CALLS IT A COPING MECHANISM.

THERE IS A FAMILY DAY NEXT FRIDAY. I DON'T HAVE ANYBODY ELSE. I WOULD VERY MUCH LIKE IT IF YOU WOULD BE ABLE TO COME. BUT I COMPLETELY UNDERSTAND IF YOU DON'T WANT TO RISK THE EXPOSURE.

YOURS, STEVE

He reread the email again. Should he ask her to come to the family day? Why did he feel like the awkward band geek had just asked the head cheerleader for a date to the prom? He closed his eyes and took a deep breath. He wanted to believe that if he asked, she'd come. He so very much wanted to see her—

He hit "send" before he could talk himself out of it. Then he logged out of his email and logged off the computer. He would have an opportunity to read her reply tomorrow after lunch. He had a feeling the next twelve hours would pass by so incredibly slowly.

♫ ♫ ♫ ♫

HARMONY wore a dark wig and not a stitch of purple. In a Christian facility the chances of someone recognizing her quadrupled. She wore a light blue sweater over a pair of jeans and black heeled boots and had draped a blue and red scarf around her neck. She sat in an iron chair under an oak tree and waited. The chittering of black squirrels made her look up and grin into the gold and orange leaves as she watched two squirrels chase each other along a branch. She smelled the faint scent of burning leaves in the crisp air.

Every few minutes, someone would come out of the building and she would hear the excited murmur of friends or family. Finally, Steve came out of the building and onto the grounds. He had on jeans and a button-down shirt the color of the fall sky. Because of her clever disguise, he looked past her once. After scanning the crowd of friends and relatives, he looked again. She could tell by the raised eyebrows when he spotted her. Then his face lit up in an enormous smile.

He looked good. His hair had grown out some. She noticed he'd kept the sides short and allowed the top to curl a bit. It gave him a clean-cut look and made him absolutely unrecognizable from the Steven Slayer she had met so long ago. She grinned and waved.

As they hugged, she closed her eyes and savored the brief contact. Stepping back, he said, "That's a wig, right? You didn't actually color your hair?"

"Aww." Brushing her hand over the locks, she winked. "You don't like it?"

He reached out and wrapped a dark curl around his finger. "I'm happy to see you, Princess." He let her go and gestured toward a tree. "We have a full hour." They sat on the ground under the tree, close enough to touch. "What did your family say about you coming?"

She smiled. "My mother told me to be careful. Franklin is barely speaking to me right now."

"I see. And how do you feel about that?"

With a chuckle, she nudged his arm. "Been learning a few tricks in therapy I see."

"Just how to get someone to dig a little deeper." He leaned back against the tree and held his hand out. She gladly placed her hand in his and leaned back with him. They laced their fingers.

"Harmony, listen. I've been rehearsing what I wanted to say to you when we met in person again in my head and I think I just need to get this out."

He sounded so serious. "Okay. I'm listening."

"I may not say everything exactly right so forgive me if I mess it up, but here it is. I feel like you're the kind of friend I really need. I know you're the kind of friend I need to get through this." He stopped talking and stared at the ground between them.

"Is there a 'but' coming?" She prodded.

He looked up, shocked. "What? Oh. No. Sorry. I don't know exactly how to say this. It's just that, well, I'm not the kind of friend anyone needs. I am definitely not the kind of friend you need. For anything."

"That's not true—" she started, but he held up a hand.

"I'm not finished. Just let me get through this."

"Sorry."

"Just listen, okay? For a minute."

"I'm sorry. I'll be quiet until you tell me you're done."

"What I'm trying to say is like, like with Franklin. I don't want to come between you and your family, Harmony. And with my past, I would only hurt your family. I just don't want that." He paused and took three slow breaths then said, "So, it's like this. I feel like for me to truly be your friend, we can't be friends anymore. I don't want anything bad to happen to you because of me. That's all."

She waited about five seconds and said, "Are you done being all noble now?"

He grinned. "I guess."

"Okay, good. Now, you got that out of your system. Eventually you're going to realize that I'm a grown woman. I understand my family dynamics even better than you do, and I get to decide who I'm friends with regardless of what anybody thinks, please and thank you very much." She smiled a genuinely happy smile. "How do you like that?"

"So I don't really get a say is what you're saying."

"You catch on quick."

He smiled a toothless tight-lipped smile and she felt the tension leaving his body. "Okay, but what about Franklin?"

"It makes me feel impatient, even though I understand why he worries." Content, she looked up at the blue sky through the branches of the tree. "You look really good, Steve."

"It's all the red meat they feed me here."

She snorted.

"You look really brunette." She gasped out loud. A part of her wanted him to shower her with compliments about her beauty. Another part felt relieved at this sudden lightheartedness. At her gasp, he chuckled and said, "You look amazing. I've missed you a lot. I'm insanely happy you came."

"Me too."

For a few minutes, they didn't speak. Finally, she said,

"Cain Proctor really went after you in the press." She thought of the nasty comments that she'd read and how she would feel if someone had said those things about her.

Steve took a deep breath. "He said he would." After a moment he said, "Has there been another link made between you and me?"

Thinking back to the phone call her mother had received from Mrs. Cooper about the reporters asking about Steve, she gave a small shrug. "They found out about your friend's cabin, and some of them have been asking questions in town. It's only a matter of time. We move in different circles, so it will take someone who knows us both to put it together." Harmony straightened and rolled to her knees, her thigh brushing up against his hip. "What do you want to do when they connect the dots?"

He stared at her, his green eyes serious. "It'll be your reputation on the line. Not mine. I'm starting at rock bottom, remember? I got nowhere to go but up."

She lifted her chin as justified anger made her want to dare someone to challenge her. "I am not afraid."

"Fear or no fear, it will happen." He leaned his head back against the tree and closed his eyes. "I would stop it if I could."

Thinking back to the conversations she'd had with Franklin, she said, "So would everyone else in my camp."

He patted the ground next to him. "I don't want to talk about terrible things right now. I just want to sit next to this beautiful brunette and listen to you talk about things that won't make or break an incredible woman's career."

Frustrated, she turned so she could lean back against the tree again. She lay her head back and closed her eyes.

"My album's doing well in the pop charts. I have a single that's actually competing with one of yours."

"Are you serious?" He gave a small laugh. "They must have released a ballad."

"They did. It's an interesting sound. You kind of lure the listener in all soft and romantic, then you go a little crazy. By the end, I can barely understand the words and I think the bass is way too heavy." She wouldn't admit to listening to some of his music, trying to get a full picture of the "before" Steve, but she hadn't truly enjoyed any song.

"My ballads are all similar to that. They're designed to get my albums onto the pop charts and into the pop video countdowns, hoping more kids will buy them." He sighed. "I have an appointment with an entertainment attorney this week. He's coming in from LA to help me work through my business and see where everything stands."

"That's great." She picked up an acorn and rolled it around on her palm. "I wish we could still be in Oregon."

"This was good for me. I don't know if I've thanked you properly, yet, but it was good for me. You were good for me."

That made her happy. Pushing him to go to rehab hadn't been easy. She knew he could have resented it in the end. Knowing that it worked, seeing with her own eyes the true progress he had made really did wonders for her own heart. They spent the rest of the hour talking about the spiritual discoveries that Steve had made, about the Bible study his small group had started, and about his keeping a daily journal. Soon, a staff member rang a bell, announcing the end of the visit. The two of them stood, then lingered under the tree, talking until they absolutely had to stop. She turned so that she faced him, standing toe-to-toe with him. He reached out and cupped her cheek, and she wished that she knew that he would kiss her. However, she knew him and knew he would not.

"I can't wait to see you wearing princess purple with blonde hair again," he joked, brushing a strand of hair off of her forehead.

She reached up and took his wrist. "I don't have to hide, you know. I could take my wig off and let the world see us together." She raised a hand to her hair and he stopped her.

"Don't." He pulled her to him and wrapped his arms around her, resting his cheek on the top of her head. "I look forward to the day we won't have to hide."

"Me, too," she whispered.

Feeling a little sad, she left him standing under that tree. As she walked back to her car, she slipped the wig off of her head, scratching at the edge of her hair where it had itched. She tossed the wig and her bag into the car and slid behind the wheel. She took a deep breath and released it before starting the car and driving away.

♫ ♫ ♫ ♫

HARMONY rushed to the door as the doorbell rang for the third time. She opened it, surprised to find Franklin standing there, his face darkened with fury. "It wasn't bad enough before. Is that it?" he demanded.

Confused, she frowned. "Why hello, Franklin. Nice to see you. Why don't you come in?" she asked, looking beyond him into the dark of night. Moths flapped around her porch light and one darted in. She could hear crickets and frogs competing to see who could chirp the loudest in the night.

"Thank you, no," he insisted. He handed her a stack of magazines. "I'll just leave these with you." He turned on his heel and left her front porch.

Frowning, she let the door shut and looked down at the magazine on the top and gasped. The cover of a popular Hollywood gossip rag showed a picture of Steve and her hugging under the tree, then one of her taking the wig off outside by her car. She dropped the magazines on the floor of her foyer and started digging through them. Newspapers and magazines all carried the same shots. The photos must have come from a single photographer. How did they find out?

Her phone rang, muffled by the pocket of her sweatpants. She retrieved it, glanced at the caller ID, and answered. "Grandma," she said, her voice catching. "What can I do?"

Liz Harper spoke quickly and with authority. "We have a press conference scheduled for nine in the morning. Be at the office by eight."

She hung up before Harmony could even say, "Yes, ma'am."

As she sat there, staring at the photos, it occurred to her that as much as she wanted to feel upset about this, as the initial panic wore off, she kind of felt relief. Didn't she want to have the chance to visit him and talk to him without worrying about someone finding out about it? Taking one of the magazines, she walked through her spacious foyer and into her main room. A comfortable velour couch the color of a stormy sky faced two wingback chairs. Tall windows dressed with open drapes in a lighter gray looked out over her backyard. Her maple wood floors gleamed throughout the entire first floor. She walked through the room and into the kitchen.

She'd left her laptop sitting on the marble-topped island. Slipping onto one of the tall stools, she turned her laptop on. Within minutes, she had composed an email to Steve.

PRESS GOT PICTURES OF LAST WEEK'S FAMILY DAY. THEY'RE CLEARLY ME. YOU AND ME HUGGING. MY FAMILY HAS A PRESS CONFERENCE SCHEDULED FOR NINE CENTRAL TOMORROW MORNING. I DON'T KNOW WHEN YOU'LL SEE THIS, BUT PRAY FOR ME.

Suddenly, the reality of the damages to her career that her mother, Franklin, and even Melody had warned her about flashed in front of her, much like a strobe light. She didn't know what else to do but go into her quiet corner and fall on her knees, begging God to help protect her against the wolves that wanted to consume her.

♫ ♫ ♫ ♫

S TEVE followed Paul into his office. He waited while Paul pulled up a website on his computer, looking at the pictures of Paul and his wife, another doctor on the campus, that sat on the credenza behind the desk. He looked at the clock on the wall and saw that the press conference would begin in one minute. Knowing Paul broke at least three specific rules to allow him to watch the press conference, he felt nothing but absolute love and respect for the doctor who had gradually become his friend.

As the press conference appeared on the screen, Paul moved aside and let Steve sit in his comfortable leather chair. He watched Harmony walk up to the microphones. She wore a purple business suit with a silver necklace, and had her hair wrapped up in a twist on the back of her head. She looked like a woman about to take over the world. To her left, stood her parents, and to her right, her brother. Behind them, he recognized her grandparents. Another woman stood with them whom he did not recognize.

He watched the press start screaming questions at her while she waited, hand up, for them to quiet.

"First of all, I want to thank you all for coming today. I have a brief statement. I would like to dispel any rumors before they get started. Steven Slayer and I are friends. We met during his road to recovery from addiction. I'm very proud to say that he has accepted Christ Jesus as his personal Lord and Savior and is currently and voluntarily undergoing treatment in a Christian rehabilitation facility."

She cleared her throat. "I know there is a knee-jerk response to tabloid-style photos. Here are some facts. As I said, Steve and I are just friends. The embrace in the photos is a hug. No addict has any business pursuing a romantic relationship during the tumultuous road to full recovery. We both have that intellectual knowledge and are behaving accordingly." She smiled as the cameras flashed. The unspoken message rang clear. Steve watched Franklin close his eyes as if wishing to escape. "Steve has a long road in front of him. He needs our love and our prayers. He has mine."

She stepped back from the microphone and Franklin stepped forward, pointing to a reporter in the front row.

"Miss Harper, can you talk about your time with Slayer in the mountains of Oregon?"

Franklin answered, "Miss Harper and," he paused, then continued, "Mr. Slayer did not know each other when they were there. They met several days into Miss Harper's sabbatical. Their friendship formed there, and Mr. Slayer's life-changing conversion to loving and trusting Jehovah God occurred there. It is a time the two of them hold very dear—and personal—and Miss Harper will not discuss it with you."

Questions erupted again, and Franklin picked another

reporter out of the crowd. "Miss Harper, what are your plans when Slayer comes out of rehab?"

Franklin started to speak, but Harmony stepped forward and interrupted him. "I have not made any plans with Steve. Truthfully, it isn't my place. Those are the kinds of decisions he is currently praying about. He has several months before he needs to finalize his plans. Who I am to him right now is a friend who loves him and prays for him daily."

"Mr. Harper!" An uninvited voice filled the silence immediately following Harmony's remark. "You've spent decades talking about the importance of family and Christian influences, yet your very own daughter has now been romantically involved with the lead singer of a band named for the Hebrew word for hell. The man has Satanic tattoos on his skin. How do you plan to explain that to your listeners around the world?"

Steve watched as the formidable Grayson Harper stepped up to the microphone. He stood a full head taller than Harmony. Despite the accusatory manner of the question, his face looked pleasant and when he spoke, he commanded the room. "I'm so happy you asked that question, Mr. Haggarty, and may I say that I am personally relieved to see you can still find work other than just adding a few daily lines to your personal blog."

A few of the reporters chuckled despite themselves.

"In my opinion, you came into this press conference with that question preloaded, and therefore didn't listen to my daughter explain that she is not in a romantic relationship with Mr. Slayer. Be that as it may, the fact is that Mr. Slayer is our new brother in Christ.

"I was hopeful that you would be somewhat better informed about the subject of your question, and I am a bit disappointed that you appear to remain ignorant. Mr. Slayer has already resigned as the lead singer of his former band and has in fact already issued a formal statement to that effect, well, gosh, it's been a few weeks ago now, hasn't it?"

Another chuckle passed through the ranks of the assembled journalists. Grayson removed his glasses and his rich radio voice dropped a few staves lower, as if confiding an emotional point to a dear and trusted friend.

"As to what our listeners will or will not think, that is something that each of them must freely and prayerfully arrive at on their own, in their own hearts. The thing is that despite the media portrayal of Christians as callous, uncaring, self-centered, greedy folks, the exact opposite is true. We are called by our Savior to minister to the least of these and to minister to sinners. What Harmony is doing is her duty."

Grayson paused and held up his index finger then glanced around the room, ensuring that his eyes met every pair of eyes that would meet his. He wanted the last sentence to sink in before he continued.

"If journalists have any obligation to the truth in this very jaded post-modern age, you may wish to reflect upon the notion that I have just spoken the truth. My apologies if it doesn't make for a very controversial headline. As to your question, Mr. Haggarty, when Harmony met Steven Slayer, he needed a friend more than anyone she had ever met, and she felt God's calling to be that friend." He settled in more comfortably at the microphone, and Steve could see how this man had succeeded in his career in radio.

"Ladies and gentlemen, we are called to be like Christ, are we not, who one time faced suspicion and accusations when he dined with tax collectors. Who more should we give a part of ourselves to in this world? Harmony dined with sinners, and like her Lord whom she strives to emulate, she is being criticized and falsely accused today. Personally, I am proud of my daughter for the way she is representing our Savior."

He gripped both sides of the podium and leaned toward the microphone. "Rather than printing rumors and gossip, I would suggest you take the time to also pray for Steven Slayer and the other residents at his facility. They are going through things that most of us will never understand, and it will be through the power of the Holy Spirit that they will succeed."

The family turned around together and left, leaving the reporters shouting out questions. Steve balled his hands into fists. "You knew this would happen, Steve," Paul said. "It's why we talked about maybe not even mentioning family day to her."

"Yes." Which made this his fault, he knew. "But, selfishly, I wanted to see her."

"She knew the risks when she came." He pointed at a magazine. "I saw the security footage from that day. The pictures were taken by the teenage daughter of a patient using a smartphone. Our facility prides itself on privacy, which I know is one of the reasons you picked us in the first place."

Steve scrubbed his face with his hands. "I knew the news would get out eventually. I'm certain that your focus on privacy kept the news back longer than it would have in many other places." He stood and held his hand out. "Paul, thank you for letting me watch the press conference. I know you debated whether you should or not."

Paul shook his hand and smiled. "You are an

incredibly insightful person. I am anxious to see what your future holds."

What did his future hold? He looked at the now black computer screen and wondered if he could possibly have a future with the woman who had become the most important person in his life.

"In the meantime," Paul continued, "we have a new resident who is coming from two weeks at the detox facility at the hospital."

"Oh?" He couldn't figure out why he would tell him that.

"Yes. His name is Mr. Charles Zachary Acker. I believe you know him."

Part of him felt elation, another part anxiety. "Chaz? He's here?"

"He is. You should be able to see him in small groups next week some time. He's had a rough road, but he claims that your influence is what made him decide to get clean."

Remembering his friend from childhood and the disdain they both felt at their church's youth group, he asked, "Has he accepted Christ?"

Paul walked to the door, clearly dismissing Steve. "I believe that will be something Mr. Acker will have to reveal to you himself. I'll see you in a few hours, Mr. Slater. If you start feeling anxiety or the like over the press conference, please make sure you talk to one of the counselors."

Steve left Paul's office and looked down the hall at the closed doors of the rooms of the newest residents. He wondered which room contained Chaz, and pondered his coming here. His entire life, Chaz had followed Steve. He liked the same things, went the same places. Steve wondered if he knew how to be an individual. Was he here just because Steve was, or did he truly desire to be clean, sober, and a follower of Christ? If his intentions were insincere and individually motivated, then he couldn't afford to carry him like he always had. He would fail, and in the end, they both would fail. That possibility filled Steve with an ominous sense of dread.

♫ ♫ ♫ ♫

BILL Rhodes stepped outside of the arena. A semi-truck backed into the loading dock, and the stage crew immediately started unloading it. He checked the time. They had eight hours to prepare this stage, lighting, and sound for the boy band currently getting their beauty sleep in the luxury tour busses parked in the parking lot.

Still furious over the demise of Abaddon and the fact that he now had to tour with a band that catered to an average audience age of thirteen, he pulled a cell phone out of his pocket and dialed a number from memory. "Frankie," he said as Francis Dawkins answered, "I'm glad I caught you."

"I am, too. I've been waiting to hear from you since the press conference."

Bill clenched his jaw. "I don't even know what to say about that." He smiled a jovial smile and waved at the stage manager heading back into the back of the arena. "I have to get to work," he said as the smile slipped off his face, "but I need you to take your group and go deliver a message for me."

"Of course. We're ready to serve you. Tell me what you need."

♫ ♫ ♫ ♫

Chapter 13

HARMONY walked into Franklin's office and sat in the chair across from his desk. He kept writing on the yellow legal pad in front of him. She looked around the room. While she had decorated in lavenders and silver, with very feminine touches, Franklin's office looked almost spartan. The black furniture had clean lines. Cream-colored pillows on the black leather couch matched the carpet perfectly. Simple black and white photos of musical instruments hung on the walls. Only the books in the bookcase provided any color to the room. Franklin had once told her the lack of color helped him concentrate better.

Finally, she spoke. "Are you still my manager?"

His pen paused and he finally stopped writing, slowly screwed the cap back onto the pen, and looked at her. "I don't know if I've really been your manager for a while now. I think I've just been your secretary and designated whipping boy."

Her heart twisted in her chest. "Why is that?" Even before he spoke, though, she knew his answer.

He gently set the pen down on the pad and leaned back in his chair. Before he steepled his fingers, he straightened his already perfectly straight tie. "Because you stopped listening to me. For the last three years, you've made decisions completely outside of my advice or recommendation. In fact, I make recommendations and you seem to go out of your way to do the opposite. It's almost as if you intentionally buck me. It seems very personal and very disrespectful."

She fiddled with the clasp on her bracelet and contemplated what he said. Finally, she replied, "I don't think I intentionally buck you, but I do feel like you don't respect where I feel God is leading me. I know you've been my manager since I was a child, but the truth is, I'm no longer a child. I'm an adult who's been doing what I do for basically my entire life. I no longer need your protection from the big bad world. I need you to be my manager and see my vision along with me then help me achieve it."

Franklin, fifteen years her senior, stared at her with a hard face that gradually softened. Finally, he said, "You know, maybe you're right. When you were a teenager, I watched you rush into so many situations where you just didn't think things through to the end. You actually needed me to protect you back then, and I took that on without complaint." He leaned forward and crossed his arms on his desk pad. "Are you saying that you look at the big picture now, and make wiser decisions? Or do you still tend to rush forward and just hope things work out in the end?"

She could hear the condescension in his voice. "See, that's insulting, Franklin. I'm twenty-seven years old. I am a praying woman. I make decisions based on the counsel of the Holy Spirit. If I buck anything it's this annoying and unprofessional tendency you have to treat me like a baby."

"I don't treat you like a baby, Harmony." Franklin sounded tired.

Harmony went on as if he hadn't spoken. "I believe God grants me wisdom, and I believe He is leading me to reach out to a more secular audience, rather than just singing to the choir. If nothing else, I think the incredible success of the last five years have shown that I am fully in His will in that."

He nodded. "I'm proud of all of your achievements, but you realize that you're putting out more secular than religious music at this point? Albums that used to be eighty-twenty Christian are now sixty-forty pop. My very real concern is that you're letting the world influence your decisions, and since you seem to go against whatever I suggest, I find myself at a bit of an impasse."

She lifted her chin. "I'm doing what I feel God would have me do."

With a sigh, he said, "Harmony, do you honestly believe I don't pray for you and for your career? Do you think you're the only one in this relationship who prays, the only one to whom God speaks?"

With a pause, she considered what he said. Contrite, she replied, "I honestly didn't think about it."

"Of course you didn't. In my experience, you rarely think about much more than yourself." Hurt, she opened her mouth to reply, but he held up a hand. "I mean as far as your business goes. I don't mean in your personal life. I know you pray for plenty of others in your personal life from dying children all the way to me."

"I'm the same person, Franklin, with the same heart.

You don't think that same heart applies to my career?"

He shook his head sharply. "I don't. The business revolves around you and your talent. You often feel like the only one invested in it. But the truth is that I love you and I am entirely devoted to your success. I would just like you to respect my opinions and trust my instincts."

When he stood and walked around the desk, she didn't know how to respond. He took the chair next to her and reached for her hand. "I know there should be some times when we disagree over a few things. But, Harmony, I am exhausted with it being over every single thing. If we can't find a productive working relationship, then we really oughtn't continue to work together. We each have enough to do. You have your music career and I have the entire family to manage at this point. I'll be happy to find you another manager."

Harmony turned completely in her chair to face him. "That's the problem. I don't want another manager. So how about if I commit to knee-jerking less with your ideas and to talk with you more and you try very hard not to treat me like your baby sister." She searched his face and added, "But I will continue in my friendship with Steve. I'm not going to stop that."

He smiled an unhappy smile. "After father's address at the press conference last week, I don't think you should dare to stop being his friend."

"I remember all those years ago when you objected to me working with Bobby Kent and Melody Montgomery."

Franklin snorted. "Completely different. They were exclusively secular artists back then but at least they were both believers. Not satanic acid rockers."

"Exactly what is an 'acid' rocker? What genre is that?"

He held up a hand to forestall further sarcasm. "Don't worry. Dad made a good point and it convicted me."

Laughing, she grabbed him and hugged him. "Thank you for taking such good care of me."

"Always," he said. "You're my baby sister after all."

She poked him in the ribs with a stiff finger.

♫ ♫ ♫ ♫

STEVE spotted Chaz at the picnic table. His friend had lost some weight, but he mainly looked just like Chaz. After the transformation he'd made internally and externally, he'd somehow expected his friend to look different, too. "Brother," Steve said, walking up to him, "it's good to see you."

"Dude," Chaz said, jumping up and taking Steve's hand. The two men gave a quick hug-hand shake combo, then sat down across from each other. "Whoa, man. Can't believe how different you look."

"I was just thinking that you look the same." He crossed his arms on top of the table. "I owe you big for letting me use your gran's cabin."

Chaz shrugged and started using his first fingers to play imaginary drums on the tabletop. "Ain't no big thing." He looked around and said, "Dude, Cain blew a fuse. I mean that cat went well off the deep end of crazy."

With a twinge of unease, he asked, "What happened?"

"He's been telling the press all kinds of lies. Tried to take money, but you'd already locked him out of that. Now I hear he's suing you."

So, nothing he didn't expect. "He said he'd ruin me. I don't think he knows how much he ruined me already." He inspected Chaz's eyes. Everything about his friend appeared normal and sincere. "How are you, man?"

Chaz's fingers stilled. "Ain't never detoxed before. Don't ever want to do that again. No idea how you did it alone. Man, that… That. Sucked."

Thinking back to his early days at the cabin, he couldn't agree more. "Think about that the next time you're tempted to use."

"I think it even wiped the temptation away. 'Course, I never really got as into it as you did."

Steve looked around and made sure no one could hear him. "What do you think about all this Jesus jazz?"

Clearly uncomfortable, Chaz looked him in the eye then quickly shifted his eyes and looked at the table. "Actually, man, I kind of like it."

"Seriously?" Steve let himself see a sliver of hope.

"Yeah, man. Like I always felt like that there was a God, you know? And, you know, like my grandma, if anyone is in heaven right now it's for sure her. So I believe there's a heaven and a hell. Yeah. So, after getting into it, I don't know." He unconsciously tapped his fingers on the table in a staccato beat.

"So what now? You gonna' drink the Kool-aid?" Steve sneered.

His face looked pained. "Well, like, yeah. I think I will. For the first time ever, I kind of feel like I'm something other than just some dumb drummer. Tell you the truth, man, I want to learn more about God and all that—whether you do or not, man. Something I gotta do for me."

His friend had always followed, blindly and faithfully. To hear him say that even if Steve intentionally tried to make it sound like he didn't personally believe it, filled his heart with joy. With a smile, Steve said, "I have completely given my life over to God, Chaz. I'm so happy to hear that you're believing it, too."

Chaz looked all around, then started drumming the table again. "So, you know, what does that mean?"

With a laugh, he replied, "I guess we'll find out whenever we get out of here."

An hour later, Steve finished writing an email to Harmony.

DEAR HARMONY,

I'M SO HAPPY TO HEAR THAT YOU AND FRANKLIN ARE WORKING SO WELL TOGETHER NOW. IT'S IMPORTANT TO HAVE A MANAGER YOU CAN TRUST TO LOOK AFTER YOUR BEST INTERESTS. THAT IS GOOD NEWS INDEED.

CHAZ ACKERS IS HERE. HE IS CLEAN AND DESIRES TO STAY THAT WAY. PLEASE PRAY FOR HIM. HE HAS BEEN MY BEST FRIEND SINCE WE WERE TEN. THE THOUGHT THAT HE WILL COME TO KNOW CHRIST IS ALMOST TOO MUCH TO HOPE FOR.

I FIND MYSELF THINKING OF YOU A LOT LATELY—YOUR LAUGH, YOUR SMILE, THE WAY YOUR BRUNETTE HAIR SHINES IN THE SUN (KIDDING). I KNOW THAT ROMANCE IS KIND OF TABOO FOR ME RIGHT NOW, BUT THAT KNOWLEDGE DOESN'T KEEP THE THOUGHTS AT BAY. I LOOK FORWARD TO THE NEXT TIME I CAN SEE YOU IN PERSON.

YOURS,

STEVE

♫ ♫ ♫ ♫

SITTING on a vinyl couch in the counseling room off of Paul's office, Steve looked out the window as a

February snow fell from the sky. Paul had some nature sounds playing softly, coming from hidden speakers somewhere in the room. He could smell the faintest scent of lavender and knew the doctor used lavender essential oils to provide aromatherapy for some patients. That scent was new, and it put Steve on edge a bit at the idea of Paul thinking he needed to add an extra element of relaxation before this session.

"Tell me about your sister, Steve," Paul said, eyes on a notebook that sat on top of Steve's open folder.

Steve's heart froze in his chest. In all the months here, Paul had rarely spoken of his sister. "Why?"

"Because, you are cruising along nicely. Your faith is growing, you're a leader among the residents, you appear to have completely shifted your entire life, and you are now on an even keel. By all outward appearances, you are ready for the great big bad real world out there. And yet, your face froze, you have sweat beading on your upper lip, and your pupils just dilated at the mere thought of her. So, tell me about your sister."

Memories assaulted the front of his mind. He remembered visiting his mother in the hospital after she was born. He got to miss a day of kindergarten in order to meet his baby sister for the first time. As his eyes welled up with tears, he whispered, "I killed her."

Paul raised an eyebrow. "Do you honestly believe that?"

"What?"

He searched through the folder to a page way in the back and read through notes there. "When you first came here, you said your parents blamed your lifestyle for the punishment from God that resulted in your sister's death. Do you honestly believe that's what God did?"

What did he believe? He tried to sort through a jumble of emotions that threatened to overwhelm him. What did he believe? "Right after my sister's funeral, my parents came home and found me smoking pot in the basement. I'd taken about three times more than the normal dose of the pain pills they'd given me for the surgery. I was drunk, high as a kite, and when my mother showed outrage, I started laughing so hard I fell down."

Paul spoke softly. "You shared this with me before. I'm asking if you believe you killed your baby sister."

Steve remembered it like it happened right in front of him. "My father balled his fists and punched me as hard as he could. He screamed that my evil organ had killed her. That if I hadn't donated a kidney, she'd still be alive." He cleared his throat and surged to his feet, pacing to the window to look outside at the snow-covered grounds. "It's true. If I hadn't donated a kidney, she never would have developed a staph infection, and she would probably still be alive even today. People live for years on dialysis. Decades, even. Honestly, what else is there to believe?"

"True. But do you really believe her death is your fault? Your responsibility?"

His heart actually ached. He rubbed at his chest and pictured his sister's beautiful face, the look of sheer joy when she found out that his kidney would be a match to her. "I…I…," His breath hitched and he fell to his knees. "I hated them and I hated myself. I thought I could take enough drugs that I would die."

"Steve? Do you believe you killed your sister?"

Why did he keep asking that question? "If I hadn't—"

For the first time ever, Paul interrupted him. "If you hadn't donated your kidney, she wouldn't have developed staph infection. I got that. Do you believe your kidney somehow diseased her? Or do you believe that some terrible thing happened during surgery and staph entered her body and attacked an already weakened immune system? Do you truly believe that God was punishing your parents for your behavior by killing your sister, or was it all a terrible event that you were forced to carry on your little teenaged shoulders? What do you really believe, Steve? Do you believe you killed your sister?"

Steve lowered his forehead to the ground as tears streamed from his eyes. He heard the rustling of papers and the shifting of Paul's body as he came over to him. Soon, the doctor knelt next to him, an arm over his shoulders. "The fact is, Steve, you had nothing to do with her death. Your parents were grieving. Bereft. They blamed you in a time of terrible grieving, and in the end they lost both of their children, but that is their cross to bear. The fact is, you didn't kill your sister. Until you accept that, then there will always remain the risk that you'll rebound and end up back on drugs, back to trying to kill yourself, and back to being so furious with God that you try to hurt Him with your sinful life."

The words made sense, but the emotional turmoil that seventeen-year-old went through fought to pull him down and drown him. With Paul praying next to him, praying for his mind to be free and his heart to let go of the horrible event, he felt something inside of him snap. Sobs poured out of him. He didn't kill his sister, but taking the blame and the suffering all of those years ago had kept him from truly mourning her. Suddenly, the overwhelming grief nearly suffocated him as he fought the waves and struggled to not be swept under.

Eventually, his emotions stilled, and he found himself still on his knees, his wet face buried in his hands, Paul silent next to him, his arm still over his shoulders. After several moments of silence, as the tears dried on Steve's face, Paul spoke again. "Steve? Do you think you killed your sister?"

With a raw voice he replied, "No."

"Why don't you tell me about her? The only thing I know about her is how she died. Tell me about who she was before she got sick. Let me see her through your eyes."

For the next hour, he talked about Gracie, about their years growing up together. Like most females, she was a walking contradiction. She was bratty but loving. She was spoiled but sweet. She was both a tattletale and a confidante. She played with dolls and had tea parties and caught snakes and shot bb guns.

Despite the difference in sex and age, they shared a close friendship. She loved her big brother, Stevie, in a way that only little sisters can love big brothers, in a way that he could feel every waking moment. And Steve loved Gracie. He loved her enough to let himself get sawed in half for her. He never once suspected she would actually die. What kind of loving God lets little girls just die like that? Only an uncaring universe could be so cruel.

While he talked, he laughed, he cried, he smiled, and his heart finally began to heal.

♫ ♫ ♫ ♫

Chapter 14

SITTING at her desk in her office, Harmony worked her way through a stack of eight by ten photographs of her singing on stage. She signed her name with a silver marker and added the words "Romans 12:9" below her signature. The wind whipped against her window, coating the glass with freezing rain, making it look like beveled glass. She had a local Christian radio station on low volume, and quietly sang along with her favorite songs while she worked.

When her cell phone rang, she looked at the number and didn't recognize it. It occurred to her a second later that the number had a New York area code, so on the fourth ring, she engaged the call.

"Hello, Harmony." When she heard Steve's voice on the other end, she closed her eyes and silently thanked God that she had answered. Through her happiness at the call, she could hear something wrong in the tone of his voice.

"Is everything okay?"

"Not really."

"What's the problem? Can you talk about it?"

"That's why I called." He didn't say anything else.

After seconds that passed like hours, Harmony prompted, "Did you want to help me out here?"

Steve sighed. "The problem is you."

She felt her eyebrows furrow. "Me?"

"Well, us. I guess."

"There's an us?"

He cleared his throat. "I need some space. I am calling to tell you that I need to take some time away from you and just focus on me."

As much as she wanted to protest the words, she knew in her heart that he had made the wisest and best decision for him. Their friendship had gradually morphed into an unstated yet somehow understood romance, and that was wrong for now. Sadness enveloped her. "I know you're right. Still, I feel like I've done something wrong."

"You didn't. There's just this thing that we both feel. The more time we spend together and the more we communicate, the more it will grow. I have to believe it will still be there when I'm a whole person."

Her throat dry, she whispered, "I understand." Clearing her throat, she added, "If you ever need anything, please call me."

She disconnected the call before she ended up begging him to change his mind. Eyes closed, she leaned back against the cushions of her chair. Thinking of the email she had saved in her drafts folder that she'd penned to him for Valentine's Day, she realized how much she cared for him and just how many of her thoughts centered around Steve

Slater. Though she'd never admitted it out loud, she loved him.

Who knew when she had actually fallen in love with him. It had happened gradually, like water coming to a boil over low heat. That email had never gone out. She didn't even mention Valentine's Day in her email to him last week because she knew he couldn't—or shouldn't—reciprocate right now, and placing the burden of her feelings on his shoulders wouldn't help him.

The certainty in her heart that God had placed them together last summer never faltered. Since she believed that so thoroughly, she would step back and let Steve heal, let him become whom God would have him to be without her interference. In the meantime, Harmony had her own messes she needed to clean up. She needed to mend some fences with her family. She needed to visit the Mercers. She needed to catch up with her friends.

More than any of that, she needed to pray and meditate on God's word so she could understand her own feelings. Despite her protestation of a few seconds earlier, she knew with an absolute certainty that there ought to be an "us." She knew that "us" ought to be Harmony and Steve as one and the fruit of that union would be amazing and pleasing to God.

Before any of that could happen, Steve had to get right with God and his own heart. When that time came, when he was ready, she would be right there, waiting for him and also ready to love him in the way God had prepared her to love.

She picked up the phone and dialed the hospital, getting transferred to the director of volunteer services. "Hello, this is Harmony Harper. Yes, hi. I know I haven't been there in several weeks. I honestly didn't want to drag a swarm of paparazzi to your front door. I think that's died down for now and I have a few hours free this week. Is this a good time for me to come in?"

♫ ♫ ♫ ♫

IN the Salt Lake City hotel breakfast area, Steve looked up from his laptop screen and took a sip of coffee from the paper cup, putting the paper napkin into the empty cardboard bowl that had contained oatmeal earlier. He had earbuds in his ears and listened to Grayson Harper's morning radio show. The depths of the man's wisdom astounded Steve, and he wanted to go sit next to him with a list of questions and soak in his knowledge.

Right now, though, he put that dream aside and focused on his laptop screen. After four days of driving from New York, he faced the possible last day of his trip. He'd gone through the Appalachian Mountains and enjoyed a breathtaking visual of the eastern United States' splendor, ate pizza one night in Chicago, stopped in South Dakota and taken in the magnificence of Mount Rushmore, and battled a freak May snowstorm in the mountains of Colorado. Today, he tried to decide which direction he should travel.

Staying east on I-80 would take him straight to San Francisco. He could go see Chaz's mother and tell her how much good the rehab continued to do for her only child. He could drive into the neighborhood of row houses and park behind his father's truck and walk up to that door and ring the doorbell.

The idea made his stomach clench. Did he have that power? Had he reached a point in his faith walk that he could enter their home and forgive them for their mistreatment and for their lack of care, then beg their forgiveness for his disrespect?

He clicked a button and the mapping program highlighted another route. I-15 southbound would take him straight home. Ten months had passed since he last stepped foot in his home. He was an entirely different person now than the man who had stumbled in from the beach, hung over and already buzzing on a new high. Did he have the power to retake his life? To sleep in that circular bed with the black silk sheets, to open the refrigerator and clean out the beer bottles without taking a drink?

Maybe he should call a housekeeping service and have them clean out the liquor before he got there. Did housekeeping services even do that? Who would Cain call?

He shook his head. It didn't matter who Cain would call. He didn't exist as a part of his life anymore, so it was a moot point.

In his ear, Grayson bid his audience farewell for another day and the show's theme song started playing. As he pulled the wires to pop the earbuds out of his ears, he watched a young mother step off of the elevator, holding the hand of a little girl with blonde curls, a purple tutu, and a T-shirt with a purple rhinestone crown and the words "Daughter of the King" emblazoned on the front.

It took his breath away. Out of nowhere, a longing to call Harmony assaulted him. He wanted to hear her voice. He wanted to get her opinion about some decisions he'd made. Yes, he wanted to do those things; but he wanted to walk into his house and open the refrigerator without wanting one of those cold green bottles of beer, too. She deserved more than him. He needed to test his endurance for the real world before he invited her to experience it with him.

He shut the laptop lid and stood, taking the disposable remnants of his breakfast with him and tossing them in the garbage as he walked out of the breakfast area and to the elevator. After he loaded his laptop into his backpack, he grabbed his already packed suitcase and left the room. Within minutes, he'd checked out of the hotel and drove out of the parking lot.

Until he merged onto I-15 southbound, he didn't know what decision he'd made. Clearly, he subconsciously knew he wasn't ready for that meeting with his parents. Maybe after more time. Maybe after more endurance tests, when he knew he could handle the stress and the emotions.

He plugged his phone into the jack on the radio and pulled up the series of podcasts he'd downloaded. Right now, he listened to teachings on how to live like a godly man. He searched through the list and found the fifth sermon in the series and pressed play, listening to the familiar opening song of the podcast come through the car speakers.

♫ ♫ ♫ ♫

HARMONY sat curled in the corner of the couch, her feet tucked under her, a bottle of water in the cup holder in the arm of the couch. She'd already put on her pajamas and tried to wind down from a series of interviews she'd conducted all day followed by a concert in Madison Square Garden. Now her bus traveled from New York to Pittsburgh for her second show in this thirty-show tour. As she turned the page, the bus hit a bump and made her lose her place. Not really in the mood to read anyway, she set the book aside and looked up.

Franklin sat on the other side of the circular couch, feet propped up on the table in the middle. He'd long since taken off his tie and unbuttoned the top two buttons of his shirt. His rolled up sleeves showed off his anchor tattoo. He paused typing on his laptop to look at her.

"What?" he asked in answer to her stare.

"Did you see tomorrow morning's rankings?"

He winked. "I did, little Miss Number One."

Elation ripped through her and she clapped her hands in glee. "Number one? That's phenomenal!" She sat up. "What about the pop charts?"

"Harmony," Franklin grinned, "that is the pop charts."

"Wait, what? 'Are You Ready?' is an evangelical song. We didn't even plan to release it. It just kind of happened. How did it hit number one?"

"Well, after you and Sheri's duet being such a smashing success, the song inspired by her life would almost have to be. I think it's beautiful to know that so many people are listening to the Gospel message. I'm proud of you." He looked back at his screen. "Now go to bed. You have a sound check in twelve hours."

Pushing herself off of the couch, she walked out of the rear of the bus and through the narrow hall of the sleeping area with bunks on either side. She slipped into the tiny bathroom and ran a cleansing cloth over her face. She had written 'Are You Ready?' as a celebration of Sheri's deep and abiding faith in God that shone from her. As a ten-year-old who faced certain and soon death, she had never feared what would happen to her after she died. In Harmony's song, she challenged listeners to consider their faith and their walk with God, and examine whether they knew with certainty that if they died tomorrow, they'd awaken in the presence of Christ Almighty. To know that song had made number one in the pop charts and the Christian charts the same week overwhelmed her. In reverence, she bowed her head and thanked God for the inspiration for the song.

After brushing her teeth, she left the bathroom and climbed into her bunk, shutting the black curtain behind her. On the shelf next to her mattress, she had a framed photo of a "selfie" she and Steve had taken right before she left Oregon.

Franklin had told her that he'd left rehab five days ago. She'd waited to hear from him and waited some more. Every day that went by made her wonder why he didn't call or email. Maybe during the time spent not communicating with her, he'd decided he didn't want to talk with her anymore. Nothing else made sense.

She could dwell on it, lose more sleep over it, or she could get restorative sleep to help keep her body strong for the coming grueling three months. Feeling the sway of the motion on the bus, she closed her eyes and prayed to God for traveling mercies, for the people coming to her concert tomorrow night, and for Steve, wherever he was.

♫ ♫ ♫ ♫

STEVE stood in his driveway and looked at his home now that the sun bathed it in morning light. Someone had spray painted some contorted railroad symbol all over the exterior in black and red. They'd also written words in Latin. He recognized *mortem*, meaning death. *Diaboli* meant devil, and he only knew that because he'd used the word in a song before. The other words, *sanguinem*, *poenitentiam*, and *rogabitque* he'd have to look up.

He'd come home late last night after the sun set, and discovered the trashed interior—couches ripped apart, mirrors smashed, his bed gutted and coated in animal blood. He needn't worry about emptying any kind of alcohol out of the house because everywhere he walked, his feet crunched smashed bottles. The same Latin words had been gouged and carved into the drywall all throughout the house.

He closed his eyes and shook his head. The immaturity level of some former fans who thought to punish him for leaving Abaddon should surprise him, but it didn't. His groupies practically worshipped the band and the music. It wouldn't take much for someone to take the dissolution of the band personally.

He ran his finger over the substance that had dried to one of the windows. It looked like egg. As he walked along the house, he saw dozens of egg shells littering the ground. Spray paint and eggs—clearly some teenagers had a grand time.

As he went into the backyard he stopped short. The rotting carcass of some animal hung suspended by a spit over the fire pit. Skulls of the same kind of animal littered the patio. Someone had spray painted pentagrams and baphomets onto the decorative Spanish tile. He wondered if the dark stain on the concrete and in grout of the tile was blood or more paint.

At the sound of a car door slamming, he walked back to the front of the house. The police pulled a pen out of his pocket and opened his notebook as Steve approached. "Morning, officer," he said, holding out his hand.

"Mr. Slayer." He shifted the notebook and pen to one hand and shook Steve's hand, then gestured toward the house. "Looks like things got a little crazy around here."

"Slater," he corrected. "It's legally Steve Slater."

"Right. Gotcha." He made a notation in the notebook. "Why don't you show me what you have? I know you'll need a report for insurance purposes."

They documented everything they could, then the police officer gave him a number to call to get the actual police report number. Since all of the destruction had clearly happened some weeks before, he didn't hold any hope of finding out who did it.

After the police officer left, Steve ripped a piece of paper out of his journal, grabbed a pencil, and started in the bedroom. He walked through every room, opened every closet and drawer, and looked behind every door, making sure he documented everything. While he did that, he made a materials list.

In the kitchen, he cleared off the countertop, running his finger over the tile that his vandals had smashed with a hammer. The obvious rage with which these people destroyed his home bothered him on a deep level. How could so much hatred come to someone who simply chose not to sing in a band anymore?

Once he had a space cleared, he set his laptop on the counter and looked up his bank information. Cain had lived high and large on Abaddon. Aside from his percentage of the band's royalties as manager, Steve found hundreds of payments that revolved around Cain, from mortgages to car payments to airline tickets. In a desire to not have to deal with life, he'd handed every facet of his life over to Cain.

He had regular money coming in. Abaddon singles still topped charts, but not touring for the last year made his income a fraction of the year before. While he owned this house outright, the taxes he paid on it annually would buy this house over and over again if it wasn't on a California beach.

He had to make some decisions. What money he had right now after paying the exorbitant rehab bill would get him through the next few months, but he didn't think he could survive a year. He left the computer and looked around the house. Emotionally, he had no ties to the place. Any feelings he had about the destruction of his property and the invasion of his space centered around the personal attack and not the things. What he possessed in his backpack—a study Bible, his journals from rehab, a selfie photo taken of Harmony and himself—those things he cared about. The pool table that someone had used as a fireplace just annoyed him.

Maybe he should sell the house. That would give him some operating capital and the taxes would quit draining what money he had left. In order to sell it, though, he had to erase the satanic messages off of the wall. He thought they might discourage some buyers.

List made, he left the house. He'd turn in the rented car and rent a truck. That would give him the freedom to haul supplies and materials from the hardware store and not force him to rely on delivery times and availability.

♫ ♫ ♫ ♫

Chapter 15

HARMONY lifted her arms above her head and stretched her lower back. She wore a multi-layered purple skirt that fell in ripples down to the floor with a white sequined top that just barely covered her midriff. With her arms up, her purple bracelets fell to her elbows, clanking together and her shirt rose up.

As she stretched, the low ache felt relieved, but as soon as she stopped, it started with a dull throb again. Franklin sat in a chair in the green room and watched with a slight frown on his face.

"What do you think it's from?"

She shrugged. "Maybe five weeks of sleeping on the bed in the bus? Maybe I should get in one of the upper bunks instead of the lower bunk."

He gestured at her plate of pasta. "Eat. You still need to do voice warmups." As she sat down, she prayed over her food then picked up her fork. Her band had already eaten. They left twenty minutes ago to do a final sound check for the Denver show. Her opening act never ate before a show, so the two of them had the room to themselves.

Franklin squeezed a lemon into his tea. "Do you want to stay in a hotel tonight? We don't have to be in Las Vegas for four days. We could check in and relax for a couple of days, then fly to Vegas."

"Thanks. I'd like that." Normally, she would show enthusiasm, thank him for being so thoughtful, and smile. Tonight, though, she didn't feel it. Her energy had waned to nothing. She reserved any extra animation for when other people were around. Alone with Franklin, she knew she didn't have to pretend.

She slowly ate the pasta loaded with vegetables and garbanzo beans. As she reached for a piece of bread, she caught Franklin staring at her. "What?"

After a long moment he asked, "Are you okay?"

With pursed lips, she considered his question. He knew the reason for her low energy. He wasn't asking why she felt the way she did. He asked to determine if she had the stamina to continue on with the tour. Finally, she answered, "I don't think I'm okay. It's been six weeks since Steve got out of rehab, and I haven't heard from him. I'm confused, I'm a little sad, and I'm kind of concerned for him. But, I can keep working. We're halfway through the tour. I have six more weeks in me."

She buttered her bread while Franklin considered what she said. Finally, he asked, "Have you tried to contact him?"

"No, Franklin. I haven't." Setting the bread on the plate without taking a bite, she brushed her hands against her napkin. "The last contact from him he asked me not to contact him. If he wants to get in touch with me, he knows how."

Franklin took a deep breath and sighed. "Harmony, I'm sorry you're sad. In the end, though, I think maybe this works better for you."

"I know you think that, Franklin. You know how? Because you tell me every chance you get." She took a sip of her water, then picked up her fork again. She didn't feel hungry, but she knew the calories she'd consume once she got on stage and she needed to eat. "I don't agree, but I know that's what you think."

Her voice coach opened the green room door and stuck his head into the room. "Can we meet in five?"

Straightening and putting on the cheerful disposition she required of herself, she smiled. "Sure. I'll be finished with this by then."

"Great!" With a thumbs-up, he shut the door.

Harmony's shoulders slumped forward again as she took a bite of pasta. After chewing and swallowing she said, "The thing is, if he called me tonight, I'd go to him. That's how I feel."

Franklin picked up his empty plate and carried it to the bin put there by the caterers for used dishes. "We're going to be in Los Angeles in a week. Are you going to be up to going? Do you want me to cancel?"

Love for her brother filled her heart. He truly did worry about her state of mind. "No, Franklin. I really appreciate you thinking about that, though." She picked up the bread then put it down again. "I do want a pass left for him at the box office, though. Just in case he comes to the concert."

"Harmony..." he said her name on a breath. "I hate to

see you get excited then let down."

"I know. I won't get my hopes up. I just want to be prepared." Focusing on eating, she shoveled three more bites into her mouth while Franklin packed his briefcase. After cleaning her plate, she drank all of her water and wiped her mouth. "Ready?"

He nodded and held the door open for her.

♫ ♫ ♫ ♫

STEVE walked barefoot across the new tile floor and into his kitchen. New appliances gleamed under the newly repaired lighting. Every room smelled faintly of paint, varnish, or floor seal. New windows let the sun in, bathing the new white and bamboo furniture in the morning light.

He poured himself a cup of coffee, grabbed a boiled egg out of the fridge, and carried his breakfast and Bible out onto the patio. A brick grill stood in the place of the old fire pit. A wooden table with a canvas umbrella and wooden chairs provided a place to sit and watch the surf.

While he peeled his egg, he listened to the roar of the surf and the cries of the gulls. Even at his most terrible times, high or drunk or hungover, he could find peace in listening to the crash of the waves on the shore. Now, with his heart on things more eternal, he realized that the shore reminded him of the vast all-knowingness of God. God, who knew the number of the grains of sand on every beach in every planet in every galaxy also knit him together in his mother's womb and knew the number of hairs on his head. God, who could hear every whisper of every thought in his mind and heart loved him anyway.

It fascinated him that he, in all of his unworthiness, was loved by God. Jehovah had given him a purpose, had a plan for him. As he watched a heron walk into the shore and look for its morning meal, he sat back in his chair and ate his egg, contemplating the harmony and perfection of God's creation and how man had tried so hard to utterly destroy it.

Brushing his fingers against his shirt, he finally opened his Bible to the book of Psalms. In his quest to understand God's love for someone as sinful as himself, Paul had guided him into studying the men of the Bible. Right now, he focused on David. David, the adulterer, the murderer who made decisions based on his emotions, the man after God's own heart. He'd read about David's life, and he'd read the Psalms he'd written. Now he read events, then the Psalms inspired by the events, then more events. He remained in awe of the way David's faith never faltered even in the midst of the most tragic circumstances.

Like usual, as he came to a revelation, he wanted nothing more than to call Harmony and discuss it with her. In the weeks they spent in Oregon, he found out how much he loved listening to her perspective on passages of the Bible. Once he started listening to her father's radio program, he understood where she had garnered her wisdom.

He would call her when he had stabilized his life. He'd promised himself that. So far, getting the house ready to go on the market had taken so much time and energy. Thankfully, the insurance settlement kept it from depleting his financial reserves too much, but he did have some expenses he hadn't counted on. He'd hidden away in Oregon, hidden away in New York in the rehab, and now he'd hidden behind the guise of manual labor that kept him physically active every single day for a full month. With the last of the work completed yesterday, it occurred to him that the time for hiding away had come to an end. He needed to reenter the world after nearly a year and see how he handled people, temptation, and stressors. As he finished his cup of coffee, he closed the Bible and bowed his head.

"God, two important things. One, please be with me today as I face temptation. Give me wisdom, like you gave Solomon, so I don't make a stupid decision. Second, please give me a sign and confirm with me that I'm doing the right thing by waiting for Harmony. I don't want to move too quickly so that I end up hurting her, but I don't want to miss my chance with her either. God, I want to trust you. I know you'll give me a sign if she's who you made for me. Just give me a sign if I'm right for her; if I'm ready for her. Thanks. Amen."

He took his coffee cup and Bible back into the house. After rinsing the cup out, he set it in the dish drainer and grabbed his keys. Now that he'd brought the interior of the house up to standards, he wanted to work on the outside. Right now, he had a gravel bed with some arid plants. He might want to do a little more than that to make it look appealing.

He climbed into his truck and backed down the driveway. At the corner of his street, a flash of purple caught his eye. He looked up and saw a giant billboard of Harmony Harper in a purple sequined dress. Words splashed across the sign said, "Are you ready?" The date and time for her LA concert were printed below that.

With a laugh, he glanced upward as if speaking directly to God. "I guess I asked for a sign. Now I need to determine if you're asking me if I'm ready, or if you're making me ask myself." He stared at her face for a little longer and longing to see her welled up in his chest.

He knew the answer but only to the question. Was he ready? No. He was not. The answer was wait. Be patient.

♫ ♫ ♫ ♫

"LET'S take a break," Bobby Kent said into the microphone. Immediately, Harmony stepped backward and took off her headphones, setting them on her stool. She saw the producer and engineer through the glass as they both pushed their chairs away from the sound board. After a long day of recording the annual Christmas album, they all needed a break.

"Thanks," she said, rubbing her throat. "I need to rest my voice."

Melody Montgomery put her hands on her shoulders. "Are you okay? You seem like you're a little low energy today."

With a slight shrug, she said, "Mostly. I've been on a long tour. Thirty venues. After we finish this, I'm headed to the mountains for some rest."

Once they opened the door to leave the sound stage, she slipped her sweater off, knowing they set the temperature about ten degrees lower in the booth. She rolled her head on her neck as she followed Melody out of the studio. Her friend wore cowboy boots with light-up Christmas trees on them. "Those boots, Melody," she exclaimed as she filled a coffee cup with hot water, "what were you thinking?"

Melody laughed and pushed a button on the inside of the top of one boot, making the lights start flashing. "We're recording a Christmas album in August. It was either this or an ugly sweater. I needed to get in the mood."

"The mood, huh?" Harmony added honey and a tea bag to the water and sat down on the couch. "They certainly invoke some sort of mood."

Bobby Kent knocked on the window of the studio and gestured with his finger toward the door. Melody rushed over to the heavy metal door under the exit sign and opened it, letting Bobby's wife, Carol, inside. "Carol! Hello!" Melody greeted, hugging her. "What a surprise!"

Carol wore a slim skirt and a silk blouse. Strapped to her waist was a badge and her cell phone. To accommodate Bobby's schedule, they had all decided to record the annual Christmas album in Richmond, Virginia, this year, where Carol worked as a prosecuting attorney for the city. The badge on her waist made Harmony think she must have come from a crime scene.

"I wasn't going to miss an opportunity to come say hi." Carol smiled. Harmony walked over and hugged the slim red-head, wishing she could claim half of the six inches Carol had on her in height. Next to Melody and Carol, she always felt very short.

"It's amazing to see you. I was hoping I'd get a chance while we were here, but I have to leave tonight," Harmony said. "Bobby said Lisa has a school thing tonight, so I won't get to see her at all."

"I know," Carol replied, pouting out her lip. "She has an orchestra concert in a week. Their practice is crazy."

"What night is it?" Harmony asked. "Maybe I can come back for it."

"I'll text you all of the information. But, don't worry about it if you can't. There'll be lots of orchestra concerts."

Melody put a hand on her shoulder. "I bet you would know."

"Yes, I played violin all through college." Harmony had listened to Carol play violin many times and always felt like it was a treat. Carol continued, "Lisa didn't go with strings, though. She's chosen piano. In my highly objective and unbiased opinion, she is so talented."

"I can't imagine how anyone could have bias over her skill," Melody agreed. "She's inherited it from you and Bobby. Think of that talent."

Harmony took a sip of her tea and nearly choked when Carol looked at her and asked, "How is Steven Slayer doing?"

Heat flushed her face. "Why would I know?"

Her eyes narrowed as she looked at her. "I thought you two…"

Melody answered for her. "Not so much right now."

"Oh, Harmony, I'm so sorry. I just assumed when I heard that he'd left rehab that you were back in contact." Carol took her hand.

"That's okay. I thought so, too. Apparently, it's not what he thought." She felt a little embarrassed. "I've been expecting to see him or hear from him all summer long. I've almost given up." She pushed herself to her feet and paced the small room. "The more time goes by, the more I assume the worst."

Melody nodded. "James suffered a little bit that way after we met. He couldn't get in touch with me. It was three entire years from the day we met until we were together again."

"Yes, but neither Harmony nor Steve are in a coma," Carol observed dryly. Harmony gasped at the bluntness of the attorney but Melody just laughed. Carol said, "Listen, Harmony, if there's one thing I learned in my life with Bobby Kent, it's that communication between two people is the only way that the truth will be known."

Harmony frowned. "I don't understand what you mean."

"What I mean is that if I had just communicated directly with Bobby, the first nine years of Lisa's life would have been entirely different. So, either call him yourself or go see him yourself and in person, but don't just sit back and assume. Your assumptions could be completely wrong."

The thought of just showing up on his doorstep terrified her, but made her feel a little bit of giddy excitement, too. "What if I'm right?"

Carol stood and crossed over to her, putting her arm over her shoulders. "Then you'll know for sure, but the knowing will replace the doubts and wondering." She hugged her to her side. "Besides, you could be wrong. And then how glorious would that be? Maybe he's sitting back afraid you'll reject him, trying to get up the courage to call."

Harmony thought about it. "Or, he could be kicked back high as a kite and drinking himself blind."

Melody pursed her lips. "If you thought that, you wouldn't be so sad. Besides, the tabloids would have reported it. How magnificent would it be for their papers if Steve Slater, professed Christian, fell off the wagon? We'd have all heard about it from a dozen sources before we even had our morning coffee."

Harmony nodded. "Good point." She clapped her hands together. "Okay, so maybe I'll go to LA when I finish my autumn sabbatical."

"I think that's a brilliant idea." Melody stood and hugged her from the other side. "If you need backup, you just need to call us, sister. We'll be right by your side."

Harmony smiled, then laughed as Carol asked, "Melody? What is up with those boots?"

♫ ♫ ♫ ♫

STEVE sat in the cloth-covered chair. The conference table had such a high shine that it reflected the platinum records that lined every available inch on the wall. A cup of coffee that he hadn't touched sat in a gold rimmed cup and saucer. Directly to his left, at the head of the table, sat Marcus Ortiz, president of Gannon Records.

He was a thin and unassuming man. Steve had expected the president of one of the nation's most successful record labels to fill the room with a commanding presence. Instead, Marcus very calmly and quietly spoke while people tripped over themselves to do his bidding. He wore a gray suit with a pink shirt unbuttoned at the neck. To finish his look he wore a ring with the logo of Gannon Records made out of diamonds on his pinkie.

Across from him, Paulette Byrd, Gannon's attorney, scribbled on a yellow legal pad. She had skin the color of milk chocolate and wore her hair in a tight twist on the back of her head. She wore a mustard yellow business suit with a thick gold necklace.

"The fact is, Steven, you were what made Abaddon great. You. Your drive. Your talent. A solo act would be perfect. Or, if you're more comfortable in the group setting, we can get some backup band members with presence and name it Slay or Slain or something more identifiable to you." Marcus spun his chair so that he faced Steve. "We'd go with a more pop sound, drop the whole acid rock vibe. The real money is in pop these days. You cleaned up your act. A crossover to a more popular sound is very realistic right now."

Honestly, the idea appealed to him. He needed the money. He didn't necessarily want the record deal, but with a three-year contract, one that he controlled rather than one that controlled him, he could get his feet under him financially and continue to make different plans for the future. A contract in hand would mean that he was employed, and he could go to Harmony his own man.

Marcus continued, "And, knowing the legal issues that have been brought against you by Cain Proctor, Ms. Byrd has agreed to represent you on behalf of Gannon Records." Marcus pointed in Paulette's direction. She paused in her writing and met Steve's eyes, nodding in agreement. "You should know that they call Ms. Byrd the genie because she will magically make your legal issues with Mr. Proctor disappear overnight. Believe it."

He felt another burden lift from his shoulders. Intellectually, he knew that Cain had no standing in his lawsuit against him. Financially, though, he didn't know if he had the power to fight it. With Gannon behind him, it would go away.

Please God, help me make the right decision here, Steve thought has he pulled the contract across the lacquered table toward him. As soon as he finished the inner prayer, his phone buzzed. Two people had that number—Chaz and his realtor. Either one would take precedence over this meeting. "Excuse me," he said, pulling his phone out of his pocket. The message from the realtor made his heart skip a beat.

OFFER: $3 MILLION. MUST CLOSE IN 3 DAYS AND MOVE IN BY THIS FRI 9/2. YOU IN?

Thank you, God, he thought as he turned back around.

"Steven?" Ortiz prompted.

"Mr. Ortiz, Ms. Byrd, I appreciate the offer, I do. Let me be completely honest with you. I did not want to insult you by turning down this meeting, but I also don't want to enter into an agreement then watch things fall apart. I still have some things I need to get in order with my personal life. Because of that, I don't feel like signing with Gannon would be fair to you right now. I respect you and what you are doing in the industry and I would absolutely not want to waste your time or effort or undermine your trust in me. After meeting with you, I feel like you are willing to give me a hundred percent. I'm being as candid as possible with you. I am not yet in a position to return that level of effort. It just wouldn't be right at this time." He stood up and offered his hand to Marcus.

Marcus stood and shook hands with him. "Steve, I respect your talent. I also respect what you are doing with your personal life. It's important. We all believe you'll do great things. I've never said this to a talent before, but if you change your mind, the offer will stand. We'd love to have you at Gannon. We can make good music, man."

Encouraged more than he knew he needed, he said, "I appreciate that. Thank you."

In the elevator, he pulled the phone back out and sent her a text.

ACCEPT THE OFFER. AND THANK YOU.

He had one backpack to pack. In three days, he'd sell his house and bank the money, giving him the financial freedom to not only tell Cain Proctor where he could take his lawsuit, but also the stability to go to Harmony Harper and see if her feelings for him were as strong as his were for her.

♫ ♫ ♫ ♫

HARMONY walked out on the porch of the cabin and closed her eyes, letting the sun hit her face. She hadn't been here in nearly a year and had missed the solitude and serenity. Taking a deep breath and slowly letting it out, she opened her eyes, then settled on the rocking chair. Despite the cool September morning, she knew the temperatures should soar high today, so she would enjoy the cool dawn while she could. She watched a family of peacocks step out from the edge of the woods and into the sunlight. The male fanned his beautiful feathers and strutted around as if he knew Harmony watched. She smiled, hoping he would leave a feather or two behind she could collect.

The sound of a car engine cut through the quiet of the morning. With a frown, she walked along the porch to the other side of the cabin and looked down the lane. A Jeep climbed the mountain, making its way toward her. Uneasy, she wondered if a reporter had discovered her whereabouts and decided to come and sabotage her retreat. She had a few minutes, so she went inside and got her cell phone, checking to make sure she hadn't missed any emergency messages. A newly erected cell tower in Harperville opened a whole new door for communication ease in the cabin. She had no texts, no missed calls, nor any voice mails. That meant this vehicle climbing her private drive likely wasn't carrying any kind of bad news. She slipped her phone into the pocket of her jacket and waited just inside the door, watching the Jeep slowly approach from the window.

It pulled into the yard next to her Jeep. When Steve "Slayer" Slater stepped out of the driver's side, surprise mingled with sheer joy in her heart. She threw open the cabin door. "Steve!" she yelled as she rushed down the steps.

He grinned and held his arms out. Without hesitation, she threw herself into his embrace. "Hello, Princess," he greeted.

"What are you doing here?"

She broke the hug and stepped back from him. He'd put on some healthy weight. His hair had grown out, but he'd kept it cut short. While he'd looked gaunt before, he'd filled out and gained some muscle mass. She wondered if someone who had never met him before would recognize him as Slayer.

"I called you in Nashville, but your assistant told me you were gone for the next few weeks. I figured that meant you were here." He smiled. "Well, I hoped that meant you were here."

She hadn't seen him nor heard from him in eight months. "You could have called me."

He shook his head. "Didn't want to. I wanted to see you."

"I did a show in LA." Harmony tried to keep her voice from sounding like she was scolding him. "I left passes for you."

"I wasn't ready to see you back then." His voice sounded calm, assured.

"But you are now?"

"Yes. I am." He sounded so certain, so confident. "I have a lot to tell you."

"You look fantastic," she said sincerely. "How are you feeling?" As she spoke, she led the way onto the porch. He sat in the chair next to hers and turned his body toward her.

"I feel good. I left New York in May and went on home. I actually rented a car and drove the whole way. I was home in California the rest of the summer. Some angry fans apparently took out their anger at me on my house. They spray painted it with terrible graffiti and egged it several times. There was also actual animal blood in one of the rooms. Gross."

Harmony gasped and frowned. "Anger? Why?"

"Well, because I quit Abaddon, of course. Apparently, that's a sin." He settled back in the chair. "So I had to clean it up so I could get it on the market. It felt good to have to do manual labor like that."

"On the market?"

"Yeah. I sold my house."

"Because of the vandalism?"

"Not really."

Feeling a rush of understanding, she reached over and touched his hand. "Too many bad memories?"

With a smile he said, "Not particularly. Well, not that I

paid attention to. I'm just done with LA. I'm done with the lifestyle and the drugs. Done with all that. I decided to move to Nashville."

Her heart rate accelerated and a nervous, excited feeling started in the pit of her stomach. "There's drugs and all that in Nashville, too, Steve."

"That's not why I want to move to Nashville, Princess."

"Then why?"

"Because you're there." He shifted his body toward her. "I feel good now. I'm living clean. I'm studying my Bible. I actually took time to get my GED, and I'm taking some online business classes. I turned thirty-one two weeks ago, and I feel like I'm ready to actually start living my life. And, now that I've had some time to get to know who I am, I would like the opportunity to get to know who we could be."

Part of her thought she should feel upset that he would assume she had just simply waited for him for the last eight months. Another part of her brain celebrated the thought that he was finally here after waiting for him for the last eight months. That joyful side won the war inside her and she grinned. "As summer ended, I thought for sure you had moved on, away from me. Especially after I didn't see you in LA."

He reached forward and took her hand. "I have thought of you constantly, but I had to be away from you. I hope you understand."

"Of course I understand." She looked at their joined hands. "I just had this fear that once we were apart, you wouldn't—"

She didn't know how to word it. At her pause, he

smiled and said, "I wouldn't want you? Need you? Desire to be with you?" He chuckled. "Everything I've done has been with the thought that I was moving toward the goal of us having a life together." He released her hand and settled back in his chair. "I know how I lived before. Believe me when I say that I know I am unworthy of you. I am unworthy of your friendship much less your love or your affection. But I am not the man I was. I am brand new. And I would like nothing more than to prove myself to you."

Joy flooded her heart until a grin lit up her face. "Steve, I don't think you need to prove a thing to me. Now, my father," she picked up her now cold coffee and settled back into her chair, "he might be another story entirely."

He groaned and she laughed. It felt right to hold her hand out and have him take it.

♫ ♫ ♫ ♫

RAIN pummeled the windows of the cabin and she could feel the cold, damp air blowing in through the edges of the window pane. The kitchen smelled like the remnants of their spicy Japanese noodles. The warmth of the kitchen steamed up the window. Suddenly, a howling sound came from outside and the loose glass in the pane rattled. Harmony looked out the kitchen window and frowned. "Getting pretty nasty out there."

Steve looked over her shoulder. "I don't know if I want you driving out there. The wind's picking up, too." He put the last dish from the dish drainer into the cupboard then filled the kettle with water.

She barely heard the ticking noise of the gas igniting

the burner over the sound of the rain. "Well, I can't stay here, so I better just go before it gets any worse."

For a month, they had enjoyed the solitude of their mountain escape. September had given way to October, and she knew another month stretched in front of them before she absolutely had to be back in Nashville. They'd spent every single day together, but always parted at night. When the rain started earlier, she should have gone ahead and left, but she didn't want to miss sharing dinner with him. She enjoyed holding his hand while he blessed their meals. She enjoyed discussing his daily readings and debating finer points of theology.

As she turned away, he caught her by the wrist. His hand felt warm, his palm callused from chopping wood in preparation for the winter. "Stay." The intense look in his green eyes made the breath catch in the back of her throat. The temptation to stay nearly overwhelmed her.

"No." A nervous laugh escaped before she could stop it.

He sighed and let her go. "I know. You're right."

Impulsively, she wrapped her arms around him and put a head on his shoulder. "Maybe one day we won't have to say good-bye every day."

When he froze, she thought she should have kept her mouth shut. Here she was, rushing him, just like that summer before he went into rehab. He slowly but firmly pushed her away and her eyes filled with tears. She shouldn't have said anything.

"So marry me," he said, surprising her.

To her shocked ears he may as well have just said Merry Christmas. "What?"

He reached out and cupped her cheek with his hand. "I

want to marry you, Harmony Harper. I love you, and I know you love me. Let's go to town tomorrow and get married."

Excitement sent her heart into a frantic rhythm. She licked her lips and whispered, "Okay."

He grinned. "Okay?"

As tears fell from her eyes, she smiled and nodded. "Okay. Yes. But, we'll have to go to Portland. Not town. My grandfather's cousin is the clerk down there, and I just don't think—"

Before she could finish the sentence, he had pulled her to him and covered her lips with his. For the first time ever, he kissed her.

As his hand slid from her cheek to the back of her neck, she stepped closer to him, gripping the front of his shirt with one hand and wrapping her arms around his neck with the other. She tasted her own salty tears as he deepened the kiss. The sound of her heartbeat drowned out the rainstorm pounding on the shingles. Her head spun and a roaring started in her ears that soon turned to a high-pitched whistle.

Only when he lifted his mouth and stepped back did she realize the whistling sound came from the kettle. While he stepped to the stove to turn the burner off, she put a hand to her mouth, brushing her lips with the tips of her fingers, and breathed in a shaky breath. When he turned back toward her she said, "I need to go."

He reached forward and took her hand, bringing it up to his lips and pressing a kiss to her palm. Then he lay that palm against his cheek and closed his eyes. "Yes, you do," he said hoarsely.

"Tomorrow?"

He put his hand into his pocket and pulled out a ring that he slipped on her finger. The square cut amethyst the color of the deepest lilac sat surrounded by small diamonds in a white gold setting. Shocked yet thrilled, she just stared at her hand, unable to move. It was the most perfect, perfect ring she had ever seen in her life. Finally, he kissed the back of her hand and said, "Tomorrow. I'll pick you up at ten and we'll drive to Portland."

Feeling like she walked on air, she left the little cabin. As she dashed to her Jeep, the cold pelts of rain hit her, clearing her head. Before she started the engine, she looked at the ring on her hand again, it fit so perfectly. The weight of the ring on her finger startled her with every motion of her hand. The glimmer of the dark lavender gem and the sparkle of the bright diamonds surrounding it shone brighter in her eyes than any spotlight she had ever seen on any stage.

Harmony wondered how she could possibly ever get any happier. Even thinking about how Franklin would react didn't diminish her joy as she drove down the lane.

♫ ♫ ♫ ♫

HARMONY slipped out of bed. As she pulled the robe over her shoulders, she looked at the figure of her sleeping husband, who lay on his stomach with his head buried under the pillow. The sky outside the east window had just started to lighten, bathing the room in the faintest light. Giddy with joy at the idea of a lifetime spent loving Steve made her want to burst out into song. The day before, they'd driven to Portland, got married without ceremony in the courthouse, then stopped to celebrate with a late lunch at a local farm-to-table restaurant. They'd held hands, they'd kissed, they'd hugged—they enjoyed not having to hold back or restrain themselves from physical affection. They made it back to her cabin by early evening.

Not wanting to wake him, she resisted the urge to run her fingers down his back as memories of the night before washed over her and her heart overflowed with love for him. Crossing the large room, her bare feet sinking into the lush gray carpet, she slipped into her closet and quietly pulled on a pair of yoga pants and a sweatshirt. When she came out of the room, she looked at the keyboard sitting next to her desk and thought she'd like to write soon. A song played in her head that she really wanted to lay down on paper.

She'd wait until Steve woke up, though, so the sound of the keyboard didn't bother him. Downstairs, she made a pot of coffee. While it brewed, she looked at the phone she'd left charging on the counter.

Before she could change her mind, she picked it up and dialed her father's cell. His radio show began at nine, so she knew she could expect to catch him on his way to work.

"Hi, daddy," she greeted when she heard him answer, "how are you?"

"Terrific," he replied. "God has blessed me in abundance." After a pause, he added, "Something wrong, sugar?"

"I, ah," she cleared her throat, shored up the courage, and blurted out, "I got married yesterday."

After a long pause he said, "I see. I assume you are married to Mr. Steven Slayer Slater."

"Yes," she whispered. "He's been up here for the last month. We went into Portland yesterday."

"Good."

Clearly, she hadn't heard him right. "Good?"

"Harmony, Mr. Slater called me a week ago and asked my blessing. I had assumed there would be a long engagement and a wedding for your mother to plan. But she will have to settle for planning a celebration party. However, you will be the one to inform your mother since you are her only daughter and she's been planning your wedding since your second birthday as I recall."

"Okay," Harmony agreed, not really excited about the idea. "I'll tell her first thing when I get back home."

"Uh, that's not right, Harmony."

"What do you mean?"

"I mean, you are home. Right now. With your husband." He cleared his throat. "I expect you can tell your mother all about it first thing when you and your husband get back to Nashville."

Should she pinch herself and make sure she was actually awake? "Daddy—"

"I spoke to him for over an hour, then we prayed together. He actually prayed for me. I look forward to meeting him in person." She heard the sound of the door chime on her father's car and knew he had arrived at work. "You have a man who knows what it's like to accept redemption. His walk with Christ will be solid. I couldn't ask for a better husband for my daughter. And the two of you have my blessing."

"I know you're at work, Daddy. We can talk later."

"And we will. Enjoy your honeymoon, Mrs. Slater. I'll see you soon."

Stunned, she ended the call. Of all the things she thought could possibly come out of that conversation, nothing had happened like her mind had imagined.

Excited, pleased, and glowing with newlywed joy, she set a cup out for Steve, poured herself a cup of coffee, and carried her Bible out onto the porch with her.

♫ ♫ ♫ ♫

Chapter 17

STEVE gradually woke up. As his mind slowly came into focus, a smile crossed his face. Without opening his eyes, he reached out, but encountered empty bed. He lifted his head and looked at the clock, squinting to bring it into focus. Six in the morning. Apparently, his new bride rose before the dawn. That might take some getting used to.

He found the suitcase he'd packed yesterday sitting open on a padded bench at the foot of the king-sized bed. He dug through it, retrieving what he needed. After slipping on a pair of sweatpants, he left the bedroom, walking barefoot down the hall. He could see Harmony through the glass door from the top of the stairs. She sat on the porch with her Bible and a steaming mug. He started to walk down the stairs, but suddenly overwhelmed, he sat, covering his face with his hands. "Thank you, God," he whispered, "for saving me, and for giving me Harmony. Thank you for giving me my wife."

Feeling more stable, he continued downstairs and

stopped in the kitchen. He found a mug next to the coffee maker and a wave of warmth washed over him at the consideration she showed for him by leaving a mug out. After pouring himself a cup of coffee, he grabbed a blanket off the back of a chair and went outside. Harmony sat on a rocking chair, bundled up in a coat, with her feet pulled up and tucked under her. She smiled when she saw him. "Good morning."

Before he sat, he bent and kissed her, letting his mouth linger, feeling her lips warm under his. It occurred to him that they could kiss and touch all they wanted now. As she sighed, he broke the kiss and sat in the chair next to her, wrapping the blanket around him. "It would be warmer a little later in the morning," he said as he took a sip of the warm coffee. Immediately, and not unexpectedly, he craved a cigarette. A few times a day, the cravings almost made him cave. That first sip of coffee almost always triggered a craving. He studied her over the rim of his cup. "You okay?"

A faint blush tinged her cheeks as she clearly thought about the night before. "More than," she finally admitted. Then, in beautiful Harmony style, she asked, "You?"

Strangely, despite his past life of excess, last night, his marriage night, had felt completely different, like a brand-new experience. He thought of Paul's letter to the Corinthians where he claimed that if anyone is in Christ, he is a new creation. He silently thanked God for making him new, for giving him this new life. "Remarkable," he said with a wink, "and madly in love with my wife."

She grinned. "I like being called your wife." She drained her own coffee cup and set it on the ground next to her. "I called my dad this morning." He immediately pictured the tall, imposing man from the press conference. "You know, my stress level could have been alleviated if you had told me you'd spoken with him last week."

Embarrassed, he scrubbed at his cheeks. "I honestly didn't think of it. I thought about it briefly last night, but you were already asleep. I'm sorry."

She touched his knee. "My family has always been a very active part of everything in my life. You should assume I'll probably talk to them about almost everything going on with me. I know that's not how you've learned to function, but it's how I do things."

"Having a family is something I'm going to have to learn how to do. To be honest, calling anyone about anything is never my first thought." He looked out into the frosty morning. A mist lay over the ground and a hawk flew past his field of view. She had admitted that she liked being called his wife. That pleased him in a very fundamental way.

"Harmony, I don't know how to explain how I feel. It feels like my life started just over a year ago when I walked into that clearing right over there. My old life is like this distant memory that happened to someone else. When I came to know Christ right here, I felt like I was truly born again, in every sense of the word."

"There was so little to keep in your previous life," she replied.

"That wasn't life. That was death." He took a sip of coffee. "I'm ready for the living." He stole a glance at her. "And the first step would be to make breakfast for my wife."

"Breakfast would be divine." She stood and stretched. "And then I would like to try to work. I have a song in my head I want to get out on paper."

He looked at the coffee in his cup. No more steam rose

from the brew. Clearly, it had succumbed to the cold of the morning. Without even tasting it, he tossed the coffee over the railing of the porch and opened the door. "I'd like to write a song with you."

She shed her jacket as she stepped into the warm main room. "Really?" She sounded excited and happy at the thought.

After setting the coffee cup on a nearby table, he slid his arm around her waist and pulled her close to him. The blanket slid off of his shoulders and pooled somewhere at their feet. "I would. I'd like to make music with you."

With a smile, she stood on her toes and kissed his lips. "Is that what you call it?"

Realizing she flirted with him, he grinned as he scooped her into his arms. She laughed a delighted laugh as he carried her up the stairs.

♫ ♫ ♫ ♫

HARMONY stared at the tattoo that ran from Steve's right shoulder to halfway down his back. A snake wrapped around an apple, clearly designed to bring the Biblical account of the temptation of man to mind. While she stared, his muscles rippled and he lifted his head from the pillow. As he rolled over, he reached out and cupped her cheek with his hand. "What?"

She didn't know how to put what she felt into words. As her eyes filled with tears, she ran a finger over the scar on his lower abdomen. "I'm hurting for the little boy who got swept into evil."

He sat all the way up, the sheet settling at his waist. "Harmony, I wasn't a little boy. I was a man. A young man, but a man. My decisions were my own, born out of anger and pain. Nothing happened to me. I sought it out and I embraced it all." He ran a hand down her hair. "Don't cry for him. He wasn't a good guy and he would have mocked your tears."

Unable to control the sob that welled up from deep inside her chest, she buried her face in her hands. Steve pulled her into his arms, whispering incoherent words to her, shushing her, soothing her.

An hour later, he brought a cup of tea for her—chamomile tea—to her piano, where she worked to pour that emotion that had so overwhelmed her into a song. She felt raw, lost, consumed with the need to convey the feelings she had experienced into melodic notes and driving rhythm that would speak to the hearts of people who might feel the same way. Somehow, Steve got it. He didn't question her. He just set the tea in front of her, kissed the back of her neck, and let her work.

Several hours later, she managed to pull herself back into the world. A fresh cup of tea greeted her, as did a plate with apple slices and some cheese. The flesh of the apples had started to brown, and the cheese glistened with oil, so he must have brought them to her some time ago. Grabbing a piece of cheese and the tea, she wandered downstairs and found Steve at the table, a journal in his hand and a Bible open in front of him. He looked up at her as she stepped off of the last step.

"Hey. How did it go?"

"Good, I think," she said in understatement. "I'll play it for you after I eat."

He gestured toward the kitchen. "I made some potato soup." He closed the books and stacked them together. "I'll fix you a bowl."

After eating a late lunch, he joined her next to her keyboard. Though she felt a little self-conscious at first, the feeling gradually faded as she played. The music came perfectly, beautifully, full of angst and poignant emotion. The words needed a little work here and there, but Steve didn't hesitate to jump in and add, suggest, and improve. When they finished working, Harmony could see their reflections in the glass windows against the pitch black night outside.

"That is an incredible song," Steve said, sitting back against the wall, tapping a pencil against his knee. "Wow."

"Wow sums it up." She rubbed at her temple. "I think I'm emotionally done with today. I cannot wait to get into a studio and record that." She looked at him and felt her heart expand with love for him. "Will you record it with me?"

The intensity of his eyes when he looked at her nearly took her breath away. When he finally spoke, his voice had fallen several octaves. "I would be honored."

She slid off of the piano bench and crawled across the floor to him. His arms wrapped around her naturally and easily. "I want to do a whole album with you."

His chest shook with a deep, shaky breath. "I think that I would like that very much."

♫ ♫ ♫ ♫

Chapter 18

HARMONY stood on the deck of the cabin. The crisp air provided a sharpness to the late morning drizzle. She could see the bone white car climbing the curving road below her through the mist. She estimated that she had about three minutes before he arrived. She'd anticipated her brother arriving last week and wondered what took him so long to come and counsel her on her recent nuptials. With a nervous twist in her stomach, she turned and went through the glass door and back into the great room.

Steve added another log to the fire. He'd changed into slacks and a dark brown sweater. Her heart gave a little leap of love and excitement when she saw him. He fit so perfectly in this room. He fit so perfectly into her life. They'd had almost two full weeks of marital peace and bliss in this secluded little environment. However, the real world rapidly approached in the form of a bone-colored Mercedes.

He turned as she slid the door closed, smiling at her.

She couldn't believe how much he'd changed over the last fourteen months. He'd gained weight, his hair had grown back, and his green eyes shone bright with the passion for God that had so completely taken over in his life. His features looked relaxed, happy—no longer strained by the addictions and hate that had poisoned his life for so long.

While she had no desire to see the relaxed and content look leave her husband's face, they both knew that this day would come. "Franklin's on his way up. I just saw his car."

Steve stepped forward and offered his hand to her. "You're not scared, are you?"

Scared? With half a laugh she said, "Maybe a little."

"I'll be right here beside you." She stepped down into the room and took his hand, letting him pull her into his arms. "We knew this would come."

"He's not going to be happy."

He framed her face with his hands and looked down into her eyes. "Of course not. I'm a wasted drug addict who sings very worldly songs. What's there to be happy about? He'll either accept me or not. We knew this going into it."

With a sense of urgency, she put both of her hands on his chest. "Don't let him discourage you or bring you down. He's very good at verbal play."

His smile set her at ease. "Princess, I got this. Don't worry. What is it you would say to me? 'Fear is not of the Lord?'"

Standing on tiptoes, she gave his mouth a quick peck with her own just as she heard the crunch of tires on the gravel outside. "Touché."

Hand in hand, they walked to the front door and

stepped out onto the porch. Harmony's stomach twisted when she saw her mother sitting in the front seat of the car. Alice Harper did not wait for Franklin to come around to open the door for her. For the first time in Harmony's memory, her mother opened the door herself and got out of the car. Harmony had prepared herself for Franklin, not Alice.

"Mama," she said, smiling, praying, and hoping.

"Darling," Alice greeted as Franklin exited the driver's seat.

"Harmony," he began, but Alice held her hand up and stopped him.

Her mother walked up the steps and onto the porch until she stood in front of Harmony and Steve. "This is Steven Slayer? Or is it Slater?"

He didn't seem phased by Alice Harper, international best-selling author and radio personality. "Slater is fine, ma'am," Steve confirmed, holding out his right hand, keeping Harmony's secure in his left. "I shed Slayer some time ago. It's a pleasure to meet you."

She took his hand and looked him up and down, clearly taking in the holes in his ear lobes and the tattoo snaking out from beneath his right sleeve. "Is it? What makes you say that?"

"Because Harmony loves you, and I love her. That's enough to make it a pleasure for me."

"My husband assured me I would like you." Alice raised an eyebrow. "Do you have any idea what the media is saying?"

Her mother still held his hand. Harmony wondered about that. She looked away from them and glanced briefly over at Franklin, who scowled at her with cold, steely gray eyes.

Steve answered her mother. "I imagine they're all about little Harmony here and her break away from the message of Christ to shack up with a drug addict rocker. I'm sure I'm not doing them justice at the way they'd word things."

"Do you find it amusing?" Franklin bit out.

Steve pulled his hand from Alice's and slipped it into his pocket, as if knowing Franklin would not return an offer of a hand shake. "Nothing that would hurt Harmony would amuse me. However, I stand here with the grace of God, sanctified and redeemed. I don't answer to man, but to Him. They are going to crucify me and, because I love your sister, she'll hang on the cross next to mine. All we can do is stay steadfast and strong, and we'll be old news one day."

Alice tilted her head, sizing him up once again, then she gestured at the door. "Let's go inside. Harmony, dear, make us some tea. Franklin, get my bag. Steven, we have some rather urgent things we must discuss."

As Franklin carried Alice's bag into one of the guest rooms, and Harmony put together a tea tray, Alice and Steve sat on the big sectional couch. From where she stood at the kitchen counter, she watched as Alice drew out a stack of envelopes and handed them to Steve. Whatever he saw when he opened the first one darkened his face in a way that made her worry. He looked up at her but was too far away for her to read anything on his face but a flash of anger.

Harmony quickly sliced a lemon and tossed it into a bowl, then poured boiling water over the tea leaves in the tea pot. She picked up the tray and carried it down to the living room, setting it on the table in front of the couch.

"What are those?" She gestured to the stack of envelopes as she perched on the couch next to Steve.

He handed them to her. "I don't know yet."

"They began arriving the day of your marriage announcement," Franklin said, coming down the stairway. "I have no idea if your people have received the same kinds of things, Steven. I haven't been able to ascertain exactly who to contact."

"I don't really have people anymore," Steve admitted.

Harmony opened the first envelope as Alice poured the tea. She pulled out an index card that had a pentagram burned onto it. In what looked like dried blood, someone had written "DIE" across the burned image. She frowned and looked up at Franklin. "What does this mean?"

"Well, sis, I'm no expert but I reckon it means someone wants you to die. They were addressed to you, after all." His gray eyes cut to Steve. "Addressed to Harmony Slayer." His tone carried an accusatory sound.

Steve's lips thinned. "Have you contacted the police?"

"I told Franklin that was your decision. They were addressed to Harmony, after all." Alice handed him a cup and saucer. Despite his strong dislike of the brew, Steve accepted it automatically which made Harmony love him all over again.

Harmony tossed the envelopes onto the table and took Steven's free hand in both of hers. "I guess it's time to go back to Nashville."

"You need to contact the police," Franklin began, but Harmony cut him off and looked at Steve.

"What's your impression?"

He set his cup on the arm of the couch next to him and

leaned back against the couch. With a nervous finger, he tapped his knee, something she knew that he did when he wanted to have a cigarette in his hand. "I have some odd fans. I'm sure it's a juvenile prank, but I don't want to risk it being something more."

"More?" Harmony let go of his hand and picked up her cup and saucer, her hand trembling enough to make the china rattle. "Like what?"

"Like true danger. Like a real threat. This is absolutely something that should not be ignored." He reached over and cupped her cheek. "I'm sure it's nothing, though."

Despite his comforting words, she could see the worry in his eyes. She could feel his tension in his hand. Her heart gave a nervous flutter at the thought that someone might actually want to harm her.

♫ ♫ ♫ ♫

STEVE sat next to Harmony on the couch in her front room. A female detective, who had introduced herself as Nadine Cox, perched on the chair in front of them. She had dark brown skin and caramel colored eyes, with her hair pulled back in a tight twist on the back of her head. She had a tall, athletic build with long, lean fingers. Instead of a paper notebook, she carried a tablet and made notes in it with a stylus and a miniature keyboard.

Delays at the airport had kept the detective waiting for them when they got there. Because of that, Steve didn't even have a chance to see any more than this front room of the house. While the detective typed, he took the time to look around. They sat side-by-side on a soft gray couch, facing two wingbacked chairs that sat in front of a white fireplace. The same open curtains that gave him a view of the fenced backyard allowed sunlight to spill onto the gray rug that covered most of a light wood floor. Along the mantel, on the walls, and on the end tables, Harmony had showcased photos of herself with friends and family. Smiling Harmony, beautiful Harmony, loving people as only she knew how. He thought back to his old home and how there wasn't a single personal photograph among any of his possessions. He determined that he would begin recording his life of loving other people starting now.

Harmony had set a tea tray on the coffee table between them, but so far no one had made a move to pour a cup. Finally, the detective looked up from her tablet. "Have you opened all of these?" Detective Cox asked, using the edge of her pen to lift corners of the envelopes that sat on the table in front of her.

"Only two," Steve said, gesturing to the stack of five. "We wanted to maintain any kind of evidence integrity on the unopened ones."

"Good." She pulled a blue latex glove out of her pocket and, without putting it on, used it to pick up the envelopes and put them into a brown paper bag. "Did all of them come in the US mail?"

"My brother Franklin said that they all came in the regular mail to the secretary, but that they didn't have postmarks on them."

"How is that possible?"

Harmony spun her wedding ring on her finger and leaned forward, putting her elbows on her knees. "It's a big facility and it receives a lot of mail. We have a mail room and some staff that sort what department gets what envelope. We hire the mail room employees from a local adult home."

"A home?" Detective Cox went back to writing in her tablet. "Meaning—?"

"Meaning all of our employees from there have Downs Syndrome. There are other special needs in the home, but they're grouped according to need so that the supervisors can be specially trained."

Steve suddenly felt impatient. The instant craving for nicotine shortened his patience even further. Knowing the feeling generated the craving in a self-propelling spiral, he took a couple of deep breaths and forced himself to relax.

"Could someone have given one of your mail clerks an extra envelope?"

With a shrug, Harmony answered, "I don't think so. I mean, probably, but wouldn't that risk exposure? I think it's more likely that the way they sort the mail is very simplified. So, if someone wanted to slip an envelope to just me, it wouldn't be hard to figure out the system. I'm sure someone could go in there any time and put an envelope in it. It's a busy area because of mail, faxes, packages, and whatever else comes into the building. It wouldn't be hard for someone who knew what they were doing."

The detective turned her attention to him. "Mr. Slay— Slater—have you received any death threats via mail?"

He shifted his shoulders, wishing he knew the answer. "I don't know. I've been in a state of limbo for the last few months. My house was on the market. I no longer have an agent or a manager. I'm no longer with my record label. I've been staying at a friend's house then at Harmony's cabin," he paused, "but I did receive a similar message."

"How?"

"It was spray painted all over the front of my house in California, and there was the same symbol in some kind of animal blood on my bed." He leaned forward and picked up a thin folder off the coffee table in front of him. "Here's that police report. I called and asked them to email it to me today."

She took the offered file and opened it. He eyebrows knotted. "Goat's blood." He watched her eyes scan all the way to the bottom, then she set the file back on the table. "What's your impression?"

He let out a deep breath. "I have some crazy fans. The state of my house certainly brought that home to me. I don't know what to think, honestly."

"Well, we'll process these and see what we can find out. The writing definitely looks like blood to me. We'll get it typed and see what's what." She stood, closing the cover on her tablet. "I don't want to tell you not to worry, but if these are just some pranks from some kids, then there's nothing to worry about, is there?" She held out her hand to Harmony. "I am a big fan, Miss Harper."

"Mrs. Slater," Harmony corrected. "I'll be changing my professional name."

Detective Cox paused before she shot Steve a sideways glance then nodded. "I apologize, Mrs. Slater."

Steve followed her to the front door. The detective shook his hand. "I'll let you know if we discover anything."

"Thank you."

♫ ♫ ♫ ♫

Chapter 19

THE *maître d'* led the way through the elegant restaurant in downtown Atlanta, Georgia. Harmony wore a strapless deep purple gown made of the softest silk that fell to her knees, and she wore a necklace that dripped rhinestones and crystals the color of the dress. She had piled her hair on top of her head and let strands of curls fall down her temples. Next to her, Steve wore a gray blazer over a black turtleneck.

She knew they made a striking couple that made people look twice. With the second look, many of them recognized them. However, in this upscale of a restaurant, no one would make a fuss or bother them during their meal. Harmony knew that's why Melody Montgomery chose this particular establishment in the first place.

Halfway across the room, she spotted their table. Melody stood and by the time they made it to the white cloth covered table, she had come around with her arms outstretched. "It is so good to see you!" she exclaimed.

Melody wore a red pantsuit, black and red cowboy boots, and a ruby choker around her neck. She had recently gotten her dark hair cut short enough that it brushed against her shoulders. Her husband, James, wore a dark blue suit with a white shirt and a tie the color of Melody's outfit.

Harmony hugged Melody then pulled back and, with a grin covering her face, introduced her to Steve. "Melody, James, this is my husband, Steve Slater."

James stood up from the table and reached across, shaking Steve's hand. Melody didn't stick to such formalities and gave him a big hug. "It is a pleasure to meet you," she said. "Harmony is just glowing."

Steve graciously hugged her back. Harmony knew that he wasn't quite used to physical affection yet. "Harmony talks about you all the time, Mrs. Montgomery. I'm happy to finally meet you in person."

"Again," Melody corrected as she sat in her chair and picked up the menu.

"Again?"

"Oh, yes." She glanced at him over the menu. "We met at the Grammy's after-party a few years back. I think you might have actually drooled in my lap."

"Oh?" James asked, raising an eyebrow as he set his menu aside. "That sounds like a story I'd like to hear."

Steve's cheeks turned pink and he said, "I'm afraid that you are probably not the only woman who will say that to me now. Let me just say that I—"

"Are a new creature in Christ. Yes. I just didn't want you to think that we hadn't already met." She set the menu down and folded her arms over the top of the table. "Use caution in social situations, Steven darling. I think you might have upset a woman or two along the path of your destruction."

He cleared his throat and Harmony, wishing she could wipe everyone's memory away as it pertained to Slayer, reached over and covered his hand with her own. "Much like you did with me," she said with a smile.

"Sobriety makes social situations much less awkward," he admitted.

Melody waved the waiter over while James frowned. "We already ordered our entrées, and I took the liberty of ordering salads for us."

James chuckled. "What did you want to meet us about? Coming all the way to Atlanta from Nashville gives a clue that this is something important."

"We'd like your blessing to do an album together."

James spoke up. "Why do you need my blessing? I hire people like Wendell Doyle who do things like manage record studios."

"Yes, but you are the final say. Your label has a contract with me, not Steve and me for the purpose of a duet album. So, I hoped I could go into the meeting we have scheduled here with Wendell tomorrow morning and tell him that you've already blessed the project."

He stared at Steve. "What say you?"

Steve answered, "As far as a joint album goes, I think the sound is amazing. We've written fifteen songs. All of them honor God. This will be an incredible album."

James leaned back in his chair and nodded. "Very well. We'll cut a demo and see how it sounds, see if you're right. You can tell Wendell you have my blessing."

Harmony laughed and clapped her hands as the waiter

brought their salads. "Fantastic! I can't wait for you to hear it!" To the waiter who hovered at her elbow after serving the table, she said, "I want another salad like this but bigger, Italian dressing on the side, and the fruit and cheese plate."

Steve ordered next. "I'll have a T-bone, medium, with the steamed vegetables and sweet potato fries."

Harmony gave a mock gasp and he looked at her and winked. "I'll eat your way at home, Princess, but restaurants are open range for me."

Harmony smiled, delighted, then extended her hands to either side of her. Melody took one and Steve the other. Soon, they all held hands. "Let's bless the food," she said, bowing her head and listening to her husband's voice as he thanked God for the food.

♫ ♫ ♫ ♫

HARMONY leaned against her bathroom counter and looked at the white counter and sink opposite hers. Steve's toothbrush, shaving gear, and toiletries now lined the counter where she used to have a large vase full of silk flowers. She'd transferred clothes from one of the walk-in closets to another bedroom and he'd filled that closet with his clothes and shoes. His guitar sat in its stand next to his own keyboard in the room where she kept her piano. They had truly started to merge their lives into this house in just a week's time.

Three weeks of marriage and she couldn't imagine his sink empty again. She paced the bathroom, counting, going to the deep whirlpool bathtub, spinning around, walking to the walk-in shower, then spinning around again. When she said, "Sixty," she stopped in the middle of the room and looked at the little test window on the stick. While she watched, a pink line appeared.

Her heart gave a little leap, then fell into her stomach. What would Steve say? Clearly, they hadn't been able to make any contraceptive plans prior to the marriage with everything being so spontaneous. She only bought the test because Melody had made the comment about her glowing and it made her think about her calendar and how she was a week late.

She heard Steve get out of bed and quickly opened the bathroom door, holding the test behind her back.

"We're going to have to do something about your early mornings, Princess," he teased, walking up to her. "I've never been one to watch the sunrise."

"I don't mind that you sleep in."

"I don't want to miss a minute awake with you, Princess."

She ran a tongue over her teeth. "You know something we never talked about with any kind of planning?"

"What's that?" He kissed her forehead, then stepped around her and went into the bathroom to the sink, reaching for his toothbrush.

While he opened the tube of toothpaste, she said, "Having children."

Something in her voice must have made him pause, because his eyes shifted to the trash can where she had thrown away the box for the test. He spun around and faced her completely. "What's that behind your back, Princess?"

Nervousness made her stomach roll. "A pink line."

"Show me." As he approached her, she held out the test. He took it from her like it was some fragile flower and stared at the window. "Is this real?" his voice was gruff and intense.

"I believe so."

"So soon? We've only been married for three weeks."

"It doesn't really take three weeks." Before she knew he had moved, he had her wrapped in his arms. "Are you okay with this?"

When he let her go, it surprised her to see tears in his eyes. "Until this moment, I honestly never thought about it, but yes, I am definitely mostly okay with this."

Crying and laughing at the same time, she threw her arms around his neck. "I love you, Steve."

He took a deep breath and slowly released it against her neck before he said, "You have no idea how much I love you."

♫ ♫ ♫ ♫

Chapter 20

HARMONY had only visited San Francisco to perform in concerts. She'd never taken the opportunity to spend any time sightseeing in the city. When Steve suggested they go there for the New Year, it had surprised her. She knew how much emotional turmoil the city brought him, but she eagerly agreed to accompany him. They'd arrived on New Year's Eve, and for two days he took her on a tour so that she could see the city through his eyes, and so that he could reacquaint himself with his old home. After touring Alcatraz, they breezed through the Golden Gate Park and took pictures of the Lone Sailor statue at the end of the Golden Gate Bridge. Harmony made sure they took a ride on a cable car and got pictures of the two of them at Fisherman's. New Year's Day, they spent a very chilly morning touring the San Francisco Maritime National Historical Park at the Hyde Street Pier, then a slightly less chilly afternoon at Pier 39. They ended their day of sightseeing by having one of the best meals she'd ever had in her life at a Greek place off Jackson Street followed by a visit to Grace's grave.

They stood there, arms around each other, and Steve told story after story of Grace's childhood antics. Listening to him speak so freely about her when he usually stayed so closely guarded about her caused Harmony's heart to open up and her love for him grew exponentially. Steve decided, standing there in the winter evening, that he wanted to visit his parents the next day.

Back in their hotel room, they barely made it through a late dinner before Harmony fell asleep. When she woke at six, she lay there for a long time and waited for the nausea to hit her, but it never did. For the first time in about three months, she didn't feel sick this morning. Maybe, finally, she was on the end of the morning sickness phase. Thanking God for opportunity, she got out of bed and went into the living room of their hotel suite and spent the next hour praying for Steve, for his courage to stay strong in making this trip to see his parents, and for his heart to remain open to accepting them into his life should they want to come.

Just as she heard Steve's shower stop, she heard the knock on the door from room service. Hungry for the first morning in months, she rushed to the door and opened it, stepping aside as the waiter pushed the room service cart in.

"Just set it by the table, please." He showed her the items on the tray then handed her the bill. Adding a tip, she signed the bill and secured the door behind him just as Steve came out of the bedroom, buttoning his shirt.

"I ordered you corned beef," she said, lifting the silver lid. Her stomach started to do a half flip at the sight of meat, but settled itself. "I thought you deserved it."

"You're just trying to tempt me to eat because I told you I wasn't hungry," he said, kissing her neck and pulling out her chair. As he seated himself and placed a napkin in his lap, he set the plate with the corned beef on it in front of him. "I do believe it will work."

After they blessed the meal, she held his hand for just a second longer, thinking of the hurting teenager who walked away from his home so long ago. "Are you terribly nervous?"

He shrugged but had shoveled corned beef and potatoes into his mouth, so he chewed and swallowed before answering. "Somewhat. I don't really know if I want you there. I don't know how they're going to act."

She couldn't imagine the courage he had to garner to just go ring the doorbell. "You'd probably know if you called first," she said, trying to encourage him again.

"I have no way of calling them. Their number is unlisted and the one I used to know doesn't work." He poured some orange juice from the carafe. "I don't even know if they still live there."

"There has to be a way to find out that doesn't involve just showing up and waiting for them to shut the door in your face." She felt nervous for him, feeling that flood of emotion she felt every time she thought of the teenage Steve Slater walking away from his home with a guitar strapped to his back. "We have resources."

"You mean you have resources." He sighed, and she could tell that not only had he grown tired of her trying to mother him about this, his mind would not change. He leaned forward and took her hand. "Listen. They'll either talk to me or not. Either way, I have to do this." He gave her hand a squeeze and took a drink of juice. "You want to stay here? It won't bother me."

"Of course not!" She took a small bite of yogurt, pleased that her stomach seemed to accept it. "I will be right by your side. Right where I belong."

"I appreciate that more than you know." He pointed at her with his fork. "Baby Slater in there needs some corned beef."

"Ugh!" Her appetite suddenly gone, she set her spoon down and felt a sudden unwelcome rush of nausea. "Why would you do that to me?" she whined, taking a sip of water.

"Princess, I'm sorry. I was just teasing."

"It's okay." She wiped her mouth and got up from the table. "I'll eat in a little while."

♫ ♫ ♫ ♫

STEVE stood at the end of the driveway and stared up at the row house with the light blue siding and red front door decked with a pine Christmas wreath. A white staircase led from the door to the little square front yard next to the driveway. He examined the property while he held Harmony's door open. Everything looked smaller, as if the sizes and proportions had shrunk down by about ten percent.

He recognized the curtains in the window of the front room. Strangely, in all this time, those hadn't changed. A netless rusty basketball hoop still drooped above the garage door. He remembered it bright orange and brand new, hanging there Christmas morning the year he turned ten. Strange feelings of nostalgia mixed in with fear and pain. It just occurred to him how much he wanted this to go well. He wanted the relationship with his parents healed. He wanted them to be good grandparents to the child Harmony so lovingly carried in her body.

Harmony slipped her hand into his and gave it a reassuring squeeze. As much as he didn't want her here, as much as he would shield and protect her from this, having her by his side is exactly what shored up his courage to put one foot in front of the other and walk up the path to the front door. With steady hands, he reached up to ring the bell, but right before he touched it, his hand closed into a fist and he closed his eyes. Was he really ready to face their rejection? Knowing this meeting had to happen, he opened them again and pushed the button.

When his mother answered the door, the first thought in his mind was how much she had aged, and yet how much she had stayed the same. "Yes?" she asked, looking first at Steve then Harmony. For a moment, she didn't seem to recognize him. Had her heart hardened so much that she didn't even know him? Then her eyes widened and she looked back at Steve. "Stevie?"

"Mom," he greeted, slipping an arm around Harmony's waist. "May we come in?"

Her mouth moved up and down, then finally closed. She cleared her throat and stepped backward, gesturing for him to come inside. "Of course."

He let her lead the way into the front room—the room reserved only for company. A room off limits to him in childhood, a room he had entered and occupied only when his great aunt had visited from Chicago. Cherry wood tables still lined up with couches and chairs covered in a rose patterned brocade. The wood gleamed and white lace curtains let in the sunlight that revealed no trace of dust. He remembered his mother always lovingly cleaning this room.

She waved her hand in the direction of the couch. He sat, perched on the edge of the cushion. Harmony gripped his hand. "Mom, I'd like you to meet my wife, Harmony Harper Slater. Harmony. My mother, Mary Slater."

Harmony, always the gentle soul, smiled warmly. "It is a pleasure to meet you, Mary."

"You should have called first," his mother said, absently patting the edge of her straight salt and pepper hair. It fell to her chin in a harsh angle. "Your father's out of town. He left this morning."

"I didn't have your number." For a moment, an uncomfortable silence fell over the room.

"Had to change it after your first record. Reporters and what not called at all hours." His mother would not meet his eyes. Instead, she stared at Harmony. "What is a good girl like you doing with his type?"

He felt her muscles tense up as she lifted her chin. "He's a believer in Christ. The boy who walked away from here died and was reborn."

Mary looked at him, then back at Harmony. "My research tells me that most addicts don't kick anything. They just pretend for a good while. Then one day it all goes away in a binge of epic proportions." She looked at Steve again and he felt a slow steady burn of anger in his chest. Obviously, he'd made a mistake in coming here. "What do you think about that research, Stevie?"

The nickname Stevie brought back too many memories to fully flesh through. Laughing in the park, the tears in his mom's eyes the first time she caught him with a bottle of whiskey in his room, Easter morning. Good and bad memories warred for top billing in his mind. "I think that through Christ, I can do anything. Including stay sober for nineteen months." He shifted as if to stand. "Let's go, Princess. I don't think this is going to work."

"Why did you leave?" his mother blurted out. She immediately covered her mouth with her hands and her eyes filled with tears.

His eyebrows drew together in a frown. "I beg your pardon?"

"You left and never came back. We thought for months that you and Charles were dead in a ditch somewhere. Then a neighbor's kid tells us they saw you on some computer video. After that, we read stories and saw newscasts and magazine articles. Then the phone calls started, but you never came back. We had to keep up with you through the gossip magazines and Charles' mother."

Sweat beaded on his upper lip and he fought the impulse to run his finger under his collar. "You told me to leave and never come back."

"Of course I didn't mean it." She crossed her arms in front of her chest. "I was grieving, Stevie."

"Yeah. You're not the only one." He started tapping on his knee. The need for a deep drag on a cigarette clawed through every fiber of his body. It made his bones itch. "You told me to leave. I left. But after receiving Christ, I have felt the burden to come here and speak to you. I guess I've done that now." He looked at his wife who sat next to him with tears falling from her eyes. "Ready, Princess?"

As he stood, a strangled sob escaped his mother's throat and she buried her face in her hands. "I'm sorry," she wailed, lifting her face to the ceiling and raising her hands. "I'm so sorry!"

"Mom?" Unsure, he approached her. She stood and lunged toward him, putting her hands on his shoulders.

"I know you leaving was my fault," she cried, her face

a ragged field of emotions. "I can barely stand to look at myself in the mirror. I am so sorry. Please forgive me."

With the slightest bit of hesitation, he put his arms around her. "I already forgave you, mom. I can't shoulder the burden of staying angry with you anymore."

Harmony's arms came around them both and his heart opened up with love that he'd closed away long ago.

An hour later, they sat around the table in the kitchen while Mary served them grilled cheese sandwiches. As he bit into one, memories of childhood penetrated even the wall of denial he had built up in his mind. He had to put the sandwich down and wipe his fingers on his napkin. Harmony, who hadn't eaten since her single bite of yogurt that morning, ate her sandwich and slowly savored every bite as only a recently pregnant woman can.

"Charles' mom called me and told me you two were in the same rehab place," Mary said, pouring iced tea into glasses decorated with citrus fruits.

Steve looked at Harmony and clarified, "Charles is Chaz."

"Oh!" she remarked as she swallowed. "I wondered what that name meant."

"She said he's doing really good. He's home, helping her with putting in her winter garden."

Harmony nodded. "We saw him last month. He contributed to our upcoming album."

"Oh, speaking of, I have some mail for you." Mary went to a drawer and pulled it open, taking out stacks of envelopes. "We didn't know where to send them, so we just held onto them. We figured that if anyone thought you lived here, their correspondence couldn't be too personal."

She set the envelopes in front of him and he noticed

the name of the law firm Cain had commissioned. He had already received duplicates of most of them. When he reached the envelope at the bottom of the stack, the blood in his veins froze as he recognized the handwriting on the address. "When did this one come?"

"Every bit of them have come in the last three or four months," she said. "I'm not too sure about specifics."

Harmony gasped as she saw what he held in his hand. "Mary, do you have a paper bag or envelope we could put these in?"

Needing to see what specific threat it contained, he carefully opened the envelope, trying to look at it at an angle his mother couldn't see. Inside, he found a familiar piece of card stock paper with a pentagram burned into the paper and bloody words.

SHE MUST DIE

Harmony held the brown paper sandwich bag Mary had handed her open so that he could slide the contents into it. Then he curled it shut and set it on the table in front of him. He looked at Harmony, whose face had turned pale. When he took her hand, it felt ice cold. He winked at her, hoping to reassure her.

Leaving Harmony and his mother talking, he stepped outside and called Detective Cox. She answered on the second ring. "Mr. Slater. How can I help you this afternoon?"

"I received another note. It was delivered to my parents' home in San Francisco. They're not certain when it was delivered but sometime in the last three weeks." He put his free hand into his pocket and looked up at the deep blue California sky. A deep cleansing indrawn breath followed by a slow exhale helped ward off the nicotine craving.

"When are you due back?"

"I can come today, but it will be later. I'm on Pacific Time."

"Great. Let me know when you get home and I'll meet you there."

After he disconnected, he looked around the neighborhood. Different cars, same houses. He wondered how many of the same neighbors still lived there. He went back inside the house and found Harmony and Mary at the sink, washing dishes together.

"We have to go, Princess. Cox is meeting us at home tonight."

She turned from the sink and grabbed a dish towel. "Okay." Looking at his mother she said, "It was a pleasure to meet you. I hope we can get together again soon."

Mary grabbed her in a hug. "I'm sure when my husband hears about your visit, we'll be heading to Tennessee. Definitely before that baby's born."

When she hugged him, he held onto her a little longer and a little tighter than before. "It was good to see you, mom," he admitted. "I'm so sorry for anything I did that hurt you and dad."

Mary stepped back and framed his face with her hands. He looked down into eyes the same grayish green as his own. "I forgave you already."

They got into the car and drove straight to the airport. Harmony held his hand and seemed to understand his need for silence during the drive.

♫ ♫ ♫ ♫

Chapter 21

"**EVERYTHING** looks good," Doctor Justin Willis said, making notations in the chart. "Your due date is July fifth."

Harmony's heart swelled with joy/ excitement. Their baby was due on Steve's sobriety birthday. What a gift from God!

"The next appointment, we'll be able to do an ultrasound and we might be able to tell the baby's sex." Dr. Willis slipped his glasses off of his face and smiled at her. "If you want to know, of course. If not, I'm really good at keeping secrets."

Harmony looked at Steve, who stood off to the side, leaning against the exam room counter. He didn't give an indication either way. "I think we'll probably want to know," she said, running a hand over her still mostly flat stomach, "if just to know what color to paint the nursery."

The doctor nodded and left the room. Harmony pushed herself off the table and picked up her purse. "We're just about halfway through the pregnancy already," she said. "How crazy is that?"

Steve straightened and pulled her into his arms. "It's incredible to think about it."

The door opened and the nurse came in. "Here is your next appointment," she said, handing over a card. "You'll come here for your ultrasound, and you can go out the back. Your driver is waiting for you there."

Clearly, the upscale doctor's office had a lot of experience in treating celebrity patients. She thanked the nurse and allowed Steve to help her into her coat. He opened the exam room door. "Sure you want to find out?"

They walked out together, through the quiet halls and out a back door. The cold February wind bit right through her coat, and she gratefully slid into the warm back seat of the sedan and greeted the driver. Harmony answered her husband, "Sometimes I do, sometimes I don't. It's weird."

"We'll know soon enough, won't we?"

"This is true. Even though it feels like forever from now."

"You know what? A day that isn't forever from now is Valentine's Day," Steve said, taking her hand and bringing it up to his lips. "What would you like to do?"

She sighed and snuggled up to him. "I'd like to go deliver stuffed animals to the kids in the hospital. And chocolates to the ones who are allowed to have it." She looked up at his handsome face and saw his smile, knowing he would enjoy that. "Is that okay?"

"No. It's not okay. It's perfect." He pulled her close and kissed the top of her head. "Where do we get the stuffed animals?"

"I have a company I order from every year. They're

due to be delivered next week."

His phone rang and she shifted away so he could dig it out of his pocket. "Hey, Chaz."

She could hear Chaz's voice, but not his words. Steve's face didn't give anything away. "Okay," he finally said. "Yeah. Seven is good. I'll see you then."

Steve's face remained stoic after he slipped the phone back into his pocket. Finally, she asked, "Is everything okay?"

He closed his eyes and rubbed between his eyebrows. "Chaz is being pressured by Cain and a couple of the band members to go on tour with them. He doesn't know what to do."

"Why would they try to pressure him?"

"Because he's one of the best in the business and an original band member."

They pulled up in front of the radio station. Harmony pulled her coat tighter as they rushed out of the car and up the steps into the building. Just inside, she slipped her sunglasses off her face and walked next to Steve to the elevators.

"Are we on time?" Steve asked, looking at his watch.

"Just. But I think we'd be excused with a doctor's note."

The family had already gathered in the conference room. Harmony slipped out of her coat and draped it over the back of her chair. As she sat down, her mother asked, "How did it go?"

Steve answered, "It all looks good. Due date's July fifth."

"That's going to put a damper on the annual meeting,"

Dee said on a laugh. "We may finally have a good enough excuse to reschedule that month."

Stuart Harper answered, "Harmony wouldn't interfere with such a family tradition. I'm sure of that. She's a good Harper."

"Except now I'm not a Harper, grandpa," Harmony teased.

Franklin stood at the head of the table. "Let's open the meeting with prayer."

The family gathered hands and Franklin led the prayer, asking God for wisdom and guidance in conducting he business that day, in His blessing on the decisions they made, and that the Gospel message would be spread through all of the family's forms of media. As soon as a collective, "Amen," rang around the room, Franklin hit a button on a remote control and the lights dimmed while the paneling behind him rolled back, revealing a smart screen. Another press of a button produced the logo of the family business.

"We are here to discuss the launch of Harmony's and Steve's album, *Set Free*. If you all have listened to it, you know that there is an incredibly poignant theme of redemption and forgiveness throughout. I have honestly never heard such beauty in music before, and I've been doing this job for a long time."

As the family murmured in agreement, Steve reached over and gripped Harmony's hand, giving it a squeeze. She felt so proud of her husband, of his strength, of his talents. She had prayed over every song they wrote and knew God would do amazing things with this album. To hear Franklin praise it so publicly encouraged her like nothing else he could have said or done.

"You're scheduled for New York the first week of

March," Franklin said, clicking a button and pulling up a schedule of interviews that spanned from seven in the morning until eleven at night. "You two are a hot item and in high demand. It took no work to get these interviews."

Liz interjected, "You'll probably be starting to show pretty well by then. Do you want to do the big reveal at that point, or leak it early?"

Harmony looked at Steve. Lines of concentration furrowed his forehead. "I think probably reveal then. That would be fantastic and really create buzz around the same time." He looked at her. "What do you think?"

She shrugged and sat back in her chair. "Buzz is going to happen either way. Might as well make it with the album." She looked at her grandmother. "You sure I'll be showing?"

"You're like me. I didn't show until about six months. Then, suddenly, I was all baby. Grew an extra chin overnight. Nothing gradual about that. You look like you might be the same way."

Franklin cleared his throat. "We have a limited number of venues scheduled that are already pretty much sold out. They'll tour until late May, or for as long as Harmony is feeling up to it."

Steve started tapping his finger on the table. Harmony recognized the signs of internal distress. She put a hand on his thigh and squeezed. Finally, he spoke. "I'd like to look into a little bit of added security for this tour. I don't like those notes we've been receiving, and I'm concerned that something might happen."

Grayson answered, "When you do what we do for the Lord, hate mail is a part of it. I really don't believe you have anything to worry about."

Steve nodded. "I respect that opinion, sir. However, I don't think you fully appreciate or understand the level of commitment of some of my old fans. The note cards are more than hate mail. They're actually threats, written in blood, by an insane subset of a rather twisted group of people. I don't trust them, and I think you need to respect my concerns on the matter."

Rarely did anyone argue with Grayson Harper. Silence fell across the table for one second, then two. Finally, Stuart spoke. "I tend to agree with Steve. If only for this first tour, we need added security."

"Good idea," Franklin affirmed. "I'll get with the security team and see if we can beef it up a bit." He pressed another button on his remote control. "This is the schedule for radio interviews. The ones highlighted in blue will be recording you playing the songs live, and will be uploaded to their social media."

Harmony tried to focus on the schedule rather than the threats that sporadically arrived in the mail. She turned the page in the folder in front of her and shook her head as if to clear it. She knew she would feel better with some additional security, especially with the baby coming.

♫ ♫ ♫ ♫

CHAZ sipped a spoonful of the soup in his bowl and closed his eyes as if savoring the flavors. "What is this?" he asked, almost with a reverent tone.

"Black bean tortilla soup," Harmony said, sliding a tray of tortilla chips toward him. She stood in the kitchen on the other side of the breakfast bar. Since they had already had their dinner, Chaz currently enjoyed their leftovers.

"This tastes incredible."

He shoveled three more bites into his mouth before Steve asked him, "What kind of pressure are they putting on you?"

Chaz took a long drink of his glass of tea. "Just constant, man. Adolf calls me every day. Cain is constantly texting me. They keep telling me it will be okay. That they miss me."

Steve stared at him, wondering if he saw through them, worried about pressure applied at just the right places to throw Chaz off of his wagon and back into the mire. "And?"

"And I'm about to change my number. They're driving me nuts. They only want me because I'm the best in the business and they know it. If Adolf had ever said three words strung together to me before now, I might believe him. But since he's never even said 'boo' until now, I don't owe him nothing." He set his spoon down and looked at Harmony. "I talked with your friend Melody. Her drummer isn't traveling with her this year, so she's going to hire me."

Harmony raised an eyebrow. "You know she sings country music, right? Not rock."

"Yeah, man, I got it. No worries. I played with her band last week." He turned toward Steve. "Dude, Cain really wants to see you crash and burn. Like it is mega-personal with him. You need to watch your back. He still talks about it."

The idea that Cain still harbored any feelings for him at all baffled him. Eighteen months had passed—time to move on to other thoughts. He shook his head. "Why does he talk to you about it?"

Chaz tapped the side of his head. "Because he thinks I'm stupid. He's always thought I was stupid."

"That's nothing new." Chaz had always had his head in music, which made people misread him. While Steve treated him like a peer, like a friend, it never did stop the other band members from assuming that Chaz didn't have all of his mental faculties. He was actually quite brilliant when it came to percussion, and since that was the only thing important to him, he kind of let the world happen around him.

Harmony gasped. "Why would he think that? Has he never actually talked to you?" Steve adored her for seeing Chaz without the blinders of the world on her eyes.

Chaz frowned. "I don't think so," he said slowly. "Not that I remember. But to be honest, a lot of years are kind of a blur."

He pushed back his chair and stood, grabbing his bowl and glass. Steve watched him carry the dishes to the sink and found himself thanking God that Chaz had remained his friend all this time. He started thinking back, grabbing hazy memories and events. "I've not been a great friend to you," he admitted out loud.

Chaz turned from the sink and walked back to the table. "You weren't always a great person," he said in reply, "but you were always my friend, and we made it to the other side." Steve stood and Chaz held out his hand. They shook hands and hugged. "Harmony, thanks for dinner. It was fantastic. Thank you for your hospitality."

She walked around the counter to hug him, then kissed his cheek. "Any time. I mean that."

Chaz put his hands in the pockets of his coat then his eyes widened. He pulled out an envelope and showed it to Steve. He immediately recognized the envelope. "This came in my mail today. But, it doesn't have a stamp. It's a little creepy."

Harmony went into the kitchen and grabbed a plastic bag. "Is this the first time you've gotten one?" she asked, holding the bag open for him to slip it inside.

He frowned in confusion. "What do you mean? You got one, too?"

"Almost weekly." Steve felt the slow burn of anger. "What did it say?"

"She must die." Chaz shook his head. "Don't know who she is."

Harmony grabbed her phone off of the counter and sent a text. Steve could only assume she texted Detective Cox, who would come pick up the envelope or send a uniform by to retrieve it. "We don't know either," Harmony said, setting the envelope on the counter next to her phone. "We give them to the police every time they come."

Chaz looked from Harmony to Steve, and Steve could tell that he had come to the same conclusions. There was nothing empty about the threats. Scary people who would hurt them without a second thought used to worship Abaddon. Thankfully, he didn't say anything that might upset Harmony. "Be cautious, man," Steve said, walking him to the door. "I don't want anything to happen to you."

Chaz looked past him, beyond the foyer to make sure Harmony didn't hear. He lowered his voice. "Dude. What are you going to do?"

With a shrug he said, "We've hired extra security for the tour. There's not much else I can do. She won't hide away. That would be my second choice."

"Hey, man. You need me? You know where to find me. Like always." They hugged again, slapping each other's backs, then Chaz left.

Steve slowly walked back into the kitchen. Harmony had her phone in her hand. "Did she text you back?"

"Yes. She said she'd come by in the morning." She went to him and hugged him. He gladly wrapped his arms around her, closing his eyes and breathing in the scent of her hair. "I try not to stress about them, but it's hard not to."

"Stress won't fix it," Steve replied. "but caution is probably good right about now. I want you to be extra cautious. Try not to go anywhere alone."

She laughed and looked up at him. "Like I'm ever alone."

♫ ♫ ♫ ♫

HARMONY lay with her head on Steve's bare chest, his arm around her. Her mind swirled with things she needed to do. She had an appointment first thing in the morning with the interior designer who would decorate the baby's room, then an appointment to visit a little girl in the hospital, and, at some point, she had to reply to some e-mails about the upcoming tour.

While her mind wandered, she enjoyed the feel of Steve playing with her hair. She started to doze when out of nowhere she felt a fluttering in her stomach. Her heart jumped and she quickly raised her head.

"What?" Steve asked, his hand pausing on her head.

She felt it again, stronger this time. Grabbing his hand, she placed it low on her stomach and pushed against his hand then held her breath. Seconds later, she felt the fluttering again. "Did you feel that?" she whispered.

She looked at him in the moonlight and saw his toothy smile. "Yes. I felt it," he answered hoarsely.

Laughing and crying at the same time, she leaned over and kissed him. "We're going to have a baby." She grinned.

Tenderly, he brushed her hair back from her cheeks. "Yes, we are," he said.

♫ ♫ ♫ ♫

CHARLES walked out of the bus terminal into the cloudy Nashville day. The cold surprised him. Even though it was February, he thought the South meant hot. He stopped and retrieved a jacket from his bag and slipped it on as he scanned the parking lot. He spotted the woman with the bright pink hair standing next to a black SUV. He lifted his chin in greeting and approached the vehicle with nervous anticipation. Finally, he could start living without hiding behind a mask.

The woman looked him up and down as if measuring his worth. She wore a white button down men's Oxford shirt over a long-sleeved gray T-shirt, black leggings, black combat boots, and a plaid schoolgirl skirt that came to mid-thigh. Her pale blue eyes looked gray, like a corpse. She had applied her black lipstick with obsessive geometric precision. She wore piercings in the right side of her nose along with several in her right ear. She had shaved the hair on the right side of her head, evidently to better display the piercings, while her long brightly dyed hair fell like pink drinking straws on the other side. She looked lopsided to Charles, and a little bit like one of those Japanese cartoons.

"Backseat," she said with a sharp gesture of her thumb.

His heart started pounding when he opened the door and spotted Railroad in the interior. "Father," he breathed, slipping his backpack off his shoulder.

"Charles, my protégé. I am pleased to be reunited with you at long last." He patted the seat next to him. "Come, sit. Miriam, my dear, take us to our temporary home." He looked at Charles with his black eyes. "I appreciate you coming all the way to Tennessee. Until we conclude our business here, we have established a residence in a warehouse. We'll return home to California in a few months."

Love for this man overwhelmed him. If they'd been anywhere else but the back of a vehicle, he would fall to his hands and knees to worship him. "Thank you for inviting me, Father. I was so honored when I received the instructions."

"Well, you are chosen. That message was clear for me. But, Charles, I did see the news. I am displeased with the dramatic exit you made during your departure. The police will look for you with passion now."

Horror at the thought of disappointing his master filled his soul. "Father, I am so sorry. I thought you would be pleased with my initiative."

Charles watched his master take the measure of him, up and down, with reptile cold eyes. Finally, Railroad nodded. "Your parents survived the fire. At least they're not looking for a murderer. Just a teenager who snapped. I hope nothing in your home could point them from you to me?"

"Everything I have for you is inside of me, Father. Nothing has ever been written down or kept. Frankie-D taught me well."

Railroad reached over and slapped Charles on the shoulder agreeably, then gave him a painful squeeze. "I have no doubt."

ARMONY and Steve sat on stools in the radio station's sound stage. Their band had already set up, ready to play live. A cameraman had already done a sound check and sat outside of the room, waiting for the next break before he would record their song. Harmony's makeup artist applied a touch more powder to her temple, then gave her a thumbs-up and left the room. Harmony brushed at the sleeves of her lilac maternity top and leaned back against the back of the tall stool, taking a deep breath.

Above them, microphones connected to adjustable arms suspended from the ceiling. They could pull them closer, push them away, or move them side-to-side. In the sound booth, a smaller area filled with the computers and engineering boards that ran the radio station, the two DJs for the morning show prepped for the coming segment while the song they played piped through the speakers. The producer typed on a computer at his desk facing the glass wall between him and the DJs.

Steve reached over and put a hand on her shoulder, giving her a reassuring squeeze. He wore a gray T-shirt and dark gray jeans. The stylist had fixed his hair so that it looked naturally tousled. Sitting in the studio, surrounded by musicians and radio personnel, she realized that he fit. The two of them, while they came at it from opposite sides of the universe, both had a home in a radio station on a Thursday morning.

Someone tapped on the glass and Harmony shifted on the stool, bringing the microphone closer to her. As the bumper music for the station played over the speakers, Steve winked at her and murmured, "Ready?" She smiled and gave him a thumbs-up just as the red light above the door came on.

"We are back here on affirmative inspiring AIR-LUV, your home for today's best Contemporary Christian music, and with us in the studio, right here, folks, are two of the hottest names in Christian music today, Steve Slater and Harmony Harper Slater. We are so excited you're here with us today."

Harmony smiled as she talked, knowing that the smile would translate through her voice. "Thanks for having us. It's been a while since I was in your studio."

The two DJs sat on the other side of the glass in their closed studio. Harmony watched as Rudy Gomez, the large dark-haired man with the glasses and goatee, looked in her direction. "The last time you were here was right before your spring tour, and for the record, your husband has never been here."

"Yeah, I don't think that would have worked out too well before," Steve replied with good nature while everyone laughed.

Monica Bates, the petite woman with straight brown

hair, pushed herself off of her stool to talk into the microphone. Harmony remembered she never sat when speaking into the mic. "You have a fascinating story of redemption, Steve. Can you share your testimony with the listeners?"

They'd known this question would come, how the radio station had it timed for his answer, and had prayed over it. Steve was a natural in the studio. "It's an amazing story but it isn't really about me. It's a story about an amazing God. I was a mess. I was a bad person with an ugly heart doing everything I could to break God's heart. So Independence Day weekend two years ago, I was at a concert in San Francisco with several other bands, and heard Harmony singing 'Amazing Grace.' I was in bad shape back then. At that time, in that moment, just listening to her singing that classic hymn, I had a bit of a breakdown and decided on July fifth that I would quit doing drugs and quit smoking and drinking. A friend of mine let me use his late grandmother's cabin in the mountains of Oregon. While there, I spent the next several weeks getting clean."

Harmony, very pregnant and infused with hormones, felt her breath catch as tears came to her eyes remembering the first time she'd seen Steve in Oregon. Thanking God, as she did daily, that their paths had crossed, she forced herself to re-center and pushed the emotions back.

"Now," Rudy interjected, "you and I talked some before the show today, and you and some of our older listeners out there know that I used to have a problem with drugs. I can testify to you listeners out there who may not know, that what you did wasn't easy."

Steve smiled. "Nothing about it was easy. Actually, it was dangerous. I should have let professionals help me. But in my arrogance at the time, I didn't realize that. That came later. If I hadn't been so isolated, I truly don't think I would have been able to do it. The lack of transportation and the lack of access to drugs truly is what kept me sober at first."

"But you could have actually died."

Steve agreed, "I could have died. It's God's grace entirely and I thank Him every day that I lived through it."

"What happened next?" Monica prompted.

"It was a series of things, actually, but they were all in the same time period. I went into the little town to restock groceries and the old man who owned the grocery store invited me to church and an AA meeting. A minute later, I ran into Harmony, who recognized me, guessed what I was going through, encouraged me, and told me I wasn't alone. Then, in an old notebook of my friend's late grandmother's, I found my name written on her prayer list."

"Oh, wow," Monica encouraged.

"Amen," Rudy agreed.

"Out of the blue, I realized that even through the worst of my behavior, in the midst of my anger and destruction, someone was out there praying for me. Even with my stardom and popularity, some old man in Oregon had no idea who I was and yet cared enough about me to want me to come to church with him and get cleaned up. And, someone as good and pure as Harmony Harper, who knew me, knew what kind of person I was, still cared for my soul. All of that worked into a great big ball of conviction that brought me to my knees, begging God to release me from the chains of my sins."

Rudy paused before replying, "Wow." He moved the mic closer to his mouth and repeated himself with a lower, quieter voice. "Wow. That's a powerful testimony of the Holy Spirit actually present and pushing you. Isn't it?"

Harmony answered, "It was an incredible thing to witness. Everything about him changed. I have a hard time with words to describe what it was like to experience it with him, which is why we poured it all into an album."

"So," Monica said, "you two wrote all of these songs."

"Yes," Harmony answered, "on our honeymoon, we spent several weeks in this giant songwriting frenzy. And what came out of it is this album."

Rudy grinned at her. "Something else came out of that honeymoon, too, didn't it?"

Harmony blushed and laughed in reaction while Steve answered, "I'll tell you what's amazing about the baby growing inside of my wife right now. Her due date is the two-year birthday of my sobriety. God couldn't have given me a more perfect, beautiful reason to stay strong and remember that I'm not alone."

Monica sniffled. "I am so honored that you came and told us this story today." She cleared her throat. "I know you're going to sing for us from your new *Set Free* album. Stay tuned to affirmative inspiring AIR-LUV and we'll be able to hear that on the air live for the first time ever right after this break."

As soon as she sent everything to commercial, she rushed into the studio as the band members took their places. "Guys, this is phenomenal. I intentionally waited to listen to this song so I could hear it live for the first time."

Harmony smiled as she slid onto the bench of the piano and ran a hand over her growing belly. "Get your tissues ready. This song is a powerful one."

"I can't wait."

♫ ♫ ♫ ♫

STEVE ushered Harmony into the back door of the auditorium while the guards held the door open. As they went past the brick wall of the large church, a skewed railroad symbol of the letter X with Rs on each side spray painted with red paint on the brick wall caught his eye. The symbol looked so familiar. Why was it important?

The church's worship leader met them at the door and saw Steve studying the wall. "We had some vandalism last night. There wasn't time to get it cleaned before today."

Trying not to display any outward concern, Steve focused on the man and smiled. "I think the red just caught my eye." He held out his hand. "It's really good to meet you. I had an opportunity to stream some videos of your worship services on the trip. It's an honor to start our tour on your stage."

They talked as they walked down the hallway of the church, maneuvering between the giant black boxes that had carried quite a bit of the set into the building. The sound of the opening act on the stage overwhelmed any idea of speaking. Any communication had to be done almost mouth-to-ear. The further down the hall they walked, the louder the band got. Finally, they made it to the green room. When that door closed, it helped block a lot of the noise.

The worship leader made small talk for a few minutes then left, giving Steve and Harmony time to prepare before the show. Caterers had set out fruit and vegetable trays and some drinks. Stagehands sat at a corner table watching them but they did not engage them. Their own band members didn't even look up from their dinner.

"Packed house," the stage manager said, coming into the room. "Course, we knew it would be. Atlanta has always loved Harmony Harper, and after the interviews we've been seeing all week long, Steve and Harmony Slater will be new faves." He checked the time. "First act will be finished in about ten minutes so you're on in thirty after the MC does the intros."

Harmony paced to the buffet table and helped herself to some strawberries. Instead of loose maternity clothes, she wore black sequined pants and a glittery purple shirt that fit tight across her body, crisscrossed, and tied below her belly. The ends of the material hung down past her hip. Harmony looked like the picture of perfect pregnancy health and he watched as she absently ran a hand over her swelling belly. Steve prayed that she maintained the stamina to do the scheduled shows for the next couple of weeks. Her energy level remained high so far, but the doctor had to caution her to rest. She turned and caught him staring at her and blew him a kiss. Steve felt very silly and very pleased at the gesture.

It had taken an emotional toll to bare his soul to the world the last week during all of the interviews, but he knew that testimony had power, and if his testimony had the power to sway young minds from the path he'd taken in his youth, he would handle the feeling of discomfort daily if he had to.

Harmony maneuvered over to him. He smiled at her. "How you feeling, Princess?"

"Anxious for this first show." She perched on the chair next to him. Her face looked almost plastic with stage makeup on. "I know we've practiced, but I'll be glad when we're tired of doing the same show every night instead of this worrying about getting every line and every move right."

"You're a pro. You have nothing to worry about." He

reached out and snatched a strawberry off of her plate. "Now me, I haven't performed in almost two years. And it's this point in the evening when I would do a line or two of coke so that I'd be really revved up for the show. So," he shrugged, "I'm kind of wondering about this new me and what a preshow ritual is like."

"I can get you a can of Coke, if you want," she teased, running her fingers through his hair. "We are in Atlanta, after all."

He grinned, happy she caught the teasing tone of his story. At the five-minute mark, they held hands in the center of the room with the band members and prayed over the concert and the audience.

On cue, they walked onto stage, hand-in-hand, and three thousand people surged to their feet, screaming and yelling and clapping. The wave of applause washed over them. Harmony started the first song while Steve slipped his guitar strap over his head and started strumming. As his fingers moved over the strings, he found himself humbled by the love and excitement of these fans. The energy coming from them felt different than anything he'd ever felt in the past.

He'd practiced with Harmony before. He'd recorded this album with her. He'd performed with her in front of studio audiences or in radio stations. However, a Harmony he'd never seen before emerged in front of this crowd.

She soaked up their energy and returned it back tenfold, blooming and blossoming right there on the stage. Her voice started strong and stayed strong. As she spoke, the confidence in her words and her love and compassion for the people in the audience almost radiated from her. He felt himself in awe of this woman he'd married.

Her voice had a mysterious quality to it that could only

be the result of the Holy Spirit gifting her with this talent. Harmony had selected her very first ever recorded song as the opener. Having been available to the public for more than a decade, it seemed that every single member of the audience knew the words by heart, and they sang along with her, sang back to her, as she hit every note with absolutely perfect pitch. At times, the sound of three thousand singing voices overwhelmed their speakers, and at times Harmony's voice filled the space all on its own strength. At the end of each song, the crowd cheered, clapped, yelled, and whistled. The sound echoed and rebounded in the confined space and then rose even higher during the first few seconds of the next song's opening as recognition of yet another favorite dawned.

Three songs into their set, with the band quietly playing the bridge over and over in the background, Steve began to speak. "I'm Steve Slater."

The crowed fell silent except for a few whistles and hesitant claps scattered throughout the room. From center stage, Harmony turned and smiled and nodded her encouragement. Steve continued, "Two years ago—"

He never finished that sentence.

The concussion of the explosion blew the auditorium doors off as the main power failed. Steve felt the blast microseconds before he heard the thunderous burst of sound that immediately deafened him as an invisible force lifted him off of his feet. The light instantly retreated, replaced by silvery darkness and unnaturally long shadows cast by the eerie lightning flash glare of the detonating bomb.

The detonation sent explosive energy in front of the blast wave at supersonic speeds and carried fire, fury, and deadly shrapnel along with that lethal tide. Unbelievable heat washed over him, carrying with it the sickening smell of gasoline and burning plastic. Even as it registered in his mind that something had just exploded, he found himself incapable of moving as he watched one of the large metal doors fly into the crowd, ripping and tearing its way through the people in its path like a giant jagged saw blade. The shocked look on the faces of the audience stayed imprinted in his vision even after darkness completely bathed the room.

Thick gray smoke filled the room, choking them and nauseating them. It smelled like burnt orange peels, acetone, and sulfur. For a moment, Steve lay there on the stage shrouded in complete darkness, his eyes burning from the smoke, his ears ringing with a constant high-pitched tone that muffled the sounds of screams and moans and wailing all around him. Terror unlike anything he'd ever felt before overwhelmed him and made it impossible to move. Who did this? Why? How many people were hurt? Had he sustained an injury? Then, that most important question came to the forefront of his mind.

Harmony!

Where was Harmony? Had she been hurt? Was their baby okay? After what felt like hours, though in reality perhaps no more than a second or two had passed, his brain kicked into gear again. The emergency lighting flickered on and a dim reddish glow covered the stage as if pouring blood onto the crowd. He could hear nothing other than the high-pitched ringing tone. He could barely see through the smoke, just shadows and shapes that made no sense. He turned, panicked, looking for Harmony.

♫ ♫ ♫ ♫

Chapter 23

SCRAMBLING on the stage, tripping over wires and microphone stands, Steve finally stopped and closed his eyes, taking a deep breath through his nose, ignoring the burn of acrid smoke. Keeping the panic at bay, he opened his eyes again and searched through the red light and smoke until he saw her.

Harmony stood with her back to the audience, her hands over her stomach in a protective manner. He rushed toward her and, without a thought, scooped her into his arms and bodily carried her off the stage, surrounded by security personnel who belatedly sprang into action. Under their direction, they did not stop in the green room, but kept going through the hall and out the side door to their bus. The driver shut the door immediately behind Steve and drove away, a security agent standing next to him and directing him through the parking lot.

Steve gently set Harmony on the couch and knelt next to her. The ringing still muffled his ears, but he could hear a little bit. "Is anything hurt?" he asked, running his hands through her hair and over her shoulders. "Are you okay? Is the baby okay?"

Harmony nodded her head. "I'm fine. We're fine." Her breath hitched.

Steve gripped his hands over hers and under their fingers, he felt the baby moving. "I feel him," he said. He put his nose next to hers. "He's moving."

Tears ran down her face, marring the stage makeup. He looked behind him and saw one of the yellow shirted security men. "Can you get me some water?"

"What happened, Steve? A gas main or a boiler or something?" Harmony whispered.

"I'm not exactly sure." Even as he said it, Steve thought of the smell of the smoke. It did not resemble what he imagined a gas main or a boiler explosion would smell like. It was a distinctive odor, very much like the gunpowder smell he remembered from the time the members of Abaddon got a little bit drunk and fired several hundred rounds from machine guns at an indoor range in Las Vegas. He thought of that railroad symbol he'd seen spray painted in red on the side of the church. Then he suddenly remembered where he'd seen that symbol before, and prayed that what information he could remember would help the police.

♫ ♫ ♫ ♫

FRANKLIN rushed into the hotel room followed closely by Alice Harper. Tears stung Harmony's eyes when she saw her mother. "Mama," she sobbed, feeling a flood of comfort and love as Alice took her into her arms.

The comfortable couch sat in front of a gas fireplace. In the corner, a long wooden desk gleamed in the lamplight, and on the other side of the room, a dining room table with six chairs sat under a crystal chandelier. Two closed doors led to the two king-sized bedrooms and bathrooms.

Alice and Harmony sat on the couch. Steve stood next to the fireplace. Franklin spoke to him. "Is she okay?"

He nodded. "They both are. Doc cleared us an hour ago." He stepped closer to his brother-in-law. "I need to talk to the police."

"I think they'll be here soon. The venue's a mess. So far, twelve dead and so many more wounded. A bomb was set inside a van that was parked right by the glass doors of the main entrance."

Alice sniffed and straightened, running a hand over Harmony's hair. "If it had been during a break, when more people would have been milling around the merchandise and concessions, then so many more people would have died."

"As it is, you had just started performing, so most people were in the auditorium." Franklin looked at his watch. "The news channels are all over this. They're calling it a terrorist attack."

"Well, it was," said Alice.

Franklin stared at her blankly. "No, mama. It was a hate crime. They bombed a Christian concert just because it was a Christian concert."

"There's no assigning motives to evil, son. Evil is just plain evil, no matter what the media labels it."

Twelve dead? Harmony could barely breathe around the tightening in her chest. Who would do such a thing? Why? "Please don't turn on the news," she whispered. "If you must see it, go to another room."

Franklin turned his face toward her. "You can't be in

denial over this, Harmony."

"I'm not in denial," Harmony insisted. "However, since I was there, I also don't need to relive it. I think doing so is a bit ghoulish. If you must, do it away from me."

A knock sounded at the door, startling her. She jumped and quickly muffled her startled cry. One of the security team opened it to two men. She watched them show their credentials before they received access into the hotel suite. The tallest one had sandy blond hair and blue eyes. The shorter one had dark hair and dark eyes, and looked all around the room before looking at her. When their eyes met, she recognized him somehow. Searching through her mind, she couldn't place him, but he looked so familiar.

"Mr. Slater?" The tall one asked. "I'm Detective Roberts. This is my partner, John Suarez." She watched as Steve shook their hands. "You free to talk now?"

Her mom leaned over and kissed her cheek. "I'm going to go see about a cup of tea. Call me if you need me." She stood and walked to the door. Franklin followed.

Steve turned to the two men. "Harmony and I have been receiving threatening correspondence. I have a police report in Nashville about it."

Detective Suarez nodded. "We got a call about that from Nashville Detective Nadine Cox when the news broke about what happened tonight. She e-mailed the reports. Did you receive anything today at all?"

Harmony shook her head, but Steve spoke. "Not on paper, but I believe that I saw something on the way into the building."

That surprised her. She looked at her husband, but he

didn't turn. He kept his eyes on the detective. She could see a muscle tic in his jaw.

Suarez pulled a leather notebook out of his pocket. "What was that?"

Steve gestured at the notebook. "May I?"

Using the detective's pen, he sketched a convoluted looking railroad symbol with a pentagram in the center. Harmony recognized it from a documentary she'd seen about Steve's band Abaddon that had released about a year after he quit the band. This symbol had appeared in the upper left corner of their second album cover and also appeared as graffiti in random places in every city where the band played. "Last spring when I got out of rehab, someone vandalized my house. The graffiti on the outside included this symbol."

Harmony tapped the notebook. "Steve and I watched an unauthorized documentary about his old band and the satanic influences in it. Remember Steve?"

She watched his eyes narrow as he thought. "That's right. Some kind of urban legend after this symbol appeared on our second album cover." He snapped his fingers, unconsciously snapping the opening drumbeat to one of Abaddon's better known songs. "The documentary was so vague, kind of hokey, and no one knew the exact meaning of the symbol. They made it out to be demonic, like a boogie man thing, but they just guessed. The truth was less interesting. Something about a roadie everyone called Railroad. This was his symbol, I think."

Roberts frowned. "Why is that significant?"

"On our way into the building tonight, I saw this symbol on the side of the building, painted in red. I didn't recognize it immediately. It's been a while and it was so out of place. I wasn't expecting it."

"Do you think your old roadie's responsible for this?" Suarez took the notebook back and turned the page.

With a shrug, Steve said, "I have no idea. I don't know the guy, but he's just a roadie. Seems like a stretch."

Harmony said, "According to the documentary, this railroad symbol would appear at some location whenever Abaddon would get to a town, and people would come and perform satanic rituals before or after the concert."

Steve snorted. "More like they'd meet up there and score his comp concert tickets or T-shirts or whatever he had on him. Or he'd probably pick up drugs and booze and...." He stopped talking.

Harmony finished for him. "And possibly underage girls?"

Steve shook his head. "And *groupies*, and escort everyone backstage for the after-party."

"Any of them underage?" Detective Suarez asked quietly, keeping his voice overly nonchalant.

"Never asked to see any ID," Steve answered honestly. "To be honest, it never occurred to me that some of them might have been minors until after I cleaned up my act."

"Nice," Suarez observed sarcastically.

"Not sure I like your tone, Officer," Steve observed.

"Not sure I care what you do or don't like when it comes to underage girls," Suarez said, unconsciously lowering his stance.

Roberts interjected, "Let's get back on track, folks. Bomb? Twelve dead?"

Suarez and Steve relaxed a bit but neither spoke. Harmony remembered the intentional darkness depicted in the film they had watched. "The guy Railroad was painted as some sort of urban myth. Like some kind of phantom. No one could even identify him."

"Or maybe no one would," Steve corrected. She reached over and took his hand, giving it a reassuring squeeze. "I don't know anything about him. I just remember that symbol from my house."

Roberts nodded. "Can you think of anything else?"

Steve looked at Harmony and she nodded. They'd already discussed this. He looked at the detectives. "Do you know anyone I can call to help arrange some private security for Harmony? We'd already added to our own security and had them present at the church tonight. Clearly we're out of our league."

"You intend to keep going on your tour after tonight?" Roberts asked, his voice incredulous.

"No," Steve answered simply at the same time Harmony said, "Of course." They met each other's eyes and silently agreed to discuss it later in more detail.

"Actually," Suarez said, pulling a business card out of a slot in his notebook, "I do know someone you can call."

When Harmony read the business card, she realized how she knew him. She looked at the card in Steve's hand to confirm. "Nick Williams? Detective Suarez, are you Aria's brother?"

He looked directly at her, his eyes lit with surprise. "How...?"

"Bobby Kent and I are good friends. You and I met at his wedding. I've met Aria and Nick a few different times." She tapped the card. "I thought Nick did corporate security and, in partnership with Montgomery Enterprises, data security. Does he handle individuals?"

"Not usually," Suarez answered, "but I feel like he

might in this case."

"Why?" Steve asked.

"The subject matter." Detective John Suarez flipped his notebook pages back to the drawing. "I am more than sure Nick will be very interested in the occult angle."

"I appreciate the thought of an angle as it applies to my family's safety," Steve said abruptly, "but I need personal protection, as in someone who knows how to protect a person. How useful is someone going to be who's used to dealing with corporate espionage?"

Suarez smiled for the first time since entering the room. "Nick Williams is the only person I would call if my wife were in danger."

Roberts laughed. "I'd call your wife."

"Yeah, well, Jen's rather tied up at the moment. That whole China Sea thing, you know." He capped his pen and closed the flap of his notebook. "I promise you, Nick is your man. He'll probably be here by morning if you call now."

The security guard opened the door again and Harmony watched as Melody Montgomery rushed into the room and stopped short. "John? Jerry?"

"Mrs. Montgomery," Suarez greeted, holding out his hand. Instead of shaking his hand, she hugged him then hugged Roberts.

She turned to Harmony. "You are in the best hands. Honestly. The finest Atlanta has to offer." In Melody fashion, she grabbed Steve and hugged him. "I know you're probably going out of your mind right now."

When she let him go, he rubbed the back of his neck. "I have no words."

"I imagine not." She gestured behind her as James walked into the room. "James knows, though. If you need an ear, he's your man."

As James Montgomery walked into the room, the detectives left, stopping to share greetings with him. As the door shut behind them, James shook Steve's hand. "You have a good team there."

Steve held up the card. "Detective Suarez recommended Nick Williams for getting Harmony some protection."

"Definitely. I was going to recommend him myself. Him or Jen Suarez but she's out of town. I bet you Nick would be here by morning if you call him now."

"That's the second time I've heard that. I'll make the call."

♫ ♫ ♫ ♫

Chapter 24

HARMONY felt the headache before she opened her eyes. She'd complained about it last night, but refused to take anything for it. Now it was stronger, more insistent, and kind of vibrated from the base of her skull, making her whole body feel like it was throbbing. Frowning, she slowly opened her eyes, wishing she could sleep pain-free for a little while longer.

The man standing next to the couch startled her. Her heart leapt in her chest and she let out a strangled cry. He smiled as if to reassure her. "I didn't mean to startle you. The guard let me in."

As her eyes cleared, she recognized Nick Williams. He wore khaki slacks and a light blue button down shirt with the sleeves rolled up to his elbows. She imagined that the April weather in Nashville was likely a lot more hot and humid than that of Portland, Oregon, where he had flown in from. "Nick," she greeted, her voice hoarse as she sat up. "It's good to see you again."

"Not the very best of circumstances, though," he said with a smile, his green eyes still sober. "I was already on a plane coming here when your husband called." He gestured toward the bedroom door. "He's sleeping. Franklin told me he hasn't shut down since it happened. I convinced him I needed his mind clear and alert and the only way to achieve that was to sleep now."

After setting a canvas bag on the coffee table in front of her, Nick unzipped it and withdrew a slim laptop. At the prompt, he manually keyed a code to unlock it. While it booted up, he said, "You're pregnant and you just woke up so I know you probably have to go to the restroom. Go do that, then we'll talk. I have a team in Nashville already. Some are pulling your police reports, and others are searching your home and offices. Tell me everything you know. Then we're going to go back and see what it is that you don't know you actually know."

♫ ♫ ♫ ♫

AT noon, Steve came out of the bedroom. He wore a pair of jeans and a black T-shirt that stretched across his broadening chest. He hadn't shaved since yesterday morning, and with an intense look on his face and the tattoos running down his arms, he looked fierce and angry. Harmony left Nick on the couch and walked up to him, slipping her arms around him. He hugged her back, tightly, as if he could protect her with his own body.

"Hungry?" she asked, looking up at him.

He frowned slightly then smiled. "Strangely, yes."

"It's not strange. You haven't eaten in more than a day."

He ran his finger down her temple. "Your head still hurting?"

"Terribly." She stepped back and gestured toward the kitchen. "I'll put together a lunch menu and then go lie down. Mom and dad are in their room." As she walked back over to Nick, she absently ran a hand over her belly. "I wish I had the words to thank you for coming."

Nick stood. "Just glad I was available. That's not always the case."

He held his hand out and she took it in both of hers, gripping it warmly. "I'll just leave you to talk with Steve. I'm going to order lunch and lie down while I wait for it to arrive."

She used the phone in the kitchen to order lunch, adding some red meat for Steve and Nick. As she hung up the phone, she rubbed her temple, wishing the headache would go away. Before she went back into the main room, she drank a glass of water and contemplated taking something for the headache, but thought maybe she would try lying down with a cool washcloth on her forehead first. Resting her hand on the swell of her stomach, she prayed for God to protect them in the face of whatever evil lurked after them.

When she went back into the room, she saw her mother and father.

"Hey there, Sugar-pie," Her father greeted.

Her mother looked concerned. "Feeling okay?"

"Not really. I ordered lunch," she said. "I think I'll just go lie down while I wait for it to get here."

Steve followed her into the bedroom. Heavy drapes blocked the afternoon sunlight from coming into the room. She slipped under the covers. He leaned over and kissed each temple. "Try to shut your mind off."

She thought she just closed her eyes, but when she

looked at the clock, she couldn't believe that it read two-twenty. Feeling slightly better, she rolled out of bed and went to the bathroom to splash some water on her face. When she looked in the mirror, she noticed the dark circles under her eyes and the strain around her mouth.

When she came out of the room, Steve stood up from the couch and approached her. Tears suddenly sprang into her eyes when he put his arms around her. Overwhelmed, she squeezed him tightly to her. "Any news?" she whispered.

"You don't want to hear this, but another person died this morning. Extensive injuries, they said."

"That makes thirteen dead."

"The talking heads are all gleefully reporting it that way, too. 'Thirteen slain at Slayer concert' or words to that effect. You know. 'Unlucky Thirteen' and all that."

"That's just ghoulish," Harmony gasped.

"We have to do something more for the families than we already are," Steve said. "Maybe anonymously."

"Great idea. We can arrange that through legal. Any idea who set the bomb? Did Nick find anything out?"

"Nothing concrete. Nick's going to coordinate some security for us. He doesn't want you going anywhere alone."

"What about you?" She looked up into his green eyes. "I don't know if—"

"No one's threatening me, Princess, just you. I'd rather have all of our attention on protecting you than looking in too many directions at once."

"But—"

Nick spoke from the chair by the couch. "You and I

both know he'll hardly leave your side, so any argument about splitting security between you is rather moot."

Her mother came out of the kitchen, carrying a steaming bowl and a plate. "I thought I heard you. I heated up some tomato soup and made a sandwich for you." She set them on the table. "Melody Montgomery called. She said if we plan to stay in Atlanta any longer that we're welcome in her home."

The idea of eating didn't have any appeal, but she knew the baby needed nourishment. After she sat in the chair and took the first bite, hunger pains gripped her and she took three bites of the grilled cheese before she spoke. "I love her home, but she has several children. I'd rather not take this there."

"That was my thought as well." Alice left briefly and returned with a glass of water and a steaming cup of tea. "Eat. Steve's waiting on a call from the police to see what kind of arrangements we need to make."

"I'd like to go home," she said around a mouth full of food. She swallowed and took a sip of the tea. "I know there's still a lot to do to settle things here, but as soon as that's done, at the earliest possible moment, I want to go on home."

"Okay." Alice nodded. "Well, here's what needs to happen. When you're ready, you and I and Franklin and your husband, we're all going to the hospitals. Drivers are standing by and Nick's on personal security. We're going to offer to pay for all of their medical bills. We're going to pray with them and pray for them and love them."

"Good," Harmony said.

Alice sat back a bit. "Then, tomorrow, there's a memorial service for the dead. They're expecting a lot of press and a lot of protestors. Anyone and everyone with an axe to grind will probably crawl out from under some rock and try to make it about their personal agenda instead of about paying respects."

Steve walked into the room and made his way to Harmony's side. He had clearly caught the last part of Alice's speech. Harmony explained, "When I was a kid, this activist atheist group protested mom's second book. Everywhere she showed up to do a book signing, these people were there with signs and ugliness. It was awful. I know what it will be like, and if I'm honest, I will admit that I don't want to go."

"We have to go, Harmony."

"I realize that," Harmony acknowledged with a hand draped over her enlarged abdomen.

"If I'm honest, I would rather not take one step inside a hospital again for the rest of my life, but I'm going to this morning." Steve slipped into the chair across from her. "There's a big motorcycle gang that's announced they're going to keep the protestors contained. That's a first in my experience. There are also a bunch of other groups, church groups and all, that have announced plans for an anti-demonstration of the demonstrators. Of course, the Governor plans to appear and personally offer his condolences, so there will be a hefty number of state police nearby, and Princess, I will be with you and right beside you every step of the way."

Harmony closed her eyes. "So, no show tomorrow night then, for sure."

Alice shook her head. "Franklin canceled tomorrow's show. Already issued refunds."

Steve added, "The fans all understand, Princess."

"Okay." Harmony nodded.

Steve's mouth thinned into a tight line before he said, "But he also said we need to get back at it next week."

"That soon? Do you agree?"

Steve shrugged. "He says we can't let fear and terror win. I agree in principle, but in my heart I don't like it."

"Then we should probably wait to see what next week holds, shouldn't we?" She swallowed some more soup. "How can we even consider filling another building with people at a time like this?"

As she spoke, Franklin came out of his bedroom. "You needn't worry about that. We have Nick here who will personally coordinate the security there. Local police will be briefed ahead of time. This won't happen again."

"Franklin—"

He stopped at her chair and put a hand on her shoulder. "Harmony, for just a moment try to remember that I was there, too. I know." He squeezed her shoulder and let go. "I know." Releasing a breath, he looked at Nick. "What is the process, Mr. Williams?"

Nick set a file folder on the table and stood. "I have quite a few things to go over with you all. When I'm finished, you'll have a good idea of what we'll do from here." Nick pulled out the chair at the head of the table, flipped it around backward, and straddled it before he opened the folder. It took only a few seconds for Steve to realize that Nick probably had at least one invisible handgun tucked at his back that he intentionally didn't block with the back of the chair.

Nick suddenly commanded their complete attention, as if the air around them held some kind of electrical charge that turned their eyes to his. "We're pretty secure in here. Viscolli security is top-notch. Likewise, inside the actual hospitals, we're in pretty good shape. The high risk times are when you find yourself on foot between entering and exiting the cars and entering and exiting the buildings. I need each of you to follow a specific protocol at those times, so let's review that."

♫ ♫ ♫ ♫

HARMONY sat next to Steve as he maneuvered through the Nashville traffic. Nick followed them in another car. "It's nice to be alone again."

He reached over and took her hand. "It's been a long couple of days." At a stoplight, he turned toward her and brought the back of her hand up to his lips, brushing a quick kiss over her knuckles. "I feel confident about Nick, though. Don't you?"

"I do." As he turned his attention back to the traffic, she said, "What do you think this is about?"

"I think on the surface it's probably about my leaving Abaddon and changing my genre."

When he paused, she said, "But?"

"But I think it's deeper than that." After several long moments, he finally said, "I think it's spiritual."

The idea terrified her. She knew that supernatural beings fought an unseen spiritual war all around them. The Bible clearly mentioned that, but having it manifest in the physical realm where it affected her family and her fans, and killed innocent people in a venue because of her—that thought filled her with dread. However, the words didn't surprise her. Reflecting on her time answering questions, she said, "That's almost the same thing Nick said."

"Yeah. He and I talked at length about the significance of the notes written in goat's blood and ash." He quickly stole a glance at her. "I haven't quite figured out why someone would paint the railroad symbol on the church or on my house. I'm going to talk to Chaz and see if there's something more about it that he can remember."

"Do you think it's the guy Railroad?"

"Maybe, but why would he be doing this? I always thought he was just a roadie." He turned onto the street that led to home. The guard at the gate waved them through, but Steve came to a stop and rolled his window down. "Afternoon. The car behind us is with us."

"Sure thing, Mr. Slater. I let another vehicle in about an hour ago. A black SUV. They had the credentials you mentioned."

"Thanks." He hit the button to roll the window up as he moved forward. "That's what I need to talk to Chaz about. Maybe he knows more about Railroad than I do. There's clearly something about all this that is off of my radar."

As they pulled into their driveway, Harmony noticed a black SUV parked out of the way of their path to the garage. As Steve pulled forward, the garage door opened. Before he came to a complete stop, two men came out of the house via the garage door. Harmony did not recognize either one of them. The tall dark-skinned man walked past them and toward Nick, while the shorter Japanese man stopped at the hood of their car and waited. Steve got out and walked around the hood, pausing to very briefly greet the man before coming to her side and opening the door. As soon as he helped her maneuver her pregnant body from the low sitting position, he turned back to the man.

"Harmony, this is Kazuki Tanaka. He's on Nick's team."

She smiled and held out her hand. "It is a pleasure to

meet you."

"Ma'am. We've secured the house for you. You can go on in." He surprised her by having a Tennessee accent. "I'm going to go debrief with my team and then I will see you inside."

Out of habit, she turned to help Nick get the bags out of the trunk. "I got this, Princess. Why don't you go in and make some of that gross tea?"

"Good idea." She went inside, but instead of going through the utility room and into the kitchen, she moved through the house and went upstairs to their bedroom. Her purse slipped off of her shoulder as she used the padded bench at the foot of the bed as a brace, maneuvering herself to her knees. As soon as she put her elbows on the bench and clasped her hands, sobs welled up inside of her.

She intended to just pray for continued protection, for the families of those who had died in the explosion, and for clarity and wisdom for the police and investigative units that spanned two states. But she found she could utter no words. Instead, sobs ripped out of her as if contained in a too-small pressurized environment that had just burst open. She knew that the book of Romans said that the Spirit would pray for her. She relied on that and just let all of the bottled up hurt and fear out.

By the time her lower back ached from the position, she no longer sat on her knees supported by her elbows. Instead, she sprawled over the bench, sitting flat on the floor, her face buried in her arms. She raised her head, feeling lighter and spent, and saw that sometime during her prayer, Steve had brought in the bags. He must have sensed that she needed to be alone with God right then and hadn't interrupted her. Fresh tears started to fall as she considered how well he knew her and how much he supported her in such a short time.

With a stop in the bathroom to wash the tears off of her face, she went downstairs and found Steve in the kitchen, pouring boiling water into a teapot. As she slipped onto a stool at the island, he looked at her. She noticed the lines of strain around his mouth and eyes.

"Feeling better?" he asked, setting the pot in front of her.

"I think so. Yes." She watched as he pulled two cups out of the cupboard. "Surely you're not going to have some tea, too."

He laughed and walked around the island, stopping by her stool to kiss her forehead. "Uh, no. That's for Nick, actually." When he sat on the stool next to her, he pulled out his phone. "There's a meeting at four. I'm going to try to go."

She immediately understood the code he spoke. When he first got out of the rehab, Harmony knew that he went to a Christian version of Narcotics Anonymous twice a week, and NA five days a week. He gradually let the daily NA meetings fade away during the plans and preparation for the tour. She knew, however, that any kind of stressor could start an internal avalanche from which he might not recover if he didn't have an outlet with those meetings. "Okay." She turned in her stool and leaned toward him, putting her feet on his footrest and both hands on his thighs to brace herself. "Be careful."

He cupped both her cheeks with his hands and kissed her. When he pulled away, he ran his thumbs under her eyes and caught her tears. She straightened in her stool and poured tea into her cup. "I'm sorry. I'm just a hot mess. I'm just pregnant and full of hormones and I just can't stop."

"It's okay, Princess. I'll be careful and you'll relax. Nick is a pretty impressive guy and I feel like you're absolutely safe."

"What about you?"

As he walked by, he paused at her stool. "I'm perfectly safe, too." He gave her one last kiss and ran the flat of his hand over her belly. "The last thing you need to worry about is me. I need to go consult with a higher power in my own way right now."

As he walked out of the kitchen, Nick walked in. Harmony smiled at him and poured the tea. "Let's move into the living room. This stool hurts my back."

♫ ♫ ♫ ♫

Chapter 25

STEVE sat in the back row on a metal folding chair in the basement of the church, and listened to the man speaking talk about waking up next to a girlfriend who had overdosed. His stomach rolled in a shared feeling of relief that he'd never actually woken up to a corpse and horror at the destruction of his previous life. While he listened, he prayed. His prayer may not have had the physical release Harmony's had, but the passion behind it was just as intense, regardless.

He wondered, questioned, analyzed, and still couldn't make sense of what could cause someone to do this. The vandalism to his house could be explained by passion and heat-of-the-moment. The planning and execution that went into the notes and the attack on the church made no sense to his rational mind.

He knew that meant he had to think about it without rational thought. Perhaps, as Nick suggested, this was something far more sinister than simply enraged fans. The idea of a spiritual battle manifesting into physical attacks in the material world terrified him. What did he do about that? It was all well and good to take up the Armor of God in battle against a spiritual Satan, arm himself with the Word, and shield himself with the Truth, but what did he do to protect an innocent audience and his family from car bombs?

When everyone slowly stood up from their chairs, he realized the meeting had ended. He had barely listened to the speakers. He stood as well and walked back to the table that held the coffee pot, cups, and packaged pastries. As he reached for a bottle of water, the man next to him did, too, the cuff of his shirt rising up to reveal a tattoo of a railroad symbol on the inside of his wrist. Steve's heart skipped a beat. Trying not to react outwardly, he nodded at the guy and opened his bottle of water. He turned his back and pulled his phone out of his pocket, accessing the camera. Putting it to his ear, he acted like he answered the phone while he slowly turned in a circle and took pictures.

"Hey," he paused, "yeah, it's just dismissing. Don't worry. I won't be late." Spinning in a full circle, making sure that the man with the tattoo made it into several pictures, he put his phone back into his pocket and took a long drink of water.

When the group leader walked up to him, a momentary sense of panic hit him. He expected him to challenge him on taking the pictures in an anonymous meeting. Instead, he held out his hand. "It's been a while since I've seen you."

"It has." They shook hands and Steve made a point to look at his watch. "I've cut my meetings down to twice a week right now while work has gotten crazy."

"You doing okay?"

"Honestly, yes."

"Saw the news yesterday. If you need to talk about anything, I think you have my number."

The man slapped Steve on the shoulder in a friendly way, then turned to a new face and warmly introduced himself. Taking advantage of the opportunity, Steve slipped out the door and rushed to his car. It felt like the drive took forever as he drove through the Nashville traffic toward the police department, but soon he found himself sitting at Detective Nadine Cox's desk.

"Tell me why you think this is significant," she said, scanning through the pictures on his phone.

"The symbol I saw on his wrist was identical to the one on the side of the building at the church and one painted many times over on my vandalised house in California," Steve explained. "I'm certain of it."

"You think this is our guy?"

"I don't recognize him," he sat back and tapped his finger on his knee, "but I honestly don't know for sure that I'd recognize some urban legend known as Railroad." He sighed. "I wish I'd paid more attention, been a little more sober."

She connected his phone to her computer and initiated a download of the pictures. "They could be working together. Forensics says the notes were all written on different kinds of paper, with the blood of different goats. Even different kinds of goats. There's no reason to think that this isn't a group of individuals rather than just one person."

"A conspiracy?" He asked, incredulous. She nodded slowly. "That's a terrifying thought."

As she disconnected his phone and held it out to him, she smiled at him. "I will say that what you did was exactly right and I'm impressed by your quick thinking."

He accepted his phone back. "Thanks." They stood together. He looked around the busy police station then back at her. "I also plan to show this to Nick Williams."

She raised an eyebrow. "I would expect nothing less. Bringing him on has greatly expanded my team and given me a whole new fresh set of eyes. From what I know of Nick Williams, you can rely on him and you can trust him. I would."

They shook hands and she walked him to the front desk, where he returned his visitor pass and signed the exit log. He looked at the people passing by on the street and wondered if someone followed him. Clearly, that's what the presence of the tattooed man at the meeting meant, right? Refusing to become a slave to paranoia, he walked to his car and slipped inside.

♫ ♫ ♫ ♫

IN the living room, sitting on the couch next to Steve, feeling the baby dance in her stomach after eating spicy eggplant for dinner, Harmony watched Nick's face as he looked at the pictures he had printed from Steve's phone. She wondered about the dichotomy of how she could be so physically secure but at the same time feel so very afraid.

Steve slipped his arm around her shoulders as he spoke to Nick. "What's your knee jerk?"

One side of Nick's mouth lifted in half a smile. "'Knee jerk' isn't really in my repertoire of strategic responses." She felt Steve start to reply but Nick continued, "However, my initial reaction is the same as yours. He clearly followed you there."

Nick stared at the edge of the tattoo seen on the man's

wrist as he took a drink of water. He couldn't make out any details, but Steve had described it in enough detail. He tossed the pictures onto the table. "So, now we wonder if all of the group have similar tattoos, or if he is just an anomaly."

"What does it matter?" Harmony asked.

Nick pursed his lips. "Just intel. Like a unit patch or a flag. Helps identify the enemy."

Harmony let out a deep breath. "The thought of an entire group of people following us, targeting us. How do we even reconcile this?" She sat up straighter, disengaging herself from Steve's arm. "It was scary enough thinking it was just one person. Now we have an organized group?"

"Looks that way." Nick stared at her with piercing eyes. "Fits the evidence better, too. I've already discussed this with Steve. I think you're waging a spiritual battle."

Harmony met Steve's eyes. He nodded and Harmony observed something in him that she had always known existed. This time, she recognized it. She recognized wisdom in her husband's eyes.

"Scary as that may initially feel, try to remember Who's on your side. Try not to let it discourage you." Nick smiled again. "You're truly as safe as you can be, and my team is the best. Your home's secure. We'll get into your office building tomorrow. And you're getting covered in prayer. So, for now, don't be afraid."

Nick turned his eyes toward Steve. "What decision has been made about the tour?"

Steve, who had most recently consulted with Franklin, answered, "I was all for canceling it. Then we met with the injured and the families of all the victims in Atlanta." Steve took a second to swallow hard as he remembered that very long, very hard day in Atlanta. "We went to that memorial service and the families put us right up in the front row. All those people who got hurt or lost loved ones. The one thing they had in common? They don't blame us. None of them think this is our fault. They all know this was the work of a crazy person. Or, crazy people, I guess."

Steve turned to Harmony. "I talked with Nick about it a little. The fans are, mostly anyway, they're believers. They're all professing Christians. Nick thinks, and I agree, that the Holy Spirit spoke to each of them. Like the Holy Spirit revealed to them that their loss and their suffering is due to this very real spiritual war that is raging all around us."

Nick interjected, "And the Holy Spirit did what the Holy Spirit does. He comforted them. Just like He's comforting the two of you."

"So, to answer the question, as long as Harmony's doctor clears it, we'll continue with the tour." Steve clearly didn't like it. He reached out and put a hand on Harmony's knee. "We both know hiding out and holing up at home under this siege is not going to win a spiritual battle. Our biggest concern right now is Harmony's health and that of our baby. As long as those things remain good, and the ticket holders continue to support us, we'll keep going."

Harmony ran her hand over her belly. The baby had finally settled down. "I feel fine."

Nick gathered up his papers and stood. "I absolutely honor that decision. I'll get teams together and organized. One will travel with us. One will go ahead of us. I'll be in your offices tomorrow, so I'll stop in and chat with Franklin and get specifics on everything then. I'm going to go get ready. Steve, we can leave in about thirty minutes if that works for you."

"That works."

As Nick left the room, she turned her body so that she faced Steve on the couch. "Leave? Where are you going?"

He sighed and rubbed the back of his neck. She could see the lines of strain around his eyes and mouth. "Nick and I are going to go talk to an old band member of mine."

"Which one?"

"Adolf. Bass player. Big bushy beard?"

"Right. The Viking looking guy."

"Yeah. If anyone knows the details about someone named Railroad, he will. He was always in thick with the crew." Steve furrowed his brow as if trying hard to remember something he should already know.

"Where is he?"

"Outside of LA. We chartered a plane. We'll fly down tonight, then turn around and come back tomorrow."

Fear tried to curl its tendrils around her heart. "Is that a good idea?"

He shrugged. "I have nothing to fear from Adolf. He was a companion for many years, and you have nothing to fear from my going to see him."

Knowing he was probably right, she nodded. "Good thinking, taking a picture of that guy. It kind of makes me feel like a little progress was made today."

"Hopefully, there will be a little more made tomorrow. Or even a revelation that leads to arrests." He leaned forward and kissed her. "I want this over."

He left the room, and she looked at the empty fireplace. "Me, too," she whispered, shifting her body to get more comfortable on the couch.

♫ ♫ ♫ ♫

Chapter 26

STEVE and Nick found Adolf where Steve knew they would, out by his pool. In the decade he'd known the man, unless he had a bass in his hand, he planted himself near a pool, on a beach, or on the deck of a boat. He had on a pair of blue and red Hawaiian print shorts, and had his long blond hair pulled back into a pony tail.

"Slayer!" Adolf grabbed Steve and hugged him. Immediately, the smell of marijuana smoke filled Steve's nostrils, tempting him while simultaneously almost gagging him. How had he smelled like that all the time? "It's been too long, man."

Adolf glanced at Nick, from his black-lined eyes to the black T-shirt, the ripped and dirty jeans, and the toes of his biker boots. Steve had barely recognized Nick when he emerged from his hotel room earlier. He clearly passed the visual inspection as Adolf extended his hand. "Adolf Judge, man."

"Nick." He looked around the yard and deck, at the tropical plants, fountains, and tiki bar in the corner. "Nice digs."

"My haven from the world." Adolf ducked behind the bar and reappeared with three beers. Steve felt his mouth go dry. He suddenly felt very, very thirsty.

Steve held up his palm. "Not me, man. On the wagon and all. Thought you might have heard."

"Seriously? Not just for show?" Adolf looked as if Steve had just informed him that Hitler really won the war.

"Dead serious."

Adolf stood perfectly still with an expression that conveyed both shock and puzzlement. Nick, snatched a bottle from his hand and twisted the cap off, breaking the tableau. "Thanks, man. Don't mind if I do."

They settled into chairs under an oversized canvas umbrella and looked out at the pool. Finally, Adolf said, "What's up?"

Steve looked at him. "I wanted to know if you remembered a guy called Railroad."

Adolf grinned. "Bill! Yeah, man. You trying to tell me you don't remember him? We all know roadie Railroad. He was on the light crew. Remember, Slayer?"

Nick spun the beer bottle on the glass topped table. Steve noticed he hadn't actually taken a sip from the bottle. "Seen him around lately?"

"Have I seen him around?" He made it sound like a statement, as if it came from far away, then his eyes glazed over and Steve realized he was high on something. He met Nick's eyes and gave a small shake of his head.

Nick replied, "Yeah. He's the best. Hoping to see if he

maybe wants to do some work on Steve's new tour."

Adolf's eyes cleared and he took a long pull of his beer. "Right. You're steppin' back out there, right? Doing God music. Jesus jazz." He narrowed his eyes. "Why are you really here, man?"

Steve shrugged. "Just trying to put together a crew, dude. Like working with the best."

"You mean like Abaddon? We were the best, right?" Adolf stared at him for several seconds, then looked out at the pool. "You should probably go, Mr. Clean Jeans."

Steve opened his mouth, but Nick stood. He set his untouched beer down on the table. "Thanks for the beer, man. Appreciate it. Honor to meet you."

♫ ♫ ♫ ♫

"HEY, Bill," Adolf said, staring into the still blue water of the pool. He caught himself zoning out at the image of the sun dancing on the surface before he remembered the importance of the call. "It's Adolf."

"I'm aware," Railroad replied. "Why are you calling me?"

"Dude. Slayer was just here with some other dude. Asking about you, man."

"Oh?" Despite the haze of narcotics, Adolf felt a chill at the tone of Railroad's voice. "That's fascinating. And what did you tell him, Adolf?"

"I told him to leave."

After a long pause, Railroad very coolly said, "Well done."

Nothing indicated the end of the call. After a few minutes, Adolf looked at the phone, surprised to see that the connection had ended. Anxious, feeling like he'd just done something terribly wrong, he abruptly stood and rushed to the tiki bar. He found his leather pouch behind the glass pitchers on the bottom shelf. Feeling like a thousand ants danced inside his stomach, he unrolled the pouch on the bar's surface and fingered the little package of white powder. Almost feeling calmer already, he slipped the syringe out from under the elastic band.

♫ ♫ ♫ ♫

Chapter 27

HARMONY picked up her cup of tea, but at the first sip realized it had gone cold. With a shudder, she set it back down. She looked at the clock and frowned. Had she truly sat there for the last forty minutes, staring off into space? She sat back in her chair and glanced all around her office. Despite the security team's best efforts to return all of her items to their previous positions and locations, a few things just looked slightly out of place. For example, they had returned books and photographs to the proper shelves, but not in the proper order.

Frustrated, annoyed with her lack of concentration, she pushed herself to her feet and walked over to the window and looked out at the Nashville morning. She could see the thick flow of traffic on the streets below and didn't envy those commuters trying to make it to work on time given the current state of construction in the downtown area.

"Why are you here?"

Surprised, she spun around and put her hand to her heart. "Daddy, you startled me."

Grayson Harper walked into her office and set his briefcase on a chair in front of her desk before coming over to stand beside her at the window. He leaned down and kissed her temple before saying, "You don't need to work right now, you know."

"What else is there to do?" She put a hand on the side of her swelling belly. "I want to work, anyway. There is so much that needs to be accomplished before the baby comes, and for a good bit of the next few weeks, I'll still be on tour."

Grayson raised a silver eyebrow. "So you made the decision to continue?"

She took a deep, confidence forging breath. "Steve has concerns, but we want to stay on tour. The staff is split, but on principle we really don't want to give in to fear. 'God has not given us a spirit of fear.' So, we've added the security Nick Williams provided, and we're praying every day. That will have to be enough."

Her father's light blue eyes bored into hers for several silent seconds, then he nodded. "Where's your next stop? Charlotte?"

"Yes. Saturday night. Nick already has a team securing the location and vetting the volunteers with additional background checks. He's also giving them all some training on things to look for during the event. Nick says he doesn't expect them to try anything there. It would be too soon after their last attack so they would have a much lower chance of success due to our higher vigilance, and Steve agrees."

He reached up and put a hand on the back of her neck, giving her a gentle, reassuring squeeze. "Be careful traveling. How are the headaches?"

Her eyes came together in a frown. "I just realized I haven't had one for a couple of days."

"Good. That's good." He looked at his watch. "I have to get down to the studio and get set for today's show. I look forward to hearing about Charlotte when you get back."

"Thanks, Daddy," she replied, moving back to her desk. She appreciated his constant concession to Steve's decisions as they pertained to her. She knew that a part of him wanted responsibility for those decisions back, just as much as he knew it was no longer his place. As he walked out of her office, she pulled her chair out and sat back down, sighing at the stack of correspondence she needed to personally address. She pulled a letter off of the top of the stack and started reading it.

An hour later, Steve sauntered into the office. "Good morning, Princess," he greeted with a smile.

She glanced up and grinned at him. "I tried not to wake you. I know it's still early for you."

"I think you may have somehow affected my circadian rhythms. I found myself wide awake at seven this morning, yet no bride by my side." He leaned over her desk and gave her a long kiss before sitting in the chair across from her.

"I know. I wanted to get through this stack of letters before we leave tonight."

"You can take them with you, you know." He laced his hands behind his head and kicked his feet in front of him. "They make stylish little bags designed for the sole purpose of transporting work between your home and office. Knowing your affinity for bags, I'm surprised you don't already know that."

With a grin, she put the cap back on her pen and leaned back in her chair. "Cute, but I never take paperwork from the office to home. I'd never work on it, I might forget it at home, and it would never get finished. Best to leave it here in my little bubble of productivity rather than get lost in a song writing fury that ends in me not even knowing what day it is."

With a wink he said, "You do have that beautiful artist brain to contend with. You're right." He sat up. "I have some calls to make. Have you eaten breakfast?"

With those words, her stomach growled. She laughed and lay her palm on top of it. "Apparently, not enough."

"Meet me in my office in a few minutes? I brought some biscuits."

"I knew I loved you." She uncapped her pen. "Give me ten minutes."

"You got it." He stood. "What time's our flight tonight?"

"I think Franklin and Nick worked out a charter. I don't think it's a scheduled flight." She lifted a stack of envelopes and saw the email she'd printed. "Here's the info. You probably have an email, if you'd turn on your computer."

"You're the only person in the world I've ever e-mailed. I'd rather keep it that way." He gave her hand a squeeze as he took the paper from her. "Ten minutes. I'll have hot tea and biscuits."

"My hero." She watched start to him walk out of the office, her cheeks bunching up under the silly grin on her face.

He paused in the doorway as Franklin came in,

carrying a newspaper. "Have either of you seen the news this morning?"

With a frown, she shook her head. "No. The paper wasn't there yet when I left."

He handed the newspaper to Steve. "Apparently, your former band member, Adolf Judge, was found dead yesterday afternoon."

"Dead?" Steve flipped the paper open. "How?"

"Overdose. He'd evidently died earlier this week."

Harmony watched the frown darken his face as he read the story.

"I just saw him three days ago," Steve breathed. "That's about when they think it happened."

"Should you call the police?" She slipped out from behind her desk and walked over to peer at the paper. She could see a color picture of Adolf Judge playing the bass on the open page.

"He lived in California. I wouldn't even know who to call."

"Maybe start with Detective Cox?"

He pursed his lips then nodded. "Probably. I'll go call her right now." Absently, he brushed his lips over her forehead. "Don't forget breakfast," he said as he turned to leave.

♫ ♫ ♫ ♫

THE flash of lights and the whine of video cameras assaulted them as they stepped out of the car and onto the sidewalk outside the funeral home. Steve kept his hand in Harmony's as they walked up the path to the door. As they approached, two men in navy colored suits opened the doors for them. Stepping over the threshold and onto the maroon carpet, Steve took a deep breath then slowly let it out. The need for a cigarette nearly overwhelmed him.

He stripped off his sunglasses, tucked them into his shirt pocket, then looked around. He saw dozens of faces he recognized but couldn't match to names. Harmony squeezed his hand reassuringly and they walked into the room.

"Steve!" Chaz called and began to make his way to them from the other side of the room.

"Hey, man," he replied, gripping Chaz's right hand as they hugged and pounded each other's back. He turned then to Harmony, and she stood on her toes to give him a hug.

"When did you get back in town?"

"This morning. We're staying at the Viscolli tonight, then heading up to my parents' house in the morning."

"Well, if it isn't the artist formerly known as Slayer." Steve's neck muscles tensed when he saw Cain Proctor walking toward them. He wanted to push Harmony behind him and shield her with his body. Cain walked up to stand directly in front of them and his eyes went to Harmony. "So you're Harper."

Before Steve could interject, Harmony said, "No. I'm Mrs. Slater. I assume you are Cain Proctor, the same Cain who has been orchestrating a smear campaign against my husband. Since you and I have never actually met, I can't imagine we actually have anything to discuss, Mr. Proctor."

Without another word, Cain turned to Steve. "Why did you come?"

"Because the departed was my bandmate and friend

for a long time." He put his arm over Harmony's shoulders and pulled her close. "We're here to pay our respects."

"He would have had zero interest in your respects. You know you're not welcome here. Why did you really come?"

"Funny. That's not how he acted when I saw him a few days ago. He was genuinely happy to see me. Of course, I can truthfully claim with absolute certainty that I didn't give him the drugs that killed him. Can you make the same claim, Proctor? Maybe *you* shouldn't be here."

Cain's eyes narrowed to slits. "I've been meaning to give you some advice, Slayer—"

"Actually, I've been meaning to give you some advice," Steve interrupted. "Lose the soul patch. Either shave it off entirely or else man up and grow a real beard. You're over thirty and you're scaring all the annoying teenage girls who follow you on FriendFace." He applied gentle pressure with his arm and he and Harmony turned away from Cain. Over his shoulder he tossed out, "Later, dude."

As they got out of earshot, Chaz laughed. "You should have seen his face when you turned away from him. I thought he might actually explode."

Steve shook his head. "I take no delight in his misery. I wish he'd just ignore me like all these other people are."

Harmony slipped her arm around his waist and hugged him close. "Coming was the right thing. Now no one has to speculate why you kept your distance. Let's go find Adolf's aunt and properly pay our respects."

Anton Ramirez stood next to Adolf's aunt. He wore a gray suit and had pulled his dreadlocks into a kind of strange ponytail behind his head. Steve barely recognized him. "Slayer!" He said, holding out his hand. "It's been too long."

"Anton." He rather gently shook the keyboardist's talented hand and then turned to Harmony. "This is my wife, Harmony Slater. Harmony, Anton Ramirez, my former keyboard player."

"Harmony, I've seen so many pictures of your beautiful face, I feel like I already know you." His island accent charmed her, Steve could tell, and she smiled warmly at him.

"It's very nice to meet you, Mr. Ramirez. I wish it could have been under better circumstances." She slipped her hand back into Steve's. "I'm very sorry about your friend."

Anton pressed his lips together and softly nodded. "He had a lot of bad habits, but we'd been friends for a long time." The receiving line moved forward, and Anton slapped Steve on the shoulder. "Good to see you, man. Don't be such a stranger, hear?"

He nodded. "I hear you. Take care, Anton."

After offering their condolences to Adolf's family, they found seats and sat through the funeral. Adolf, not one for anything contemporary or normal, had a funeral that could basically have been a concert of who's who in the hard rock billboard charts. The speakers often didn't make a lot of sense as they reminisced about parties or concerts or benefits, with various clips of Adolf riffing on his bass guitar in between brief sets of music.

Steve had separated himself from that life so thoroughly that he found little to no enjoyment in the memorial event and, instead, felt great relief when it finally ended. He hoped that his eventual funeral would not reflect this kind of legacy. He and Harmony made their way out of the building, not speaking to anyone else. They walked back through the throng of reporters and made their way to the car that waited for them at the curb. As their driver pulled away, he looked at Harmony. She absently rubbed her large belly and toyed with her pearl necklace. So much love for her swelled in his chest that it almost took his breath away.

Suddenly, she looked over at him and reached for his hand. "Are you okay?"

Was he okay? He searched his heart to find a way to explain how he felt. "I came so close to overdosing too many times. That could have very easily been my body in that coffin. At the time, I would have told you that I didn't care. In hindsight, I know that's not true. I would have cared, because I knew the truth. I didn't *not* believe in God; I was angry with Him and running away from Him. It makes it hard to think about how close I came to destroying, wasting, and ending the one life He gave me."

She brought his hand up and pressed it against her cheek. "I am so thankful for your heart."

"I'm thankful that my heavenly Father, in His wisdom, had the mercy and the grace to keep me alive." He turned and met her eyes. "And I love your heart, Princess."

♫ ♫ ♫ ♫

Chapter 28

THE stress of waiting for something to happen during their concert in Charlotte really took a toll on Harmony's ability to relax and enjoy ministering to a crowd of people with her style of gift. She felt uneasy, unnatural, and every time she spoke, it sounded forced and stilted. Steve's remarks about seeing the venue full of fans didn't help. Had they truly expected no one to come? Why hadn't anyone discussed that with her?

Her headache had returned full force by the end of the concert. She sat in her tour bus, kicked back on the couch in the back, with an ice pack on her forehead and her feet above her heart. It would take another hour before they could leave and head for Richmond. She looked forward to seeing the Kents tomorrow and impatiently checked her watch. Just as she tossed the ice pack aside and swung her legs around to sit up, Steve climbed onto the bus.

"Ready to head to the airport, Princess?"

Feeling a bit like a petulant child, she stuck her lip out. "Can't we just ride the bus?"

Steve widened his eyes and spoke quietly as if sensing her mood. "It's a five-hour drive, or a one-hour flight. What would make you more comfortable?"

Hot tears sprang to her eyes. "Getting rid of this headache." She pushed herself clumsily to her feet just as he approached. Without hesitation, she went into his arms.

"How about we fly back home and see about getting you in to see Doc Willis tomorrow?"

All of the planning and preparation for the tour ran through her mind. "No." Taking a deep breath, she pushed away. "Our timeline is too tight. I'll see if Carol can recommend someone in Richmond."

He smiled warmly and brushed the hair off of her cheek. "Your call. We can cancel this whole thing on your word and it will be okay. I even think the ticket holders will understand."

"I appreciate that, but I don't think it would be okay. I think it's important that we continue with the tour for as long as possible just like we originally planned. I'd rather not give the appearance of fear or intimidation. Isn't that why someone would bomb a building full of people? To invoke fear and inspire intimidation?" She brushed by him and carried the ice pack to the kitchenette's sink.

He followed her, leaning his shoulder against the corner of the wall. "So, the Harper family won't negotiate with terrorists?"

With a giggle, she reached up and gave him a peck on the cheek. She felt slightly better, and almost a little embarrassed at the overwhelming crabby attitude that led to such pouting earlier. "I think I do want to fly. It will get us to the hotel quicker and I want to lie down in a bed in a building instead of one that has to roll down the highway."

His sweeping arm gestured toward the door. "Your chariot awaits."

♫ ♫ ♫ ♫

STEVE stood on the ranch house porch and looked out over the rolling green hills, the Virginia sunshine warming his face. He could hear faint voices coming from the nearby barn and the low buzz of a motor somewhere beyond his sight. As the breeze shifted, he caught the scent of horses and hay.

The door squeaked open behind him and he turned his head to watch Bobby Kent step out onto the porch beside him, carrying two steaming cups of coffee. "Carol just called. They're on their way back. She said Harmony left her phone here."

He gave a small smile as he took an offered cup. "She always forgets her phone."

"Always has. For as long as I've known her."

"How long is that?" Steve asked, accepting the offered mug.

Bobby wrinkled his brow. "Man, that's been a while back. She won her first Grammy about a week later so I guess maybe ten or eleven years? Doesn't seem that long."

Bobby took a sip then gestured to the furniture on the porch. Steve took it as an invitation to sit next to him. He crossed the porch and sat in a chair facing a paddock that contained rails and boards set up for jumping.

"This is an impressive operation," Steve remarked.

"Thank you, sir." Bobby pulled his phone out of his back pocket and set it on the table before he sat down and stretched his long legs out in front of him. Butter soft and well worn light gray cowboy boots clad his feet beneath comfortably soft and worn looking boot cut blue jeans. "My granddaddy's daddy built it. It's grown over the years, of course. The success of my singing career helped my father grow it a lot. Modernized some things. After my mom passed, Lisa wanted to live out here. It felt right. She picked up that horse bug of my dad's that seemed to skip my generation."

As if on cue, Steve watched Bobby's daughter Lisa lead a horse out of the barn into the paddock. An older looking man in a cowboy hat walked beside her, gesturing at the jumps, clearly instructing her. "Outside of the circus, I can't ever remember being this close to a real live horse in my life," he admitted, "but out here feels good."

Bobby sipped his coffee and scowled before setting the hot cup aside to let it cool. "You don't ride, then, I take it."

"Wouldn't even know where to start," Steve confessed.

Bobby nodded. "No shame city boy. I didn't learn until I was in my teens. Karl over there's a really good coach. He could give you a few lessons on one of the gentle mares."

Steve considered it. "I might take you up on that, Bobby. It might be fun to ride with Harmony."

Bobby made a noise in his throat and sarcastically offered. "You'd have some serious catching up to do. That girl is part horse when she's not 'parasitically oppressed.'"

Steve had to translate the actual words spoken in that nearly incongruous Southern drawl to realize that Bobby was referring to Harmony's pregnancy. By the mocking tone of voice when Bobby sprinkled the vernacular phrase referring to unborn human beings as parasites, Steve deduced that Bobby appreciated irony, loved babies, and hated certain political world views. Steve took it as a compliment that Bobby felt comfortable enough to assume that he would pick all that up from a simple turn of phrase and had no reservations about speaking his mind.

Bobby retrieved his cup and took a sip, looking more satisfied this time. "Harmony's always loved coming out here. You two are welcome any time."

Steve smiled. "We'll be three soon."

"Can't imagine what it's like, to wait in such anticipation for the birth of your first child. Lisa was almost nine the first time I met her." He paused. "I guess she was nine. It was her birthday party."

Confused, Steve asked, "Is Lisa your stepdaughter?"

Bobby smiled, but it never made it to his eyes. "No. She's all mine, a hundred percent. It's a bit of a long story." He sat up straighter, looking at the paddock. "Look at her. She's such a natural." As he spoke, Lisa's horse jumped the wooden fence. The horse and rider moved in perfect harmony, as if they made up a single being with just one mind. He had never seen such equine beauty before.

"Does she compete?"

"Oh, yes. As often as possible, and I have all the bills to prove it. Matter of fact, we leave for a competition in Kentucky Friday night." He stared hard at Nick. "What's the latest news about the bombing in Atlanta?"

"I wish I knew everything. Scratch that. I wish I knew anything." Unable to sit still, he stood and turned to face Bobby, leaning against the porch railing. "The police are looking for a guy who used to be part of my team. There's actually an FBI agent assigned now since this thing spans several states. This guy they're looking for, he had something to do with the symbol painted on the church. My house in California was vandalized with the same symbol."

"What kind of symbol?"

"There's a weird thing like a railroad crossing sign and a pentagram."

Bobby suddenly tensed. Steve could see it happen the instant he finished speaking. His already baritone voice sounded even lower and he prompted, "Pentagram?"

"Yeah, you know. Abaddon was a hard rock group. The label always marketed us using all kinds of occult imagery. A big portion of our fan base were goth types."

Bobby relaxed a little bit and sipped his coffee. "Well, Steve, I know a little something about pentagrams. I'll just tell you this. It might not have anything to do with demons or the occult."

"What do you think it means, then?"

"Could mean anything or nothing at all, but it might just be a crazy person is trying to kill you. I know a little something about that, too."

"Nick Williams doesn't think this is a single person."

"I see. Well, in case you didn't know it already, Nick is the right man to see y'all through this."

"I happen to agree." Steve took a long drink of his coffee before he spoke again. Despite the seductive aroma, he had expected bitter, like instant, or stale and cheap store bought. This was a surprisingly good cup of coffee. It tasted fresh and dark and rich and not at all sweet or creamy. It relaxed him a bit to savor the flavor of it. "The notes came from too many places all over the country. The symbol keeps appearing. The threat is too pervasive with the vandalism and now the bomb. There's definitely more than just one person behind it all."

Bobby raised an eyebrow. "Symbols? Vandalism? Bombs? What does that all mean?"

"That's the million-dollar question, isn't it?" He crossed his arms over his chest. "I get the distinct impression that there's some sort of evil cult or something attached to it. It's all very creepy and a little scary." He gestured at the SUV parked partway down the drive. "Hence the protective detail."

"Nick's good. The best. If anyone can help you, he can."

"How do you know Nick?"

"His wife, Aria, and my Carol are really good friends. They go way back. Went to high school together, even." He upended his mug and polished off his coffee. "Nick would probably be interested in the whole evil cult theory, too."

"Yeah. He absolutely is. He's actually in Atlanta right now with the detectives investigating the bombing. He seems to know them." With a short laugh, he added, "And everyone seems to know him."

Bobby pursed his lips and nodded. "It would seem that God has placed a lot of intentional people in your life on purpose. I think that's good. But you know something? I find that whenever I actually see God's hand at work it's always fascinating."

Steve looked into his cup, seeing the reflection of the white puffy cloud in the sky on the dark surface. "It'll be good when this is all over. It's been present for almost our entire marriage, and the threats have escalated throughout her pregnancy. I'd like my wife to have some peace and quit feeling so afraid."

"I understand." After several silent moments, Bobby said, "You know, you and I met once before, too."

Embarrassment heated his cheeks. "Do I want to know?"

With a loud, barking laugh, Bobby replied, "Probably not. Let me just say you look a heap better nowadays. And I'm happy for you. Happy you got your act together."

Steve poured the remaining swallow of his coffee out onto the bushes below the porch. "It wasn't all me. I have the blood of Christ and the love of a good woman."

Bobby raised his empty mug in a mock salute. "Amen to that, brother." He stood as a vehicle came into view. "Here come our good women, now."

Steve watched the pickup truck roll down the paved lane and pull right up to the house. Before the engine even stopped, he had Harmony's door open. "Hello, Princess. How'd it go?"

"My blood pressure's up a bit. She thought that might be causing the headaches. Everything else looked good. So, when my head starts hurting, I'm supposed to lie down, elevate my feet above my heart, and relax." He helped her out of the truck and she leaned into him, wrapping her arms around him. "I can think back now and associate the headaches with high stressors, so it makes sense."

"How do you feel right now?"

"Well, I have to pee, of course."

"Of course."

"And I am flat starving." She laughed and stepped

back. "I'm ready for lunch."

♫ ♫ ♫ ♫

LORNA Moses, age twenty-four, normally stood about five foot five, though she could pull off five foot eight in a good shoe. She kept herself slim and fit and she dyed her already dark hair jet black. At the moment, she wore absolutely nothing other than a crimson satin robe and she crouched on all fours. Her bare hands and feet felt cool against the capped cement floor of the dim warehouse. Candles flickered all around her, and the candlelight cast dancing shadows on the cool floor before her eyes. She very, very slowly knelt further down until her lips kissed each of the bare feet of the man standing before her.

Raising up slightly, she whispered, "We failed you, Father."

Bill Rhodes leaned down with open hands and let her place her fingertips in his palms. He lifted her up and brushed her thick black hair out of her eyes. "You did a wonderful job setting that car bomb off at the church. I couldn't have asked for a better team. The failure is not your responsibility. I blame Jehovah for protecting them."

"I hate Him!" Lorna Moses declared.

Softly, Bill Rhodes intoned, "I hate Him too, my child." More forcefully he demanded, "What are you prepared to do in our master's service to make up for this near miss?"

"Anything for you, Father."

"Anything? Because what I'm going to ask you to do is going to be a sacrifice."

"I am ready, Father." Lorna Moses prepared to strip off her robe, to bare everything, every inch of flesh. Some part of her would be required as a living sacrifice to make an atonement for this error. She had prepared herself to make that sacrifice.

Bill Rhodes shook his head. "Don't misunderstand me. You will make a small sacrifice of something that you won't even mind surrendering. It will take you a few days to learn how to do it right. You will do this so that the proper sacrifice can be made. Our master has revealed to me what that sacrifice must be and I must work to execute his will."

"What sacrifice does Lucifer demand of me, Father?"

"Your freedom, child. But freedom is such an illusion. It is not so much to ask, is it?"

Her eyes filled with tears and she sobbed out, "I love you, Father. Anything!"

He looked over at the two men, her partners who had helped set the car bomb, and who had earlier made similar declarations, then put his arm over her shoulders and sideways hugged her to him. "Very good, child. I hope you're ready to learn everything we're about to teach you."

"Thank you, Father," she whispered.

♫ ♫ ♫ ♫

HARMONY slipped onto the bench at the piano and ran her fingertips over the keys. She grinned as Lisa sat next to her. "Ready, kiddo?"

"You haven't been here in a while," Lisa said with a smile. "I've had a lot more lessons."

"And hours of practice," Carol said, flipping the latches open on her violin case. "Hours. Or, to say it like Lisa, 'airs'."

Harmony laughed, kind of looking forward to arguing with her own child about piano lessons. "Well, then, let's let this girl take the lead." She grinned up at Steve as he slipped his guitar strap over his shoulder. Bobby tuned his guitar next to him. "I've missed being in this home," she observed, tears filling her eyes.

Carol started playing her violin and, within seconds, the rest of them joined in. Harmony sat back, her hand on Lisa's back, and let the teenager play the song while she, Steve, and Bobby sang. For the first time in two weeks, she relaxed and the stress of constant wait and worry gradually left her. Her smile felt real, the fist clenched around her heart loosened its grip, and she felt her spirit strengthen.

They sang old hymns, they sang new songs, they sang duets they had recorded years before. It felt amazing to let go. By the time they finished the last song, she nearly couldn't remember what had stressed her out so badly before.

"I needed this tonight," she said to Carol as they carried glasses into the kitchen.

Bobby's wife squeezed her shoulder in a comforting touch. "I know what it's like to live like someone's lurking around every corner. The stress is inexplicable. Please remember to find ways to relax, to pray, to know when you're safe. Remember that your body isn't the only one suffering when you suffer."

As if on cue, the baby stretched and moved, pushing against her right side. "You're right," she said, feeling the little kick against her palm. "I don't know what to do more than what we're already doing, but I do feel so much better tonight."

"I'm glad you have Aria's husband running

interference for you and I'm very glad our home could be a place of sanctuary." The kitchen door swung open and Bobby and Steve came through, carrying platters and bowls.

"That's everything," Bobby said, setting the stack of empty platters on the counter. "I honestly don't know how the five of us consumed that many sandwiches, though."

"Some of us are eating for two," Steve said with a wink.

Harmony scoffed. "And some of us get a whiff of meat and don't know how to say no." She slipped her arm around his waist. "I'm exhausted. I think I'll sleep well tonight."

"Good. You need a good night's sleep." Steve steered her toward the door.

Harmony said, "Good night. Thank you for your hospitality."

They left the room on the heels of Bobby and Carol wishing them good night in return and made their way, arm in arm, to the guest room Carol had made up for them.

♫ ♫ ♫ ♫

Chapter 29

DETECTIVE Nadine Cox looked through the one-way glass at the woman handcuffed to the scarred metal table. In the room next door, she could hear one of the men who had come in with her screaming for an attorney. She looked at Detective John Suarez. "How much have they confessed to?"

He looked at the suspect then at her. "Everything. Goat blood, notes, bombing the church." He opened a file. "They had the addresses of everyone they delivered notes to, how they managed to go from San Francisco to Nashville to Atlanta, how they infiltrated the offices and mail room of the Harper Industries building. Everything."

When the door at the end of the hall opened, the suspect's screaming got louder. Nick walked out, rubbing his ears. "Well! The gentleman in there is just barely on this side of insane."

"I hope you didn't hurt my confession with any untoward tactics," John said, eyes narrowed at his brother-in-law.

Nick held up both hands in defense, a look of unblemished innocence on his face. "No tactics, brother, no tactics. Just a few simple questions. I assure you, I wasn't the one who asked him to completely lose his mind."

"You know that entire exchange was recorded?"

Nick smiled. "Good. Use it for training purposes. Maybe you'll learn something useful." He shifted his attention to Detective Cox. "I found no evidence of a tattoo on any of them."

"What does that mean?" John asked.

"I think it means that either they just wanted to be part of the Railroad cult, so they painted the symbol on the wall of the church, or else they're just patsies. But, they confessed to everything, and he doesn't seem to be lying to me."

"Maybe they just have a thing against tattoos," Nadine said, opening her file to look at the tattoo Steve had photographed at his meeting. "Or maybe this was a permanent marker. Or maybe only certain ranks get tattoos. It's possible that these suspects are too low in the food chain, just hovering down at minion status."

"Which, of course, means that there's still a threat," Nick said. He sighed and rubbed the back of his neck. "A small part of me wants to distrust these confessions. We asked Adolf about the existence of Railroad—that day he dies. Three days later you have a full confession? To everything? When is a bombing case ever this simple? This pat?"

"Maybe," John said, taking the file from Nadine, "or maybe it wasn't ever as complicated as you made it out to be. You do tend to look under rocks an awful lot, Nick."

"My job is to look under all the rocks." He slipped his hands into his pockets and looked at Nadine. "It's just gravy that I enjoy looking under them. What say you, Detective?"

She let out a long breath. "I say let's step forward cautiously and keep our guard up."

"It might be hard to convince them to continue with a twenty-four-hour guard when the threat appears to be gone," John suggested.

"Say that's right, John. Don't suppose that's the reason we were meant to *think* the threat is all gone, do you?" Nick asked his brother-in-law.

"Even if this threat is the real threat and now it's gone," John murmured, concentrating, "that doesn't mean this group won't motivate some copycats. So, either we have a live threat and these guys are patsies, or we have a live threat from imitators."

"Steve seems to have a good head on his shoulders," Nick replied. "I think he'll do what he needs to do to protect her."

Detective Cox nodded and studied the woman at the table again. Despite the impossibility of such an act with a one-way mirror, the woman appeared to look up and meet her eyes. The evil Nadine faced there made her stomach go cold. "I hope you're right, Mr. Williams." She handed him a slim file. "We checked the records the company used for lighting. There was consistently a lighting guy named William Rhodes. Since your buddy Adolf called Railroad 'Bill', we checked into that angle, but he doesn't seem to exist anywhere except a bank account where paychecks go into and nothing comes out of."

Nick opened the file and read the summarized report. "Interesting," he murmured.

Nadine nodded. "We thought so."

♫ ♫ ♫ ♫

THE banner blew in the wind, exclaiming, "Welcome to the family!" Another banner hung off the porch roof proclaiming, "It's a girl!" Harmony took a sip of lemon flavored water and smiled with joy at the sight of a dozen children climbing in and around the big wooden playground in the center of the backyard. She laughed as a little red-haired girl—the guest of honor—darted between her and Melody.

"Careful, sugar," Melody cautioned with her thick Southern drawl, "lots of people around."

"Yes, ma'am!" the girl said from a distance, then dashed over to the slide.

"What a joy." Harmony grinned. She gingerly lowered herself onto the picnic table. "I'm so excited for you and James now that the adoption's official. You're going to have to build a bigger place soon."

Melody winked. "Those plans are already in the works." They watched as two boys chased each other over a rope bridge that spanned two wooden forts. "As many as we can handle, we'll make our own. It's important to us."

The bright sun shone down on the Atlanta backyard. Harmony, never one to enjoy the heat of a southern day anyway, fanned herself as her pregnancy made her feel so much hotter. She had piled her hair on top of her head and wore a loose fitting cotton sundress the color of amethysts. "I know. I so admire your loving these children so much."

"Look who's talking. I don't know how you minister

to terminal children. I believe that must take a very special gift from God, because it would completely destroy me."

Feeling sadness at the thought of the children she had seen die, she felt the burn of tears in her eyes. "Maybe. It's probably a little destructive, but they need me, and so do their parents. Maybe it is a gift."

"Never doubt it." She looked up. "Oh! Look who's here!" Melody hustled in the direction of the latest arrival, a short blonde woman with Hispanic features. "Aria! What a surprise!"

Harmony watched as Carol, the beautiful slim redhead, and a petite blonde crossed the yard. "Aria's here visiting Nick. I hope you don't mind that I invited her," Carol explained as they approached.

"Of course not!" Melody rushed to both women and hugged them. "I haven't seen you in years. How are you?"

"Good. Writing and conducting full time now." She made her way to Harmony. "I didn't think you could be more beautiful than you already are, but look at you! Why couldn't I look this good when I was pregnant?"

"Oh, hush," Harmony said, blushing and laughing, "what a surprise! I don't think I've seen you since Carol's wedding."

Carol sat down on Harmony's other side. "Has it been that long? Weren't you at Lisa's thirteenth?"

Aria shook her head. "No. I missed it. Mom was in the hospital that week. Remember?"

"Wow, so it has been since my wedding."

Harmony said, "Nick has been amazing." She lifted her hair off of her neck and let some of the spring breeze cool her off. It surprised her how much hotter Atlanta felt than Nashville. "I know you must miss him."

"Our jobs both have us gone for long stretches." She waved at a blonde girl yelling at her from the top of the slide. "We work on juggling kids between trips and savor every moment we can be together."

Melody nodded. "James splits his year between Atlanta and London. Most of the time, we go with him, but sometimes my schedule doesn't allow it. At that point, all I can say is thank you, God, that my sister lives here and loves my kids." She looked at Harmony. "Will you and Steve keep touring together as a duo, or are you going to launch his solo career?"

Harmony pondered her answer. "We don't know yet. We're still technically honeymooning, so the idea of being apart from him for more than a day or two is wholly unappealing." The ladies laughed. "But I'm sure there'll come a day when we tour separately. I guess it depends on what God has in store for us."

"I think we can all handily say 'Amen' to that," Carol added dryly.

♫ ♫ ♫ ♫

NICK leaned against the marble mantel studying Steve. He kept his voice even and steady. "Your call, brother. You know that. It's been two weeks, and nothing. No notes. No threats. No attacks. We can stand down. Or we can slim down. Or we can pull up stakes completely and leave you and Harmony in peace."

Bobby took a drink of his lemonade. "I don't envy you having to make this decision, but you know you have whatever support you need from us."

Steve tapped his finger on the arm of the couch and looked at James, who had just returned from the kitchen after giving instructions to the caterer. He had trouble reading James. The man looked like he had his head in the clouds, but in reality he took absolutely everything in all the time. "We don't need to talk about this today, James. This is your celebration, after all."

"Sentiment should never interfere with common sense, Steve." James gestured toward the wall of windows that looked out into the backyard. "This is the best time to talk about it. The girls are out there, relaxed and happy, and you're among praying friends in here. This is both the place and the time to seek wise counsel."

"I'm still new at the praying friends network." He cleared his throat. "What, uh, is your gut feeling, Nick?"

Nick silently stared out the window for several seconds before responding. "I'm inclined to feel that no real relief will come until this Bill Rhodes guy is located. The evidence definitely places those three suspects the police have in custody in the van. They are definitely the ones who attacked your concert. Now, they also claim to be the ones who sent the notes. Since their incarceration, you appear to have been left alone. It's possible Rhodes was a rabbit that we started chasing down a blind hole."

"But you don't think so," Bobby observed in his rich baritone voice.

Nick gave a slight shrug of his shoulders. "Just a feeling, but no, I do not."

"If I may interject," James said. "Knowing what it's like to have a wife terrorized by someone, I don't blame you if you want to continue to guard her with diligence for the time being."

Steve nodded. "Harmony told me about what happened to Melody."

"I wasn't speaking of my current wife, actually,"

James said without any trace of emotion. "My first wife, Angela, was brutally murdered along with a number of her coworkers. The same man came after Melody, but he failed to take her life, though his attempt cost him his own."

Nick didn't move. He continued to stare out the window. "Jen shot and killed him, you mean."

James glanced toward Nick but his expression did not change. Jennifer Thorne had worked closely with Nick for years prior to all of those long ago events. She had since married Atlanta Detective John Suarez, who happened to be Aria's older brother. James added, "Regrettably, yes."

Nick allowed himself an ironic grin. "Jen had no regrets."

James turned back to Steve. "That man died without knowing Christ. He didn't have to die that day. He made a poor choice. I feel certain it cost him his eternity."

Steve had only heard of men with this kind of nobility in their hearts. James Montgomery genuinely regretted that the man who had murdered his first wife and terrorized his second wife had died without coming to a place of understanding, acceptance, and salvation. Christ, when beaten to the point of death with spikes driven through the radial nerves of his hands and the dorsal nerves of his feet, then raised up on a cross to suffer and slowly die; Christ had asked His Father God to forgive the very men who did all that to him. In this same way, James was truly Christ-like in his own personal capacity for mercy and grace. In that moment, Steve determined that he would grow and mature in his own faith walk until he came to a similar place of maturity in his spiritual life.

"The man was evil. He left Jen no choice. Believe it," Nick said. "The fact of the matter is, I believe the current threat is real, and I believe the people targeting Harmony are evil. I honestly believe this won't end until they are either all behind bars or dead, but I also believe they are regrouping at the moment. Their next move probably won't come until they think we've let our guard down considerably."

Steve sighed and looked at Nick. "I don't want you to have to be with us any longer than necessary. I mean, I appreciate you and what you do, and I enjoy your company, but your wife and kids would rather have you home, I'm sure."

Nick chuckled. "So you got my first bill?" When Steve opened his mouth to protest, Nick held up his palm. "Just joking. Yes, if we continue surveillance, the best thing I can do is hire someone locally. I can also screen services, and you can have someone escort her when she's not with you, or I can just provide extra security for your tours. Whatever you want. I think we can relax a little bit, keep looking for this Rhodes guy, and stay diligent."

A cook came through the back door carrying a platter of steaks. Smoke from the brick grill in the backyard followed him in. Steve's stomach rumbled and his mouth watered. "That smells amazing."

"You are probably a man who appreciates a good steak at this point, aren't you?" Bobby laughed.

Steve smiled. "I don't mind vegetarian. I've come to enjoy it, actually. However, I can say with certainty that I will never, ever become one."

The men laughed. As the caterer went through the room into the dining room, James stood. "Let's all pray over Steve. Right now. Let's pray protection for Harmony and their unborn child. Let's ask God to give Steve wisdom about all this. I know he feels caught in a catch-22. Let's see if we can help lift his burden."

Bobby removed his cowboy hat and tossed it into his chair. Silently, the men came together and joined hands in a circle of prayer. For a long time, no one spoke as their heads were bowed and their eyes were closed. Then, one by one, they began to pray in turn.

♪ ♪ ♪ ♪

BILL Rhodes pulled the red hood back from his face and looked out at the sea of his disciples. Despite his nakedness beneath the satin robe, sweat dripped down his temples as he walked down the aisle among their applause. Once through the crowd, he slipped through a side door in the back of the abandoned church and found his team of advisers waiting for him.

"How did it go?"

"Our source inside the Atlanta police department says it went without a hitch. Forensics and surveillance cameras back them being in the van. Claiming responsibility for the letter writing makes enough sense that the cops shouldn't look any further."

"Good. Well done." He accepted a bottle of water from an assistant and twisted the top off. "Now, we need to figure out what we want to do next."

"Father, do we want to do anything? The cops got a little too close last time."

Sudden rage surged through Rhodes as he stared at the man who had offered this opinion. He punched the wall and his fist flew through rotted drywall. "Slayer changing sides like that! It can't go ignored! There must be a reckoning!"

Foolishly, the man spoke again. "We didn't ignore it.

We blew up—"

"Silence!" He looked to Charles who stood on his right holding the ceremonial dagger. "Get him out of my presence or I'll find a reason to drain the blood from his body and offer him up as a sacrifice." As Charles and another man ushered the fool away, Bill took a deep, calming breath and announced, "Now, we need to figure out what we want to do next. I think that the appropriate absolution will come in the form of a blood sacrifice. What say you?"

♫ ♫ ♫ ♫

Chapter 30

GRAYSON Harper sat in a leather chair in the sitting room of his father's house. Harmony remembered her grandfather always sitting in that same chair, the patriarch of the family. She looked over at her father as he studied his book. He had just finished a game of chess against her Aunt Dee at a small table by the window. Harmony realized that more and more often, her father had started taking over as the family patriarch.

"How has the investigation gone?" Grayson Harper asked.

"The police feel confident they have the culprits. All three of them plead guilty and will be sentenced sometime next month." Harmony sounded more confident than he felt. Steve reached over and slipped his arm over her shoulders. She snuggled as close to him as her large stomach would allow and continued, "We've toned down the security for now. No reason draining resources when there isn't an open threat."

Grayson nodded. "This certainly has been a trial. How are you holding up, son?"

Harmony felt Steve's arm tense but squeezed his thigh reassuringly as he answered, "I find myself wanting a cigarette more than any of my other vices. However, as the stress has lessened, so has that desire for even a smoke. I feel like if I got through the last few months and stayed clean and sober the whole time, nothing can knock me down now. But, I have to admit, I don't think it was all my doing. I honestly believe the Holy Spirit carried me through the hardest parts."

For a moment, Grayson just stared at him with penetrating eyes, then he nodded once and said, "Indeed. That's what the Holy Spirit will do when you surrender yourself. Knowing what you know, I guess your confidence in your sobriety is as solid as possible." He pointed at Harmony. "And how are you feeling, daughter of mine?"

"Like I'm going to explode. Except, I'm not allowed to for another two months." She shifted her body, uncomfortable. "I don't know how I'm going to handle two more months."

"It's because you're so petite. The baby has nowhere to go but out. Your mother was exactly the same way with Franklin, and even though you were smaller, it was just as bad the second time around."

Harmony couldn't even think of another child after this one right now. "Well, that's encouraging."

Her father grinned. He folded the paper in his lap and set it on the table beside him. "You'll figure out that it's all worth it just as soon as you deliver my grandchild. How's the blood pressure lately?"

"Now that no churches are exploding around me?

Better." She sighed. "I wish we could continue on with the tour, though. We only had three more weeks scheduled. I still think we could have finished up."

"While I think eight venues in three months was just as much as your body would take," Steve said.

"I know. And at the time I agreed. But now I'm restless. Maybe they'll let me sing at church on Sunday just to get my performing fix."

With a chuckle Grayson said, "Maybe."

She smiled and pushed herself to her feet. "Sitting is killing my back. I'm going to go see if mom and grandma need any help in the kitchen."

Franklin stopped her halfway across the room. "Dee and I need five minutes of your time. Steve, too."

"Okay. Sure." She looked over her shoulder and beckoned Steve. He nodded, said a few more words to her father, and joined them. They followed Franklin onto the porch, where they found Aunt Dee sitting at the glass topped table, typing on her laptop. When she saw them, she looked up and smiled.

"What's up?" Steve asked.

"I've been fielding a serious inquiry into producing a major motion picture about your faith journey, Steve, and the more I look at it and the director interested in taking on the production, the more I like the sound of it."

Franklin picked up an envelope that sat on the table. "This is an outline of the proposal. I'd like you two to look it over and pray about it."

Steve's lips thinned as he glanced over the top sheet. "Okay."

"I told them I'd get back with them by the end of the

week," Dee said as she closed her laptop lid and took off her reading glasses.

Franklin added, "I think this would be an amazing story of redemption that could, and likely would, affect the lives of anyone who saw it. This director is Adam Suarez. He is a big name and has a good reputation in both the secular and the Christian markets."

Steve held out his hand and Franklin shook it. "I'll let you know before then."

♫ ♫ ♫ ♫

HARMONY lay back on the couch, her feet in Steve's lap. She closed her eyes and almost purred while he rubbed the swollen appendages. "What do you think about what Aunt Dee and Franklin had for us?"

She cracked open an eye and stole a glance at his very serious face. "I think it would be an absolute invasion of privacy." His hands stilled and she pulled her feet out of his lap. "I imagine that the truth would be told, and that the world will see how bad the bad really was. Are you willing to open yourself up like that?"

He put an elbow on the arm of the couch and fisted his hand, gently tapping his lips with his fist. He didn't answer for several moments. Finally, his hand stilled and he breathed in a deep breath and slowly let it out. "I think that my redemption will give people hope. Either hope for themselves or hope for someone they love—maybe hope for the truth and power of God's word. So, if the cost of that is some invasion of privacy, then shouldn't I be willing to pay that price? What did my personal redemption cost Christ?"

Harmony sat up and shifted closer to him. "Steve, if you feel this is something God wants done, then just tell me how I can help."

He put a hand on her cheek. "You know, it occurs to me that I have done absolutely nothing in my miserable life to deserve you."

With a cheeky grin, she slipped her arms around his neck. "No? Maybe you just banked a big debt to pay off, then."

"Likely." He put his arms around her and pulled her close. "I think this movie is right. I feel like it's right."

"Then we'll go with that." She rested her cheek on his shoulder.

Steve asked, "What about you? What about your privacy?"

She grinned. "I've lived in the public eye my entire life. Invasion of privacy is just part and parcel."

♫ ♫ ♫ ♫

STEVE opened the door and immediately recognized Adam Suarez from the research he'd done on him in the last couple of weeks. He stood as tall as Steve's six-foot height, with dark brown hair worn slightly long, and olive skin. He had on a pair of aviator sunglasses, a green golf shirt with the logo of a sports company embroidered on the chest, and a pair of khaki pants. He slipped his sunglasses off, revealing dark brown eyes, and smiled.

"Mr. Slater? Adam. It's a pleasure to meet you."

"Steve, please," he replied, opening the door wider. "Come in."

Harmony had left with her mother fifteen minutes before, leaving him alone for the first phase of this interview. He led Adam into the living room and gestured at the couch. Steve sat across from Adam in an arm chair.

"So," Steve said, "you aren't Rolling Stone or Playboy. I don't know how this will work."

Adam smiled and pulled out a notebook and a slim digital recorder. "I'm going to let you talk this time. Next time, I'd like to ask specific questions, fine-tune some details, and video record it. But for now, I just want you to tell me about your life. I'll kind of guide you and let you guide me." He set a pen on top of the notebook and said, "But first, it's been a heck of a morning already, and I think I'd like to pray right now."

Steve bowed his head and listened to Adam pray for God's blessing over the project and for the people who could potentially be touched by the message. As the prayer ended, he found himself a little emotionally overwhelmed and slightly panicky. Did he really want to do this?

"Steve, I'll be honest with you. Nick Williams is married to my baby sister, Aria."

He felt only mild curiosity. Steve had never met Aria. Somehow, he thought he might have known that Adam Suarez was related to Nick William's wife. Harmony must have mentioned it at some point. "Okay."

"I want to let you know that your business dealings with Nick are entirely coincidental. He's never broken any confidence, I assure you, and we've never talked about you. Not once."

He raised an eyebrow. "I get the impression Nick is pretty good at keeping secrets."

Adam paused then smiled. "You clearly know him pretty well already. I came across your story when I saw the coverage of the funeral footage for Adolf Judge. I've been neck deep in a project in New Zealand for the last two years, so I haven't been up to date with current celebrity gossip. Once I got the taste of your story, I knew

I needed to tell it. I've never done a movie like this before, but I absolutely feel like the Holy Spirit is driving me. Consequently, I don't get to say no because He's my boss. And, clearly, you must feel the same way."

It surprised him to have his feelings so simply acknowledged. "I initially didn't like the idea, but once I prayed about it, I felt like I had no choice."

Adam nodded and half chuckled. "Glad we're on the same page." He picked up the notebook and pen, then pressed the button on the front of the recorder. "I did some research into your family and discovered that you had a sister who tragically died when you were a teenager. What was she like?"

Instantly, he felt himself mentally transported to the basement of his childhood home. He was twelve, Gracie was six, and she had a little pink play guitar. He helped her put her fingers on the strings as best he could and she got so frustrated with herself for not properly playing the chord. Smiling at the memory, realizing that he just thought of Grace without pain or fear for the first time in over a decade, he settled back in his chair and started talking.

"She was full of light and life. I was six when she was born. I remember holding her in the hospital and just being completely amazed at her little face. All of her life, people were drawn to her. Strangers would smile at her out in public. She was everyone's favorite, and that didn't bother me because she was my favorite, too."

He talked for two hours. Adam filled his notebook with notes. When he reached the last page, he turned off the tape recorder. "I have never really been through this process before," he admitted. "My films are usually products of my own imagination, not the retelling of a real life. This was both easier and harder than I thought it would be."

Steve, weary, rubbed the back of his neck. "It's kind of draining."

"I think this is a good place to stop. Thank you for seeing me so quickly, Steve. I think we are going to do great things in His name."

They stood and started walking toward the door. Steve said, "Franklin and I both agree that now is a good time to get as many of the interviews in the can as possible. I'm kind of in downtime mode until the baby comes."

"Okay. Well, my crew has the reshoots covered in New Zealand and the dailies don't take long. See you tomorrow same time?" When Steve nodded, Adam held out his hand to shake it. "I'll see you then."

♫ ♫ ♫ ♫

HARMONY finished tying a silk scarf the color of dried lilacs around her neck and turned sideways to look at her entire outfit in the mirror. She couldn't believe how big the baby had gotten in just the last three weeks. From her profile, her stomach jutted out. Just five weeks left before her due date. Little excited butterflies danced around in her chest at the thought of finally getting to meet baby Slater.

Steve walked into the bedroom and stopped when he saw her. "I wish you would stay home," he said, carrying on their conversation from the night before.

"It feels good to get out. Besides, I'll be with my mother, grandmother, and aunt. It's not like I'll be alone." She turned from the mirror and picked up her bag. "Adam said he didn't want to talk to me today, so it's better if I just get out of your hair." She walked toward him and stopped, standing on her toes to brush a kiss against his cheek. Her stomach bumped up against him. "I'll be home after lunch."

He set his coffee cup down on the dresser and pulled her into his arms. "I find myself worrying about you when you're not with me. I hope this is just impending fatherhood jitters."

She hugged him tight then pushed away. "I will be perfectly fine." She got her purse off of the bed as her phone signaled a text. "Mom's here with the car. I love you!"

With as much grace as her awkwardly large body could handle, she waddled through the house and out of the front door. As the driver opened the back door for her, she spotted Adam's rental car. She ducked her head into the car and said to her mother, "Give me thirty seconds."

Intercepting Adam on his way to the front door, she held her hand out to him. "It's good to see you," she said. "I saw you're scheduled to talk to me at the offices tomorrow."

"Yes, without Steve," he replied. "I want to bring you guys back together again next Monday and do dual interviews." He gestured at her stomach. "I realize time is becoming somewhat of an issue."

With a laugh, she said, "Hopefully, not a lot of time left. But, if you finish with Steve and me, then you can do all of the peripheral interviews after the baby is born."

"That's exactly the plan."

She gestured at the doorway. "He's waiting for you inside. Have a great day."

As she awkwardly got into the car, she leaned over and kissed her mother on the cheek. "Good morning, mama."

"Good morning, darling." She looked at her watch. "Your Aunt Dee is running late this morning, but your grandmother is already at the studio. She spoke about her upcoming book on the show this morning."

The show aired live starting at nine every morning. "Isn't Dee working with Adam some?"

"I'm not certain what all she's doing. I know they've talked, and Franklin was a part of the talks. He'd know more, or just ask her yourself."

"Yes, ma'am." Harmony looked out of the window and watched the buildings grow closer together as the car approached the downtown area. "I have a final list for you for the baby shower invitations."

"Wonderful. We'll finish mailing those out this morning." She opened her portfolio on the seat between them and pulled out a single sheet of paper. "Speaking of which, the caterers have given us a final menu. I tentatively approved it."

Harmony's eyes skimmed over roasted eggplant, hummus, chickpea salad, and a series of other vegetarian options. "What about pizza?"

Her mother raised a perfectly trimmed eyebrow. "Craving pizza, are we?"

"Like you wouldn't believe," Harmony said with a groan that turned into a laugh.

"I've done this twice, my dear. You'd be surprised what I'd believe." The car rolled to a stop in front of the office building. Alice leaned forward and spoke to the driver. "Do you have any other trips this morning?"

"No, ma'am," he replied.

"Good. Go ahead and park in the garage and stay available on the first floor. If Harmony wants to leave early, I don't want her hindered."

"Mother, I—"

Alice put a hand on hers. "Let me worry and fret over my very pregnant daughter, please." As the door opened, Alice slid out of the car, followed by Harmony. The late spring heat reflected off the sidewalk, rising up in waves, and felt almost like a solid form as she exited from the air conditioned car. As she turned from saying thank you to the driver and headed toward the door, she spotted the chalk drawing of the contorted railroad symbol on the sidewalk. Fear froze her steps. She opened her mouth to speak to her mother, who had kept walking, obviously not realizing Harmony no longer walked next to her.

She heard a feral cry as a woman and a man came from the side of the building, carrying buckets. The woman had hair dyed a bright pink and wore black leggings and a black T-shirt with the railroad symbol airbrushed on in a pink the color of her hair. The man, teenager really, was tall and thin with slicked back brown hair. He wore ripped jeans and an Abaddon shirt.

Before Harmony could move, the woman, screaming obscenities at her, threw the contents of the bucket on her. The warm liquid hit her in the face and chest and immediately all of her senses filled with the smell and taste of blood. Nausea rolled up in her stomach and she found herself on the sidewalk, desperately scraping at her face and helplessly losing the battle against getting sick right then and there as the man dumped his bucket on her head.

Chaos erupted all around. The driver tackled the man to the ground and knocked against Harmony. A leather booted foot kicked her right in the stomach as women screamed and feet ran toward them. She looked up, her vision blurred and red from the blood. She made out a security guard whisking her furious and struggling mother into the building. Another guard raced toward Harmony's assailant with his radio to his mouth. As the first pain enveloped her stomach, she stayed on her knees, wrapping her arms around herself.

♫ ♫ ♫ ♫

STEVE sat back and considered the question Adam just asked. What caused the decision to get sober? "I think," he said slowly, "that it was the fact that I was facing mortality. The doctor had just informed me that the strain on my remaining kidney and my other organs was getting to be too much, and very soon the next time I got high would be the last time. Because I'd been churched as a child, because I knew that Jehovah God was very, very real, and because I knew how fallen and sinful I was, I couldn't die like that. I realized I had to get sober. Now, none of that was conscious thinking or realization. I think it was really more like a spiritual revelation. All of it was on some deeper spiritual level. It's not like I sat on the table in the hospital and thought, 'Gosh. I need to get right with God.' But, in hindsight, I know that's what it was."

Adam nodded and wrote in his notebook. "What did consciously cross your mind?"

As he pondered and tried to remember that July day, his phone rang. He recognized Franklin's number and rejected the call. What crossed his mind? "A desire to be someone else. I hated the man I was, the sinner I was. No. Hate isn't right. Like, I loathed myself." Again, his phone rang, and this time he recognized Grayson's number. As he rejected the call, a text came through in the preview screen.

HARMONY HAS BEEN ATTACKED. ANSWER YOUR PHONE.

Without a word to Adam, he answered the next call before his phone even had a chance to fully ring. "What happened?"

"She was attacked on the sidewalk in front of the office. She's being taken to the hospital. I don't know anything else." Franklin spoke very rushed. "I'm about to get on the elevator. Just meet us there. I'll text you the address."

He looked at Adam, almost surprised to see him there. "I have to go." As he stood, he dialed Nick Williams' number.

"Williams."

"Harmony was attacked."

"I know. I'm en route. I'm two hours away if traffic is moving on I-24 when I hit it."

Adam followed him to the door. "Would you like for me to drive you?"

For a moment, the words didn't make sense through the buzzing in his ears. Finally, he shook his head to clear it and patted the pockets of his shorts. He didn't have keys. "Yes, please."

♫ ♫ ♫ ♫

DESPITE the fact that she had taken a long, hot shower, she still felt like she could taste and smell the blood. She had scrubbed at her nose so much that the skin felt raw to the touch. Now, all she could smell was the very distinctive smell of the "fragrance free" hospital soap. She'd thrown up five or six times and still felt sicker than she'd ever felt in her life.

Contractions came every six or seven minutes. She turned her head and stared at the paper slowly running through the fetal monitor. The graph showed the spike of contractions and the baby's heart rate. If possible, she would will the contractions to go away entirely. Instead, she watched the needle start to jerk as she felt her muscles tightening in her abdomen.

With both hands on either side of her belly, she lay her head back and closed her eyes, breathing slowly, deeply, and intentionally. After a few minutes, her muscles started to relax. When she opened her eyes again, her mother stood next to her bed. Suddenly, she felt sorry for herself. "Why is this happening?" she asked, hot tears filling her eyes. "What have I done to bring this on myself? I've always been good. I've always done what's right."

"Harmony, darling, you have done nothing. You're not being punished. You're being attacked." Alice leaned forward and put both hands on her shoulders. "Please don't think that you have somehow done anything wrong."

Tears slipped out of her eyes and ran down her temples. Closing her mouth to try to hold back a sob, she breathed in through her nose and smelled blood. As her stomach rolled with nausea, she scrambled for the bedpan. Alice held her hair as she got sick again. Only, nothing remained in her stomach, so she dry-heaved until she didn't think she could stand the pain.

Sad, miserable, and scared, she leaned back against the pillow. Alice picked up the washcloth that had fallen to the side and stepped into the bathroom. A second later, Harmony could hear the water in the sink. Her door burst open, and Steve rushed in.

"What happened?" he asked, a look of frantic panic covering his face. "Harmony, Princess, what happened? Are you okay?"

Self-loathing welled up inside of her and she turned her head away from him. "I don't want you here."

He reached out and brushed at her temple and she

slapped his hand away, pushing herself up on her elbows. Even as she spoke, even as the words spewed out of her, she knew she didn't mean what she said, but some stupid pregnant hormonal surge made the vileness come out of her anyway. "This is all *your* fault. Get out! Go away. Don't come back."

He straightened. An angry stony look crossed his face. Her breath hitched in her throat as she realized she had said the same thing his parents said to him after Grace died. He pivoted on his heel and stormed out of the room as Alice came out of the bathroom. With a sob, Harmony said, "Mama, stop him. I can't believe I said that!"

She watched as Alice rushed out of the hospital room.

♫ ♫ ♫ ♫

Chapter 32

S **TEVE** heard his mother-in-law calling to him, but did not slow his pace or turn around. He rushed through the halls. "Steve! Don't make me chase you. I'm too old to run. Stop!"

Instead of waiting for an elevator, he threw the stairwell door open and took the flight down two at a time. Soon, he couldn't hear Alice anymore.

It was all his fault. Of course it was. He was a worthless human being not worthy of someone as good and kind as Harmony Harper. If he had left her alone in Oregon years ago, she wouldn't be lying in a hospital bed after being attacked by his groupies.

He didn't deserve her.

With long strides, he burst out of the hospital stairwell door and into the Nashville sunshine. Adam had dropped him at the front door and driven off to find a parking space. He had no one and nothing but the shirt on his back and the cash in his wallet. Without plan or purpose, he walked along the hot sidewalk for over an hour. His phone rang in his pocket almost continually. Without even pulling it out, he finally reached inside his pocket and powered it off.

Turning a corner, he saw the crime scene tape, bloody sidewalk, and the flashing lights of police cars in front of the Harper Ministries office building. He hadn't even realized the direction he'd walked until he arrived right there on that very spot.

Detective Nadine Cox ducked under the tape and came toward him. "Mr. Slater."

"What happened?" he demanded.

"Two Railroad groupies threw buckets of fresh goat blood on Harmony. When her driver tried to restrain the man, he kicked Harmony in the stomach. We have them both in custody. They're charged with everything from animal cruelty to aggravated assault to littering." She narrowed her eyes at him. "Why are you here instead of there?"

"Good question." He looked at the chalk drawing of the railroad symbol. "How does this stop?"

Her phone rang in her hand. Patting him on the shoulder, she said, "Head of the snake," before turning away and answering.

Heat pounded up at him from the pavement and his mouth felt so dry. His head hung and his eye caught the stylized snake tattoo that coiled around his right arm. He knew he had another serpent on his back. Head of the snake? Would that be Railroad or would that be Steven Slayer? Which head needed to be severed to end this? With laser like precision, he raised his head and his eyes took in the nearby forbidden fruit.

Knowing that every step he took, he took a wrong step in the wrong direction, he crossed the busy street and stepped into the sports bar on the corner. The dim, cool interior provided a welcoming relief from the harsh, bright noonday sun. He slid onto a worn leather stool and nodded at the bartender. "Single malt. Top shelf. Neat."

The bartender showed him the green glass bottle and, after Steve nodded his approval, uncorked it. "Make it a double," he ordered. As the bartender poured the amber liquid, Steve reached into his pocket for his wallet. Instead of cash, he pulled out the gold coin that he'd received on his 18-month sobriety date. With a sigh, he set that on the bar and picked up the glass of Scotch.

♫ ♫ ♫ ♫

HARMONY sent text number thirty to Steve.

I LOVE YOU. I'M STUPID AND SORRY. PLEASE COME BACK.

Still no reply. She gripped her phone in her hand as if her life depended on it and sniffled as fresh tears fell down her cheeks.

"Honey, you really must calm down," Alice said, stroking her hair. "Right now the most important thing you can do is calm down."

"Mama," Harmony said, "I was absolutely stupid. I have no idea where those words came from. What if he—"

"His actions are not your responsibility. Steve has to make his own choices despite what happens around him." She wiped her daughter's face with a cool rag. "But nothing will help if your blood pressure doesn't come down. You have to calm down. Get ahold of yourself for the baby's sake, Harmony."

The on-call doctor came into the room then, reading notes from a tablet he carried. "Contractions have slowed down. I conferred with your OB, Willis. We're not really comfortable sending you home, just yet. We're going to keep you here for at least tonight, if not longer. I want to see your blood pressure stabilize a bit." He typed something on the tablet then finally looked at Harmony. "Are you in some kind of pain?"

She pressed her lips together and shook her head. "Nothing physical."

"Okay. That's good. Very well, then." He cleared his throat and tapped her on the foot. "I'll send the nurse in if you'd like. Otherwise, I'll see you in the morning."

As he walked back out of the room, Alice stared at his retreating back. "Could have a little more bedside manner, couldn't he?"

"I don't think he was expecting the emotional mess he saw when he looked at me." She stared at her still silent phone and willed Steve to call. "I want to calm down, mama. I really do. Will you please pray with me?"

Alice took both her hands and nodded. "I will. Then I will take your phone away from you and I will bring it back tomorrow."

"But, mama!"

"But, you need to rest and quit checking your phone every four seconds. And I'm going to tell you something. Sending him four hundred texts is not going to help this situation. He knows where you are. I will send him a message and let him know I have your phone. Now," she said on a sigh, "close your eyes and imagine yourself entering the throne room of God."

Alice's voice lulled her into the imagery of her kneeling in God's presence. This helped wipe away any worry and thoughts she still had in her mind. God was bigger than anything she might face. His presence is what changed Steve's life, not hers. As her mother's prayer surrounded her, with an inner voice she added more, begging God to protect her husband and bring him back to her, whole and forgiving.

♪ ♪ ♪ ♪

STEVE spun the coin on the bar and watched it form a perfect spinning top precession. It looked like a solid oval mass until it started to slow and wobble, and suddenly the edges of the top could be clearly made out until it finally fell to the bar and clattered before it stilled completely.

He ignored the man who slid into the seat next to him until he spoke. "So, what's good here?"

Surprised, he turned to stare into the ice cold blue eyes of Nick Williams.

"How—"

"Detective Cox saw you come in." He set his sunglasses on the bar next to the sobriety coin and laced his fingers. "Two hours ago."

Steve picked up the coin again and set it spinning. "That long? I always did lose track of time in bars."

"I'd probably buy that if you'd actually had anything to drink besides that ice water." He gestured at the coin. "What's stopping you?"

He sighed and slapped his hand down on top of the coin. "The concept that my sobriety is not connected to the matter of whether my heart is intact or not."

"That bad, huh?" Nick let out a low whistle then

reached out and took the glass of Scotch. "Man. That's the good stuff, too. I admire your restraint." Leaning forward, Nick set the glass on the bartender's ledge under the bar. "I'm happy you didn't drink, Steve. Now, let's get you a decent meal, no bar food, then we'll head on over to the hospital."

"I'm not going to the hospital," he admitted. "Harmony doesn't want me there."

"Funny," Nick said. "You really don't look stupid, and here I was impressed with how smart you were for not drinking."

Steve sighed.

"Of. Course. Your wife. Wants you there. Husband." Nick leaned forward until his nose nearly touched Steve's. "Let me tell you something about pregnant women." He put his hand on the back of Steve's neck and gripped it firmly, as if proactively stopping him from moving his head back. "They're a little bit insane. Part of the time, they don't even know what their mouth is saying until it's said. Their hormones surge and their emotions go completely out of control, then suddenly snap back. Then their emotions are even more out of control because of the stupid thing they just said."

"Are you serious?"

Nick sat back. "Have you noticed that Harmony has been acting a little scatterbrained lately? A little forgetful? You told her something and she forgot it minutes later? She's asked you the same question over and over? Annoying, isn't it?"

Steve sat back, his eyes widening. "Holy cow!"

"It's called 'pregnant brain,' brother. Or 'placenta brain,' but I think that sounds gross. Thing is, every man who has ever lived with a pregnant woman knows what it is."

"I didn't know! Nobody said a word. Is there a book or something?"

Nick grinned. "Harmony wants you there, even if her pregnant mouth said otherwise."

"I…"

"You'll listen to the man whose wife has done this three times. Three." He let Steve go and sat back in the stool. "Honestly, I'd rather have a showdown with IRA terrorists in Belfast than cope with an upset pregnant Aria." He slid off the bar stool and slipped his sunglasses on. "And I've done both, so I know what I'm talking about. Let's go. There's a really great Italian place on the next block. Looks like a dive on the outside. Best chicken parm in this hemisphere inside."

♫ ♫ ♫ ♫

Chapter 33

HARMONY lay back against the pillow, silent tears streaking out of the corners of her eyes and soaking her hair and the pillowcase. In her mind, she cursed her vile tongue. How could she have said that to the man she adored so much? If only she had let him comfort her, he wouldn't be in some unknown place. He'd be sitting right there next to her bed, holding her hand, making them both feel better.

Stupid woman. Ugh!

She fisted her hand and pounded the mattress. Why?

A light tap-tap on her door made her heart soar. Maybe he'd come back! Maybe he would accept her absolutely sincere apology and forgive her for lashing out at him— the person she loved most in the world.

The sight of the nurse in the pink and blue scrubs coming into the room made her heart fall again. She couldn't even find the energy to smile at her.

"Hi. I'm Jill. Keeping your breathing slow and

steady?"

Nurse Jill gently took her wrist and stared at the monitors.

"I'm fine. I'm just upset with myself," Harmony said, sounding like she may sob at any moment.

"Try to relax. The doctor prescribed you a light magnesium drip to try to get that blood pressure down," she said, pulling a syringe out of her pocket.

Harmony looked at the dark window and back at the nurse as she frowned. "I thought that was what that bag hanging there was. Why would he change something so late?"

Jill pointed toward her monitors as if they meant anything to Harmony. "You're not really responding. Doc wants a higher dose." She fiddled with Harmony's IV tubing, then injected the contents of the syringe into the tube in one even movement. "He just came out of labor and delivery, or we would have gotten word hours ago."

Harmony felt whatever was in the syringe hit her blood stream. It felt really hot in the veins of her arm, like acid or lava. As the prickly warmth flooded up her arm and spread across her shoulder to her chest, she spotted the Railroad tattoo on the inside of the nurse's wrist and finally and correctly interpreted the gloating smile on the woman's face.

"Nighty-night, HARM-ony," Jill sneered.

Just as Harmony opened her mouth to scream, her world went completely black.

♫ ♫ ♫ ♫

STEVE sat in the waiting room next to Alice. Her shoulders shook with silent sobs while her husband stood with his hands in his pockets, his back to the room, still as a statue staring out into the black night. Nick sat across the room on a green vinyl couch, typing into a tablet. Next to him, Franklin sat with his elbows on his knees, face resting in his hands, silently praying. The door opened and Detective Nadine Cox rushed in.

"Here's what I know," she announced, "and I'm going to give you all the details despite protocol, because I know I'd personally be going a little crazy at this moment myself." She pulled out a notebook. "The duty nurse was found unconscious on the floor behind the desk by another nurse returning from dinner break. Harmony is gone. Her bed was found at the door of the ambulance bay. That same symbol we've been seeing was written on the white board in her room. The guard on duty in the security office was also found unconscious, and all recordings for the last two hours have been wiped clean. We are currently working with the security staff to see if any of the hourly upload to the off-site backup location happened before they wiped the drives."

The despair that gripped his chest felt almost physical. What could they do?

"Nick said we could have traced her phone, but I—" Alice's breath hiccupped into a sob. With shaking hands, she pulled Harmony's phone out of her purse. "I took it away from her."

"Taking it from her was the right thing to do." Steve surged to his feet. "She needed to calm down."

"She needed you here!" Alice slapped her hand over her mouth and looked shocked at the words that came out of her mouth.

Franklin stood. "Mother—"

Steve pursed his lips and replied, "She's right. Instead,

I was sitting in a bar—"

At Alice's gasp, Nick interrupted him. "Not drinking." He glanced up at Steve. "Heck, not even smoking. Lest we inadvertently give anyone the wrong idea."

"No one needs to be given any idea," Steve said. Self-disgust roared inside his chest. "There's nothing they can think that's worse than the reality. The things I—"

"The reality is," Nadine interrupted, "that we have traffic cameras working on finding whatever vehicle took her away. If any of you hear from her kidnappers, come find me while you're still on the phone, if at all possible. I will be with my team down the hall, but the officer at the door will know where I am at all times." She put her hand on the door knob and surveyed the room. "I understand the level of anxiety and stress in this room right now. Turning on each other will help exactly no one. I encourage you to band together and pray rather than lash out at each other."

After she left the room, Steve took a deep breath and slowly let it out. He paced to the far side of the room and sat away from the group. Slipping both hands into his pockets, he slumped down in the chair and stretched his legs out in front of him. *God*, he prayed silently, *help me. Please.*

The door opened again and Chaz came in. He scanned the room, looking at each Harper before zeroing in on Steve. "Dude, what can I do?" he asked, holding his hand out. Out of habit, Steve took it, surprised to feel a piece of paper in Chaz's hand. Palming it from him, he slipped his hands back into his pockets and shrugged.

"I don't know what we can do," he said. "We don't know anything. Maybe if we knew something." He pushed himself to his feet. "I'm going to go find a cup of coffee. Anyone want anything?"

Nick set his tablet in his bag. "I'll come with you."

"I don't need a babysitter," he crossed the room and put his hand on the doorknob, "or a drink. I just need coffee. I can go by myself."

Nick raised an eyebrow, but didn't say anything. Relieved, Steve slipped out of the room and nodded to the uniformed police officer sitting in a chair next to the door. "I'm going to get coffee. Would you like some?"

"I'm good, thank you sir," the uniformed officer answered.

Steve strode down the hall and casually pulled the note out of his pocket. In Chaz's chaotic handwriting, he read:

THEY TEXTED ME. NO COPS OR SHE'S DEAD. WAREHOUSE ON BRANON STREET NEAR THE DOCKS. ALONE

Heart racing furiously, he walked to the elevators as slowly and calmly as he could manage. He nodded to the various detectives and police officers he saw, and hit the down button. As soon as he stepped into the elevator, he furiously hit the "close door" button, worried someone would follow him. When the doors slid shut, he breathed a sigh of relief and closed his eyes. Now to get to Branon Street.

♫ ♫ ♫ ♫

HARMONY lay perfectly still, her eyes closed, terror beating in her heart. She could smell the sick smell of burning incense. The odor overpowered her until she felt like she couldn't escape the smell. Somewhere far away she could hear the sound of one of Abaddon's songs. Even through the distance, she recognized Steve's voice singing. Someone sat near her bed. She could hear the recognizable sounds of haptic feedback on the screen of a smart phone. The way the sound moved in the building, she knew someone had moved her from the hospital, but fear kept her from opening her eyes and discovering her surroundings.

Thick leather straps chafed her wrists. When she tried to move her legs, she felt the same material on her ankles. They'd strapped her to this bed. A faint headache started vibrating in her temples and a contraction gripped her stomach. What would happen to her? What would they do to the baby?

"Anything?" A man's voice echoed in the large space around them. Harmony almost jumped, but forced herself to lie still.

"She's been awake about ten minutes but HARM-ony's pretty good at playing 'possum." A woman roughly nudged her shoulder. "Ain't that right, Princess?"

The mocking tone of Steve's nickname for her scared her as much as the straps binding her limbs. Defeated, she opened her eyes. She immediately recognized the woman who had taken her from the hospital. She still wore the nurse's uniform. As Harmony turned her head to look at the man, she saw the high ceiling, metal joists, concrete flooring, and metal walls of the warehouse. A man in jeans and a tan T-shirt stood at the foot of her bed. He had black hair pulled back from his face and a black goatee. From the angle she looked at him, his eyes looked black to her.

"Well, good morning," he said with a smile that did nothing to warm his face or eyes. "Glad to see she didn't overdose you with the sedative. We'd prefer to have you awake for this." Her tongue felt thick. She opened her mouth to ask a question, but the fog in her brain from whatever drug the nurse had given her stilled her thoughts like sludge in a stale pond. He clucked his tongue in a sympathetic manner. "Lightweight, aren't you? No worries. You'll probably be thankful for the dulling drug when we perform our ceremony." He squeezed her foot as if to comfort her. "Slayer will be here soon. Then we can get started."

He clapped his hands loudly. "Where is my altar boy?"

"Here, Father," a young voice answered. Harmony watched as a tall, lanky teenager with slicked back brown hair came into her line of sight. He wore a black robe and carried an unlit candelabra. "I'm setting up the altar to your precise specifications. We're almost ready."

"Well done, Charles." He cupped the boy's cheeks with both of his hands. "You will be rewarded."

"Thank you, Father," the boy whispered. When he looked at Harmony, she felt the hate emanating from him, felt a chill settle over her. "But I will have reward enough."

The man let the boy go and he moved out of her line of sight again. "Who says kids in this generation don't have a good work ethic?" he laughed. "Now you," he said, patting Harmony's foot again, "just chill. Hubby will be here soon and then we'll get the real party started." He looked at the nurse. "Go ahead and start the Pitocin."

Panic surged through her and she fought against the straps. Pitocin would put her body into full labor. Tears fell from her eyes as the man laughed and walked away. The woman next to her spoke. "You did real good. Best to just keep quiet, let him talk."

Finally, her tongue reconnected to her brain. "Jill, why are you doing this?"

The woman giggled. "You are really dumb, aren't you? My name isn't really Jill."

"Why is this happening?" she asked, her voice low and

hoarse.

"Atonement," she said matter-of-factly. She fiddled with the IV bags hanging next to Harmony's bed. Her task complete, she settled back into her chair and picked up her phone again. "You'll understand in time."

♫ ♫ ♫ ♫

Chapter 34

STEVE stood at the entrance to the street and stared at the warehouse. An overgrown railroad track ran along the side of it and just stopped at the road. End of the line.

Early morning darkness settled around him. He could hear something rustling in a bush along the edge of the railroad track. Frogs, crickets, and night birds fought with each other to see who could make the loudest cry.

A light shone from a high window. He knew Harmony was inside that building, but he didn't know anything else. Would walking in blind and unarmed be the wisest decision? Should he call Nick and wait for the professionals?

No. The note said no cops. Come alone. He couldn't risk them killing Harmony over his inability to follow their simple directions. That didn't stop him from turning his location settings on his phone on and setting the phone on the ground. He imagined Nick had already started to search for it.

Taking a deep breath, then whispering a desperate prayer for courage and protection, he walked up to the warehouse door. It sat propped open by a broken brick. Someone had spray-painted the contorted railroad symbol on the door in red paint. Drips of paint looked like dripping dark blood in the faint light generated from a distant street lamp.

All of his senses heightened, he pushed the door open and walked into the warehouse. For a moment, he saw Harmony in a hospital bed in the center of the room. She had her head thrown back, panting, as sweat poured from her face. He could see her arms stretched out wide, connected with leather to chains fastened to pillars on either side of her. Taking a deep breath, she screamed in agony.

Steve stepped forward. The room plunged into darkness, the only light coming from the candles in stands and candelabra all around Harmony. From the far side of the room, he saw a cloaked figure carrying another candle walking in his direction. Confused, scared, angrier than he had ever been in his life, he rushed toward Harmony.

He reached her, placing a hand on her soaking head. She jerked and screamed then looked at him, recognizing him.

"Steve!" She gasped and her whole body tightened up. Panting through gritted teeth she said, "They induced labor." Moments later, she relaxed. "Contractions are on top of each other. I don't know how long I can—" before she could finish her sentence, she tensed up with another contraction and a low groan emanated out of her throat.

He put his hand on the buckle of the leather strap around her wrist when a woman in scrubs stepped into the circle of light, a scalpel in her hand. She placed it against Harmony's neck and said, "Move back. I don't mind killing her. I can get the baby out in time." He could see the railroad tattoo on her wrist.

"You might want to listen to her. She's killed hundreds of unborn children over the course of her career," Bill Rhodes said from somewhere in the darkness.

"Thousands," the woman corrected, then gave the skin on Harmony's neck a little cut. It bled more than Steve thought a cut that size could bleed.

"Apologies, my child. I don't mean to diminish your accomplishments."

Horrified at the words, unable to comprehend exactly what they meant, Steve raised his hands to show that he wouldn't touch the buckle again while he looked around him, frantically trying to figure out a way to get them out of there.

"We're so happy you could join us," the cloaked figure of Bill Rhodes said, finally reaching them.

"Railroad?"

He pushed his red hood off. "In the flesh." He laughed as if he'd made a joke that only he understood. "I know the show seems a bit—dramatic," he set his candle down on the table next to the bed, "but my lord likes the drama. It makes the younger followers feel like they're truly engaging him."

Harmony screamed through her teeth. Railroad clicked his tongue. "Poor girl. If only her puny deity could save her. But you know what? Jehovah doesn't really care what happens to his followers here in this world. Didn't even care about His own Son, come to think of it."

Rhodes patted her bare foot with the dry skin on his

left hand and Harmony, even through the pain of the contraction, jerked her body, trying to get away from his touch. "You know, Princess, daughter of your uncaring King, you're only experiencing this painful labor right now because your buddy Yahweh punished Eve for her crime of seeking knowledge. Don't you know that? Her so-called *sin* made him punish all women with the pain of childbirth from that day forward."

"I'm experiencing labor right now because you nutcases kidnapped me and drugged me!" Harmony yelled.

Rage poured through every cell in Steve's body. "What are you doing?"

Railroad snapped his fingers and held out his hand. The woman in the nurse's uniform handed him a purple blanket lined with gold thread, then went back to her station at Harmony's head, scalpel at the ready. "Why, I'm heralding a prince into the world. Then I'm going to sacrifice that prince to my lord on the stone altar I've built. My master has loved child sacrifices since the dawn of time. This will please him, and then your debt will be repaid."

"My debt?"

"Steve—" Harmony's whole body tensed up and she fought the restraints holding her arms out. "Oh God, please help me," she prayed.

"Your abandonment of Abaddon destroyed a very lucrative career." He unzipped his red gown and slipped it off his shoulders. Steve wanted to recognize him so that all of the pieces would fall into place, but the truth was, he didn't know this man.

"That's a load. People leave bands all the time." He looked all around for some weapon he could use.

"Yes, but they don't very publicly leave Abaddon for Jehovah God." He spat out the last word like it tasted vile on his tongue. "You didn't just leave. We could have recovered if you had kept the faith, dude. But no! You publicly switched sides. People started looking to you as some kind of role model, started turning to Yahweh in droves. They were clinging to your putrid testimony. And exactly what were you doing? Making an idol of your wife? Your wealth? Your fame?" He put his hands on either side of Harmony's belly and closed his eyes. "Soon, child, you will be born."

Harmony screamed and struggled.

Railroad continued, "I have covens in every major city. Followers and disciples listened to my every word. I carried drugs and product from city to city. I only had to say the words and I had money, women—" He looked at Steve with vicious hatred. "And then you stopped. You disappeared. For months, no one went anywhere. I still traveled to each location, but without your band backing me up, it all felt very watered down. Then it came to me. Your music fed their souls. Your arenas were their tabernacles. No one else could generate the kind of mindless worship you could.

"Despite everything I am and could do, you were the catalyst, the center, for my followers. And then you made your little announcement."

He screamed the next words, stabbing a finger in Steve's face, eyes wild, nostrils flaring. "My world fell apart! You will *apologize* to the world, denounce your uncaring god, and reclaim your rightful position with Abaddon. Or we can sacrifice your child. That will cleanse your offense. That will even the score. Those are your only two options."

Harmony wailed and cried out to God for help. Steve's mind whirred as he tried to process all he had just learned.

"The altar is ready, Master," a teenager in a black robe announced from the edge of the circle of candles.

"Wonderful, Charles, let's make the final preparations." He turned his back on Steve and Harmony and walked away with the boy. The nurse walked over to a portable cabinet and opened the top drawer. Steve took the opportunity to put his forehead to Harmony's. "I'm going to get you out of this, Princess," he whispered, fiddling with the buckle on the leather strap. As soon as he freed her arm, she threw it around him and sobbed. Reaching over her body, he unstrapped her other arm and found himself held tight against her.

"Don't you dare turn your back on God. No matter what," she said, her teeth clenched in a contraction. "No matter *what*, Steve. Remember Isaac and Abraham."

The nurse stood at the foot of her bed. "I'm going to check you now. I think you might be ready to push."

"Don't you touch me," Harmony shrieked. "I'll tell you when I have to push."

The nurse lifted an eyebrow. "You're hardly in a position to give me orders." She unstrapped Harmony's feet and Harmony immediately kicked her in the mouth. She stepped back, a shocked look crossing her face. Spitting out blood, she stepped forward again, scalpel gripped in her fist. "Why you little—"

Before Steve could talk himself out of it, he balled his hand into a fist and punched her as hard as he could right in the jaw. Her eyes widened in shock a split second before she fell to the floor. He turned back to Harmony, who ripped the IV out of her arm and sat up, clutching her stomach. "Let me help you," he said, bending to scoop her up.

"No, I have to stand. I have to walk. The pain is so bad." She stood up then turned and used the bed to support herself as she breathed through another contraction.

"We have to get out of here," he insisted, looking around but seeing nothing beyond the dim candlelight. "I don't know how much time we have."

"You have no time." Railroad stepped back into the circle of light, back to wearing his red hood. The teen appeared next to him, his black hood pulled up over his face. He clutched a long knife in both hands.

With a roar, Steve grabbed an iron candelabra and swung it like a baseball bat. The heavy base hit Railroad across his stunned face less than a second before he fell down. With a feral roar, the teenager lifted the knife and charged. Swinging the candle stand again, Steve knocked the knife out of the youth's hand. He heard it clang and skid across the concrete floor.

The teen roared in pain and fell to his knees, clutching the arm struck by the iron candelabra. Almost without thinking, Steve attacked him, throwing him all the way to the ground. As he pressed on the screeching teenager's back, the overhead lights came on, flooding the room with a harsh fluorescent light. Steve blinked and squinted while his eyes adjusted to the brightness. He heard shouted orders and the chirp of radios. He looked at Harmony, who leaned against the bed, crying and panting.

"Sounds like the cavalry just rode over the hill, Princess," he said.

She turned her head to look at him and her eyes widened. She screamed, "Steve!" a second before intense pain flooded his lower back.

Something felt very wrong. It almost felt as if he had just had the kidney pulled from his body again, but different. The pain was so immediate and intense that he didn't really react to it. His shirt and pants began to feel warm and wet. Suddenly, staying upright didn't seem so important and he felt himself relaxing, falling. As he fell forward, he heard a gunshot and Railroad landed on the ground beside him. Steve slowly reached behind him. His fingertips felt the handle of a long dagger sticking out of his back. He looked down and saw the blood covered sharp tip of the blade extending out from his stomach about an inch.

"Don't!" Nick yelled, rushing forward. He kept the gun in his hand trained on Railroad. "Don't mess with it, Steve. I know it feels completely wrong but leave it in. Leave it right where it is. Let doctors take it out."

He knelt next to Railroad's body, the muzzle pointed at the man's skull while he fingered his neck. As soon as he confirmed the absence of a pulse, Nick slipped his gun into his shoulder holster and retrieved a thick zip tie from somewhere. "Looks like someone just made some pretty permanent poor decisions."

As Nick approached, Steve slid off of the teenager's back, sitting next to the boy who struggled as Nick used a zip tie to secure his wrists. "Try not to move, Steve. Take slow, deep, even breaths."

"This is nothing. I've had worse cuts." Steve started to chuckle at his own ironic humor, but the pain stopped him. He wondered if he was going into shock. He looked down and watched as his very own hot blood spread across the front of his shirt and stained his blue jeans. He felt dizzy and looked up at his wife. "Harmony," he whispered as his vision tunneled. She used the bed as a support to work her way to him, then knelt on the ground next to him.

"It's over, Steve," she sobbed, wrapping her arms around his neck.

The area flooded with police officers. As the EMT's arrived, Detective Cox knelt next to Steve and looked at the teenager's face on the ground next to him. "Well, Charles Galton. Nice to meet you. I have a Federal warrant for your arrest for the attempted murder of your parents and the arson of their home." She grabbed him by the upper arm and hauled him to his feet. He jerked and kicked at her, snarling like a wild animal. "Of course, we'll have to bring charges against you here, first, before we send you on back to California."

With the help of a uniformed officer, she took the kicking and screaming boy out of the building as the EMT's wheeled Steve to the ambulance escorted by Harmony, who had to stop just once and pant through a contraction.

♫ ♫ ♫ ♫

"YOU know, Mr. Slater, if you had a kidney right there, we'd be having a very different conversation," the doctor said. "Actually, I'd probably be having one with your widow." He typed something into the computer suspended near the bed. "I'm going to have the nurse bring you something for the pain."

"No." Steve sat up and swung his legs over the side of the bed. The pain nearly overwhelmed him as sweat broke out over his body. "I don't want anything."

"Uh, yes you do. You were just stabbed in the back with a ten-inch blade," the doctor said, turning to find Steve standing on shaking legs. "You are going to want pain relief."

"No, I'm not. I've been in worse pain before, and in

the same general area of my abdomen as you could tell, but I don't want any drugs." He modestly held the back of his hospital gown closed with one hand and made his way to his feet. He held onto the bed for dear life with the other.

"Mr. Slater, we can give you non-addictive medications."

"Doc, thanks for getting that blade out of me. I honestly appreciate it. But now I find that you aren't listening to me. So, let me be clear. I don't want any drugs. None. What I want is directions to the delivery room. My wife's having a baby."

The doctor stared at him, obviously seeing the determination on his face. Finally, he nodded. "Let an orderly take you in a wheelchair. I don't want you collapsing and ruining three hours' worth of world-class surgery."

♫ ♫ ♫ ♫

STEVE reached over and ran a finger along his infant son's perfect cheek. Little Isaac never moved, secure in his tight swaddling. Harmony leaned forward and rested her head against Steve's shoulder. He sat back and slipped his arm over her shoulders, moving slowly and gingerly, afraid to move too fast because of the pain any movement caused.

"He's so beautiful," she whispered.

"You're beautiful. He's handsome. Like his dad."

Harmony grinned. "You are handsome. Like it makes my heart stop sometimes."

Steve pressed his lips against Harmony's temple and closed his eyes, inhaling the smell of her shampoo. When he felt like he could speak, he said, "I'm so sorry all of this happened."

She shook her head. "You weren't the cause of any of it. It was evil, pure and simple, attacking us. Attacking God." She looked up at him, her eyes swimming with tears. "I'm the one who's sorry. I was stupid, and crazy, and stupid—"

To shut her up, he kissed her. "And beautiful, and wonderful, and forgiven." He gave her another long kiss before he pulled away.

"It's truly over now, right?"

Pulling her tightly to him, he looked at Isaac and nodded. "Head of the snake," he whispered.

♫ ♫ ♫ ♫

THE old oaks standing guard over the granite stones offered protection from the September sun. A light breeze blew the leaves and a wind chime sang somewhere in the distance. It provided a lovely yet melancholy ambiance to the somber feeling of the graveyard.

Harmony spread the blanket on the ground and settled down, putting baby Isaac in the cradle of her folded legs. She looked at the polished marble headstone.

SHERI ROSE MERCER

BELOVED SISTER AND DAUGHTER

STAR

As a tearful smile lit up her face, Harmony reached into her bag. "Hey Sheri. I have been dying to know how this book ends. We never did get to finish it."

As she flipped to the last chapter of the book, she leaned forward as if conspiratorially. "I don't know if you paid attention to the news or anything, but I found my Almanzo. He's exactly what we described. Tall, blond, with a beautiful heart. I think you would be proud and I know you would have loved him. And, Sheri, his tattoos really aren't that gross." Taking the moment to press her lips to baby Isaac's sweet smelling head, she shifted to a more comfortable position, cleared her throat, and began reading the last chapter of *These Happy Golden Years*. "Little Gray Home in the West...."

THE END

French words/phrases

maître d'—also, *maître d' hotel*, meaning headwaiter, or majordomo. Person who runs a large house. One who runs an organization or project.

Jargon

amscray—pig-latin for scram

ricki-tick—immediately. Phrase popularized by US Infantrymen during the Vietnam war sounds similar to the Vietnamese words for "now."

Latin words/phrases

mortem—death

diaboli—devil

sanguinem—blood

poenitentiam—penance

rogabitque—atonement

Deprecamur, ut sanguis—We bring you blood

Deprecamur, ut in carne—We bring you flesh

Nos vobis inimicus—We bring you your enemy

♫ ♫ ♫ ♫

Discussion Questions

SUGGESTED questions for a discussion group surrounding *A Harmony for Steve*, part 4 of the *Song of Suspense* series.

In bringing those He ministered to into an understanding of the truth, Our Lord used fiction in the form of parables to illustrate very real truths. In the same way, we can minister to one another by the use of fictional characters and situations to help us to reach logical, valid, cogent, and very sound conclusions about our real lives here on earth.

While the characters and situations in the *Song of Suspense* series are fictional, I pray that these extended parables can help readers come to a better understanding of truth. Please prayerfully consider the questions that follow, consult scripture, and pray upon your conclusions. May the Lord of the universe richly bless you.

♫ ♫ ♫ ♫

Discussing her desire to help Steven stay sober, Harmony Harper told her mother that the Bible did not say to do things to avoid being the subject of gossip, only not to gossip.

1. Some translations of 1 Thessalonians 5:22 suggest that we are to refrain from even the appearance of evil. Do you think this disqualifies Harmony's statement?

2. Do you agree that even her placing herself in the company of someone with such a bad reputation doesn't make her responsible for what other people think?

♫ ♫ ♫ ♫

Over and over again, Steve and Harmony mention that Steve is a brand new creature in Christ. 1 Corinthians 5:17 says: *Everyone who is in Christ is a new creation.*

3. Do you believe that someone can truly become a new creation in Christ? That the old person dies and a new person is reborn?

4. Do you think that so much of a person's heart and mind can change that his or her entire personality is affected?

5. Have you ever witnessed such a transformation? Did that kind of transformation happen for you?

Ephesians 6:12 says *For our struggle is not against flesh...*

2 Corinthians 10:3-4 says, *³ For though we walk in the flesh, we do not war according to the flesh. ⁴ For the weapons of our warfare are not carnal but mighty in God for pulling down strongholds.*

6. Spiritual warfare is a continual theme in this story. A satanic cult is bent on destroying Steve and Harmony because of his turning toward God. Do you think that we are truly involved in spiritual warfare right now? Or do you think that kind of war is restricted to the time in which the New Testament was written?

7. Do you think that a battle in the war was won by the end of *A Harmony for Steve*?

8. Steve mentioned that they couldn't fight the battle with weapons, and that he would continue to serve God even in the midst of the battle. Do you think that Christians actually face that kind of warfare today?

♫ ♫ ♫ ♫

Steve wanted to make sure that he could stay clean outside of rehab before contacting Harmony.

9. Do you think Harmony should have forgiven him on the scale she did?

10. Do you think that they got married too soon after his release from rehab? Do you think that the skills he learned in so many months in a Christ-centered rehabilitation facility will equip him for the years to come?

Steve believed that because he had spent so much time living a lifestyle and singing songs that actually led his fans away from God and away from the light, that God would have considered him "enemy number one" and that he was unforgivable.

11. Do you believe that even though the bible says *whoever believes in Him [Christ] should not perish but have everlasting life* (John 3:16), that there are actually some people God would not accept?

12. Do you believe that Steve's sins were so bad that the Holy Spirit would not have convicted him?

13. Do you think that Steve's forgiveness of his parents for the way they treated him is a good and healthy thing?

♫ ♫ ♫ ♫

Charles Galton believed he became possessed by a supernatural being, and that it gave him supernatural strength. The Bible mentions several incidents where Jesus or his disciples cast demons out of people young and old. Matthew 8 tells the story of men possessed by demons who had to live in caves:

"When he had come to the other side, to the country of Gergesenes, there met Him two demon-possessed men, coming out of the tombs, exceedingly fierce, so that no one could pass that way. Matthew 8:28

Mark 5 tells the story of a man who could not be bound by any chain:

> *And when He had come out of the boat, immediately there met Him out of the tombs a man with an unclean spirit, who had his dwelling among the tombs; and no one could bind him, not even with chains, because he had often been bound with shackles and chains. And the chains had been pulled apart by him, and the shackles broken in pieces; neither could anyone tame him. Mark 5:2-4*

14. Do you believe that people can still be possessed by demons today?

15. Do you think that Charles was actually possessed and actually did have supernatural power as a result of his demonic possession, or do you think he was merely insane?

♪ ♪ ♪ ♪

SUGGESTED luncheon menu to enjoy when hosting a group discussion surrounding *A Harmony for Steve*, part 4 of the *Song of Suspense* series.

Those who follow my Hallee the Homemaker™ website know that one thing I am passionate about in life is selecting, cooking, and savoring good whole real food. A special luncheon just goes hand in hand with hospitality and ministry.

If you're planning a discussion group surrounding this book, I offer some humble suggestions to help your special luncheon talk come off as a success in this section.

♫ ♫ ♫ ♫

The Vegetables:

MEDITERRANEAN
GRILLED VEGETABLES

The first meal Harmony and Steve share is grilled vegetables over rice with a salad. If you don't have a grill, you can make this recipe under the broiler of your oven.

INGREDIENTS:

$^3/_4$ cup olive oil

$^1/_4$ cup red wine vinegar

2 cloves garlic, minced

1 teaspoon chopped fresh rosemary

1 teaspoon fresh thyme leaves

1 teaspoon chopped fresh basil

1 teaspoon chopped fresh oregano

1 eggplant

1 zucchini

1 yellow squash

1 red bell pepper

1 green bell pepper

1 red onion

2 large portobello mushrooms

$^1/_2$ teaspoon salt (Kosher or sea salt is best)

$^1/_2$ teaspoon freshly ground black pepper

SUPPLIES:

Bowl with lid

Whisk

Grill or sheet pan

Tongs

PREPARATION:

Mince the garlic.

Whisk the oil and vinegar together. Add the garlic, spices, salt, and pepper.

Slice the vegetables about $1/2$ inch thick. Place in bowl and cover. Toss with the marinade.

Heat a grill or set the oven to broil, or bring to about 500° degrees F (260° degrees C).

DIRECTIONS:

Grill over flame until grill marks appear on the flesh of the eggplant. Or, cook under broiler just until the flesh starts to sizzle and brown. Using tongs, turn the vegetables over and repeat.

♫ ♫ ♫ ♫

The Rice

BROWN RICE

This rice is perfect to serve with the roasted vegetables.

INGREDIENTS:

1 $3/4$ cups vegetable broth

1 cup brown rice

1 tablespoons olive oil

$1/2$ teaspoon salt (Kosher or sea salt is best)

SUPPLIES:

2 quart pot with lid

PREPARATION:

Stir all ingredients together in the pot. Bring to a boil over high heat. Cover with the lid and turn heat to low.

DIRECTIONS:

Mix all ingredients in the sauce pan.

Bring to a boil. Reduce heat to low.

Cover.

Simmer, covered, for 45 minutes.

♫ ♫ ♫ ♫

The Strawberries:

CINNAMON GLAZED STRAWBERRIES

INGREDIENTS:

2 tablespoons sugar

1 tablespoon butter

2 teaspoons lemon juice

$1/2$ teaspoon ground cinnamon

1 lb strawberries

SUPPLIES:

Saucepan

Bowl

Wire rack and sheet pan

PREPARATION:

Wash the strawberries. Remove the stems.

DIRECTIONS:

Heat the sugar, butter, lemon juice, and cinnamon in the saucepan until the sugar melts. Toss the strawberries in the sugar mixture.

Place the wire rack on top of the sheet pan. Put the strawberries on top of the wire rack to drain and cool.

Serve alone or with whipped cream.

♫ ♫ ♫ ♫

With more than half a million

sales and more than 20 books in print, Hallee Bridgeman is a best-selling Christian author who writes romance and action-packed romantic suspense focusing on realistic characters who face real world problems. Her work has been described as everything from refreshingly realistic to heart-stopping exciting and edgy.

A prolific writer, when she's not penning novels, you will find her in the kitchen, which she considers the "heart of the home." Her passion for cooking spurred her to launch a whole food, real food "Parody" cookbook series. In addition to nutritious, Biblically grounded recipes, readers will find that each cookbook also confronts some controversial aspect of secular pop culture.

Hallee loves coffee, campy action movies, and regular date nights with her husband. Above all else, she loves God with all of her heart, soul, mind, and strength; has been redeemed by the blood of Christ; and relies on the presence of the Holy Spirit to guide her. She prays her work here on earth is a blessing to you and would love to hear from you.

You can reach Hallee via the CONTACT link on her website or send an email to hallee@halleebridgeman.com.

Newsletter Sign Up: tinyurl.com/HalleeNews/

Author Site: www.halleebridgeman.com

Facebook:
www.facebook.com/pages/Hallee-Bridgeman/192799110825012

Twitter: twitter.com/halleeb

A MELODY FOR JAMES

MELODY Mason and James Montgomery lead separate lives of discord until an unexpected meeting brings them to a sinister realization. Unbeknownst to them, dark forces have directed their lives from the shadows, orchestrating movements that keep them in disharmony. Fire, loss, and bloodshed can't shake their faith in God to see them through as they face a percussive climax that will leave lives forever changed.

♫ ♫ ♫ ♫

AN ARIA FOR NICK

ARIA Suarez remembers her first real kiss and Nick Williams, the blue eyed boy who passionately delivered it before heading off to combat. The news of his death is just a footnote in a long war and her lifelong dream to become a world class pianist is shattered along with her wrist on the day of his funeral.

Years later, Aria inadvertently uncovers a sinister plot that threatens the very foundations of a nation. Now, stalked by assassins and on the run, her only hope of survival is in trusting her very life to a man who has been dead for years.

A CAROL FOR KENT

BOBBY Kent's name is synonymous with modern Country Music and he is no stranger to running from overzealous fans and paparazzo. But he has no idea how to protect his daughter and Carol, the mother of his only child, from a vicious and ruthless serial killer bent on their destruction.

♫ ♫ ♫ ♫

A HARMONY FOR STEVE

CHRISTIAN contemporary singing sensation, Harmony Harper, seeks solitude after winning her umpteenth award. She finds herself in the midst of the kind of spiritual crisis that only prayer and fasting can cure. Steve Slayer, the world renowned satanic acid rock icon, who has a reputation for trashing women as well as hotel rooms, stumbles into her private retreat on the very edge of death.

In ministering to Steve, Harmony finds that the Holy Spirit is ministering to her aching soul. The two leave the wilderness sharing a special bond and their hearts are changed forever.

They expect rejection back in their professional worlds. What neither of them could foresee is the chain of ominous events that threaten their very lives.

♫ ♫ ♫ ♫

**Available in eBook or Paperback
wherever fine books are sold.**

FICTION BOOKS BY HALLEE

Find the latest information and connect with Hallee
at her website: www.halleebridgeman.com

The Virtues and Valor series:

Book 1: Temperance's Trial
Book 2: Homeland's Hope
Book 3: Charity's Code
Book 4: A Parcel for Prudence
Book 5: Grace's Ground War
Book 6: Mission of Mercy
Book 7: Flight of Faith
Book 8: Valor's Vigil

The Jewel Series:

Book 1: Sapphire Ice
Book 2: Greater Than Rubies
Book 3: Emerald Fire
Book 4: Topaz Heat
Book 5: Christmas Diamond
Book 6: Christmas Star Sapphire

Standalone Suspense:

On The Ropes

PARODY COOKBOOKS BY HALLEE

Vol 1: Fifty Shades of Gravy, a Christian gets Saucy!
Vol 2: The Walking Bread, the Bread Will Rise
Vol 3: Iron Skillet Man, the Stark Truth about Pepper and Pots
Vol 4: Hallee Crockpotter & the Chamber of Sacred Ingredients

EXCERPT: ON THE ROPES

WHAT happens when the gloves come off and a bruised boxer's fist takes hold of a delicate doctor's fingers? Please enjoy this exclusive excerpt from Hallee Bridgeman's new standalone Christian suspense story, *On The Ropes*.

Mara Harrison fanned her face with the ball cap, then took the end of her ponytail and wrapped her hair into a bun before settling the cap back on her head. The humidity and lack of breeze coupled with the Florida summer sun beating down against the gravestones made her feel like she'd spent the last hour working in a sauna. As she reached for her little shovel, she noted a faint pink tinge behind the freckles on her arm. With rich red hair, pale white skin, and freckles, she hardly had the complexion to work outside in the midday Florida summer. However, she had promised the pastor she would have the cemetery weeded by Friday, and she still had two sections to do.

"Time for a break, Mara," Pastor Ben Carmichael chided. He pushed the graveyard gate open with one hand while clutching two water bottles with the other. Despite the fact he'd spent the last two hours sitting on a riding lawn mower, he looked cool and crisp in his light blue golf shirt and khaki shorts. Even though his Florida Gators ball cap covered blond hair, his skin had tanned to a rich bronze since spring, while Mara's freckles provided the only color on her skin other than an occasional burn.

In the six months since Mara had relocated to the little village on the western coast of Florida, she and Ben had become good friends. The twenty-six-year old pastor had bought the long-abandoned and dilapidated church they were working at with money inherited after the death of his grandfather. Over the last year he had spent most waking moments restoring it and building the congregation.

Mara worked from home, doing medical transcription for four different doctors. That job gave her ample opportunity to volunteer during daylight hours at the church. She and Ben had lain carpet and tile, built shelves, planted bushes, weeded, and painted until she couldn't stand the thought of painting anymore. Under their love and care, the church bloomed, the congregation quadrupled in size, and Mara knew Ben's feelings for her had grown.

Part of her wanted to return his feelings, but a small part inside her held back. She knew she could never put him at risk. She didn't think she could live with herself if anything happened to him because of her. She also knew she could never enter into a romantic relationship predicated upon deception and misdirection.

Despite that, she liked him. A lot. Whenever he managed to get up the courage to profess his feelings for her, she hoped he wouldn't end their friendship over her rejection. She so desperately needed his friendship right now.

"Thanks," she smiled, accepting a water bottle from him, "it's hot out today."

"Too hot to be right out in it." He gestured at the sun directly overhead. "Why not stop for now and pick back up later this afternoon?"

She drained half the bottle before answering. "Can't. Have mandatory training about some changes in medical coding at three." She used her burning forearm to swipe at her damp forehead. "You have your first funeral here tomorrow. We need to get it finished."

He smiled at her, his brown eyes warm. "Had a feeling you'd say that." He gestured over his shoulder with his thumb. "That's why I rounded up some volunteers."

Three teenage boys from the youth group ambled into the cemetery. They all wore swim trunks and tank tops advertising a national fishing supply store. She knew the tallest boy, Jeremy, had a pool and guessed they'd spent the morning there before coming to work at the church. "Hi, boys," Mara said with a smile as Ben headed back to his mower, "ready to get to work?"

"Yes, ma'am," Jeremy replied, always the outspoken one of the group. "Mama said we had to spend four hours here and you'd give us the Wi-Fi code she texted pastor this morning."

"We tried going to our house," one of the two Cantrell

brothers said, "but Jeremy's mom had already conspired with our mom."

Mara laughed. "The Bible says to serve God with a willing heart."

The youngest of the three grimaced. "We're willing, ma'am."

Mara showed them the section of the graveyard to weed and gave them a wheelbarrow and tools. Once she saw they had it under control, she doused herself with more sunscreen, traded the ball cap for a floppy wide-brimmed straw hat, and went back to attacking the weeds covering the hundred-year-old grave of, according to the inscription on the stone, a beloved grandmother. The new hat offered much more protection from the sun and the bottle of water she'd consumed helped energize her. Letting her mind wander, she found herself thinking about what the air would feel like a thousand miles away in Manhattan right about now.

"Mara!"

The panic in the boy's tone pushed every other thought from her mind. One of the brothers rushed toward her. "A snake bit Jeremy!"

Heart pounding, she rushed to where she'd left the boys working. She found Jeremy sitting on the ground staring at the still twitching body of the headless rattlesnake. One of the boys had killed it with a hoe. The snake looked enormous—five feet long at least.

Despite the six-month hiatus, her medical training took over. She retrieved her pocket knife as she crouched next to Jeremy. He sat on the pine straw covered ground, clutching his right hand with his left. "Is that where it bit you?" He looked dazed. "Move your hand," she ordered, "let me see."

Taking his hand in hers, she lowered it closer to the ground to get the bite below his heart. "My shin, too," he panted. Inspecting his face, she witnessed his pupils dilate. His breathing came short and quick. Looking at his calf, she saw the other bite. "Which first?"

"Hand," he said on a breath.

"Call 9-1-1," she ordered the youngest Cantrell, "and go get Pastor Ben." She touched his cheek to get his attention. "Listen, Jeremy, I need you to calm down. We're going to move you to this bench right here." She helped him up then settled him on the stone bench. "Keep your hand down. Below your heart." She inspected the wounds and checked his vital signs, wishing she had a blood pressure cuff.

She looked up at the older Cantrell boy. "EMTs on the way?"

"Yes ma'am," he confirmed.

Ben and the younger brother rushed onto the scene. "What happened?"

"Two rattlesnake bites." As she spoke, Jeremy turned his body away from her and vomited into the grass behind the bench. "Jeremy, that's just the venom making you sick. Try to take slow deep breaths. We need to try to keep your heart rate down." She pressed her fingers to the jugular on his neck then double checked the distal pulse at his wrist, looking for a discrepancy. Two minutes had passed. With every heartbeat, the venom moved further into his body. She couldn't wait any longer. "Give me your shirt," she said to the youngest brother. He slipped it over his head and held it out to her. "I need two sticks," she said to no one in particular. "About six inches long. Strong. Hurry!"

Pulling out her pocketknife, she cut the tank top in half. She tied half of it right below Jeremy's elbow in a surgeon's knot, and the other half right above his knee. "Where're my sticks?"

"Will these work?" Ben asked, offering four oak twigs about half an inch in diameter.

She snatched them with a nod. Picking up the running ends of the tourniquet below his elbow, she tied a square knot on top of the stick, trapping it between the square knot and the surgeon's knot. Then she twisted the stick like turning a spigot, tightening the makeshift tourniquet until as much of the venom as possible remained trapped below his elbow, away from his heart. Finally, she secured the stick in place with the ends of the shirt.

Using another stick, she repeated the process above his knee; the wound furthest from his heart and the snake's second strike, making it the lower priority. Jeremy moaned. "I know it hurts," she agreed, her heart aching a bit at causing him so much pain, "but you're tough and I hear the ambulance."

As sirens sounded in the distance, she checked the tightness of the tourniquets and felt his pulse in his neck and wrist again. The flesh around the fang marks on his hand had gone from red to a purplish black. The venom had already started to denature the protein in his flesh.

"What can I do?" Ben asked.

She swiped at her forehead with her forearm. "Pray."

A Note from the Author...

I'm so glad that you chose to read ***A Harmony for Steve***. I pray that it blessed you.

I'd love to hear from you. Leave a review for this book where you bought it or leave a comment online at my website. Your feedback inspires me to keep writing.

www.halleebridgeman.com

May God richly bless you,

SIGN up for Hallee's monthly newsletter! Every newsletter recipient is automatically entered into a monthly giveaway! The real prize is you will never miss updates about upcoming releases, book signings, appearances, or other events.

Hallee News Letter
http://tinyurl.com/HalleeNews/